Shiloh Spring

KEVIN GETCHELL

outskirts
press

Outskirts Press, Inc.
http://www.outskirtspress.com

ISBN: 978-1-9772-7855-5

Library of Congress Control Number: 2025901793

Cover Image by Kevin Getchell

Outskirts Press and the "OP" logo are trademarks belonging to Outskirts Press, Inc.

PRINTED IN THE UNITED STATES OF AMERICA

"Duty is the most sublime word in our language. Do your duty in all things. You cannot do more. You should never wish to do less." — Robert E. Lee

Dedicated to Larry DeBerry and other descendants of the children of Shiloh who lived on the land that became the battleground.

Authors Note: Certain passages are drawn from autobiographical material of Mark Twain and Henry Morton Stanley

Contents

1

Inferno

The night sky vibrated with lightning. Tripping on a root in the dark, Dennis was thrown down a wet hill and rolled rapidly like a log until he bumped against something in the ravine. It was long and covered with cloth. He turned his head to find a stark white face staring back with fixed glazed eyes. Its mouth was frozen in an o-shape as if surprised at Dennis's sudden arrival. The thunderstorm illuminated the landscape and revealed a vale clogged with other corpses.

Numbed, he rose and climbed back up the embankment to get his bearings. He trudged in the mud down a farm road in what he hoped would be the way to Shiloh Church. His ears rang from the periodic bursting of shells coming from the gunboats on the Tennessee River; dizziness made him feel like a toy top. His mouth was parched. He licked at rain droplets catching on his lips, but it was not enough to quench his thirst. All across a field, he could hear distressed cries of the wounded.

"Water! Water! Oh please, could someone just bring me a canteen…just a little…please just a drink." Then, as if heaven answered, came a downpour.

Along the road among the trees were clusters of men bivouacked around stacked rifles, nursing sputtering fires. Solitary soldiers shivered, huddled against tree trunks, trying to sleep. Miserably wet Confederates stood guard over cheerless Union prisoners sitting on the soaked ground with knees pulled up under their chins. Then came a long whistling shriek of a cannonball. It exploded in a concussive wave slamming him into a dense thicket.

Incredibly, he remained conscious, but his left ear was bleeding. Others were not so lucky. He made out a tall oak split from top to root with a human leg dangling from a branch. Grabbing bushes to raise himself, he pushed his way through the tangled underbrush back to the road. He took hold of a handful of leaves, only to feel a jelly-like substance. He screamed with horror at the human remains and wretched.

Emerging from the undergrowth, he could see at least a dozen men, both Yankee and Rebel, contorted in death as a result of that one explosion. Dennis staggered through the mud as the outcries of the wounded and groans of the dying created a strange orchestra amidst the storm, a symphony of the damned. He broke into an arm-flailing, mud splattering run. As he distanced himself from the massacre, he slowed up with chest heaving. He cursed God unrestrained; as he did, he heard his mother's religious admonitions. *Never use the Lord's name in vain. Don't blame God for the sins of man.* There came a panicked repentance, and he begged forgiveness for his blasphemy. A quiet set in, and he could only hear the squishing of his shoes in the sludge. It was a short reprieve. There was a great racket, and a wounded but magnificent white horse, blood streaming down its back, burst out of the bushes with a throat rattle, snorting like Apocalypse fulfilled. Could the other horses of the Revelation be far behind? Indeed, he found them as he walked on. Two artillery horses floundered, still in their harnesses on the ground, emitting shrieking whinnies, but then something familiar. A dapple gray animal lay heaving on its side, breathing out labored snuffles in the mire. That was the crowning horror for him. The beautiful animal looked to be his family's lone horse.

"Bobby! Bobby!" he cried out to the horse his father had named after the Irish revolutionary, Robert Emmet. "Oh, Bobby, what have they done to you?"

Falling to his knees, he threw himself over the side of the animal, sobbing. Its huge mid-section quivered then relaxed. As the horse expired, steam rose from its hide, and the horse's warmth ironically revived Dennis in the chill of the rainy night. He rose sobbing, plodding on, hoping it was westward, but not knowing which point of the compass he might be facing. He passed destroyed cabins. Neither Union nor Confederate armies had spared the domiciles around Shiloh. What had happened to the residents? Especially, what had happened to *her*? A strong resolve came over him. It did not matter that he, too, might die tonight; he had to keep going as long as he was alive and find out what had happened to her. Scant hope drove him. Jane might be out here somewhere in the miles of altered landscape. Now maybe the Great Jehovah would answer prayer. He fell to his knees and begged.

"Dear God, Dear God. If you would only help me find her, please help me find her!"

He kept repeating it, hoping a God of love who rescues out of trial would miraculously answer, but his mother's words loomed in his mind again as he said "amen." "God helps those that help themselves," his mother had repeated time after time.

That's how Dennis was helping himself, by pursuing Jane, but she discouraged him not to go after that girl. His mother intimated that girls like Jane were not wholesome enough, not devout enough. She implied that he would help himself by leaving Jane alone. How could he have brought her home anyway into the house where, of course, his father also resided? That man of unpredictable temperament possessed peculiarities that at times were embarrassing or even revolting. He himself had taken his father to a lunatic asylum in New Orleans. He reasoned that if Jane had seen any of his father's idiosyncrasies, it would have made any chance of being with her a moot pursuit.

He should have ignored all that when it came to Jane. He should have gone after her. He shouldn't have displayed reluctance about her in the earlier years. If he had, she would have looked upon him as more than a mere friend. He would not be in this place right now, searching for his unrequited love. He was going after her now under the worst possible circumstances. He would find her somewhere out here. He would run to her. He would hold her. He would tell her all he had ever wanted to tell her. He would take her away from this now wretched place.

The distinctive trickling of water interrupted his ruminations. Its sound in the darkness brought an overwhelming realization. He knew where he was. He was where he had first met Jane. At Shiloh Spring.

He staggered into the little stream, then tripped and fell head first into the gurgling water. He coughed as he drew in the sweet liquid. He splashed in it vigorously, careless of enemy eyes. The perdition of the night seemed to melt away as the rivulets of cold water soothed his parched tongue and burning throat. His heart beat slower with the succor of water. Hope returned and merged present with past, transporting him back to that wonderful day when he met her at the spring years before.

2

Jane

The gurgling of fresh artesian spring water next to the Corinth road below the Shiloh school and church escaped from underground through a rock escarpment, producing a little waterfall that created a small creek farther below. Dennis plunged his head into the pool, sapped from the heat and humidity of the west Tennessee autumn morning. It was a long walk to here from his house, more than five miles south near Hamburg landing. The cold water quenched his thirst, but the refreshment also helped him clear his head after the latest disturbing incident at home with his father. Rising, he wiped the water from his eyes. Droplets from the bangs of his auburn hair dripped onto his red gingham shirt, so he shook his head back and forth. In so doing, he became aware of a blurry feminine form across the creek.

He squinted. Then lightly tapping his breast pocket, he retrieved gold rimmed spectacles. Slowly, he curled the ear pieces around each ear, blinking away the droplets still on his long eyelashes. How he hated those glasses. With the round lenses sitting in place on his nose, the person across the water came into focus. It was a petite blonde girl, no older than himself, about 15 that day in early September 1859. She gazed at him quizzically for a moment and then whirled around marveling at trees, birds, and sky, blurting out, "I just can't wait for class to begin at the new school! Can you?"

She smiled at him, and he noticed one of her blue eyes was slightly askew. The look perked him up.

"It's so glorious. Have you been up there? The walls and roof are all finished, and the logs smell so wonderful, the fragrance of fresh cut oak just floats to the road and makes your nose tingle."

"I…uh, I just got here. I was on my way up there," Dennis stuttered uncharacteristically. His attention went from her eyes to her smile

"My name is Jane. What's yours?" she asked and came down to the creek bank in her long red gingham dress. She cupped her hand into the spring, drew it to her mouth, sipped, and then winked at Dennis. The wink discombobulated him, and he could not speak.

"No name?" she teased. He remained flummoxed. Then a bell started clanging. They both paused to listen to the pealing as it resonated from up on the hill. She turned back to Dennis, waiting for his reply, but they were interrupted again as a whole raft of youngsters came excitedly around a corner where a farm path intersected the main Corinth road next to the creek. The noise of the oncoming crowd quashed further conversation between them.

Almost all of these kids lived on the Shiloh plateau that stretched out from Pittsburg Landing on the west side of the Tennessee River. Small children came skipping, singing, and some running. Older boys strutted like roosters. Girls in calico and striped dresses giggled at them. After the bulk of the crowd had passed, another blonde haired girl appeared, who seemed to be more independent than the rest. Seeing Jane at the creek, she called out:

"I wondered where you had gone!"

"Abby!" Jane called back and hastened up the embankment to her friend. They hugged, and Jane whispered something in Abby's ear while motioning her head toward Dennis. As they walked uphill at a distance behind the other students, Jane called out to him, "I guess I'll never get *your* name!"

"Dennis! Dennis O'Brien," he called out with a twinge of awkwardness.

The brief encounter left him with both a sinking and exhilarating feeling. He watched the blonde girls move up the hill, each with a distinctive gait. Abby had a confident stride and slight sashay back and forth at the hips. Jane had a pronounced bounce, and he could not keep himself from looking at her derriere.

With the crowd passed, and Jane and Abby far the up the incline to the school, he stood alone at the spring lost in thought. Minutes slipped by, the school bell had already rung, so he was late, but it could not be helped. He needed time to compose himself. There was the violence of his father upon awakening, and there was being left behind by his older brother, who had taken the family horse and left him in the lurch in order to get to the school far ahead of him. Now he was especially affected by that girl. She had branded his brain.

Shiloh School was not the closest to his home. There was one in the village of Hamburg where his family lived. His mother had tried getting him on the rolls of the school at Hamburg, but the teacher there had said he could not handle any more students there this year.

"It's just as well," she decried. The school was being held at the "hard shell" Baptist church, and his mother could not abide the hellfire preaching there. She'd vowed long ago to stay away from a denomination of that persuasion. When she found that her sons, Dennis, his older brother John, and youngest Adam, could not attend because of overcrowding, it was a relief. Not that the Methodist Church which held sway up here at Shiloh was more attractive to her. Tongue in cheek she would say:

"*Dyed in the wool* Methodists are just *hard shell* Baptists who can read."

When she heard there was a schoolhouse separated from the church structure at Shiloh, she was pleased. The attendance at Shiloh school would be packed as well, but Ida O'Brien knew the teacher and convinced her to let her children attend. Adam, the youngest of the three O'Brien boys, would be schooled at home until there was a vacancy.

Today, Dennis's older brother John had maddeningly taken the family's horse and loped away, so Dennis could not ride double behind him. He often did things like that to Dennis, a way to keep his sibling under his thumb, but this morning had been especially difficult for Dennis. His father had had a spell so bad that his raving had shaken him to the core. While John was already on his way to make new friends, Dennis was left behind to deal with the aftermath of destruction in the wake of their father's crazed episode. It seemed he was always the one left to comfort his mother. It was up to him to bring his father down from the exhausting maniacal incidents.

On the journey up to the Shiloh school, it was easy to get turned around in the terrain along the Tennessee River. He had hiked the area around Shiloh church and Pittsburg Landing, but one had to have a good memory and keen sense of direction to avoid getting disoriented among branching farm roads, thick hardwood forest with its underlying vegetation and multitude of ravines. The virgin forest along the road comprised a broad variety of trees. There were dogwood, poplar and cedar, white oak, red oak, red maple, sugar maple and sweetgum as well as wild blackberry bushes and other vining plants climbing up the trunks and encircling branches like boa constrictors.

After John sped away on the horse, Dennis half ran, half walked to Shiloh. He was exhausted and angry at his brother. School began about 9:00, so he was pressed for time. The rapid pace caused him to cough and wheeze. It was an affliction that other boys did not seem to suffer.

The quiet bell confirmed his tardiness. He jumped the creek and headed north up the steep incline to Shiloh Church and School. The ground leveled, and there stood the church with the school across the road. Neither were large structures, maybe twenty by forty feet in size. The church's logs were darkened, moss having gained foothold. He was surprised to see no cross mounted on the peak of the roof.

On the other hand, the wooden structure of the school contrasted with its freshly sawed logs perfectly notched to hold the structure together. The roof's shingles were so fresh they shouted in the brightness of the sun. There was a small cemetery north of the school. Several horses were tied up to a split rail fence on the south side. There with the others, stood Bobby, the O'Brien's horse, a dapple grey gelding. Dennis' father had named him after Robert Emmet, the leader of the 1803 Irish Rebellion. The horses name had allusions to his father's murky past. Three wagons were parked in front of the school. A water trough was off to the north side with three buckets stacked each inside the other. A single step fashioned out of a large log lay in front of the doorway.

He was late the first day of the term. The consequences loomed large. With trepidation he put his foot up on the log step. As he did, there was a galloping thunder behind him on the Corinth Road. Several militia men wearing butternut brown outfits pounded up the track on fine horses, past the school and church toward Pittsburg Landing. Everyone in the schoolhouse turned at the commotion, but it caused all eyes to focus on him. He wished he had taken off his glasses.

3

──⊰⦿⊱──

Angst

The atmosphere inside the schoolhouse was buzzing like cicadas in the sweet gum trees outside. The militia's passing caused disorder in the room. Some boys began to pantomime gunplay. A short, stocky, dark-headed kid pulled a mock pistol from his imaginary holster and pointed it at another boy while making a shooting sound, and with glee, shouted above the din of the other kids.

"Pow! Pow! Take that, you Yankee! That'll teach y'all not to mess with us southern men!"

Everybody burst into laughter. A towheaded boy grabbed the teacher's pointer leaning against her desk. The boy raised it like a sword and walked deliberately toward Dennis. He flourished the make-believe sword and poked the stick at Dennis' chest:

"Don't take another step furthah, you pissant. I am Lieutenant James Barnes. We'll be tolerating no Lincolnites in this district! Stand down, or else you shall feel the effect of this cold steel!"

Student laughter exploded again. It was made worse by the fact that his own brother John was nearby, chuckling at him with the rest of the crowd. He tried to deflect the bullying with humor. Pushing the stick away from his chest and brushing his shirt off, he feigned being a preacher, quoting the King James Bible:

"Sir, I am a man of the cloth. "Put up again thy sword into his place: for all they that take the sword shall perish with the sword!"""

The classroom burst into applause, and now it seemed they were on his side. Dennis watched the "lieutenant" return to his seat, stiffly. He had just made an adversary in James Barnes.

Having tolerated the horseplay until then, the teacher stamped her feet and her cross face shouted, "Enough of this, children! Enough! Everyone take your seats, all of you! Yes, and that includes you, Mr. O'Brien. Take that seat over there!" she demanded.

The class came to attention. She chalked her name on the slate board at the head of the room.

"Children! You will address me as Miss Sornby. You there, the ones in the third row! Move over and let young O'Brien sit down," she commanded.

He was pleasantly surprised as she pointed to a place immediately behind the blonde girl he had met at the spring, whose hair came to her shoulders and turned up at the ends. Jane turned to look at Dennis with those blue eyes and whispered, "Hi, Dennis. Let's talk later."

"All right!" he whispered back, not noticing the stares of two boys sitting on either side of James Barnes. It became clear that they were in league with James Barnes.

"Psst! Jim, are you goin' to let that pass? He's after your girl."

James whirled around startled, looking back and forth between Dennis and Jane.

"Stay away from her, or I'll stomp your tail!" he rasped at Dennis.

Dennis looked into Barnes' eyes unflinchingly. His left eyebrow rose in anger, Irish dander flaring.

"You two Wicker boys settle down now, and that includes you, Mr. O'Brien."

He gritted his teeth, stung by Miss Sornby's rebuke. Jane turned and gave him a sweet smile, then whispered, "Don't bother about any of it with Jim. He's always like that."

The statement produced angst because it betrayed Jane's familiarity with this Barnes. Barnes made a fist and shook it at Dennis.

"That will be enough of this ruckus. I will not tell anyone again to settle down! The next one to make a disturbance will have to stand in the corner. Enough, enough, I say. I will call roll now."

Though Barnes was trying to intimidate him, the budding rapture he felt about the girl with the flaxen hair, bouncing exuberance, and mischievous intelligence behind those slightly crossed eyes had overridden Barnes' threat. However, something else did interfere. "Stop it!" he told himself. He tried to imagine escape from the cold, iron bars of familial responsibility, but felt only a crushing burial of aspirations for any hope for him other than duty. He rubbed his temples. He looked out the window, and tried to force this awakening attraction for Jane away from himself, but it was for naught. She was like the Shiloh Spring. He savored the feeling during the roll call as students responded, standing up briefly as they replied saying:

"Present, Miss Sornby!" or "Here, Miss Sornby!"

He tried to memorize the names. He did not know Jane's last name. He waited to hear it with full attention. There were more boys than girls.

"Barnes. Mr. James Barnes. Mr. Larkin Bell. Cantrell, Mr. Ira Cantrell. Mr. Nicolas Chambers. Miss Elisabeth Cloud. Miss Abby Davis. Miss Elsie Duncan."

The monotony of the roll call lulled Dennis into a daze. He could only hear her name in his head, over and over again. Jane. His thoughts went rapid fire every time he glanced at the sheen of her yellow hair. He caught the scent of her ivory neck slightly perspiring in the morning humidity.

"George Hagy. Isaiah Glover. Benjamin Howell. Clifton Jones. McCuller, Mr. Allan McCuller. Miss Darla Mulberry." Miss Sornby was calling his name now. "O'Brien. Mr. Dennis O'Brien!" He snapped out of his daze.

"Present!"

"We shall see about that, Mr. O'Brien. You do not look so present at this moment!" She watched the distracted look he had with a faint smile and continued on with the roll.

"Overshot, Miss Kathryn Overshot. Perry, Mr. Lawrence Perry. Rhea, Miss Mary Rhea. Seay, Miss Lorraine Seay. Mr. Bradley Sowell. Spain, Mr. Patrick Spain. Tilghman, Mr. Lawrence Tilghman. Wicker, Mr. Bruce Wicker. Wicker, Mr. William Wicker. Mr. James Wood, and Mr. Barry Woolf.

Jane's name had not come up. He wondered why. Then Miss Sornby announced, "Oh, this last one I apologize for. I somehow got it out of order. Pardon me. Winningham, Miss Jane Winningham."

Spoken out loud, Jane's full name startled him. He whispered to himself, savoring the sound of it. "Winningham…Winningham… Jane Winningham."

4

4

Trapped

Dismissal released a torrent of pent up energy. The students flooded away from the schoolhouse in all directions. Before he could even speak to her, Barnes took Jane by the wrist, and out the door they went. From the window he stifled his feelings as if it did not matter. He watched some kids pass through the cemetery, slapping at tombstones and playing tag. He caught sight of his brother with Abby, pulling at early turning autumn leaves. Some girls screamed into the woods to hear the reverberation of their voices. The Wicker boys continued the earlier charade of gunplay. Miss Sornby exited quickly, walking with purpose across the road to the church where the preacher stood expectantly.

Crestfallen, he turned to examining the rugged construction of the new schoolhouse. Like Shiloh Church across the road, the community had come together to build it. The walls were hand-hewn white oak timbers, corners connected by snugly cut dovetail notches. The floor was sturdy yellow poplar boards, but there were cracks between the boards and you could see the ground beneath. The rafters were simple poles. Plate boards were nailed atop the rafters and these in turn were topped with split-cedar shingles. The fresh cut aroma of all this wood permeated the room with a heady effect. The crevices between the horizontal logs were sealed with red Tennessee clay. The rude backless benches were hewed logs supported by two angled peg legs on either end. There were four rows of benches, on both sides of an aisle in the middle, a bit of standing room in the rear.

Then he heard his brother John's voice, and John leaned in through the door.

"You won't mind running the traps today, will you?"

Dennis whirled around angry.

"I've run them for the last two weeks."

"Well, then it won't hurt you to run them one more day, will it?"

"And why can't you do it?"

"Aw, come on, Den! There's this girl named Abby. You've seen her. I told her I would give her a ride home on Bobby."

"Yeah, what's that to me?"

"Oh, come on, give me a chance with this girl. I promise I'll take care of the traps the next three weeks, alright? Come on, you don't have anything else to do."

"Don't have anything else to do?!" He gritted his teeth. "Don't have anything else to do?!"

John condescended, "Oh, poor Dennis. Look! I'm the oldest, got more responsibility than you. The oldest son always bears the brunt. Oh, poor Dennis, poor little Dennis!"

Dennis felt powerless. If he said no to check the traps, his brother would take off anyway and leave him to it. It was galling that John claimed he was giving Dennis a choice.

"Okay. Go! Just go. I'll run the traps!"

John wasted no time crossing the yard confidently to where the horses were tethered and Abby stood waiting. He mounted Bobby and pulled her up behind him on the horse. They sauntered southward down the Corinth road, talking as Dennis looked resentfully on.

To his surprise, Jane came bounding up to the door and came in.

"Dennis! Good. You're still here. I hoped we'd talk before you went home."

He was befuddled again.

"What's the matter, Dennis, cat got your tongue? Dennis, I just talked with Miss Sornby over at the church. They are going to use the church for teaching the younger ones, and the school for the older kids because it's so crowded. Did she tell you? Some of us older ones will help with the younger ones, teaching English and History. She said that you and I will be part of it!"

Skeptically, he replied: "Really? You heard her say I would be part of it? She didn't seem pleased with me today."

"Yes, yes, Dennis!! You're smart. Look how you matched wits with James. He thinks he's smart, but he didn't get asked. It was so clever the way you acted like a preacher. Oh, isn't it just wonderful, Dennis, the new school and all, and now this great opportunity to help Miss Sornby?"

Not waiting for him to answer, she turned and bounded back out the door. He went to see where she went and saw several teens gathered at buggies. Among them were James Barnes and the Wicker Brothers. James held Jane's hand.

Dennis set out north on the Corinth road on the way to the trap line. About a quarter mile up the road, it crossed Hamburg-Purdy road. Here he would cut through the woods off the west side then down to a creek bottom. From behind he heard horses clopping and jingling harnesses. A buggy approached, and he heard the chidings of the Wicker brothers.

"There he is fellas, there's the preacher man!"

The wagon churned dust into Dennis's face. They derided his spectacles, hooting and hollering:

"Haww Four Eyes!! Haww! Haww!"

Then came a wagon filled with girls. They squealed with delight when they saw him, but he did not see Jane among them. This was followed by another buggy. Jane was sidled next to James Barnes. His heart sank. It was true. She was sweet on that boy. Dennis turned to walk off into the woods, but she called out to him.

"Hey, Dennis! Let us give you a ride!"

James pulled up on the reins, perturbed and glowering while Jane urged him to jump on.

"Come on, Dennis. Just jump on!"

"Can't! Have to run my father's trap line."

"Too bad, Denny-poo!" James said contemptuously.

Having James belittle him in front of Jane raised Dennis's hackles, but he only repeated:

"I have to check traps. Thanks for the offer."

Disgusted, James clicked his tongue to urge the horse, and with a quick shake of the reins, they were off. Jane turned back and waved. He should forget about this girl, she was already involved. He waved back and dropped off into the woods.

"Jane…. Jane Winningham," Dennis said under his breath as he stepped into the forest with rumpled ground and fallen leaves. His mood began to correspond to the diminished light. *Yes, best just forget the idea of ever getting close to that little gal.*

The first trap had no prize. He reset the mechanism, but experienced the same result all down the creek. Then came a pond with tell-tale signs, felled saplings on the hillside. A little waterfall spilled over the top of a beaver dam. One slapped its tail and dived, then there was only a breeze through the trees and lapping water. Sunlight filtered through the breaks in the leaves in slanted beams. He sat down and waited for its reemergence. Finally, the placid surface broke as a nose poked from underneath sending out concentric rings. Dennis stayed still as the critter paddled toward shore.

The beaver went to work gnawing on a slender trunk. It weakened, snapped, and fell into the water. The beaver towed the sapling across the pond. Suddenly, the quiet was broken by shouting, "Hey, Dennis, whatcha doin' down there! Think you're a trapper?!"

Dennis was relieved, thinking his brother had come back to help. Then he heard the voice again. It wasn't.

"You won't have to worry about this anymore! This trap line is my territory now!"

The timbre alarmed Dennis, and he rose, grabbed a stick and raised it threateningly. How did this interloper know his name? There was a familiar laugh.

"Oh, you plan to defend yourself with that stick?"

To his relief, he recognized Frank Walker, a neighbor of the O'Briens who lived near Hamburg. Frank was the same age as John. He was a tall, strong, brown-haired boy of seventeen. He was fair-minded, straight talking, and never ridiculed, in some ways the brother that he would have liked to have. And he, too, wore spectacles. Frank had his own trap line and had given the O'Briens pointers on catching game. But what was this he was saying about not being the O'Brien's territory anymore? He figured it was a joke as Frank sidled down the bank, his feet pushing soil downward as he descended.

"You're never goin' to make money this way. Look at you, you're soft on killin'. Y'all have been workin' this stretch so long, and little to show for it."

It was true. His father had tried valiantly to succeed, made a few dollars with the pelts and meat, but overall it had added little to the family's estate, which mainly consisted of farmland granted to Charles O'Brien's for his service in the Mexican-American War. Dennis's heart sank as Frank went on.

"I talked with your Daddy this mornin'. He's a smart man, but he just keeps slippin' back. I offered him twenty dollars for the line, and he took it."

"Twenty Dollars? Twenty Dollars! Why the line is worth a couple of hundred at least, Frank! How could you offer so little?"

"Look, Dennis, the line might be worth that much if it had been properly worked, but you and your brother don't get all of the ins and outs. You have to make constant adjustments because of the wiles of these critters and move the traps around. Just look at this beaver dam. You're so sentimental you can't even bear to put a trap in here. I checked just a little while ago to see if you had, then I decided to wait in the trees 'til you got here. I'm sorry, Den, but I made a square deal with your Daddy."

Dennis knew it was true. This was just another failed venture since that fateful day in Corinth. Something odd had happened. His father had a good government job at the post office and just left one day, disappeared from his duties. When found, he was sitting limply in the family buggy near the railroad crossing, staring into space with some stones in his palms repeatedly saying, "These are the answers to all my problems. These are the answers to all my problems."

Once home his mother had cried, saying, "You boys are going to have to look after our needs now. Your father has gone beyond the pale, and I fear he is never coming back."

Frank put his hand on Dennis's shoulder.

"Dennis, Dennis. Come out of it. It's not so bad. It's twenty dollars, and now it belongs to your Daddy. And you can come with me on the line anytime. If you do, I'll pay you. Come on, you can go home now. You can do what you want for a little while. Go after that girl I saw you talking to. The boy she was with is a toad. Go after her."

So Frank had seen him at the encounter with Jane and James. You never knew what eyes were watching around here, never sure anything you were doing was not being observed.

Frank kept talking, but Dennis didn't hear, he only saw his mouth moving.

"Thanks, Frank. I'll see you around. But could you let the beavers alone awhile?"

"Sure, Dennis, sure," and Frank clambered back up the bank.

Dennis sat back down, reflecting on what had just happened. Something else would come along. His father would find something else. His father would try again. His father would fail again. He watched the beaver surface. It pulled another fallen sapling into the water.

5

———— ⚬ ————

Dread

He scrambled to the top of the ravine, grabbing at the hillside, then clapped and wiped his hands off on the butt of his trousers. By position of the afternoon sun, he reckoned it was five o'clock. On the road two slaves in a freight wagon loaded with cotton were heading northwards toward Pittsburg Landing. At the crossroads, he hailed them down, and they reined in their mules hesitantly.

"Hey there! Any chance you have seen a yellow-haired girl with a boy in a buggy?"

"'No, young massuh!" said one.

"No suh, we ain't seen em!" the other said cautiously.

Their reluctant response reminded him blacks had to be settled in before dark. He thanked them as they hurried the team of mules along with a coaxing shout, "Hep! Hep, mules!" Their sense of urgency heightened his own dread about what he might find at home, so he increased his pace on the road that led southwest to Hamburg.

In less than a mile, on the right, was a field with a large house. There was someone in a paddock by the house, brushing down a horse. Pushing his spectacles up on his nose, Dennis stiffened at seeing James Barnes. Then there was a shrill call from the house, James was being called to supper. Dennis briskly moved along the road glad that his passing went unnoticed. Enough of that kid for one day. Dusk was closing in, and he had to move along.

Because of the trap line, he knew some who lived in these home-steads. Diagonally from the Barnes' place, at the crossroads of the Eastern Corinth Road was the home and wheat field of Daniel Davis. Next to the wheat field, woods separated the Davis farm from the cotton field of the widow Sarah Bell. The eastern corner of her farm was positioned at another junction. At this junction he headed south, passing between the fields of Noah Cantrell and Larkin Bell. A bit farther south, McCullers's field was dense with apple orchards. Allan McCuller was enrolled at Shiloh school, another blonde kid like James with a high opinion of himself.

Past McCullers's, Lick Creek meandered through the bottom-land, finally draining into the Tennessee River. Up in the hills west was Shake-a-Rag slave church. Whites had acceded this place to negroes to practice their boisterous brand of Christianity apart from the white man's world. It was here where Beulah attended.

Beulah was a Negro woman who had become part of the O' Brien household after Charles found her washed up along the Tennessee riverbank. Charles, wandering in an aimless mental fog one day, discovered her near-lifeless body. In an emergency he could somehow rally to normalcy. It worked that way with Charles. Dennis's father had performed medical support during the Mexican War and possessed basic medical skills. She sprawled as stiff as the dead men he had carried from the field at the battle of Chapultepec. Retrieving the same green wool army coat that he had worn in Mexico, he wrapped it around her and coaxed her to consciousness.

She coughed up brown water, and looking into Charles's eyes said, "Please, massuh, jus' lets me be...I's jus' wants to go to the

Lawd. I been ketched befo and don't wanna be ketched agin. Jus' let me go to the Lawd."

She had leapt from a steamboat shortly after it had disembarked, distraught from being forcibly separated from her husband and children. Charles made up his mind that no one was going to take this woman back to bondage. Over time, she became like a family member to the O'Briens, but they had to keep up pretenses. Beulah had to act like a slave if visitors came. Bringing Beulah into their household enriched it and contributed a measure of stability to his father's erratic personality.

Charles was such an unpredictable man. Some days he was loving and considerate. Other days he stormed around the farm fields like a man possessed of a demon. This created irreverent and ironic humor in his boys. They had learned to treat anything their father did, even the unpredictable violence, like it was a farcical event. Dennis, though, was affected more deeply. The contorted nature of his father's spells, overblown reactions to loud noises, certain subjects, words and smells, and a tendency to talk to himself in an argumentative way were disconcerting to say the least. Dennis yearned for ways to fix his father.

As for the family farm, it was a precarious gamble. The precious forty acres of bottomland stood the chance of flooding in minimal rainfall. If flooding came at the time when the cotton bolls were bursting and ready for the gin, it meant disaster. The little cotton that they had grown this year still needed harvesting. Now that the trap line was a thing of the past, he and his brothers would be doubly concentrated on the crop, while dealing with the vagaries of their father's diminished capacity. Dennis broke into a run the last two miles to home. By the time he neared home, it was twilight, and the trees cloaked in Spanish moss looked menacing, like hobgoblins. There was a formidable rumble as he came over the hill on the path that led down to the little farm. The door to the cabin opened briefly. Screaming and shouting emanated from the open door. The sound reverberated off the bowl shape of the land, and he knew it could be heard even on the other side of the river. He was thankful that evening that Jane's family place was not near.

He crossed the pebbled path in front of the house, gravel crunching under his feet. When his shoes thumped on the porch planking, the raving inside the house stopped. Dennis pulled the door open, and hearth fire and yellow lamplight made him squint. As his eyes accustomed, the aftermath of another of his father's rages was evident. Things thrown to the floor, dishes broken, and his father, panting in the shadows with his arm across his brow. His mother Ida, his brothers John and Adam, sat nervously at the dinner table. John gripped the edges of the table, and his face was strained, as was Adam's. His mother, Ida, sat straight as a board, eyes fixed, and her lips twitching. Beulah was at the stove, vigorously stirring a pot. Then she started humming in a deep spiritual tone that sounded like a bow on a cello. It was what the family needed, a calming effect. Although the peak of the explosion had passed, Charles stomped out the door and slammed it behind him.

"Do you know what caused it this time?" Dennis asked his mother.

"He came back from Corinth today, agitated. There is a lot of war talk going on, and a cannon was brought into town and displayed in the square."

6

Class

The next day Charles was in bed in a stupor. This was always the case after one of the explosive releases. Unavailable to help with the cotton crop which urgently needed to be brought in, everyone would have to help. Ida wanted at least one of her children to go to school. As Ida served them breakfast, she insisted, "Someone has got to attend. I tried so hard to get you both into that school with Miss Sornby. If both of you stay home, there's a chance she will give your places to someone else."

She wrung her hands, rattled from still another night of family chaos, then drew her youngest, Adam, under her arm and directed her attention to her oldest.

"John, look what you did to Dennis. He was late to school, then late getting home. You stay here today. Dennis, you will go to school. You boys and your father are going to be the death of me."

John's eyes got big. It spoiled plans he had made with Abby. He turned to Dennis resentfully and mockingly breathed his usual, "Poor Dennis. Poor baby Dennis."

Dennis bristled, but he was angry at himself, feeling that he could have somehow prevented his father's episode. Dennis had a way of talking his Irish father down from his histrionics. *If he had only gotten home earlier, it would not have happened; he could have cajoled his father. Never mind that he walked home yesterday while John did whatever he had done with Abby; never mind that he had worked part of the trap line. If he had only been here last night…too much time at the beaver dam. Forget pursuing Jane. Duty, nothing left but duty.*

Then came a surprise from John, "She's right. I should be the one to stay home. You go to school, Dennis. Sorry I abandoned you yesterday. I just thought Frank takin' over the trap line, things would make a difference."

"You mean you knew Da sold the line, and you didn't tell me?!"

"Yeah, well…"

"Yeah, well nothin'! It's not fair! It's not fair! You do these things to me, you lie, and you cheat me out of things! You, you…" Dennis stifled curse words and headed for the barn. His brother had pranked him about running the trap line when he didn't have to at all.

Dennis put the bridle on Bobby, jumped on bareback and prompted the horse uphill. They loped off to Shiloh School. Once there he was mortified. It turned out he was the first student there. Being too early was as bad as being late. Miss Sornby was chalking the first lesson of the day. She turned to look at him. He braced himself for a lecture, but her demeanor was much different than the day before.

"Dennis," she said gently, "I have an apology to make to you."

"What do you mean, ma'am? I don't know any reason for you to be sayin' you're sorry," though he was still smarting from the previous day's reprimand.

"You know what I am talking about, Dennis, I wronged you."

Her rigid demeanor softened to the point her face looked younger. It was not every day someone in charge said they were sorry. Puzzled, Dennis replied, "It was nothin' ma'am, think nothin' about it."

"No, sometimes you take the easy way out to get things under control. But I was wrong. You had not caused any ruckus in class. Some of other boys did. If I believed in the Devil, I would say they were acting like him."

"I'm sorry, ma'am? You don't believe in the Devil?"

"Let me clarify. I am a Christadelphian. We don't believe the Devil is a real person. We believe the Devil is just a characteristic that hides inside every man. So really, I was wrong in what I said. Never mind, Dennis, I shouldn't be talking religion here, my religion anyway. If the preacher across the way heard me say this, I would be put out of my job. It was those other boys that were the problem. They just can't shut up. Especially Bruce Wicker, he's a real cutup and can't help himself, always showboating. Now excuse me, I must get back to preparing for the day's lessons."

She returned to the board, then she turned back with a fond look for Dennis and stated, "I have one true problem with you, Mr. O'Brien. You must start putting the letter g at the ends of words that end with i-n-g. You are an intelligent boy, don't say goin', nothin', or 'bein' or you will find yourself going nowhere, doing little, and being nothing."

A red-haired boy named Benjamin Glover entered the room, and Miss Sornby assigned him to ring the bell. Students gradually lined up at the door.

"Students! Students! The time has come! Please come in and take your seats!" instructed Miss Sornby. When Jane entered, she scooted to her spot in front of Dennis without saying a word. As others came in, Dennis wanted to say something to her, but he couldn't get it out. Jane spoke without turning around.

"Dennis O' Brien, don't you greet a lady when she enters the room?"

Dennis forced out words.

"Sorry, Jane. Didn't mean to be rude."

Jane turned to him and said, "Oh, stop it, Dennis. I'm just kidding. We're going to be friends."

He was warming to more conversation when James and the Wicker brothers barged through the door and stormed to their places on the benches. James glared at Dennis.

"Miss Sornby. Miss Sornby!" James demanded. "I think I could learn better if *Denny*, over there, and me switched places!"

The Wicker boys chimed in, "Yeah, teacher, make Denny-boy and James switch places!"

Dennis's left eyebrow rose in anger. Miss Sornby watched to see if it would go any farther. Her eyes cast a piercing warning, and Dennis sat down. The other boys scowled, but did so as well.

After all had filed in, Benjamin silenced the bell. As teaching proceeded, the temperature of the Tennessee September morning rose. Flies buzzed and kids swatted at them. Mud daubers were establishing a nest high in the rafters. Like others, Dennis smelled of horse sweat. By contrast, Jane in front of him, had a light cologne fragrance emanating from her perspiring neck. A breeze flowed through the room, and the smell of manure wafted in from the paddock. A young slave worked at cleaning it up.

Miss Sornby passed out slates and chalk. After reading and arithmetic lessons, the rest of the morning was spent writing. The older students were instructed to first write repetitively their names in cursive.

Jane lifted her slate to show Dennis behind her. *Jane, Jane, Jane.* Dennis displayed. Dennis, Dennis, Dennis. Miss Sornby strolled the aisle, checking everyone's progress. Then she walked to the board and chalked a sentence with all letters of the alphabet: *The quick brown fox jumps over the lazy dog.* Everyone groaned but became engrossed in perfecting the pangram.

At midday, the teacher looked at her watch and called a halt to penmanship. Clapping her hands, she announced, "It's dinnertime, girls and boys. Go outside and enjoy yourselves."

Dennis had raced away without food. He made for the shade of a big oak and sat down in cane grass and dry leaves and regretted his hasty departure from home. Some small boys were shooting marbles. Two girls sat under a large cedar tree to themselves. A clique of students sat around a gingham picnic cloth in sunshine, including Jane who was attempting to sit ladylike with two other girls. Abby sat down next to Jane, not caring that her bare legs showed. Jane was seated across from James, and they were engaged in a loud, animated conversation. Dennis could hear them clearly.

"Those Yankees had better not ever show their faces anywhere around here!" James said with conviction.

"Oh, really?" said one of the girls indignantly across the quilt. "I will have you know that my mother is Philadelphia born. Just what will you do the next time you see her?" This was Nellie Devine. She lived near the O'Brien's on a small plantation. Her father and Charles had been in the same regiment in Mexico and sometimes visited one another.

"Now, Nellie, honey," James teased the big bosomed girl. "She is now just as much a Southerner as the rest of us." The flirtation seemed blatant, but Jane didn't seem to notice, maybe she didn't even care. The conversation turned livelier.

"Captain Yerger came down to our farm with some militia on horseback last night," Allen McCuller proclaimed.

"Oh, yeah! He came by our place, too!" piped up Stephen Sowell, who had sauntered over. "Yeah, he was recruiting a company of partisans for independent operation and constant movement against the Yankees. He wants my Daddy to join up. My Daddy is going to do it, too! It is the only right thing to do. Otherwise, those Yankees will be down here and take everything, including our women! If they want war, we'll give 'em war!" Dennis snickered at how whiskerless Stephen parroted the adults, but talk of militias sobered him.

War was certainly no stranger to the O'Brien family. Charles, at twenty two, had arrived in America from Ireland after fighting British rule. In New Orleans he met and married a young and vibrant Ida. He felt his new country founded on "life liberty and pursuit of happiness" could do no wrong. He signed on for the fight with Mexico in 1846, despite having a young family. He returned home two years later with a war medal, but the experience had produced a man Ida no longer knew. The return also produced a new baby. By 1850 Ida looked old and haggard though she was only thirty six.

As he grew, Dennis liked to go through his father's trunk and try on the green army jacket his father had worn in Mexico. He admired his father's service medal, feeling proud and patriotic when he tried them on. However, he was also torn because his mother had pacifist sentiments. Periodically, she would proclaim to all three of her sons that she would never see them off to fight in a war.

When everyone went back to class, a sense of responsibility overwhelmed him. He asked Miss Sornby for permission to leave early to help with the crop. It was granted, and he retrieved the dapple gray horse from the far side of the field where it grazed. He was surprised when Jane came running up to them with his schoolbooks.

"Dennis, oh Dennis, wait! Miss Sornby sent me with these. I'm sorry you have to leave so early!" He reached for the books and felt the palm of her hand as she did.

"Thank you, Jane," he said, trying to hide how the smoothness of her skin sent a chill up his spine.

"I suppose you will be off with James after school?"

"No, not today. He said he has something to do."

Opportunity was begging Dennis to seize this moment. If he had been his brother, he would have thrown responsibility away in order to stay and take her to her home. He was not his brother.

"How will you get home?" he asked.

"I will find a way. I hope to see you tomorrow, Dennis. I really do."

He searched her face. Was her statement more than courtesy? Was she feeling any of the electricity he was feeling? She walked backward a few steps toward the schoolhouse, waving goodbye, then turned and disappeared inside the schoolhouse. Reluctantly, he clicked his tongue to head Bobby toward home.

7

Beaten

From the ridge road above the farm, Dennis surveyed the scene below. The whole family was at work on the last of the cotton crop. He couldn't believe it. Even his father was picking and stuffing a burlap bag. He trotted Bobby down to the barnyard. Dismounting, he was buoyed that his father was apparently better, and the harvest was near finished. John raised his head on seeing Dennis and dropping his cotton sack, came running. He hurdled across the rows of denuded cotton plants in uncontrolled exuberance, then tripped on the last one and fell face forward into red clay. Unperturbed, he scrambled over to Dennis and ecstatically proclaimed, "It came! I got the letter! The apprenticeship! They are going to take me on in Cincinnati!"

The long awaited answer to an inquiry brought sudden bewilderment to Dennis. It meant John would be leaving and soon.

"Really!? Really!?"

"Yeah, yeah! Can you believe it!? The letter came with the mail this morning on the steamer *Iatan*. Da picked it up at noon at the Post Office in Hamburg!"

This apprenticeship had been a subject of wrangling in the family. John, seventeen and restless, had glommed onto the idea that he wanted to be in the newspaper business. He glowed about how exciting it would be to be a correspondent. His enthusiasm conjured up covering stories of riverboat boiler explosions, drownings, hangings, and other sensational events.

Charles, who part of the time could be quite rational, was half amused and pointed out that much more was involved.

"John, you will have to work from the bottom up. They will start you as an errand boy and broom pusher before they even let you be a mere typesetter. That is a tedious, dirty job. Have you thought of that? Have you thought this through?"

John retorted, skewing up his face to look important. Ignoring the admonitions, he thrust out his chest and proclaimed, "Oh, and I would be writing about the elections, too. You know: Lincoln, Douglas, Breckinridge, and all those other politicians."

Dennis wondered if he really wanted to be a reporter. What he did know was that John wanted out of cotton picking, out of Shiloh school, and truth be told, he mainly wanted to be away from this family. He was like a colt at the starting line, and this letter had fired the starting gun.

After the stunning news, Dennis stifled mixed feelings and gave into celebration with his older brother. Adam came running. They jumped up and down together, shouting with joy, their arms around each other's' shoulders. Then in a rare occurrence, as Ida and Beulah approached, the brothers hugged.

Charles looked across the rows, appearing well-pleased, but was quaking inside at the prospect. He lifted his slouch hat off his prematurely white hair, forcing a grin while shading his eyes from afternoon sun. Acutely aware his behavior had played a huge role in this, he would not stand in John's way. In fact, he had facilitated getting John the opportunity. Charles had written in behalf of

John to Archibald Cox, a fellow Mexican War veteran, now editor of the *Cincinnati Daily Gazette*. Charles had saved his life during the Mexican War. Wounded, Charles carried him on his shoulders across an open field of fire to safety. He had only been doing his job, he would say to his sons when they pressed him to tell a "good war story." He rebuked the boys in his Gaelic accent, "Dunnot be callin' any war story good."

Archibald Cox was a good war story. Those were the days when Charles was clearheaded under duress, and his young body and mind seemed to withstand anything. Now, his inability to retain that kind of composure, to keep a steady job, or be a good father, weighed heavily on him. With this request granted, at least he had done something worthwhile for his son, even if it meant losing him to an uncertain and divisive world.

John abruptly broke away and ran to the cabin shouting. "I'm going to pack. The last steamer will be at Hamburg Landing. I want to be on it. I won't bring much. Thanks, Da, for the twenty dollars! I don't want to miss the boat!"

This couldn't be. It was happening too fast. Dennis went emotionally flat, looking wanly at the tree line with leaves turning color. The afternoon sky was hazy. The changing season made him ache. John's absence would mean increased struggle for the rest of the family, more responsibility for himself. Even now with John's hasty preparations, it fell to him and Adam to bring the packed cotton bags and tools to the barn. And that twenty dollars? His father had given John all the money Frank had paid for the trap line. Charles stepped over the plucked cotton rows and went to the house to help John get ready. The cotton plants were drying up, soon to be plowed under like the portion of John's life he was leaving behind.

Back at the house, Beulah watched the hurried packing. With hefty arms across her plump chest, she hummed a tone of pride mixed with resignation:

"Mmm, Mmm, Mmm, Mmm. That boy John gonna *be* somebody."

Ida wept, and as Beulah put her arm around her, she sobbed repeatedly, "He's going. He's really going. My baby, my boy."

The next two hours were a blur. When Dennis and Adam came in, they tried to help, but John packed wildly, and took some of Dennis's belongings. In helpless dismay, he watched John take his red gingham shirt.

"You don't really need this shirt, Dennis. I need an extra," and he stuffed it into his rucksack without looking at his brother's distressed face.

The steamboat whistle split the air, announcing impending arrival. It echoed off the bluffs of the Tennessee River. Normally the comings and goings of riverboats brought a kind of reassurance, a way of marking time, but now, for the O'Brien household, it produced a mournful noise. To Dennis it sounded ominous.

The goodbyes were far too quick. In anguish, Ida ran back into the cabin and Beulah followed. Charles and John rode tandem, loping up the hill with John's belongings thrown over Bobby's rump. When they topped the ridge, they stopped briefly. John waved a last goodbye to Dennis and Adam. On the Hamburg road, they broke into a gallop in order not to miss the boat.

Charles came home in the twilight with typical tell-tale signs. He arrived in the yard in the closing darkness, his eyes glaring, fists clenched, berating himself. With little time to spare, Dennis called out to his younger brother, demanding, "Adam! Get in the house! Quick!" Dennis steeled himself, approaching his father who was by this time raving in slurred speech.

"I'm no good! Might as well be dead. Look at what I did to John. I am certainly dead to him. Why go on? Too much struggle. Now that he's gone, the rest of you boys will follow. I have nothing, nothing but five pitiful bales of cotton."

KEVIN GETCHELL

Dennis took Bobby's reins from his father's hands and tried to help his father down from the horse, but Charles fell in a clump on the ground. Surprisingly unhurt, he got up and continued, "I'm no farmer. Just an Irish Catholic lout, a foreigner in a Protestant land! Why am I here? I have no friends! Why am I even alive?"

He was not a practicing Catholic, but he could not bring himself to set foot inside any other church. In this tight knit Protestant community, it was difficult to get other farmers to warm to him. His erratic nature didn't help. Dennis attempted to comfort his father.

"Da!" he said empathetically. "You need rest. Go in the house and get some supper," but the innocent exhortation released some unseen banshee in his father's mind.

"Just shut up and dun not tell me what to do! Go get ta work on those sacks of cotton in the barn and start puttin' them on the wagon!"

His father started boxing, swinging in the air at some horrible invisible foe. Then he started smacking his own face with his fists. Dennis tried to prevent him. That only served to make Dennis the personified demon of Charles's mind. He got up, removed his belt from his trousers, and started flailing it about in fury. Dennis tried to get out of the way. The belt hit Dennis across the head, buckle first. It rose again in his father's hand, then shot snakelike across his back, ripping his shirt and flaying a long strip of flesh. His father dropped the belt for a moment, and Dennis dived for it, but Charles was faster. Maniacally, his senses heightened, and in a truly altered state, Charles grabbed it again and continued the uncontrolled lashing. His eyes were bulging, and his mouth was frothing with spit. He hit Dennis again and again. The belt buckle opened a gash over his eyebrow, but he did not cry out. Ida looked out the window, screaming at what she saw. A moment later, she burst out of the door frantic, followed by Beulah and Adam.

"Stop! Stop! You're going to kill him!" she screamed. Her voice vibrated as she ran toward them.

Charles kept on. Ida reached them, but he continued to whip. A strike glanced off her shoulder. She got in front of him, and started pounding her husband's chest.

"Stop it! Stop! In God's name, stop it!"

Charles seemed to come to. A look of horror passed over his face, realizing what he had done. He crumpled to his knees and wavered.

Her voice steady, Ida said, "Go to the house now, Dennis. I'll be there in a minute with some liniment."

"Mama, I'm alright," Dennis strained as he rose, first hands on knees, then upright and dizzy. His mother looked at Dennis uncertainly. Beulah examined him up and down, then gave him a careful hug.

"Why, why does it have to be like this?" Charles whimpered, stuttering slowly into silence.

Dennis asked himself the same question, "Yes, why, why does it have to be like this?" He climbed painfully up the ladder to the loft where he usually slept with his little brother. Grimacing, he began examining his body with odd wonder in the lamplight. He was throbbing all over. Bright red rivulets ran down his chest, intermixed with darker wine colored blood streaks. He lowered his pants, twisting around to look at his backside. Black and blue bruises mottled his hips. He mused at the multi-colored shades, but his head was now spinning. He slumped to the floor, unconscious.

8

Prophecy

The next day when the pink sunrise glowed over the river bluffs onto the little amphitheater of the O'Brien farm, the beating had compromised Dennis's resistance to infection. He had developed a raging fever. Adam gingerly poked his brother's sweat-drenched body. Opening glazed eyes, Dennis with limp hand, motioned at something

Adam called out. "Ma, he's sick! Ma! Real bad sick - dreaming! He keeps reachin' out, pointin' and sayin' a name, but I can't tell what it's about. He's sayin' it over and over!"

Ida climbed the ladder. Dennis's delirium continued as she pressed a cloth to absorb beads of fevered sweat from his forehead. Adam clambered down the ladder and scurried over to Beulah preparing a breakfast that no one had much interest in. She stirred lard into eggs and potatoes in the iron pan and called out, "Dat boy done takin' too much this time. Lawd, have mercy!" Then under her breath she muttered. "When dis kind of beatin' all gonna end?"

She glared over at Charles who was lolling on the bed below the loft. He had taken laudanum. The drug had him groaning, uncomprehending of the magnitude of damage he'd wrought.

"Dennis is a tough one. He'll be alright." Then before he succumbed to the mind-deadening effect of the drug, he called out, "Adam, Adam, you're goin' ta haf to be the man t'day. I cannot get up."

Adam seized on his father's incapacitation. He yanked at Beulah's sleeve and called out in the pitch of a ten-year-old, wishing his father to hear him through his stupor, "Coffee! If I am going to be a man today, I get to drink some coffee!"

"Why, Yesssuh, young Adam, dere is coffee, and it's just like my man, Jack. Strong and black!" Beulah chuckled. "Yesssuh! So black, he like a sapphire in the sun. Mmm, mmm, mmm, black and delicious."

The attempt to lighten the atmosphere and spirit in the cabin belied a more sobering situation. Her husband had been sold down the river deep into Mississippi, yet Beulah still hung on to hope they would one day be together again." Mmm! Mmm! Young Adam, dat coffee gonna put hair on ya chest, and ya gonna be strong like Jack!"

Adam laughed, so did Ida up in the loft, who looked for a response in Dennis, but there was none. Dennis continued desperately ill. The fever would break only to return, leaving Dennis drenched in sweat. After a week, a red rash spread over his body, his tongue strawberry colored. He continued muttering a word that had now become clear, and fitfulness evidenced disturbing dreams.

"Jane. Jane. Jane."

For several days Adam remarkably shouldered the brunt of necessary chores, while Ida and Beulah attended to Dennis. Charles continued downing his medicine and residing in an opium universe.

"Lawd, have mercy!" cried Beulah, after climbing up to the loft the next day. Seeing the color of his tongue, she exclaimed, "Dat tongue! Dat rash on his body. He gots da Scarlett fever. I seen this a hundred times! He look like a ball on a Christmas tree! Lissen, Miss Ida, we got's ta to get dis boy outta dis hot loft fore he starts bleedin' from da ears."

Ida and Beulah carefully moved Dennis closer to the ladder. Ida put her arms under Dennis's armpits, and Beulah stepped onto the ladder backwards carrying his legs. Carefully, she stepped to the next rung and then the next. Adam helped his mother as they came to the bottom. Dennis had lost weight and his ribs were showing as they stretched him out naked on the kitchen table.

"We gots ta get' him cool, his brain 'bout to explode."

Adam ran to the well, returning with a sloshing wooden bucket. Ida and Beulah ladled the cool water over Dennis. Rivulets poured off his overheated body onto the rough wooden slats of the table, then dripped through cracks in the floor. It roused him and he drank, but he still kept losing consciousness.

"They is infection in dem wounds. We gots ta do somethin' bout it!" decried Beulah.

Storming quickly out the door, she hurried to the woods and gathered some wild medicinal herbs. She ground them into a poultice. She and Ida carefully smeared the medicine on his wounds. As the fever raged, hallucinatory dreams controlled Dennis's mind.

He found himself alone on a raft on a river with no current, smooth as a mirror. He looked down into the water and saw his face. When he looked up, there was a man sitting on the bank in a throne-like chair. Robust, he wore a white shirt with a blue military jacket over one forearm. The man's hair was reddish, and he had a roughly trimmed beard.

"Who are you, sir? And can you tell me what place this is?" asked Dennis in the phantasm.

"Look back into the water," the man instructed him. He saw Jane's face next to his own, and beyond their faces, a storm was raging behind them.

"There is the restless sea of mankind," the man declared.

"If you please, sir, may I have your name?"

"You will know my name, but not now," came the stern reply.

Dennis insisted, "I am sorry, sir, please tell it to me."

The authoritative figure proclaimed again: "All in good time. Look into the water again."

"Blood?" he asked in horror.

""It is coming," the man said firmly. "It is coming."

When Dennis awakened, September had slipped into October.

9

——◦《◉》◦——

Bonds

In a couple of days, the fever left him, and his consciousness returned, but he was too weak to even stand. Dennis was more than anxious to get back to school. He missed so much, but he had his books, and to the extent the illness allowed, he devoured their contents. Through a trusted neighbor, Ida had sent a letter to the teacher about all the trouble and John's departure. Miss Sornby returned correspondence and sent word she would hold Dennis's place in class for as long as she could.

On a balmy autumn afternoon, Dennis, having regained some strength, walked tentatively along the riverbank that was the eastern boundary of the O'Brien property. The moon was visible in the sky while the sun was still up. Seeing him, Beulah lifted the coarse brown cloth of her skirt and moved awkwardly through the dried cotton plants until she got to Dennis. She said to him lovingly, "I'll walk down da rivah wits ya, hunny. I gots sumtin' ta sho ya."

Dennis held out his fingers weakly to her. Beulah took them gently with her doughy white palms, and they gingerly walked hand in hand down the riverbank, their feet making squishy, sucking sounds in the mud. They sat down, side by side, on a driftwood trunk of a long cypress tree. Beulah patted the top of his hand.

"Do you see 'em?" Ida asked in a whisper.

"See what?" Dennis replied.

It was an hour or so before sunset, and afternoon sunbeams were split by the trees on the bluff. The beams splayed across the bowl of land and onto the Tennessee River. In the middle of the river glided a pair of elegant black birds.

"Ain't dem swans beautiful, Dennis? Ain't dey jus beautiful?" Beulah clasped her hands together and her dark eyes sparkled with unadulterated joy.

"Black swans! I've never seen *black* swans!" Dennis muttered too loudly, and the birds became alarmed, flapping their wings, threatening to fly.

"Shush, shush now. Did ya know dat swans marry fuh life?"

Dennis whispering now said, "My Da once told me so, Beulah."

"Dids he tells ya dat swans be livin' longest o' birds and dats dey be married until dey die?"

"Yes, but I have never seen black ones."

"Dat's cause dey be frum places fah 'way, cross da big watah. Dese swans 'scaped frum sumbody. Dey is like my people. Taken 'way frum dey homes far 'way. Yes, suh, Dennis, wen I see dose black swans I sees me and my husband, Jack. Him'n me jumped the broom twenty years ago."

"Do you know where he is?"

"Yesssuh, I do. Rights here in muh heart, but I heered he wuz on a plantashun somewhere. But I's gonna finds him sum day."

"When was the last time you saw him?"

"Twenty year ago we wuz wed. Five year latah on da same day o' da year, da massuh took him ta auction. It wuz a day jus like taday. Moon was risin' while the sun still up, just like now. Da air wuz jus like now, warm, buts not too much wetness. An wen dey took Jack and my two yung chillun down river on the barge, there was two black swans in the watuh, jus like now."

Dennis looked into Beulah's face, expecting to see tears flowing down her cheeks. Instead, there was a confident look of determination.

"Yes, suh, young Dennis, I see dem black swans, an' knows Jack and me is gonna be together agin someday. But really, we is together now." They sat quietly while the light began to fade. "Well, young Dennis, I's goin back up ta da hous. I's gots a cake ta bake fuh the walk-aroun. Stays and enjoy dem swans. Yous not be seein 'em agin fo' a long time."

The sun had not fully set, but darkness was fast closing in. He watched the swans as they turned in unison in the waning light. A moonbeam shown down and reflected in the river. He and Jane. Could they be as swans?

There came a crack and a boom of musket fire in the distance across the river. The startled swans lifted broad wings from their sides and flapped, moving with increasing speed across the water until their webbed feet were just skimming the surface. Rising slowly, they flew low above the river until they disappeared in the moonlight.

10

CakeWalk

D ennis awoke to a honey sweet aroma permeating the air. Feeling a renewed strength, he climbed down from the loft. Sitting on the stove was a moist golden cake Beulah had baked for the harvest festival, specifically for the cake walk also called the walk-around. Everyone had eaten breakfast, allowing him to sleep, but there were biscuits and an apple for him on the table. Going to the window, he pushed back the blue checkered curtain to see all four of them loading the wagon with the precious sacks of cotton. He watched his father particularly, and he appeared mellow.

At the wash stand, he poured water from the white ceramic pitcher into the matching bowl, cupping hands to draw up water to splash his face. It made him feel better, but his mind was grappling with ways to manage his father. Patting his face gently with a towel, he examined in the oval mirror the lingering evidence of his injuries. The miracle he had prayed for had not been granted. Though much of the bruising had turned yellowish, darkness still encircled the orbits of his eyes.

He carried the cake carefully toward the loaded wagon. Charles

O'Brien kept his back to his son. When he spoke, Dennis detected a hint of shame in his voice.

"Good to see you about, Denny. Tis a fine day. You'll be happy to be seein' all your friends up at the school, I'm sure." With his voice slightly wavering, he said. "Tis good to have friends."

Dennis would just let it all pass as he had before. He had learned after much experience with his father's episodes that extreme forbearance was the best way to continue coping.

By contrast, his mother was perkier than he had seen in a long time.

"Dennis, Dennis! I can't wait to see you with all of your friends up at the school. I can't wait to meet them and see Miss Sornby again! Come, get on the wagon! Hand Beulah the cake!"

Beulah cried, "Mmm, mmm, massuh Dennis. You's gonna have a good time today!"

He cringed over Beulah calling him master, but Beulah would have to act that way while at the festival, safer because of factions at Shiloh. Shiloh Church was a breakaway from anti-slavery Union church at intersections of crossroads to the north. Shiloh was a microcosm of what was taking place all across the country.

"Come on, Denny!" Adam shouted. "Get on the wagon!"

The O'Briens headed north. Charles clicked his tongue and coaxed Bobby. The wagon bounced and jolted while Beulah protected the cake. When they got to Lick Creek, Charles became jovial and sang an idyllic Irish ballad. The Tennessee autumn was a balm to them all with the changing leaves, apple and peach orchards, and crisp air. Adam pressed Dennis about who lived on the farms along the way.

"That's the McCuller place over there," he said dryly, thinking of Allen McCullers's sarcasm at school. Cut from the same cloth as James: clever, brash, good looking, and he knew it. As they drove on, he pointed to a lop-sided sign on the left.

"There's Larkin Bell's. His oldest boy is named after him and is in school with me."

They came to a fork in the road where lay a large cotton field. At its edge was a split rail fence. A few slaves were bringing in the last of the cotton. They sang as they picked the bolls. In a commanding baritone voice, a tall muscular Negro intoned:

"Oh, my Lawd! Oh, my good Lawd!"

The rest answered in low mournful reply.

"Keep me from sinkin' down!"

The spiritual continued with the call out and answer:

I tell you what I mean to do! (Keep me from sinkin' down!)
I mean to go to heaven too! (Keep me from sinkin' down!)
I look up yonder and what do I see?! (Keep me from sinkin' down!)
I see the angels beckonin' me! (Keep me from sinkin' down!)

Piles of cotton sacks stood at the end of the rows. Charles eyed them enviously.

"If we had property the size of Sarah Bell's and as many slaves…" he stopped, suddenly struck with guilt over Beulah. Current cotton prices were thirteen and a half cents per pound. The O'Briens had harvested about 1400 pounds, two hundred dollars' worth. Every penny counted. It had to cover debts and expenses for next year's crop.

Approaching the crossroads of the Eastern Corinth and Hamburg-Purdy roads, Dennis got uncomfortable. It was, of course, where James Barnes lived. No one seemed to be at home, probably already at the festival. As they rolled along past the admirable log home, Charles commented, "B' gosh and begorrah! Would ya look at that place? Somebody has a little bit o' heaven! Imagine the crop they brought in!"

Closer to the school, Dennis adjusted his hated spectacles. He smoothed with his finger his blackened eyes, as if his touch might somehow wipe away their discoloration. He cringed about being seen with his family, then felt sorry he felt that way. He wanted to be proud to be with them. He loved his brother Adam. He loved his mother. Certainly, he loved Beulah. But as for his father? Would something trigger him? The man was like a weeping willow, lovely to look at when the wind did not blow, but a frightening, thrashing, howling banshee in a storm. Love his father?

In order to distance himself from the family as they approached the school, Dennis dropped softly off the wagon and walked several paces behind. Adam was puzzled and called out, "What are you doing all the way back there, Dennis?!" It dawned on Dennis he was acting like his older brother John, but he shushed him with a finger to his lips. When they got to the schoolyard, Dennis watched his father help his mother off the wagon. She blossomed like a tulip looking around at the crowd. Beulah wrestled herself down off the wagon with the assistance of Adam.

She spied Dennis hiding, and shook her head, "Mmmm, mmmm, mmmm!" she hummed disapprovingly. It made him regretful. There was no getting around it. You cannot choose the family you are born into. There was a major chore that needed to be done before they could fully get involved in the celebration. The wagon was going to have to be taken to Wood's Cotton gin.

"Da!" he called, now not caring who heard or observed him. "Let me take the wagon to the cotton gin with you."

"Oh, Denny boy. 'Tis a fine shindig here. I'll take it me self. Go on! Have as much fun as ya can."

Dennis tried to insist, but his father would not have it. Hoping for the best, he watched his father roll away down the Corinth road towards Wood's cotton gin.

Attendance was swelling, maybe as many as three hundred, not counting slaves. Dennis meandered among the boisterous crowd looking for Jane. He paused among a group that had gathered to watch a rousing game of horseshoes. Farmers needled one another about skill; hurrahs went up when there was the clang of a ringer, laughs or moans when there was an overshot. He zigzagged, trying to be nonchalant, but every time he encountered someone, young or old, there were remarks about his bruised face. "Whoa! Where did you get that shiner?" "If you look like this, what does the other boy look like?" "Hey, raccoon!" "Who are you planning to rob, Bandit!?" If it was not the teasing, it was suggestions of how to treat black eyes. One old man with snuff dripping out of one side of his mouth suggested he try chewing and smear some tobacco juice on them.

Over on the side of the schoolhouse, a bunch of boys were pitching pennies. Dennis reached in his pocket and found an Indian head cent. Mulling it over, he heard his mother quote Scripture in his head. "He that tilleth his land shall have plenty of bread; but he that followeth after vain *persons* shall have poverty." He looked at the coin and decided to violate the holy admonition. To prepare for the gamble, he removed his spectacles, cleaning them with his shirt sleeve.

"What are you planning on doing with that penny, Dennis? Make a fortune?" came an unmistakable feminine voice from behind.

"Yes, Jane. I plan to fill my coffers." He turned around, looked her in the face, and she saw his condition.

"Oh, Dennis, you've been hurt! I'm sorry." He was dismayed that she had seen him like this and pretended nonchalance.

"It's nothing, fell off my horse," he stated flatly. She could tell he was lying and chuckled.

"Now, Dennis, it's cute. You kind of look like a bandit with a mask."

There it was, that lame joke, but here she was, talking with him after being away from Shiloh for so long. He searched for the next thing to say, then suddenly blurted, "Would you go to the cake-walk with me? Go with a black-eyed bandit?"

She appeared surprised. Thinking it over, she replied playfully. "Mmm, not a bandit. *I* would say "highwayman," and I would be glad to go with a rogue like you!" The answer seemed too good to be true.

The cake walk was quite a spectacle for the residents around Shiloh. Mr. Cherry had brought some slaves from his Savanah plantation to perform. It started out simply enough to the accompaniment of a small band of slaves on fiddle, banjo, and flute. Decked out in hand-me-down finery from their masters, the participants started out with a bow and curtsy. Then they circled in stately promenade. Each time a round was completed, the slaves added a new step such as a kick, another circuit and there was a jump, next a twirl around. The dance evolved further. The black couples began competing and their dancing became wilder with hilarious jumping and gyrating. Onlookers applauded, laughed, and clapped time. When the music stopped, everyone, black and white, seemed unified in merriment. The music picked up and continued. Jane and Dennis stood at the edge of the encircling onlookers.

By evening, families began drifting away. Before the crowd thinned too much, Mrs. Cherry appealed to them to vote for the best contestants. She called for cakes to be brought forward and presented to the winners. Beulah brought hers and waited happily. Mrs. Cherry looked at it disdainfully and selected instead a more elaborately decorated cake with white icing. Looking over other cakes, she clapped her hands together and cried out, "Oh look, there are plenty of cakes for all the darkies."

Beulah deferred to Mrs. Cherry, "Yes ma'am. I's gonna gits dis here one over to dem over dere," and she pointed to a gray headed couple in the circle. Mrs. Cherry gave her a condescending nod.

The preacher came forward and raised his voice. "So let us adjourn this gathering with prayer!"

Amens were said, and people went their respective ways. Someone bumped into Dennis hard, forcing him into the crowd, separating him from Jane. He nudged people out of the way, only to find James Barnes pulling Jane away briskly. He started to pursue them angrily. Not realizing that his mother had been watching him with Jane, she came up next to him, "Don't get so worked up. Besides, she is *not* the kind of girl for you. Look your father is back! It's time to go home."

11

━━━━━◦◉◦━━━━━

Cousins

In the weeks following the fall festival, the cotton crop's financial gain brought tentative peace and security in the O'Brien household. At school Dennis had to numb himself about Jane. Though they continued friendly interaction, apparently James was still her beau. In order not to see affectionate interactions between them after class, he quickly exited the school house each day and cantered away on Bobby. The last day before Christmas recess he came home to a familiar unsettling scene.

Charles had walked to Hamburg and returned disturbed. As Dennis entered the cabin, his father threw a rolled-up newspaper at the wall. It exploded, its pages fluttering like wings of disturbed pigeons. With a sarcastic Irish lilt, he announced:

"Governor McMillie, of the great State of Mississippi, has just given his message, sayin': "The Democratic party of the State, representin' an overwhelmin' majority of the people, have adopted the followin' resolutions!"

Then he spit into the fireplace, venting Irish curses.

"*Amhas!* That lout McMillie! He's a shame to his forefathers!

And that legislature?! *Pla ar do theach!* A plague upon their house! Just look what they have proposed!"

He picked up the front page of the paper and flourished it in front of the family. They braced themselves.

"Look!" he hollered. "Look what it says here!" running his finger across the headline, then handed the article to Dennis to read. Dennis took courage since his father's outburst was not directed at any of the family and began reading.

The CORINTHIAN
December 21, 1859 Corinth, Mississippi
Secession Looms!

"Resolved, That in the event of the election of a Black Republican candidate to the Presidency by the suffrages of one portion of the Union only, to rule over the whole United States upon the avowed purpose of that organization, Mississippi will regard it as a declaration of hostility, and will hold herself in readiness to co-operate with her sister States of the South in whatever measures they may deem necessary for the maintenance of their rights as co-equal members of the confederacy."

"Listen to that!" Then came another curse. "*Go n-ithe an cat thu, is go n-ithe an diabhal an cat!* May the cat eat you, and may the devil eat the cat!"

Political pontifications usually posed no threat to the family, mainly venting, but they braced themselves. In some ways it was humorous, the English translation of Gaelic curses having lost intrinsic power. Dennis and Adam tried not to snicker. Beulah turned away to kitchen chores, giving a wide-eyed knowing look. Ida put her hand over her brow to hide a "here we go again" rolling of her eyes. Charles ranted on.

"These Fire-Eaters, listen to 'em! They are calling Lincoln

a Black Republican candidate?! Why the no good so-and-so's *Briseadh agus brú ar do chnámha!* May all their bones be broken! Lincoln, a Black Republican candidate? It's a double meanin' they are suggestin'...That he's not only evil, but has black blood in him."

Charles checked himself and looked over at Beulah, embarrassed that he had repeated the bigotry of the newspaper article.

"Beulah, now I apologize."

She replied, "No suh, don' you never no mind about it. Don' you never no mind."

The tirade now turned dangerous. He slammed his fist into the log wall. Ida rushed to see what he had done to his fist. Taking his hand, she wrapped his bloodied knuckles. Charles simmered down.

"Denny, Denny. I hope you understand what I'm meanin' by these words. Ya see boy, the jingoists are on the march again. In my life, first it was the British treatin' the Irish like cattle. Then I went to Mexico, thinkin' I was goin' to fight fer the land of the free and the home of the brave. Turned out it was about gettin' land and more land, this time, from brown skinned people..." Charles trailed off muttering more Gaelic and slunk out the door dis-spirited. Dennis followed him. If his father's mood took a turn for the worse, Dennis wanted to be a buffer for the rest of the family. More importantly, he wanted to understand the secrets of his father's experience in Ireland and Mexico. Was there anything he could do to help his father get better? As he had done at other times, he spent the next two hours just listening to his father as he paced back and forth in the barn, spewing wild words. Staggering revelations bled from his father's wounded mind. Revelations in sessions like these were part of what had helped him endure his father's assaults.

As was the case after most of these spells, there was a reprieve, and Charles seemed to be in control of himself. "Well, Denny, the morning is gone. Go over to Albert's place and stay the night. You'll be havin' a fine time with your cousins. I talked to your mother last night, and she said it would be good for you to get away."

Dennis could hardly believe his ears. Albert Moore was Ida's first cousin. Randy was Albert's middle son, so second cousin to Dennis and the closest thing to a best friend he had. The Moores lived about 10 miles by road from the O'Briens. Albert was a widower, and frankly, he was a rascal who operated a still. His three boys were just as wily as their father. They had gone to school as little as possible, but all of them managed enough reading, writing, and arithmetic to keep shrewd accounting for the family business of making white liquor. They were all experts at dickering prices with customers of all social classes, whose arrivals were as consistent as the distilled drops of moonshine coming out of the still. It was cash on the barrel head for some, barter for family necessities with others. It was rumored that Albert had a fortune stashed away somewhere, but the appearance of the place did not reflect the amount of coin that was transacted there. The quality of the booze was storied. Allowing him to go the Moore's place betrayed inconsistencies in the way his mother looked at things. Ida could put up with scalawag relatives. The Moores might be bad association, but Dennis reasoned she was thinking blood is thicker than water. Besides, she could handle Albert Moore. She could tangle with anybody when she was riled.

It was late afternoon, New Year's Eve, as Dennis trudged to the Moore's house. The wintry sky was a pink chiffon curtain behind the silhouettes of denuded trees. Dry bronze leaves lay thick in an unbroken blanket across the forest floor. As he moved, there was an ever present white noise of his shoes shuffling through the leaves, and the snapping of dry twigs underfoot. Of course, he thought of Jane. From the day he met her, he began to develop a mental callous about her relationship with James. This hardening made him feel that it would be impossible to be "with" her. Had she not said merely, "Let's be friends?" If that is all that she wanted, could he live only with that? In the bleak existence that was Dennis's life, he could not afford to lose a bright spot amid the on-again-off-again tyranny of his father, the encouraging but smothering control of his mother, and his own relentless sense of duty. Jane was a little light in the darkness. He had to keep her in sight no matter what might happen.

As Dennis tromped across the widow Howell's field, his breath became vapor in the cool of the evening. When he came to the northwest corner of the field, he paused at a bluff that overlooked the prettiest little valley. The creek that ran through the bottom of the valley was the reason Albert Moore had set up his moonshine operation here. The tell-tale signs of distilling were rising from a sizable shed near a large cabin. Dennis smiled to see the wisp of steam rising in the crisp evening air, and the sweet smell of corn mash wafted up the bluff.

The hillside was about a forty-five degree angle, making it hard to descend. He grunted as he grabbed dry cane grass on the hillside to steady himself, but finally got to the creek below. In the dark he perceived two silhouettes standing in front of him on the other side of the creek. They were cradling sawed-off shotguns.

"Hold it right thar, mister!" came Randy's voice, not yet recognizing Dennis. "State yur 'n ten-shuns!"

Dennis laughed at the twang of his cousin's accent.

"And, what's sooooo funny, buddy?! It ain't gonna be funny around heer in a minute!"

Dennis replied ruefully and took on his cousin's accent. "Well, I just figured if I snuck down here, I might find you snogging on a jug, full as a tick, happy as a dead pig in the sunshine."

"Wheeeeee! It's Denny! If'n it ain't fer the fact I was expectin' ya, I'd of peppered yur behind. It's been a long time, cousin! We're gonna have some fun ta nite!"

Randy lowered the shot gun and handed it to his brother, Walter, next to him. Walter was near-deaf and more dangerous because of it, so Dennis stepped back. Randy patted the big boy's shoulder, got up close to his ear and hollered in a voice loud enough to create an echo, "Let ur bee, Walter!! It's jus' cousin Denny!!"

Walter took the weapon, so he now had one in the crook of each elbow. Randy jumped exuberantly across the stream and embraced Dennis with a bear hug. Dennis held his breath, stiffening as Randy squeezed as hard as he could. It was a contest.

"Is that all you've got?" Dennis laughed and reciprocated with a bear hug of his own, lifting Randy off the ground. Randy grunted and responded with the nickname he'd given Dennis. "Not bad, Possum. Now come on over to the cabin."

On the other side of the creek, Dennis went up to Walter, looked up into the tall boy's eyes, and mouthed his words that so he could read his lips: "Hello, Walter. Good to see you."

Walter responded with a grin of acknowledgment and blunted baritone because of his life-long inability to hear, "Uhh, Denny, gooood toooo see youuu, too!"

Walter was the youngest but tallest of the three cousins. He survived at birth, but his mother had died. Soon after, he developed ear infections in both ears that left him deaf. It was not the only thing he lived with. He was born with a club foot. Dennis slapped him on the back lovingly, and they all turned to go up to the cabin, Walter limping.

"So what's cookin' besides liquor?"

"We got a smoked ham hangin', an sum o that fine fresh bread widow Howell brings over heer. Ya know, I think she's sweet on pa. But ther'll be somethin' better than vittles tonight. Walter heer is gonna stay an watch things while we go over yonder." He pointed vaguely west. Randy always had a mysterious plan when Dennis came over. The fun they had had together forged a strong bond between them.

"Great, I tell you, I'm hungry. I haven't eaten since breakfast. Where's your pa and your brother Gunnar?"

"Daddy an Gunnar are deliverin' a batch over ta Purdy. They's won' be back tanight. They's gonna stay with pa's sister, Aunt June. You know how good Walter is about watchin' things. He's gonna watch the new batch cook while you an me go over' ta hill ta Robert's plantation."

The one-room cabin was smoky inside from a stone fireplace with poor chimney draft. It wasn't enough to make him cough, but the haze and permeating wood burning smell caused Dennis to wave his fingers in front of his face. There were two hickory wood bedsteads, one for Gunnar and their father, and for Walter and Randy in the other. Old quilts sat in rumpled piles on the beds. In the middle of the room was a roughhewn oak table with benches on either side. Dennis couldn't help but wonder what this family would have been like had their mother lived. Would Randy speak with better diction with more schooling? Walter may have had better treatment for the ear infections. Maybe Albert Moore would have sought more respectable means of living. Then Dennis thought of the way things in his own family had turned out. You can't pick being born, you can't pick the family you were born into.

"Quick! Heer, take this and slice off a piece o' that ham!" Randy said, pulling a knife from his belt, whipping it deftly into the hanging ham.

"Think you're Jim Bowie?" Dennis said, pulling the knife from the hog leg and slicing off a thick piece. From a loaf on the table, he tore off a chunk of bread. Truly famished, he scarfed down the food. Walter took the rest of the loaf and silently slipped out the door to go watch the still.

"What's going on? Why are we going to the Robert's plantation and why so late?"

"You'll see. Ur really gonna get an awakenin' tonight. I been thinkin' bout you. Been heerin bout you, somebody said yur all doe-eyed bout some slip of a gal named Jane."

Randy had heard about Jane? It was a reminder that somebody was always observing and tattling. He didn't want to pursue the subject with Randy just now. When Dennis finished the rugged supper, he wiped his mouth on his sleeve and looked at his cousin. It was hard not to slip into an accent with Randy.

"Whadda ya got to drink?"

"Boy, howdy, have I got somethin!"

Randy picked up a white and brown stoneware jug by the door. He plunked it down in front of Dennis at the table. Dennis looked at it long and hard. He was thirsty and wanted water, fresh cider, or milk, not this.

"Watcha lookin' at? Think it's gonna drink itsef?"

"Look, Randy, this won't quench my thirst. Just give me some water."

Randy brought a wooden bucket, reached down and pulled up a ladle of water. Dennis reached for it, but Randy held it back teasingly. Dennis reached again. Randy drew it back once more. Finally, he let Dennis have it with conditions.

"Promise me yur gonna take a sip uh this jug. It's some my Daddy's best, what he saves fer his best customers."

Dennis stared at the jug. He had had alcohol before, but never hard spirits. His mother had forbidden that. The O'Briens made their own hard cider and crock wine, but this stuff of Albert's? His mother told him it was poison. It was peculiar that she let him be around the still when he was younger, but when he'd come over then, he was more interested in the mules that were pastured on the property, and fishing, hunting snakes, and pretending to "Remember the Alamo" with the cousins. He once had gone into the shed where the still was, however, Albert caught him and warned, "Your mother'd kill me if she found you in here. Now git!"

"Okay, Denny, pick er up and slam 'er down yer gullet," Randy demanded.

"Slam? Slam it? I don't think so. You think I'm crazy. I'll taste it, that's all."

"Okay, possum, jus' try it."

Randy still liked to call him "possum" from the days they played Alamo or Injun fighter. One would shoot with a pretend musket and the other would fall down. Dennis was better at playing dead than Randy. He could stay so still, show so little breathing, move so little that it would alarm Randy. Shaking him hard to see if he was really okay, Dennis would pop his eyes wide open and say, "Hah! Just playing possum!" It had stuck with Randy all these years.

Dennis picked up the jug. He pulled the cork out of the neck of the bottle, sniffed, and then cautiously touched his tongue to it. Randy stared at him, studying every move.

"Yep, that's right, there ain't nothin to warry about."

Dennis picked up the jug in both hands and was bringing it to his mouth when Randy came around the table and said:

"No, that's ain't the way ya do er. It's like this."

He picked up the jug with a finger through the handle, and with the bottle against the top of his forearm, cradled it in the crook of his arm, then took a short swig and held it in his mouth. His face squinted, his eyes clinched up. He swallowed hard. A visible shiver went through his body, and he growled and shook his head.

"Whweeeweees doggy! Whew, that's good!" Then he stomped the floor.

"Good!? Good? It looks like you swallowed a weasel!"

"Here, watch again." Randy took it up over his arm again. It produced a similar reaction, only this time Randy put his palm into his armpit and made a farting sound, then clicked his tongue.

"Now, it's yur turn."

Dennis thought it best to get it over with quickly. He hoisted the jug and took a deep swig. The liquid hit his tongue and felt like it burned off every taste bud. It went down his gullet like angry hornets and wound up in his belly feeling like a hot coal. He put his head on the table and slapped hard.

"Whaa! Whaa! Whaaa! Whaat in the…!"

Randy beat his chest hysterically, howling and stomping, having coaxed Dennis into trying the hooch. After a couple of minutes, Dennis felt the effects and a wave a euphoria swept over him. What was this? He raised his head and looked at Randy, who had calmed down, but was smiling at him knowingly.

"Pretty good, huh?" Randy now chuckled.

"Mmm, I don't know."

"Oh, come on now, Denny. You cain't tell me there ain't anything like this in the whole wide world?"

"Mmm. Mmmph," was all Denny could reply.

"Come on now, Denny, just take 'nother lil sip. It'll do you more good. You already feel it, don't ya? "

Randy picked up the jug and took another sip. He handed the jug back to Dennis. Dennis, not so cautiously this time, took another drink. This time it was not as wrenching. The euphoria increased. He had never felt finer than he did at this moment.

Dennis and Randy continued to pass the jug back and forth between them. Stories of their past came up.

"Ya member when we threw mud at those girls in their Sunday-go-to-meetin' clothes down in Corinth?" and he rolled, laughing.

"Yeah, I do. We must have been about six years old. It was fun, but my Daddy used the belt because of it." Dennis laughed, thinking about how he had padded his pants to lessen the effect of the strikes. He recounted another incident.

"Yeah, and do you remember the time we snuck in the church and smeared honey on the pulpit? We hid and waited for the preacher to come in and practice his sermon. His paper got stuck on the podium and there were so many flies, he cussed."

The stories continued, and the jug passed until Dennis and Randy were thoroughly soused. It was then that they decided to head out to the Robert's plantation.

The Robert's plantation was not by any means the largest plantation in Tennessee. Some were several thousand acres with more than a hundred slaves. This one was several hundred acres. It was close in size to the Cherry properties around Savannah. The Cherrys and the Roberts each kept a little more than twenty slaves. The plantation was a mile west of the Moore's house on a well-drained plateau, and Dennis and Randy made an unholy pilgrimage that night.

12

$$\text{---} \ll\!\langle\!\langle\textbullet\rangle\!\rangle\!\gg \text{---}$$

The Yaller Gal

I t would have taken less than thirty minutes to get there during the day, but it was night, just a quarter moon, and they were drunk. It took an hour and a half. Somehow managing to climb up the western bluff behind the Moore's still and cabin, they staggered through some canebrakes, holding each other up, and finally got to the edge of Robert's sizable cotton field. The rows were laid out east to west. The cotton had already been picked, leaving the dead plants dry and prickly. Dennis and Randy were so woozy and wavering that they struggled to communicate. Dennis said slowly with slurred speech, "Sooooo, buddy boy...are we here yet?"

Randy, fighting a rising urge to vomit, replied, "Yup, yup, we's here. I think it 'ud be better ta get down an' go hands and knees below these bushes an' sneak."

Dennis agreed. They got down and crawled for some distance parallel to one another in separate rows until Randy flopped down on his belly, then rolled over on his back. He screamed, "Denny, ain't it great! Ain't we a pair! We shud be doin' this all the time, playin' hide and sneak!"

"Shhh, Randy, be quiet. Shhh!"

"I um bein' quiet as I kin, Denny!"

"No, you're not. If you keep yelling like that, you'll draw attention, and they'll catch us."

Immediately, a hound began to bay.

"Randy, Randy, you hear that? See? They know we're here. We might as well turn around and go back. Randy! Randy!"

There was no answer because Randy had apparently passed out. Dennis crawled over to Randy's row to check him. He patted Randy on his cheek gently and rasped, "Wake up. Wake up, Randy!" There was no response, not even a twitch. Dennis patted harder. "Come on, Randy. Come on! Wake up!" Still no sign. He fell back off Randy, his head swimming. He began to imagine the worst. His mother had been right, the stuff Albert made *was poison*!

At that Randy popped up like a jack-in-the box and snickered, "Just playin' possum, Possum!"

Dennis pushed him back down. Randy sat up again and pushed back at Dennis. It turned into a wrestling match. They kicked and half choked each other, rolling over two stands of dead cotton plants until they found themselves in mud. The shock of the wet made them stop struggling with each other and give in to suppressed laughter. They sat for a while in damp pants, feeling content in the buzz of inebriation.

Contentment was short-lived, however, as the drunkenness brought waves of vertigo and nausea. Their bellies finally rebelled. Dennis retched and threw up. Randy heaved, trying to direct the spew into the next furrow, but part of it got on Dennis's cheek. He wiped his face with his sleeve, complaining disgustedly. Randy stood up unsteadily and burped.

"We gotta gets goin,' Denny. We're late, and there's sumthin' speshul up ahead."

Something special up ahead? Randy's words "sumthin speshul"

triggered a memory of when they were both twelve years old. It was before things had disintegrated for the O'Briens, when they had lived in a nice clapboard home in Corinth Mississippi. Randy was staying over for the night. It was a hot, humid evening, and they had sneaked out to go to a much finer home in town down the street. Soon Randy was standing on his shoulders, trying to reach the decorative balustrade of the second story. "Come on, once I git up, then I'll pull you up an' show you sum thin' speshul."

In short order he and Randy were clinging to the narrow ornamental shelf, peering through a clerestory window into a bedroom. They perilously waited. Before long someone entered and lit a lantern, slowly turning up the wick until the room was fully illuminated. It was a beautiful raven haired girl, about eighteen. She stood before a long oval mirror just looking at herself. Then she began to disrobe down to her frilled undergarments. Dennis and Randy were transfixed. Randy was almost drooling, and as for himself, he felt a strange sensation below his belt. The balcony began to creak. "Jus wait, Jus wait," whispered Randy.

The girl loosened her corset and placed it in a chifforobe, her smooth naked back a creamy color in the lantern light. Then she turned and stepped out of her pantaloons, and it bared all her glory as they stared. She looked up at that moment and saw them looking through the window. She screamed and then the railing gave way. They remarkably survived the fall with no injuries, and they shot away like panthers in the night, while the girl's father shouted and waved a shotgun.

Dennis jolted out of the memory. With the contents of his stomach dispelled, his head felt clearer. Why were they here in this field? Where were they going and to what purpose?

"Randy, hot spit and monkey vomit, that white liquor is powerful! What happened? It's like we were somewhere else a minute ago. Now we're in this field."

"Well, Denny, you always was a bit "gone in the haid," Randy cackled.

The suggestion that he was "gone in the head" hit his clearing brain bitterly. It cut through the residual alcohol fog and sliced into the fear he had about his father and himself. "The apple doesn't fall far from the tree." Isn't that what people were fond of saying? Now, the person he felt closest to was mouthing all was not right with him. A rage came up in him. He got up, whirled around, and headed back down the row in the direction of the Moore's place, though having come this way while drunk, he had no way of knowing which direction he was headed.

"Denny, Denny, whar ya goin?!"

"You said I'm crazy! Leave me alone," Dennis began to run.

"Naw, Naw, Denny, now come on, I didn't mean nothin' by it!"

Randy went after him. The hound bayed again, and more dogs joined in a chorus. Alerted by the noise, someone appeared between the Corinthian columns on the lighted porch of the mansion. Another couple of lanterns brightened in the area of the slave cabins.

"See, Denny, looky down thar, don be runnin' away! They'll sic the dawgs on us. If ya run, they'll tear ya up! They know me, but they'll git you!"

Dennis froze. He came back under control, but he shook from both receding anger and remnants of intoxication.

"What do we do?!" Dennis asked, fighting panic.

"Calm down, calm down now, they're expectin' me, b'sides the Roberts are over in Savanah for a New Year's party at the Cherry Mansion. I told Elmore, the overseer, I'd be comin ta nite. Thas him on the porch. Ifn I call out, he won't loose the dawgs, and they'll settle down. We need ta stand up an walk slow ta the house and show ourselves, Elmore will recognize me."

"Okay, okay, lead on, but why are we doing this? What've I signed up for? What's this "somethin special?"

"Well, I cain't tell you everthin just now, jus trust me, it's goin ta be speshul. No, fer a fact it's gonna be fancy, (hee hee), and Fancy is her name."

Fancy? Who was this Fancy? Blast conscience and blast his mother, he had gotten drunk for the first time. Why not see where Randy's scheme would lead with a mysterious girl? He would seize the opportunity. What difference would it make? Jane was not going to be his anyway.

He kept on his cousin's heels, walking steadily toward the plantation complex. When they arrived at the edge of the cotton field, they encountered a man of medium build holding back a leashed hound pulling and growling. In the sliver of moonlight, the man's skin was as white as an elephant's tusk. He wore a rumpled hat and had an irked expression on his face.

"Elmore! Did ya get that lil gift I sent over this mornin'? An', oh yeah, this is my cousin, Denny." Randy came prepared for the hound. He pulled a piece of ham from his pocket.

"Heer Blue, heer ya go, ol' boy!" The dog sniffed then scarfed the chunk of meat in one bite. The man loosened his firm grip on the hound. It began to slowly snuffle Randy's and Dennis's legs.

Elmore looked Dennis over and grunted that he had received "the little gift," then said, "You're late and you'd better hope to heaven all the noise you made didn't wake Mr. Roberts. He didn't go the Cherry's for the New Year's celebration because he wasn't feeling so good. You made a lot of noise. You'd both be dead meat if he'd a heard ya."

"We're sorely sorry, Elmore. Does that mean everthin' is all off fer ta nite?" The overseer didn't answer, only turned around and motioned with his hand to come on. They walked softly across the compound toward the group of slaves' cabins. Seeing now where they were headed, Dennis backed off and whispered gruffly, still buzzed by the liquor.

"What's going on? What is this, Randy?!' protested Dennis, and the dog began to growl at him because of his agitation.

Elmore pulled the dog away and said, "I fulfilled my part of the bargain. I'm doin' this only because you gave me that hooch. I should've made a better deal. This octaroon gal is pretty fine. If Mr. Roberts knew I was doin' this, I'd be out of a job, he might even shoot me. This kid with you is skittish. Now, you wanna do this or not?" The dog became more unsettled.

"Dang it! Dennis, come on!" Randy grabbed Dennis's wrist and pulled him forward in the direction of a cabin set off from the others. Still dulled, Dennis stumbled along as Randy towed him.

An old black man opened a creaky door and shone a lantern into the yard. The overseer waved a warning, and the slave lowered the wick, then slowly turned around going back inside, shaking his head.

Elmore told them to be about their business quietly, while he stayed outside with the dog. Randy pulled Dennis up on the porch, still whispering.

"Now, Denny, dang it, I was gonna go first, but look at ya, yer all tensed up and gnarly! Just git in thar and do what nature tells ya ta do."

Dennis hesitatingly opened the door. Randy gave him a little shove, peeked in for a look, and then slapped Dennis on the back. Then under his breath whispered, "Have at her, you Tennessee stud!" and closed the door behind Dennis.

He found himself standing on a rag rug near a hearth with subdued fire. On a brass bed, looking into the flames, was a naked and shivering slave-girl, her skin amber in the glow of the fireplace. Her head was bowed, she had one hand between her legs and a forearm drawn across her breasts. This was way beyond being peeping Toms with Randy in Corinth. Dennis stood frozen, then finally said awkwardly, "I'm sorry, ma'am."

The girl looked up, puzzled. "What are you calling me ma'am for? No white man ever calls me ma'am."

Mortified, he wondered what Beulah would think of him if she knew he was here. It was clear that this young slave had been through this many times, with no way to say no. She took his dumbfounded expression to mean something about her appearance.

"Oh, you are looking at my skin? Have you never seen a yaller gal, an octaroon?"

Averting his eyes, his throat went dry. Why had he allowed himself to get into this situation against what he had been taught? He had heard the phrase "yaller gal" before, however, his mother had not allowed him to use it or "octaroon" because it made a person sound like a thing. Hoarsely, he said:

"Look, I'm sorry. Can I simply call you by your name? My cousin says your name is Fancy, am I right?'

"My name is Elizabeth. Don't you like what you see?"

All he could say was, "My name is Dennis."

"Well, come and get what you came for," and with that she simply lay back limply on the covers, exposing her nakedness in full view.

This was wrong. How many times had this girl been forced to submit to this? How many times had Elmore been in here, in this cozy room? How many times had Mr. Roberts betrayed his marriage here? Even Randy. What, why, and how had he sunk to this? The girl stared up at him with stiff anticipation, steeling her body for what she expected to come. There was a quilt laying over the brass foot rail. Dennis covered his eyes with one hand, then moved forward gently. He covered Elizabeth's entire body with the quilt and backed away. Incredulous, she looked up at him and said, "What are you doing? No one has ever done that before, young massuh. Thank you."

"Don't say that...please, don't call me massuh." Sick to his stomach, he turned and stepped out of the cabin, and was immediately confronted by his cousin.

"Hey, how was it, Denny?" Randy asked greedily. "It was like watermelon in summer, wasn't it?"

Dennis grabbed Randy by the collar and fairly yanked him off the porch. "I'm taking you home! *Pla ar do theach! Go n-ithe an cat thu, is go n-ithe an diabhal an cat!*

Surging rage gave him unexpected strength. He slammed Elmore with his elbow, causing him to lose his grip on the hound's leash. The dog lunged at Dennis, but he deftly kicked the dog in the ribs as hard as he could. The dog gave out a piteous, elongated yelp, and ran off whimpering until it disappeared in underbrush. Lights came up in the Big House. Dennis yelled as loud as he could, while glaring at Elmore. Without the dog he was not so intimidating.

"You deserve what's comin' to you, Elmore!" He clapped his hands and gave a long shrieking whistle.

"Hey, Mr. Roberts! The Yankees are coming! The Yankees are coming!"

He dragged his cousin across the yard, down between the cotton rows, into the darkness.

13

————)◊(————

Baptism

January 2, 1860, Dennis turned sixteen. He felt aged and washed out from the New Year's eve experience with his cousin at the plantation, but he'd felt old long before that because of his father. Weary from trying to figure him out, and weighed down by thoughts of Elizabeth's subjugation, he was changed. Yelling had lowered his voice by an octave.

At the schoolyard paddock, he dismounted, then reached in his pocket for a lump of sugar. Bobby snuffled it out of his palm. He leaned his head against the horse's neck. It brought warm comfort to his forehead and penetrated his careworn brain. Then to his surprise, Jane came bounding toward him across the little meadow wearing a new blue and white calico dress and with a joyous voice, cried out:

"Hi, Dennis! What did you did you get for Christmas?"

"Gold, frankincense, and myrrh," he joked. She chuckled.

Jane then expressed surprise at the timbre of his voice. There was a subtle change in her blue eyes as she looked at him.

"My, Dennis, what a manly voice you suddenly seem to have. Where did that come from?"

"Have you ever heard of clergyman's throat?" he quipped.

"No," she replied puzzled.

"You see, I was practicing being a preacher, shouting hellfire and damnation. I worked myself up to a crescendo like at a brush arbor revival, my vocal chords popped, and I started sounding like this."

She burst into laughter. "Oh, Dennis, that's hilarious! Just what church do you belong to?"

Dennis mentally choked. He was joking about his "clergyman's throat," but religion could lead down a rocky road. His family did not go to a church. His father, raised as Catholic the straight up Irish way, had stopped going to mass long ago, and anyway, there wasn't a Catholic Church anywhere near Shiloh. Moreover the "church" his mother favored did not actually believe in hellfire and damnation. She always quoted scripture: "God is love" and *a God of love could not condemn people to everlasting torture.*" There were other beliefs that ran counter to most denominations in the area. He identified somewhat with Miss Sornby who was hesitant to admit openly to being a Christadelphian. It seemed good to be cautious with Jane. Best not get into doctrine, so he quickly turned the question back on her:

"We don't call it a church, but what about you? Do you go there at Shiloh?" Jane turned pensive.

"Don't call it a church? You sound something like the Campbellites. They make a point to say the church is the people. I have been going with Abby over at Purdy. I like it, and gave my life to the Lord on my 15th birthday." Her eyes rose wistfully to the sky. "They call it the Holiness Church." The religious Pandora's Box was open now. Catholics, Methodists, Campbellites, Christadelphians, Holiness, and whatever, were just a fraction of the denominations he knew about.

"Yes, it's called Holiness, but I get confused. I turned my life over to the Lord, but they keep preaching something called a second work of grace. I can't seem to reach it. I really don't even understand what that means. The preacher says it's because I like boys too much."

She lowered her eyes from heaven and her face flushed. With that charming slightly askew smile, she carefully searched Dennis's face. Maybe this was an opening to build something more substantial with Jane. Not just puppy love. Then came an interruption.

Across the meadow stood Allen McCuller and Abby Davis. Abby started toward him and Jane, but Allen stayed back, looking at him condescendingly. To his dismay, Jane abandoned their conversation. She met Abby halfway and exchanged a few words then walked up to McCuller. Jane's demeanor toward Allen betrayed something was going on between them. Abby continued across the meadow to talk with Dennis.

He gritted his teeth. "Where's James, and what's up with Jane and Allen?"

"Over Christmas recess Jane and James had a falling out. They aren't together now. Allen has been paying attention to her. You are a good guy, Dennis. You just need to be a little more forward!"

"Yeah? I'm a good guy, great! La de da!" He threw his hands in the air and sarcastically quoted an old Irish proverb: "So may the sun shine all day long, everything right and nothing wrong!"

"Oh, Dennis, stop selling yourself short. You had her full attention."

She was right. He wanted to kick himself for missing his opportunity.

"Dennis. How is your brother John? I thought he liked me. I went with him different places, did things he liked, and then he left so quickly. I heard he went to Cincinnati. He didn't even come and say goodbye. Do you hear anything from him?"

Abby's brown eyes showed a vulnerability, mentioning John. She was usually self-possessed, confident. She could have had any boy she liked, but she was attracted to his brother. He was proud John had taken to Abby. He had a fantasy that their relationship would somehow rub off onto him and Jane, and the two O'Briens would be with the two most fetching girls at Shiloh School.

"We got a letter from him. He is doing well in Cincinnati, learning about the newspaper business. He asked about you."

John had not specifically asked about Abby in the letter because it would have brought a sour reaction from his mother. John had cloaked a greeting to Abby, giving a post script to Dennis to give his regards at Shiloh School. He watched Abby's eyes go downcast.

The bell clanged, and Dennis and Abby walked together to class, and he wondered why he was not attracted to Abby the way he was to Jane. As kids engaged in the usual horseplay, Dennis looked to the back of the schoolhouse. Allen McCuller and Jane were up close to one another. Abby took her hand and placed it over Dennis's eyes and led him away from the sight saying, "You have to do something dramatic to show her how you really feel."

For the rest of the morning he tried to concentrate on class, but it was difficult. He couldn't get New Year's Eve out of his mind. There were rumors of war in the newspaper. Never mind, he had to find some way to change his friendship with Jane into something stronger.

Miss Sornby announced lunch, and all headed out of the school. How could Dennis catch Jane's attention before McCuller could corral her? He looked at the church across the road and saw the preacher talking to Miss Sornby, and it gave him a giddy inspiration. He buttoned up his collar like the preacher and strode across the yard to where everyone was eating lunch. He resolved he would risk a parody.

"All right, brothers and sisters, gather round!" His tone was righteous. "Yes, yes, you there and you! Listen to me! Are you listenin'? If you are, Say Amen!" He repeated, "Yes, yes, you there and you! Listen to me! Are you listenin'? If you are, Say Amen!"

Abby looked quizzically at him, and he winked at her. Seeing that something was up, she gave the first "Amen." Others caught on, joining in a small chorus of amused "Amens."

"Come hear the sayings of righteousness!" he demanded. The audience chortled, and said "Amen" every time he called out. He looked for Jane's reaction. She was puzzled, but followed Abby's lead. James Barnes and Allen McCuller and the gang that hung about them began to razz. He ignored them and continued.

"You there, brother, you haven't been saved? Well, you had better get down on your knees and pray. And you there, sister, have you been down to the river? Come with me, we will go down to the river right this minute." He grabbed Lorraine Seay and pretended to baptize her.

Then another, Michelle Rhea, came up to him and pleaded sweetly, "Preacher, I want to be baptized, too!"

He grabbed her and plunged her under imaginary water. When he lifted her back up, she swooned. This was fun. Dennis was oblivious to Jane now. Jane, watching other girls being "dipped" by Dennis, grabbed Abby's sleeve.

"What's he doing?" she asked. "I have never seen Dennis like this before." Abby slapped her knees in the hilarity. More girls in class lined up to participate in the false sacrament. This proved too much for Jane. She cut in line in front of a couple of other girls, and said, "Baptize me, Preacher! Please, Dennis. I mean, Preacher, baptize me, too."

Uninhibited, Dennis took her in baptismal stance and leaned her down, holding the small of her back. Her blonde hair cascaded onto dry grass, her bosom near his face. He brought her back up gently. Their eyes met for more than a moment. "Amen!" shouted Abby.

He did a couple more "baptisms," bowed to the crowd, and walked to the schoolhouse amidst applause. He felt more confident that there was yet time to close the gap between him and Jane. There was time, plenty of time, wasn't there?

As he entered the schoolhouse, there was a commotion. Down Pittsburg Landing road, came a man prancing a fine sorrel stud. He was in a gray uniform with fancy epaulets on his shoulders. Enthralled, students ran up. The preacher called out, "Hail, Captain Yerger! Hail dear old Dixie! Hail our hearths and homes! Hail God and Country! God is with us and all the southland!" Students joined in the cry.

14

Ambushed

The moment he had held Jane in his arms when pretending to baptize her gave him a glimmer of hope, but there were rivals aplenty. A whole cadre of Shiloh boys felt they owned the available girls, and if a boy came from outside their invisible boundary, there was trouble. Hamburg was outside that boundary.

Dennis was walking home one afternoon in late February because Charles needed Bobby at the farm. As he approached a wooded area, James Barnes, Allen McCuller, Larry Tilghman, Joe Hagy, and Bruce and Will Wicker emerged from the trees and encircled him on the Hamburg-Purdy road, halfway to Barnes field.

"So you think you're good enough for Jane, do you?!" said James, getting up in his face and then pushing him into Larry Tilghman.

"Yeah, you stupid Mick. Who do you think you are? Jane is way too good for the likes of you!" and Larry, pushed him into Allen McCuller.

Allen rasped a taunt in his ear, "Jane's lips taste good. You thought you could play my part didn't you, what with that baptism stunt. She's like butter on bread with me."

The next push was into Bruce Wicker. It was sort of pathetic to see the usually comical Bruce try to be a bully. He was no strong man though he was stout. He pushed Dennis into his brother Will.

"Think you're really something don't you, four eyes?" and he grabbed for Dennis's spectacles. Dennis resisted, shielding his glasses, so Will pushed him once again over to Larry. Larry popped Dennis in the nose, and immediately blood dripped. Then Larry pushed him back into Will, who this time succeeded in pulling Dennis's spectacles off his face and threw them to the side of the road. Dennis stumbled, looking to retrieve them. James walked over, crushed them, and kicked them into the field. They all laughed derisively, then the group broke up, heading in different directions toward their homes.

He got down on his hands and knees and found the earpieces of his spectacles, splayed out from the frames with lenses gone. Searching the grass, he found pieces of one shattered lens. He kept fingering through the grass, and found the other lens miraculously intact. He forced it back into the frame, then bent the earpieces as close to their original form as he could. Dusting off his dungarees, he resumed his journey home with bloodied nose and shirt, broken glasses, and clenched fists.

He walked on to the southwest corner of Widow Bell's cotton field, where the slaves were singing when his family was on their way to the cake walk. At the fence, a large black man was leaning over, watching him casually with his elbows on the fence rail. It was disconcerting to find a single towering slave, bent over, looking at him in the late afternoon, not averting his eyes as was typical. And then he spoke in an accent different from the area's negroes, "Hello, young Massuh!"

The size of the man, with pectoral muscles nearly splitting his smooth white shirt, put Dennis on guard. It was unsettling for a slave to speak without being spoken to first. He repeated. "Yes suh, massuh. It shore is a nice afternoon."

"I've had better. What's your name?"

"Well, now, let's see. Around here they call me Toby, but my real name is Douglas."

"Douglas. That is not a name you hear for a field hand."

The black man dropped his southern accent completely. It was startling to hear. "No sir, it is not."

"You kind of speak like a Yankee."

"Well, sir, two things. I am a free man, and I was born in Massachusetts."

"Not a slave? Massachusetts? Have you got papers?"

"Oh, I have papers. Do you want to see them?"

He reached into his hip pocket, produced a wallet, and held it out to Dennis. Dennis took it, and carefully pulled out the contents, including some paper money. He indeed had free black documentation, certified by a court. Dennis handed it back, somewhat relieved.

"Massachusetts. I have always wondered about that place. Plymouth Rock and all. Isn't it still a bit dangerous traveling this far south, even with these papers?"

"Well, sir, you do have that correct. I always introduce myself to the local authorities when I come to minister, and I don't talk this way around here. Slave catchers are a problem. Still have to be out of sight at night. Still not good to be found alone in a place where you have nobody to vouch for you."

"Minister?"

"I am serving the Shake–A–Rag church just now. Down the road apiece."

"Of course. Do you know Beulah?"

"Yes sir, I do!"

"Then you will know of my family. The O'Briens." With that Dennis reached out to shake the black man's hand.

"It's best not to do that. You'll get us both into trouble. Yes, of course, I know of your family. All of us know your family through Beulah."

"By "all of us" you mean?"

"Every black person in this region knows who you are."

"How could that be?"

"Your reputation precedes you among black folks. Beulah, of course, communicates it to all. The group of us that you found singing in this field know your character. Beulah tells all she knows in the language we speak."

"Language that you speak?"

"Mr. O'Brien, language is not just a mother tongue of a particular nationality. It is also communication that occurs as a subtext within a given dialect. Only those that know the subtext understand it. The black men you met in the wagons on the road know your character, as does Elizabeth."

"Elizabeth!?" The shock hearing her name was like lightning.

"Best keep your voice down. "Little pitchers have big ears" as they say. We should not have to worry about such ears. One day we shall no longer have these concerns. The derogatory words people use will be archaic slang, consigned to large dictionaries rarely consulted. One day, there will be no North, no South, no East and no West. There will be no discrimination or hate, but only a recognition of glorious diversity under the Kingdom of God!"

The words mesmerized Dennis. He had rarely heard anyone speak with this kind of power and diction.

"Listen to me, Dennis. I hope I am not too forward to call you by your first name. I know what you just went through down the road. You are a good man, Dennis O'Brien, but you must unclench those fists and seek the higher road."

Dennis looked down, not realizing that he had not relaxed his hands. He had clenched them so tightly he could barely open them.

"You see how balled up your fist is? Lift your fingers one by one out of that ball. It's like those boys down there who roughed you up. Lift them one by one; you will prevail."

"What do you mean? Track them down one by one and fight them each alone?"

"You could do that, Dennis, and I do think you might win a round or two, but remember, I said "lift them up" one by one. The Good Book would say it another way. To the Romans – 'If it be possible, as much as lieth in you, live peaceably with all men." Now Dennis, the sun will be down soon, we both must move on."

Douglas lifted his muscular arms off the fence rail, turned and headed off into some woods. The scripture resonated. *If it be possible, as much as lieth in you, live peaceably with all men.* "If it be possible?" Dennis reflected. It was not long before he would be tested in this. There was someone waiting at the corner of the cotton field. Dennis braced himself. As he drew closer, he could see through his one lens, Bruce Wicker. He had attempted to be a tough guy this afternoon. Was he going to try and prove himself again? Dennis braced himself for the unpredictable encounter, but Dennis could not see himself hitting Bruce. He called out, "Is that you, Bruce?

"Yeah, it's me, Dennis."

"You wanna go at it again?" Dennis raised his fists weakly, suggesting a tussle.

"Nah. I don't know why I did what I did." Dennis lowered his fist, and Bruce blurted out a half sorrowful confession "You know, I want her, too! She can have any boy she wants!"

"Well, Bruce, I can't say I want you to get her, but nobody controls her. Sometimes I think she sees me, you know what I mean? Other times not."

"Oh, I get that. It just turns out she only sees me as the class clown. I've decided it's never going to happen with me. I have to move on."

"I think we all may have to move on. My brother is in Cincinnati.

God, I would hate to live there, but this place has limited possibilities. You know what I mean?"

As he listened to Bruce, he could not help but feel a little sorry for him. So the class clown was in love with Jane, too. He was also sure that Bruce would never "get" Jane. That's the problem with being a jokester. Maybe that was the way it was with himself. She had not taken him seriously. Dennis had that time with her at the cake walk, but had she only taken it as fun? The day she had come bounding across the paddock, apparently glad to see him, she took up with Allen. He had spent day after day with her, tutoring the younger ones; and through some serious conversations, he had come to know her better, yet she still had not given any sign that she thought of him as more than just a friend. He had played out the fake baptism, and that time she had looked intently into his eyes. But was it just about fun again? Or was it a glimpse of spirituality?

"I'll see you tomorrow, Bruce. No hard feelings."

Bruce held out his hand to Dennis, and they shook.

"I'm sorry, Dennis. I am sorry about your glasses especially. I will make it right. I have some at home that my grandfather left when he died. I will bring them to you."

Bruce turned and walked north on the Hamburg Savannah Road that would take him home. It was only half a mile for Bruce, while for Dennis it would be another five miles south in the direction of Hamburg. It would be after dark when he got home. He was truly relieved that he would get a replacement for his glasses. If his father found them missing, it could mean dire consequences. He would just pretend that he had left them at school. That would work, wouldn't it? Or if he was on the laudanum, maybe he wouldn't notice at all. And there was time, plenty of time for everything.

15

---※◉※---

Almost

The latest news had come from back east. The editor of the Corinth newspaper did not print it verbatim from the original sources, but transmitted his own version for the local population. That latest issue now sat in Charles O'Brien's limp fingers.

The Corinthian
March 21, 1860
Lincoln's Outrageous Oration

"On February 27, 1860, at the so-called Cooper Union, the blackguard Abraham Lincoln of Springfield, Illinois accused our beloved South. Take note of what he said:

'Your purpose, then, plainly stated, is that you will destroy the Government, unless you be allowed to construe and enforce the Constitution as you please, on all points in dispute between you and us. You will rule or ruin in all events...'

The gall of Lincoln. We in the south were the first in freedom in the war of independence from England. We here in the South say that you, Mr. Lincoln, are the pot calling the kettle black, no, nay, we say the northern states are the blackest of kettles, the blackest of pots, unable to get clean of the very things of which you accuse us so violently.

Any other time, this kind of article would have triggered a rant, but there was no expression on Charles's face. His eyes were glazed. He looked like a rag doll. Would he come out of it and explode or would he stay in this state of mutism? Ida finally announced, "So be it. It's business as usual. You will go to school tomorrow, Dennis!"

Dennis rode slowly that early spring morning. Oak trees were in bud, the cedars had put forth fragrant new needles, and dogwoods were in delicate white bloom. It gave him a spirit of optimism. He found the replacement glasses on his bench, and his hopefulness lasted the day through to the last recess. He went up to Jane feeling playful.

"So, Jane, what do you plan to do once school ends?'

"Oh, I don't know. Why? We will probably go up to Nashville and visit kin."

"No, no. I mean when we graduate next year."

"Well, I submitted my application to the ladies academy in Clarksville, and Miss Sornby wants to help me get admitted. Isn't that exciting, Dennis?"

"Clarksville, eh?"

"Yes, Dennis, Clarksville."

"The Ladies Academy, eh?"

"Yes, Dennis, the Ladies Academy in Clarksville. What's wrong with you? "

"Hmmm....The Ladies Academy in Clarksville. That would not by any chance be the Clarksville in New York?"

"Do you think I would go to a Yankee Academy? Shame on you."

"A Yankee Academy? What's wrong with a Yankee Academy?

I understand they are quite good," he said with a twinkle in his eye.

"Now what are you up to, Dennis O' Brien? You know very well I am talking about the Ladies Academy at Stewart College, in Clarksville, in the great state of Tennessee."

"Well, I think you should go to Clarksville, New York," he harrumphed.

"Oh, stop it, Dennis"

"How about if I contribute a dime for you to go to the Yankee academy?"

"Now I know what you're up to, Dennis! Don't you dare!" She began hitting him with her quill pen. Dennis fended off the feathery attack and promptly planted a kiss on her cheek.

"And there, my Dear, is the contribution of my Yankee dime!" Before she could say anything further, recess ended, but she blushed as they re-entered the classroom and seemed to be looking at him with different eyes.

It was with suppressed exhilaration he had touched his lips to her cheek, but he also felt a pang deep in his chest. If her dream of higher schooling came true, Jane would be 150 miles out of reach. It might as well be Clarksville, New York. He wanted to fully open up to her after school and tell her how he felt, but as had happened so many times before, someone else grabbed her attention before he could. This time at least it wasn't another boy, but Miss Sornby wanting to discuss her desires to go to the Academy. It pained him and he turned to go home. He didn't feel like mounting Bobby. Instead he walked the dapple gray horse away from the school. He came to a freshly scythed field and dropped reins to let Bobby graze. The grass lay thick across the acreage waiting to be raked into haycocks. The sweet smell of the first spring cutting was so potent that he bent over and sneezed three times. It was then that he was surprised to hear the familiar feminine voice of Jane calling to him. She grabbed his hand and begin pulling him forward.

"Come on, Dennis! Let's run!" and she dragged him into the deep cuttings.

Then she broke away and bounded like a sprite across the open field. Dennis took off after her and was about to catch up when the pungency of the new mown hay caused him to explode into a sneezing fit again. Jane delightedly watched.

"God bless you! God bless you! God bless you!" She chortled, then took off again until she stopped, out of breath.

Dennis reached her and in the spur of the moment put his arms around her and lifted her off the ground, swinging her around and around until she was dizzy. Finally, he let her down lightly. She staggered a bit, and he steadied her. They stood looking into one another's eyes, laughing. The mown grass lay in long lines. Spontaneously, Dennis reached down and gathered up an armful.

"What are you doing now?" Jane asked quizzically.

"Wait and see."

With that he began spelling her name in sprinkled grass letters on the ground: JANE. For him it was a proclamation of his feelings for her. Then in a moment that he thought might never come, she reached down and gathered up a grass sheaf of her own, and letter by letter she spelled out: DENNIS.

It was happening. At long last it was happening. She knew how he felt about her now. Surely she knew how he felt. Suddenly, something came over Jane, and she ran off towards the road.

"Where are you going?" Dennis cried in a mix of surprise and desperation.

"I left something at school, my letter to Clarksville! I'll see you tomorrow, Dennis! Never forget how we wrote our names in the grass!"

Though the afternoon ended the way it did, Dennis's heart was bursting. He mounted Bobby, feeling giddy, clopping down the road, bouncing in the saddle. He raggedly remembered the lines of a Longfellow poem that had summed up his pent-up feelings until now.

> Who love would seek,
> Let him love evermore
> And seldom speak:
> For in love's domain
> Silence must reign;
> Or it brings the heart
> Smart And pain.

He was done feeling that way. He would not be maudlin anymore. Just look what was happening with Jane at long last! In the euphoria of it all, he stopped along the way to take in the smells of redbud blossoms, white dogwood petals, and the heady scents coming from occasional beds of yellow daffodils. Unfortunately, it resulted in more sneezing, yet even the sneezing felt delicious. He had actually kissed her lightly. He had swung her around, and while so doing, held her breast to his. They had written their names in the grass together. There were a few days of school left, and surely there would be time enough to completely end the unrequited nature of his love for Jane.

As he got farther down the Hamburg road, these thoughts were supplanted by the realities of what might be waiting at home. It did not take long to find out. He entered the cabin to find his father pacing back and forth, holding a letter in his hand. He was not angry, but rather was shrugging repeatedly. He handed the letter to Dennis.

"Look at what your brother has gone and done," then he went into the yard outside muttering in Gaelic. On the other hand, his mother was bouncing on the balls of her feet with excitement.

"Read it! Read it out loud again! Your brother is making something of himself!"

John's letter had been sent three weeks earlier.

Cincinnati, Ohio
March 1, 1860

Dear Father and Mother,

I hope you are all doing well. I am fine and I am most anxious to tell you I have a new job. Mr. William Russell, Mr. Alexander Majors, and Mr. William Waddell have started a company that will be transferring mail by swift relay riders from St. Joseph, Missouri to Sacramento, California. I will be carrying the latest newspapers and letters. It will be miraculous. It is figured to take just ten days' time. Mr. Cox feels that since I am from Tennessee and am good with horses and that I am a good Christian young man, he would recommend me to Mr. Majors. Mr. Majors is a religious man and has resolved by the help of God to overcome all difficulties that will present themselves on the way. What with fierce Indians, floods, wild animals and the like, he presented each rider with a special edition Bible. To show you there is nothing to worry about, I signed an oath which is in my special edition Bible. I repeat the oath in this letter.

I, John O'Brien, do hereby swear, before the Great and Living God, that during my engagement, and while I am an employee of Russell, Majors, and Waddell, I will, under no circumstances, use profane language, that I will drink no intoxicating liquors, that I will not quarrel or fight with any other employee of the firm, and that in every respect I will conduct myself honestly, be faithful to my duties, and so direct all my acts as to win the confidence of my employers, so help me God.

Your son has been blessed by God to work for a company that will be doing the work of the Kingdom. Hug Beulah and Adam. Tell Denny to give my regards at Shiloh.

Your Loving Son, John

After reading the letter out loud, his mother gushed over the contents. She effused what a good boy John was, what good people he would work for, and how she wished she could see the Pony Express Bible. *How nice for John*, Dennis jealously thought. *What a bunch of palaver.* He didn't really know what to say to his mother, so he went outside to check on his father. He found him kicking dirt. Dennis ventured a cautious inquiry, wondering whether his father was on the verge of violence, "Da, this is quite a thing John is doing, eh?"

"'Tis, 'tis actually wonderful," came the surprisingly positive reply along with a Gaelic proverb: "Encourage young people and they will get there."

It was a remarkable thing to hear from his father's mouth. He had gone to great effort to effect employment for John with his friend, the editor Archibald Cox. Now John had abandoned what he was previously excited about and was off on some grand adventure.

"Da, you're not disappointed?'

"Your brother is young and like a stag in the rut. It is his time. Let us let him choose. He who travels has stories to tell."

This was a little more than Dennis could take. It was enough that his brother had left him holding the bag, but here was his father and mother glorying over John's grand adventure, and in his mother's case, some convoluted sense of it all being God's will. Going off to the barn in a huff, his father called after him, "Don't worry Denny! Your time will come, your time will come!"

16

—◦◦◦—

Picnic

Awakening the next day in the loft, he stared up at the rafter boards re-living the moments of what had happened on the field of grass. He couldn't wait to get to school, but on arriving at the table for breakfast, it was clear that yesterday's moments of normalcy with his father had subsided. His father was silent, not touching his food. It caused everyone to have a loss of appetite.

"Da, do you want me to stay home today?" Dennis asked, trying not to feel crestfallen over the prospect.

His father did not answer. His limp state reflected internal struggle. Dennis was intuitive about such things. No doubt inside Charles's brain, a debate was going on. He had flipped his attitude. The optimistic Irish proverbs about encouraging the young people "to get there" and "those who travel will have stories to tell" ran counter to a fatherly selfish hope. If he was not going to follow through with being an apprentice, his oldest son should return home to help care for the family farm and keep the family whole so that Charles could build a legacy with an intact family, one that he had never had. He uttered under his breath a different Gaelic saying.

"Ní neart go cur le chéile"- There is strength in unity. We are better together." Then he clenched his jaw and balled up his fist. Ida tried to soothe him, and her touch seemed to help. She helped him to the bed where he lay down, turned over on his side and groaned.

The nature of these spells was unpredictable. Would they plummet into wishes for death, or soar to a superlative optimism that he could not sustain? The worst scenario was the violence that could surface, though the ferocity was never truly directed at the family. Even when he had beaten Dennis, Dennis had not been the true target of his fury. Charles never intended the family to be the victims of his lack of control, but they inexorably were.

This morning was only a ripple in the pond of Charles's mental malady, so everyone resignedly went about the business of another day. Dennis sought permission from his mother to take the letter from John to school, claiming that he primarily wanted to show it to Miss Sornby, but he had other reasons. He could not help himself. He was proud of his brother.

Dennis arrived at Shiloh fully expecting to find Jane anxious to see him, but as the horse sauntered into the schoolyard paddock, she was nowhere to be seen. For that matter, there was no sign of activity at all. No horses, no buggies, no students anywhere. Uneasily, he jumped down off Bobby, entered the schoolhouse, and found it eerily empty. Not even Miss Sornby was there. Like a bolt of lightning, he suddenly remembered this was the day for the last social event of the school term. The picnic was to be held at the Rhea farm, the same area where he had first met Jane by the spring. He made a frenzied ride for the farm.

Drawing up the horse upon arriving, he surveyed the scene. There was a cluster of teen girls higher up a sloping meadow. Along cheery Shiloh Creek that ran through the property, two little ones were trying happily but fruitlessly to catch minnows with cupped hands. On level ground across the road from the creek, another group of kids danced ring-around-the-rosie. A game of baseball was being loosely organized, and shouts of approval or dismay rang out each time someone was picked for a team. He did not see Jane, but he caught sight of Abby. After dismounting, he headed toward her, exchanging jocular greetings with others along the way. He called out, "Hi Abby! Quite a jamboree!"

"And, hi to you, Dennis! I was beginning to wonder if you would make it here today."

Patting his shirt to make sure the letter was still there, and finding it was, he removed it and held it out to her.

"I have something you would like to see."

"What's this?" she asked.

"It's a letter the family got from John. I wish I could say that I had another one to deliver especially addressed to you, but I don't. But there is something in this that I can say was meant for you."

Abby's face was enraptured. She carefully unfolded the letter and began reading. Dennis watched her lips as she read in a whisper with an occasional gasp. She stated the word Pony Express out loud, then she stopped incredulous and looked at Dennis.

"When you reach the end of the letter, you will see something that looks like a mistake. Like the quill bled on the paper, so that my mother wouldn't see it. You would have to know my mother to understand why."

When she finished reading, her eyes welled up. "Do you really think that the splotch on the paper said something about me?"

"I would swear to it. He really liked you."

"Liked? Liked? I loved him, and he went off without a word. Now he will probably find someone else, and I will never hear from him again. Either that or he will get himself killed riding cross-country!"

Dennis, unaccustomed to seeing this kind of emotion from Abby, put his hands on her shoulders and said "Abby, you are always telling me, you know what you always tell me…there is time. There is time."

Abby wouldn't allow herself to show any more emotion. "You know, Dennis, the boys won't let girls play baseball. I'm going to change all that!"

Dennis watched as she swiftly crossed the road. When she reached the ball field, she singled out James Barnes, who had apparently organized the game, pushed him back like she was ready to fight him, then took her index finger and began poking him hard repeatedly in the middle of his chest. A laugh fest ensued. In short order the game was reorganized, and Abby and four girls had been added to the teams. Jane was not among them.

Perplexed by her absence, Dennis visited clusters of students. Two or three had seen her talking to Mary Rhea, another said she had been with Lorraine Seay. Then little Elsie Duncan ran up and pulled at his shirt and pointed to a shaded place up the slope. There sat Jane alone on a picnic blanket. Relieved at finding her, he climbed the hill, and as he came closer, he could see she was preoccupied reading a book.

All sorts of superlatives about yesterday gushed into his mind about what to say first. He checked himself, remembering something Beulah had said about liking a girl, "Young Dennis. 'Member dis. Too much waterin' kin make da blossom fall off."

After a moment, she looked up pleasantly at Dennis.

"Oh, Dennis, it seems you appeared out of nowhere."

"What book are you reading? It's got you quite absorbed."

"It's a memory book for people to autograph. I have just been reading over some of the things our friends have said. I want you to sign it for me, too."

She seemed unmindful about the previous day, and he was disheartened. Nonetheless, he pressed, "Jane, there are some things I have been wanting to tell you."

Unexpected at that moment, Katie Jones came up behind him and poked the ribs on both sides of his body. He almost leapt out of his skin.

"Did she tell you, Denny? Did she tell you about what she's invited to, the cotillion?"

A debutante ball? He tried to mask his dismay at what was probably already a certainty. The only question was at which cotillion an eligible Jane would be presented. A dark emotional curtain descended on him, with the mention of a southern spring rite of which he knew he would never be a part. The Roberts and the Cherrys were the only ones in the Shiloh vicinity of the social stature to put on such an affair. Taking it for granted it was one or the other, he asked Jane which. He prayed that at least it would not be at the Roberts'.

"No, Dennis. I will be at neither the Cherry's nor the Roberts.' I'm sorry I didn't fully tell you my plans. I told you I was going to see kin in Nashville. My cousin in Nashville wants to take my hand for the presentation at Belle Meade. Can you imagine? Me, a country girl at Belle Meade?"

He did not want to imagine and could not bring himself to answer Jane. He was full of hate that Jane was going to this cotillion. In a frenzy of what to say or do he improvised a little pantomime. He turned to Katie and said.

"Well, Katie! Let me take *your* hand, won't you? We can go to a cotillion, too."

Jane watched him kiss Katie's hand as a gentleman might. He raised Katie's left hand with his right and then put his other hand on her waist. They proceeded to do a little two step waltz on the hillside. For her part, Katie was delighted, but after a brief whirl, she insisted that Jane get up and take over.

Jane was in his arms again. He sensed that this was the last time. What was happening at home bode that he too would probably be going away, only in the opposite direction. His father was broken, and if he was to be salvaged, he needed a special kind of doctor. He and his mother had discussed it, and that kind of doctor could only be found in New Orleans. Abby had said there was time, but time had run out. She was going to Belle Meade where an unknown young man, albeit a relative, would escort her into higher Southern society. Sometimes cousins married. As he and Jane awkwardly danced, he tried to find words that could sum up how he felt about her without sounding like a fool.

"Well, there isn't much use in me telling you how much I've enjoyed knowing you."

"Oh, Dennis you talk as though we will never see one another again. I will come back after summer." He could not bring himself to talk about his father and New Orleans.

"Well, no matter what happens in the future, know that your friendship has added a lot to me."

"Dennis, stop talking this way. Of course, we will always be friends."

"Friends...yes, friends." He spoke the words blandly though he felt as if a great earthquake had just taken place and a chasm was now between them. In a tone that exhibited that a kind of divorce had taken place in their relationship, he broke away from her and started walking down the hill. He had had enough picnic for one day. She called out to him,

"Dennis! Wait I need you to autograph my memory book!"

He hurried to distance himself, not wanting to hear her voice. Yesterday had meant little to her. He was hurt and could only mutter into the air when he got far enough away from her:

"Jane, I think you're great. You do have a lot of potential, I hope you don't waste it. You're smart, and with that smile, you can have anything you want. But it's clear you want me only as a "friend." I wanted something else for the rest of our lives, so take care of yourself," and then in a note of resignation he whispered, "I love you."

17

———◦《◉》◦———

Chapultepec

The weather matched Dennis' mood as he raced away from the picnic on Bobby. Rolling thunder started low and slow like kettledrums of an orchestra. He headed in a direction away from Hamburg. A quarter mile north of the school, they shot through the intersection of the Hamburg-Purdy and Corinth roads. Fifty yards later he veered right, towards Pittsburg Landing. Bobby's pace exhilarated him, and he goaded the powerful horse on to greater speed. He responded like he had been waiting for this moment to arrive. Hurtling up the road, Dennis lay forward, gripping Bobby's mane. The pounding hooves produced a cadence. Dennis heard the rhythm transformed in his head: "This too shall pass! This too shall pass! This shall too pass!"

They traveled over a mile. Then Dennis dismounted Bobby, dropping the reins so the horse could drink from a creek. After he'd had his fill and cooled down, Dennis walked him instead of riding up the road. They arrived at another crossroad. North went to Savannah and Pittsburg Landing, south to Hamburg and home. Dennis flirted with the idea of continuing northward and abandoning all responsibility. He did not want to go home.

The alternative was to continue east on a farm road that cut through a large field and led to some mysterious Indian mounds above the river. After tying Bobby to a tree, he clambered to the top of the largest mound where he had a grand view of the Tennessee River and the unending forest beyond. The panorama was awe inspiring. The vantage point revealed the river was on the rise. He unburdened himself into the air, shouting about all the things that were tearing him apart. A wave of animosity against God and heaven swept over him.

He turned to descend, but tripped and somersaulted back down the mound and was knocked unconscious. Coming to, he found himself staring up dizzyingly into the inky eyes of an immense black man with a musket.

"Hello, young Dennis," said Douglas in his deep velvet voice.

It took a moment to realize it was not a figment. How did the freedman get here? Then Douglas extended his giant hand and pulled Dennis to his feet woozy, glasses missing. He fruitlessly slapped his pocket see if they were there, then knuckled his forehead. *Not again!*

Douglas opened his hand and held out the intact spectacles. Kindly he spoke, "Looking for these?" Ever so relieved, Dennis thanked him and returned them to his face, but now felt embarrassed that someone had witnessed his little debacle. Douglas only looked around at the surrounding compound of hills and ruminated.

"An interesting place, this. Makes a person introspective. We all need introspection. "Know thyself," said Socrates about 400 B.C. That is all good and well, but as you and I know, it is not an easy proposition. Furthermore, if one succeeds in such a quest, then comes the conundrum propounded by Polonius in Shakespeare's *Hamlet*: "To thine own self be true." What do you think, Dennis? Can a man know himself, and upon gaining that knowledge, be loyal to principles that he knows are true and good?"

Recovering from his tumble, it was difficult to try and comprehend the oddity of this well-read, intelligently reasoning black man, showing up out of the blue. To top it off, this still unfamiliar Negro was posing questions quite close to the ones he had just been hurling into the atmosphere. He spoke with some alarm.

"Where did you come from? I didn't see you on the road. Why were you following me? Did you see my horse? How come you're not preaching somewhere? Last time I saw you was weeks ago at the Widow Bell's fence line. You walked off in the woods and now you reappear like some kind of phantom!"

Douglas was amused. "I see what you mean. I will explain. First, I was not following you. A free black lay preacher must find ways to be self-sustaining, so I have been hunting feral pigs. Mr. Cloud, who owns that large field, supplied me this musket to protect their upcoming crop from wild hogs. There are a couple of big razorback boars rooting around. If they had found you knocked out at the bottom of this mound, it would have been unfortunate. I was tracking them and came upon your horse. Then, I heard your troubled voice. I am correct, you are troubled?"

"Troubled to say the least. I would not know where to start. For one thing, there is a girl who, who…is killing me."

"Mmm, I know your situation."

"What do you mean?"

"If you will allow an illustration, perhaps it will help." Douglas reached into his pocket and took out some coins. He counted out seven. Six were shiny new pennies, one was a tarnished dime, and he asked which was the most valuable.

"The dull one is the more valuable. The dime. Thanks a lot, but I already get it. The girl has been choosing shiny pennies, while the dime is worth more."

"Did I say the shiny coins are the choices she makes in boys? That you are the dime, more valuable than the others?"

"Well…what are you getting at then?"

"They all have value. My intention is to say that the seven coins represent seven kinds of love. A person can possess them all, but only one is the most valuable. It is the seventh love."

"What is the seventh love?"

"I should like to discuss that with you, but I am afraid we cannot now. The light will be failing us soon, and the storm is coming. We both need to find shelter. We will meet again."

And there it was. The big black man named Douglas turned on his heel and disappeared into the woods the same way he had done the first time they met. Now he faced the dreaded possibilities of his father's situation. He found Bobby grazing. He cantered home without incident taking just less than an hour.

As he approached the farm, he saw his father staggering halfway down the farm's road to the river. Beulah and Adam were in a state of high anxiety. Dennis slid off Bobby, turning him over to Adam, who gave him an exasperated shrug of the shoulders.

"What's going on?"

"Lawd, Dennis, this is somethin' new. We all be tryin' talk ta him. Your mama be beside herself in the house. He be talkin' soft like to himself part o' the time, but other time git no rise outta him atall. Den he jus take off walkin' to da rivah."

"He's not angry though?"

"No suh, Denny, is like he back dere in Mexico."

"All right, Beulah, I'll see what I can do," and he headed after his father.

By the time he reached Charles, he had found a log to sit on and appeared to be watching something across the rising Tennessee River. Burgeoning thunderheads were turning from cotton white to chemise pink, pregnant with more rain in the late afternoon sun.

"Da?" he spoke softly, "Da, what's wrong?"

His father replied cordially. It had the effect of relieving Dennis, but he kept on guard. Patting the log next to him, Charles motioned Dennis to come over and sit down.

"Here, here, now my boy, sit with me awhile." Charles's eyes had a distant look, focusing on a vague spot across the river. Dennis tried to see what he was looking at, but there were only the flood waters, slowly swallowing the trunks of cypress trees. The water was inching ever closer to the log. Carefully sitting down, yet keeping taut, Dennis readied himself to jump away at any moment.

"Do you see them, Denny, do you see them?"

"What, Da, you mean the trees? Yes, they are getting covered up. We had best not stay here much longer, Da."

"Look over there at the wall of the castle. Do you see them?"

"Castle, Da? Where are you?"

"Denny, look at them, see how young they are?"

Dennis kept his voice low with no exclamation. "No, Da, please tell me. What is it? I don't see anybody."

"They couldn't be much older than you, Denny, just look at them up there."

"Look at who, Da?"

"The little Mexican boys. There on the precipice. Look. There are one, two, three, four, five, no, there are at least seven up there."

"What are you talking about, Da, what is it you see?"

"We're stormin'em. Look over there, Pillow and his troops! What a mornin' they are havin!! See our boys, so pretty in rows of green with their gleaming bayonets. My, ain't war so grand as when they charge in formation? Now look! See! The little Mexicans. Everyone up there on the wall of the castle. Pretty puffs of smoke! The little Mexican boys. Here they go, Denny, look! One, two, three, four! Oh, look! See how beautifully they fall? Five, six! Look, here goes the last one! Look, he is like an eagle in flight, wrapped in the flag. Isn't he beautiful?"

Dennis realized that the seven Mexican boys had become casualties. He did not want to jolt him out of his hallucination, so he remained quiet.

"The Castle! The Hall of Montezuma! Isn't it a beautiful thing?! Up there. They chose such a perfect spot to build it. Ain't it beautiful? Here they go. Watch! See the musket men making their way up the stairway?"

As the first sprinkles of rain dotted their clothes, Dennis realized his father's hallucination was the defeat of the Mexicans at Chapultepec Military Academy, the last futile defense by cadets.

"Ah, there now, Denny, they are finished, we must go over there now."

His father rose and started walking into the river. Dennis grabbed his hand and pulled him away from the deceptively lapping and rising water at the bank. Then, as if a thousand horses were pounding toward them, thunder rolled across a blackening sky

"Da, let's go back to the house now. Do ya hear me, Da?"

"No, Denny, we have to go get them. Look, see how beautiful, see how red! Look, look at his lovely hand, isn't it beautiful! It is just like my twin, when the British came! Oh well, we can put the hand here in the bag. Look! Look! There, there he is, there he is! Look, look at his face! Just like my brother! We must take him home, we must take him home. Ma is waitin,' Da is waitin', we will put him in the soil, by the wall with them."

Memories of Ireland, memories of Mexico, all tumbling together in the mire of Charles's brain. Dennis tried to salvage the truths infused in the hallucination. Incalculable, frightening, and intriguing. Allusions to Charles's twin brother, who died long ago, with so many things unclear about the circumstances. And what about his Ma and Da in the soil by the wall?

Dennis's father fell quiet and became compliant, lost in a maze of memories. Dennis was able to take him by the elbow and gently walk him back toward the cabin. When they got to where Beulah stood, she said, "Dennis, son, we's gotsta hep ya Daddy. He has done gone far. He gone far away."

Ida walked toward the three of them, head in hand as she came, her feet slipping in the wet red clay. Dennis took command of the situation

"Ma, we'll get things ready for tomorrow."

As the words came out of Dennis's mouth, a lightning bolt shattered the air, and the clouds disgorged a waterfall. Everyone was instantaneously drenched. There was no use in running. They encircled Charles and led him as quickly and gently as possible through the downpour. Ida and Beulah prayed aloud for protection from the storm.

18

Rising

That night it became evident that Charles O' Brien was on a voyage through the lost world of his past. He sat in the rocking chair by the fireplace, the firelight producing a silhouette of him against the timbers of the cabin. Staring at the flames with glazed eyes, he made grand gestures with his arms and hands and had unintelligible conversations with unseen personages.

In a search for a reprieve from the pall cast by his father's condition, Adam went out on the porch where the rain was pouring off the roof like a waterfall. Dennis joined him, and they stood next to one another, not speaking. They watched the powerful cloud burst, feeling the silent camaraderie that had been forged together by familial trial. Lightning blasts lit up the entire area of the farm and revealed the river was encroaching deeper into the bowl-like property. The house and barn were safe for now, but the rising water level bode frightening possibilities.

Simultaneously, the two brothers shouted through the noise of the storm. "We need to check Bobby!" They jumped down from the porch and raced to the barn through the downpour. Inside Dennis lit the coal oil lantern. The subdued light flowed golden over the stall. Bobby's eyes gleamed like fireballs in the lantern's light. They both moved quietly for the disturbed and twitching horse and slowly patted and rubbed Bobby from muzzle to hip to calm him. Then Adam sat down glumly in a pile of hay. The horse whinnied and lowered his head, snuffling Adam's hair.

"You stay here with Bobby, Adam. Keep him calm until I get back from the house."

As he ran back across in ankle deep mud, it was more than apparent swift decisions had to be made. Once inside, Dennis felt a new kind of estrangement from his Da as the Irishman continued traveling through the tortured landscapes of his private hellfire. Periodically, he dropped his head almost into his lap and uttered the only understandable sentence that could be made out, "Somebody kill me. Somebody kill me." Dennis decided to take control of the situation.

"Ma, Beulah, we need to pack up everything. We've got to get out of here as soon as possible. It's likely the flooding will reach the cabin by noon tomorrow. Maybe before. We should put what we don't need up in the loft. Maybe we can save some things that way."

Ida and Beulah sprang into action, gathering items to store above an unpredictable waterline while Charles now under the sedation of laudanum continued oblivious to the real time world. They needed something to carry things in. There were burlap bags in the barn. Dennis ran through the rainy slop to the barn. When he entered, he found his brother sleeping under a saddle blanket in the straw and roused him. They prepared the wagon and hitched up Bobby. There they spent the night. Through the alarming nature of the darkness, time was incalculable, but finally dawn broke, and there was a deceptive pause in the storm, indicated by a scarlet eastern horizon under a gloomy overcast.

It was time to get Charles O'Brien to a special kind of doctor.

Such a hospital was in New Orleans. Dennis left Adam with Bobby and trudged through the mud back to the house, trying to comprehend the ramifications of this drastic situation. How would they be able to pay for all of this: the arrangements associated with committing his father to the asylum? Would it mean the loss of the farm itself?

In a quiet voice, Dennis discussed all that he was thinking with his mother. They decided the best place to go was to her sister's house in Corinth. Cautious that the talk of an asylum might rouse Charles, Ida motioned at the empty bottle of laudanum on the fireplace mantle. She whispered, "We used some an hour ago. At least he's quiet for now."

Ida shook a kerchief that tinkled when she picked it up. Untying the loose knot, she revealed a stash of five twenty dollar gold pieces, money left over from the cotton crop.

"This should tide us over for a while. I don't know what we will do after that, but the Lord will provide."

Beulah pulled out a little pouch from between her breasts and emptied the contents on the table. There were five dollars.

"Dis five is my savin', my part in all dis. I don need no money, so yous kin have it all."

Then Ida eyed something that had served as a decoration over the mantle. She retrieved a tarnished silver plate, hand inscribed with hers and Charles's names. "It is our one remaining wedding present! Pure silver! Now it will be of real use. You must use this for your father in New Orleans. Untold souls are under care there. You will have some difficulty getting him in. You can sell this. The proceeds will be enough. They will surely take him."

An exhausted calm came over the household, and since the storm had abated temporarily, they all tried to get some rest before starting their arduous journey. With Charles surrendered to an opiate induced sleep, Ida and Beulah retreated to a corner together, wrapping themselves in quilts to salvage a few moments of rest. Dennis sat on the bench, and with financial concerns somewhat eased, a strange enthusiasm at the prospect of a journey came over him.

He added a log to the fire and poured himself a cup of coffee, returned to the table, and spread out a February copy of *The Corinthian*. He read old news of pronouncements against Republican Lincoln and his running mate, Hannibal Hamlin; opposite was an endorsement of Vice-President John C. Breckinridge, the Southern Democrat candidate for President. He skimmed an article with optimistic predictions about the bounty of corn, wheat, and next year's cotton crop, and perused advertisements for the local mercantile stores in Corinth. One ad by the local photography artist read: "Carte de Visites! Studio portraits, now available." When Dennis turned the page over, his heart sank. There was an announcement and discussion of the upcoming cotillion season. It was a reminder that Jane would be a debutante, so he closed the paper and threw it into the fire.

Dennis stepped outside, and the sky glowered fulfillment of the Biblical passage his mother often quoted: 'And in the morning, *it will be* foul weather today: for the sky is red ... the sign of the times."

The sky had yet to unleash another downpour; however, the river continued to rise from tributaries up-river. It now lapped at the edges of the barn. Adam had led Bobby and the wagon to the front door of the cabin. All of them loaded what they could take with them, when Dennis thought of something that might help his father. As a last act before getting underway, he retrieved Charles's military jacket from the trunk behind the wagon seat and helped him put it on. Looking at his father in the jacket, Dennis imagined a time when his father was at his best. Charles looked down at the jacket and tried to smooth out the wrinkles while saying, "This will never do. The captain will be coming for review, and I shall not stand up under the inspection."

19

━━►•«(O)»•◄━━

Bushwhack

It was twenty-two miles to Corinth, Mississippi. Bobby was pulling a loaded wagon with five people over roads so muddy that in places the wheels sunk to the rear axle hubs. To make faster progress, Dennis, Adam, and Beulah walked alongside, pushing when the wagon bogged down.

Midmorning, there was a break in the weather. The sky became startlingly blue, but meringue-like clouds on the horizon portended more rain. The serpentine road oozed red clay beneath as the wagon wheels rolled. Colonies of wild flowers populated rises in the landscape, looking like colorful rafts on a swelling sea. In the distance, slaves were turning over ground behind teams of mules. The refrains of their songs wafted on the wind.

Periodically, frightened rabbits darted across the road. It was noon when they reached a forested area near a fork in the road. One path led east toward Alabama, the other southwest toward Corinth. They paused to rest and eat. Beulah passed out biscuits and pieces of salt pork. Water from a barrel was passed between them, and they drank from a common cup. They tried to serve Charles on the wagon seat, but he was unresponsive and sat like he had a ramrod up his spine. At this point a rider emerged from a copse of trees nearby.

"How de do, folks?" the mounted man called out. He was lean, and his voice was like the banging of tin. He meandered his chestnut stud toward the wagon. He wore a slouch hat, a worn leather vest over a black shirt, and had a mustache like a spiky caterpillar. His nose gave evidence of having been broken more than once, and his eyes were mere slits below a brow crowded with locks of greasy hair that merged with bushy eyebrows. He had a hand resting on a revolver holstered on his right hip. Suddenly, he yanked it out, and pointed it directly at Charles.

"Now let's give a look see, Mister. What have y'all got in that there wagon that a man like me might make use of?"

Charles, catatonic, just stared ahead. Dennis leaped forward with his hands clenched and shouted. "Leave him alone! "

Immediately, the man swung his aim onto Dennis. "What's wrong with him?!" and he pointed the weapon alternately at Charles and Dennis.

"He's touched! You know what I mean? Touched!"

"Well, we will just see about that!" The man ambled the horse next to Charles, reached across, and yanked at his green military jacket. Charles showed no response, so the man got a firmer grip and pulled still harder. Charles tipped over and fell off the wagon face down into the mud, his green army jacket falling off of his shoulders into a large muddy puddle. Dennis ran to his father and turned him over.

Dennis screamed, "Damn you! Are you satisfied now?!"

"Okie dokie, big man," he cackled in derision at Dennis. "How's about you start to unload that wagon, so's I can to lighten your burden."

Adam rushed up next to Dennis and stood defiantly beside him. Foolishly, he shouted at the man, "Best you leave us alone! Thar's a whole bunch more of our kin ridin' behind us, so you best leave us alone!"

The man laughed mockingly.

"Is that so? I am very skeered! Just let me show you somethin'." He motioned back at the stand of trees which stood on a rise. "Take a look at that hill over yonder. I been watchin' you folks from that screen of poplars for well-nigh an hour. I ain't see no bunches of kin." Then his voice whanged, "So get up on that wagon and start throwing stuff down! And tell the nigger woman to get up there and do the same."

Ida's upper lip began to twitch. If the man searched her, all would be lost. She had all their money in her bodice. There was also the matter of the silver platter. Underneath the bench was Charles's trunk. Next to the box was the double barreled shotgun that they used for game. Ida faked hysteria.

"Lord, Lord! He's going to kill us all, Lord, Lord!" Then Ida fell backward into the wagon. She laid next to the box covering the shotgun with her dress.

"Well, looky that! You folks are gonna be easier than pluckin' chicken feathers!"

Beulah and Adam climbed up into the wagon. Beulah checked Ida to see if she was alright.

"I have a plan," and she whispered instructions to Beulah.

Adam slowly started to move bags and boxes to the gate in the back to let them down.

"NO! Not like that! I told you to throw them things off the wagon. I ain't got all day. Turn those bags upside down! Tip those boxes over! You there, black biddy, get over there and hep him!" The man snarled as Beulah and Adam reluctantly obeyed.

He rode around the back of the wagon for a better look, all the while maneuvering the revolver to keep the family off balance. Then he vigilantly eased down off his reddish brown horse and climbed up into the wagon. He opened bags and pulled out brass candlestick holders, table utensils, and kicked them off the back of the wagon.

"That ain't worth nothing. This is just junk! What else you got up in there?! You have to have some kinda real valuables, travlin' all packed up like this!"

He pushed Beulah, then slapped down Adam's pockets and inner thighs. It was clear he was going to thoroughly search everyone and everything. He poked his pistol periodically into Beulah's and Adam's ribs, then swung back around to make sure Dennis was not going to try anything. The possessions of twenty years wound up in the mud at the sides and back of the wagon. White clothing turned red in the Mississippi clay, crockery shattered, blankets fell in the sludge.

"Please no, not that!" Ida gasped.

"Go on! Push that box over here!"

He quickly flipped open the lid. Inside was a precious collection of books that had taken years to accumulate. "Books?! Nothin' but books! Wait a minute. We are gonna go through these one by one. Maybe you hid money. Flip through them pages, boy, then give 'em to me." Gradually they wound up in the road, their backs broken, an unsalvageable pile in the rutted road. Finding nothing in between any of the pages, he became enraged. Looking around, his attention was drawn to Bobby who was stamping his front legs uneasily in his harness. He growled at Dennis.

"You, four eyes! I'll have that horse. Unhitch him and bring him round to the back!"

Dennis felt an anger that he had never experienced and bellowed, "You can't have him!"

"I told you to unhitch that horse!" the man again demanded. "So you think you're a man? I have an urge to blast you, just for the fun of shootin' a goggle-eyed turtle! Now, unharness it! "

Charles was coming out of his listless condition. Trying to make sense of the scene, through half-closed eyelids, he began muttering unintelligibly. It caught the scoundrel's attention.

"He sure nuf is crazy, ain't he? Well, here folks, let me help ya with the situation!" He took a last book from Adam's hand and hurled it, striking Charles in the forehead. Dennis dashed for his father. As he did, the man fired at Dennis's feet. The women shrieked. Bobby, startled, rose up and bolted slightly forward. The robber lost balance, but steadied himself.

"Now if you don't bring that horse back around here, kid, I will put the next one through your eyeball! Do it!! Now!!!"

He kept the revolver trained on Dennis as he undid the harness and brought Bobbie to the back. The man then instructed, "Tie him off to my horse's saddle horn."

Dennis did so, but tied him loosely. The robber, too occupied with maintaining control over five individuals, didn't notice. Ida started drawing attention to herself with exaggerated wails. The man began to chuckle, "Well now, Missus, now that we dun looked through all this stuff, and there ain't nothing good, it ud be just about right that you're carryin' the valuables. Stand up!"

"I'm sorry, sir, I will oblige you if you just give me the time to do so."

"Awww, now I'm just getting tired of all o' this. Give you time to do so? If you don't stand up, I'll come over there and strip you down to your petticoat."

He moved toward Ida, who put her hand under her dress and onto the shotgun.

"No sir, you don't understand. I have to have the time to get up. You see I have the lady business."

The man recoiled. "Lady Business! You just take all the time you want."

Ida's claim she was menstruating revolted him, and he stepped back. There was no time to lose. She swiftly raised the shotgun and shoved it into his belly. It misfired, but the action made him drop his gun and fall backward out of the wagon. The man hit the road below Bobby's feet. Both horses reacted, but Bobby reared high in the air. Though the man tried to shield himself, the fury of the dapple gray's hoofs came crashing down on him. Dennis stood back as Bobby furiously pranced on the man's head and torso. Finally, there was no movement. Bobby snuffled at the man's armpit and pushed at the lifeless body.

Dennis embraced the gelding's neck. "Bobby, Bobby, oh, Bobby."

Everyone was awestruck. Beulah raised her hands to the heavens and shouted, "Lawd. Lawd, you dun delivered us by da steed! Hallelujah! Hallelujah!"

Ida got off the wagon and went to Charles's side. He had regained consciousness, but was woozy. He looked up into Ida's face not fully cognizant and said, "Captain, Captain, have we seized the day?"

Ida cupped his cheek and kissed him lightly on the forehead, then whispered into his ear, "Yes, Private O'Brien. Yes, we have seized the day."

Beulah picked up the dropped revolver and jumped down into the mud beside the corpse. She poked at it with the gun barrel. Dennis kneeled next to her. It was the first time he had witnessed the death of a man.

"What shall we do with him, Beulah?"

"Dis here beast don't deserve no decent burial. Best we uns leave him out heah fo da buzzards ta pick his bad bones clean!"

"We don't know his name. Maybe there is something in his saddlebags to identify him."

Dennis led Bobby back around the front of the wagon, but did not hitch him up. He helped his mother and Adam ease Charles back up onto the wagon seat. Then he returned to the chestnut horse.

He looked over the sheen of dark horse's coat and patted its twitching neck. Then he undid the saddlebag. He emptied its contents on the wagon bed. Beulah joined him in examination.

There was an assortment of obviously stolen items. A woman's set of ivory and silver brushes and combs, a small mirror set in silver. There was a packet of paper money tied up with a bow, two gold wedding bands, and a gold watch with a long gold chain. Beulah reached over and picked up an ivory rimmed cameo. Inside was a small tintype of a man and woman.

"These people may be dead, Beulah. If they aren't, we have to get these things back to whomever they rightfully belong to."

"Yous right bout dat, Denny. And dat dere hoss need to be returned, too."

Ida cradled Charles's head and began singing an Irish lullaby to him. She instructed Adam to help. When he got to the rear of the wagon, Dennis picked up the dead man by the armpits, and Adam and Beulah took him by the boots. They dragged him off the road.

"Adam, bring those branches. We'll at least cover him up with them!"

Beulah responded. "Mmm, Denny, yous mo righteous dan me. Ifn was left ta me, I'd jus let the buzzards have im."

They began to recover what they could from the muddy roadbed. Dennis hitched Bobby back up to the wagon. Ida took the reins. They had Charles lie down in the back of the wagon, covered by a blanket they had salvaged. Dennis and Adam insisted that Beulah ride the chestnut horse. Once more the rain started falling.

20

Relief

It was after dark when they pulled into Corinth. After the bushwhacking and traveling so many miles of bad road, they were all beat down, covered with grime from head to foot and so weary that they had hardly spoken to one another for hours. Bobby's beautiful dappled gray coat was so muddied that he could not be distinguished in color from the chestnut horse. Beulah had turned the horse over to Adam to ride, he was so given out. As they passed through the streets of Corinth late that Saturday evening, heading for Ida's sister and brother-in-law's home, they were mistaken by an inebriated man for a group of slaves out after curfew.

"You black so-and-so's better have passes! I'm gonna report you to the sheriff!" He staggered after the wagon as it rolled by and shook his fist. Lights in residences along the street came up, faces appeared in windows.

After traveling deeper into town, the sheriff along with two other mounted men did show up. It was the business district.

The sheriff demanded, "You negrahs, halt right there. You're in violation of the law, out after dark! Names and papers!"

The two deputies, lariats hanging from their saddle horns, circled the wagon. Dennis immediately came forward to the sheriff and identified who they were, making sure to speak respectfully while wiping the mud from his face to show he was not black.

"Sir, I'm Dennis O'Brien, this is my family: my mother Ida, my father Charles sitting in the back of the wagon. My brother Adam is over on the horse. That woman there is our servant Beulah. We have had a devil of a time the last two days. We are on our way to the Garrett's house, they are kin."

One of the deputies took his finger and dabbed at the mud encrusted on Dennis's face. After determining that they were not all Negroes, they let down their vigilance. However, since Charles had not responded and only stared, the sheriff pulled up close, sideways on his horse next to Charles.

"Any reason you can't speak up, mister?" Charles remained mute, so Ida spoke compliantly.

"My husband is quite pixilated, sir. Please, I beg of you not to press him. He is so ill my son is taking him to Louisiana, to an insane asylum there, until such time as he is better."

The sheriff backed off as if Charles was contagious, then began to interrogate Dennis. Breathlessly, he launched into the account of the day's events

"Sir, after being flooded out of our home up in Hamburg, we were waylaid on the road by a bushwhacker. He was killed. We have the plunder and horse it appears he took from other victims. My brother is on the horse he was riding."

"Killed? And how did the man die?"

"Trampled to death by our horse."

The sheriff instructed them to pull over to the side of the street and told Adam to get down and let him examine the horse and the contents of the saddlebag. Dennis gave a full description of the robber's appearance and where they could find the body. The sheriff scratched his head incredulous.

"Many have suffered at that marauder's hands. He is suspected in the deaths of a man and his wife near Eastport, and it's apparent that the items in these bags are the sad remnants of those people's lives. You folks and your horse have saved the lives of others had this coward continued to rampage through Tishomingo County. You and your mother must come to my office to make a full report. I will take the saddlebag with me now, but keep the horse with you for now. Bring it with you when you come. Meanwhile God bless you and good night."

Arriving after midnight at the Garrett's home, it took a while to rouse them. Robert Garrett, Ida's brother-in-law, came to the door with a shotgun and warily opened it. Seeing who it was, he laid the gun aside and Peggy Garrett, Ida's sister, pushed her husband out of way to joyfully hug Ida's neck. Becoming soiled herself as she embraced her sister, she laughed at the muck that covered them all, then brought them all into the house. All but Beulah, who refused to go in because they did not know her, and instead remained on the porch.

Robert and Peggy were aghast at Charles's condition, so they helped Charles upstairs. They cleaned him up the best they could and put him down in their own featherbed. Ida stayed with him until his eyelids closed, and Charles began to snore. After that, everyone ended up in the main room, and Robert brought the hearth to a roaring blaze, lit all the lanterns, and Peggy brought food from the pantry. The two little Garrett girls, Connie and Marcie, stood sleepily by the fireside, but as the conversation became more animated they became fully awake, especially at the presence of their cousin Adam.

Though it was late, all were keyed up and wanted to talk. They sat down in the parlor while Ida let loose a torrent of the travails they had been through. Trauma transformed to relief. Restorative laughter filled the bright and cheery room. As things wound down,

Beulah became the topic of concern. As the Garretts were filled in about her history with the O'Brien's, Peggy exclaimed, "Dennis! My land! Bring that woman inside!"

Dennis opened the door and made her come inside. Although she was now an invited guest, she still kept her distance and sat in one of the straight backed chairs in the kitchen until the proprieties could be worked out. Robert and Peg sorted out the sleeping arrangements for the night, Ida to bed with Charles, Peg in the girls' room. Adam and Beulah on pallets in the main room by the fire. Dennis elected to sleep in the carriage house, and Robert chose to join him. Uncle and nephew first looked after the horses, then made beds in the hay.

As they lay down a couple of quilts, patting the straw in place, Dennis broke down and cried. With distress after distress in the last few days, and uncertain miles ahead, he fell into his uncle and sobbed quietly into the shoulder of the only relative he had ever been able to truly confide in, "You're my favorite uncle, Uncle Robert, my favorite uncle!"

Robert put his arm around his nephew and patted his back.

"Well, Dennis, you're my favorite nephew, and if I ever have a son, I am going to name him after you."

21

———— ◦《◎》◦ ————

Windfall

The two families had barely slept when the clanging bells of a dozen different denominations started pealing, calling the faithful to church. Robert rolled over in the hay, nudged his nephew and groaned into the air in his deep baritone, "Ah, it's the LORD'S day! Yes, the Lord rested on the seventh day, so why do *we* have to get up?"

Dennis began laughing and couldn't stop. It was the first time in a long time he could remember waking happy. As they lay there on their backs, Robert reminisced:

"Well, Denny, you're not rangy any more. Last time I saw you, you looked like a beanpole. I could have picked you up and thrown you all the way to Memphis! Now look at you, all filled out and ready for a fracas."

"Yeah, Uncle Robert you taught me most of what I know about tusslin'. Remember when you used to say …" and they said simultaneously:

"I'm gonna' jerk a knot in your tail!"

"Jinx!" cried Dennis. "You know what happens next!" and they both got to their feet. Dennis continued laughing

"Let me see what ya got!" Uncle Robert said gruffly. "Give me your best shot!" and he gave him his shoulder to punch as hard as he could.

Dennis pulled back his arm to strike his uncle and then dropped it.

"No, I can't do it this time. I'm just not up for it."

"Oh, come on, Denny. Give me a good un!"

He hauled off and punched his uncle as hard as he could. It didn't faze him. It made Dennis go pensive.

"Ma tells me remember what the good book says: "turn *the other cheek.*" There are times when I just want to clean somebody's clock, like with some boys up Shiloh way!"

"Well, son, I know what you're talkin' about. Peg and your mother get that religious philosophy from their mother. It's funny though, your mama was the one that pulled up the shotgun and knocked that robber off the wagon. Just goes to show, you don't really know what you will do in a given situation. The good book also says there's a time to kill."

"That was the horse. I sure felt like killing that man, but he had a gun, and I didn't. But even if I had a gun, I am not sure I could have used it." His uncle's tone softened, and he slapped Dennis's back.

"Well now, Denny, let's hope it never comes to that," and he turned the conversation away from the previous day's grim encounter.

They left the carriage house for the expansive back yard, surrounded by a white picket fence. Robert's job as a foreman at the railroad roundhouse gave him a solid living wage, and the Garrett place reflected that. They walked and talked about the changes made since he had last seen them. It made Dennis wonder what things might have been if his father had not disintegrated. His uncle showed him the new chicken coop, with several new Leghorns on their nests clucking to announce newly laid eggs. Then he pointed to the goat pens. He went on about how he preferred goat's milk to cow's milk, winking and saying "it'll make a man out of you, put hair on your chest."

Aunt Peggy called from the back door "Come and get it before it gets cold!" Robert took a deep sniff.

"Just smell that bacon sizzlin'. Let's get some vittles."

The whole house smelled of warm biscuits, bacon, and coffee. Peggy and Ida were putting finishing touches on breakfast. Beulah was setting the table. The girls had come downstairs in their white sleeping gowns and were bouncing on their toes while Adam yawned and rubbed his eyes at the parlor door. Charles was still asleep. It facilitated a jovial atmosphere. They all settled in around a long walnut table. Robert said an irreverent grace, "Good food, good meat, Good God, let's eat!"

With relish everyone attacked the meal. The aroma of fresh coffee mixed with the sweetness of honeyed bacon. Of course, there was a pitcher of goat's milk. Biscuits stacked on a white platter tumbled over onto the checkered tablecloth, while viscous brown gravy dripped over the sides of the gravy boat. There were canned peaches, hard boiled and scrambled eggs, jam and jelly. The conversation was dominated by optimism and hope despite the reasons for the O'Briens being in the Garrett home.

When the meal was over, and the dishes were cleared, the children were dismissed to go play. Conversation turned to arrangements concerning Charles. Dennis began outlining how he was going to go about taking his father to New Orleans. As they sat there, Dennis's uncle and aunt listened carefully to him and offered suggestions, but his mother kept pooh-poohing his ideas. He became rankled and went outside. When he calmed, he came back in, put both palms on the table, and said firmly:

"Look ma, please stop treating me like a child. I know you're worried, but I can handle things. I'm really the only one who can make the decisions. I know I haven't been far away from home before, but it's not that hard to acquire tickets and ride alongside him. I know how to get there whether by train, riverboat, or coach. I know I will have to find the asylum when I get to New Orleans. I know I will have to deal with the doctor, and find people to trust. It might be hard to live by myself down there, but I'll find work and I'll feed myself. I can do it!"

Facing the inevitability of the situation, Ida broke down in tears. Peggy tried to console her sister. His uncle took him out on the back porch, and they stood silently for a while. Then Robert said, while patting him on the back:

"I know you can do it. You will do alright in New Orleans."

By evening, what was left of the O'Briens' goods had been cleaned and stored, and a sense of calm prevailed. Everyone was in the parlor when Charles found his way downstairs. He still was not really present. He had an exaggerated grin, and though they all tried, even his jocular brother-in-law couldn't cajole him into conversation. Charles picked at some leftovers that Beulah laid out for him, then he stumbled up the stairs to bed again. Soon everyone retired except for Robert. His duties at the railyard called for working odd hours; he had adjusted to having little or no sleep when he had to, and he went off to work.

Dennis and his mother took the wagon into town the next morning to turn in the stolen horse to the Sheriff. Entering the office, on the desk was a block of wood with the name Rupert Davy engraved on it between two metal stars. The Sheriff stood up and begged pardon for the mistake Saturday night. Then a revelation. He stated that a reward had been offered for the murderer and $250 rightfully belonged to them.

Ida bristled: "Sheriff Davy, we will be taking no money for the death of a man!"

"Ma'am, you more than deserve the reward!" protested the lawman.

"You, sir, are paid for your services of public safety. We, however, have already been paid by the Lord who protected us from the man that so despicably brought harm to so many."

"But, ma, we can use that money!" Dennis pleaded aghast.

"Now, Denny, you know better than that. Where does it say in the Good Book that we deserve a reward for doing only what we ought to have done, doing the right thing? That will be enough said about that!"

Gritting his teeth, Dennis slipped out the front door onto the boardwalk. *They needed this money. Why did she have to be so righteous?!* It was money that could be used for maintenance of the family here in Corinth while he and his father were in New Orleans. It would be enough to get his father into the asylum and cover his own accommodations for an undetermined amount of time while he waited to see what the doctors could do for his father. He was not going to allow his mother to reject this huge windfall. He stepped back into the office where Sheriff Davy and his mother continued to wrangle.

He got in front of his mother, cupped her face between his palms and said, "You are always saying the Lord helps those who help themselves. Can't you see the Lord is telling us we have helped ourselves, mama? Can't you see it? You are rejecting the Lord's provision. You should be saying like you always do, the *Lord has provided*."

His mother was mesmerized by the authoritative tone in her son's voice, and she nodded assent. Sheriff Davy filled out the paperwork and said he would notify them when they could claim the money. On the way back to the Garret's, his mother's attitude changed significantly. She looked up at him now a head taller than herself and said:

"Dennis, Dennis, you are truly my favorite loving son."

The town of Corinth had been called Cross City when the O'Brien's lived there years ago. Following the prospect of the windfall, Dennis had time to wander through town. The growth of the place was a marvel. Rail commerce had burgeoned the population to more than 1500. Homes here seemed like palaces in contrast to the log cabins around Hamburg and Shiloh. The neatly landscaped properties with six to eight rooms and fine brick facades with wrap-around porches awed Dennis.

Other homes were covered in smoothly finished clapboard with arched gingerbread and decorative balusters. Streets were laid out east to west. North of Main Street were 1st through 8th street, and new streets were being platted north of there. North to south the successive streets were named after American Presidents like Washington, Taylor, and Buchanan. At the edge of town, Dennis came to the monstrous three story brick building that housed the Corona Female College. He stifled thoughts of Jane, wondering that she might have applied here instead of Clarkesville.

Turning back to town, he passed the modest house where his family had once lived and considered asking the current occupants if he might look inside. Then he thought better of it, wanting to keep it frozen in time when the family had been better off, his father stable with a good job at the post office. A government job had been the best work possible, but he had not been able to keep it. Charles became eligible for The Military Bounty Land Warrant because of his Mexican War service, so he acquired the fragile piece of land that they owned in Hamburg, but it was a gamble. That gamble, of course, may now have been an ultimate wager lost.

On Main Street at the square was the two-story Corinth Hotel and next to it the Cross City Restaurant. More businesses skirted muddy streets: grocery and mercantile, leather shops, photo galleries, livery stables. Dennis wondered what kinds of places would be in New Orleans.

He went toward the railway station and arrived at the two story, balconied Tishomingo Hotel. Below the hotel, the afternoon train steamed on the track next to the boarding platform, bell clanging.

Behind the locomotive were two boxcars, three passenger cars, and five flat cars stacked high with heavy bales of cotton. His heart pounded at the thought of boarding the morning train Saturday. It would be his first experience riding the rails. Inquiring at the window, he found that the cost of fare to Memphis amounted to $2.50 per passenger.

When he got back to the Garrett's house, his father had aroused. He was still in psychosis, but now was confused at not finding himself on the farm. Robert put his arm around him and guided him toward the door, motioning Dennis to come along.

"Well, now those horses need some attention. Don't you just love rubbing down beautiful animals, Charlie?"

His soothing southern drawl and baritone voice was a tonic. For the next hour, they groomed Bobby and the Garrett's black mare. All the while Robert regaled Dennis and Charles with tall tales about growing up in the woods of Mississippi. He claimed he had fought bears and panthers, and was made blood brother to Chickasaw and Choctaw Indians

There still needed to be some way to explain to Charles about New Orleans. Dennis marveled at the way his uncle handled his father. He convinced Charles that it was his own idea. A little myth was seeded in Charles's mind that it was important to take Dennis to see where he came from. *Yes, it was of superlative importance that Dennis see New Orleans,* where he had arrived from Ireland. New Orleans, the Crescent City, the place he had met Dennis's mother.

"Now, Charlie, why don't you go on back in the house and get some more rest. You will need it for the long trip. Denny and I will take care of the rest of the preparations. Now you go on in." He dreamily did as Robert suggested.

"That was amazing, Uncle Robert. It was beyond me how I would keep him steady when he found out where we were going."

"Now, don't you worry about anything, Denny. I know you. You will figure things out as you go along. He's now got his mind set on New Orleans. I know that your challenge will be getting him into that hospital."

The rest of the evening was spent in reminisces of family history. After everyone else had gone to bed, and Robert left for his midnight shift at the roundhouse, Dennis went to the carriage house to sleep. Beulah followed him. She grabbed him by the shoulders and stared him in the eyes. "Nows when yous gets down ta New Orleans, you watch out for the Hooba Dooba!"

"The Hooba Dooba? What's the Hooba Dooba?"

"You gonna know it if the Hooba Dooba shows up. Jus knows the Lawd is stronger than the Hooba Dooba. But whatever ya do, stay away from the Hooba Dooba ifn ya can!"

Beulah then put her hefty arms around Dennis, gave him a kiss on his cheek, then went back to the house. Dennis lay down in fresh straw. He was so weary his eyelids hurt, but he could not fall asleep. He lay there staring into the darkness thinking about what lay ahead.

22

━●(◉)●━

Memphis

After painful goodbyes, Dennis and his father stood at the Corinth depot in front of the Tishomingo Hotel. Hissing steam filled the air of the warm and humid morning. The train's bell clanged its clarion call. Along with dozens of others, Dennis and his father boarded the westbound *Memphis and Charleston Railroad*. After several blasts of the steam whistle, and calls of "all aboard!" the flagman signaled the engineer, the machinery engaged, and the train began chugging on the first leg of its journey. Gradually accelerating, the train achieved a headlong pace of 30 miles per hour.

Initial excitement gave way to the hypnotic clacking of rails. The passing vistas became mesmerizing. Cabins, farms, and luxuriant fields alternated with swamps, forests, and creeks. Occasional grand plantation houses looked out over fields being worked by slaves. Herds of deer grazed in meadows, and at one point, the sky darkened with an immense flock of passenger pigeons.

The spell was broken when Dennis began observing the interior of the passenger coach where a menagerie of human cargo sat uncomfortably on pew-like benches. The breeze flowed through open windows, and body odors permeated the confined space. As his original enthusiasm waned, Dennis returned to vigilance over his father, who was in a daze quietly humming a Gaelic lament. He was wearing a smart suit of clothes that Robert had given him, and he was nicely combed and clean-shaven. It was a great improvement after weeks of little or no personal care. As for Dennis, he wore a new blue plaid shirt and denim dungarees. He mused over the fact that he, his father, and his uncle Robert now wore the same size. It gave him new confidence that his physique was now more adult. Inside the waist of his trousers was a money belt sewn by his mother. It contained the better portion of the reward. Its presence around his waist caused both vigilance and the need to appear nonchalant. There would be enough to get them to New Orleans and get Charles into the asylum, at least for a time.

Charles's humming went on for about a half-hour until other passengers became annoyed. He nudged his father to stop. He did stop, but not from the prompting. A man appeared at the door leading to the next car forward. He scanned the coach and seemed to fix eyes on Charles. He then retreated to the next car forward. Suddenly, his father rose and went rapidly after him. His father disappeared through the door, pursuing the stranger. Alarmed, Dennis got up to follow, struggling to carry their luggage. Did his father know the man? Was an unpleasant scene about to ensue?

When he got to the front of the car and opened the door, a rush of air came up from the tracks, and the coupling screeched, metal grating on metal. Going through the door of the next car, he saw his father standing in the aisle, engaged in conversation with the unknown man. There was something unusual about the interchange, the body language. Nevertheless, his father seemed okay, so Dennis decided not to interrupt them and stayed back.

The man was handsome, tanned, and nattily dressed, with a dark suit of finest quality. He wore a smart purple cravat around a starched turned-up collar. His upper lip exhibited a perfectly trimmed pencil mustache, and he kept smoothing the sides of his shiny black hair as he looked intently at Charles. Dennis decided not to intrude on an apparent reunion, so he found an empty seat and merely watched.

Shortly, the train came to a halt at the station in Collierville. Some passengers got off, leaving a seat open next to the stranger. Charles sat down next to him. Dennis fortunately found an empty row and stowed the bags. As the train took on water and loaded and unloaded goods, other passengers got on, and one immediately caught Dennis's eye, a stunning brown-eyed girl who looked to be his age. Her satin bonnet covered her tresses loosely, her nose was dainty and rounded. Her dress had puffy sleeves, and the neckline revealed gentle cleavage. She smiled at him, and he smiled in return. It was the first physical attraction to a girl he had encountered since leaving Shiloh. He politely stood up and greeted her with a "good morning" and a slight bow.

"Bonjour," she said demurely and sat down on the seat opposite him.

"That's French, right?" he said not so elegantly, taking his own seat.

"Oui, but I speak English, of course"

"My name is Dennis. I am going to New Orleans. Are you perhaps from there?"

"Oui! Yes, New Orleans." She said in a warm reply.

"I am going there now for the summer with my father. Do you think I will get by without knowing much French?"

"It is an international city. You will do well, I'm sure! However, a few words might be helpful."

"Well, I think I know one already. Bonjour. That's like a regular greeting?"

"Oui, but it is meant for the daytime. Bonsoir is the greeting at evening."

Risking being too forward, but figuring he would never see her again, he ventured, "And how would I say, "You look lovely?"

Her eyes brightened, and with a knowing look she replied.

"Tu es belle."

"Tu es belle, hmm. Tu es belle" He feigned being thoughtful, then looked straight at her.

She laughed.

"Do you know more than you are telling me?" and she began flooding him with French.

The conversation had just started when the train whistle sounded, and the conductor had cried "all aboard," when a young man came hurriedly down the aisle. He stopped where they were sitting and began speaking French in her ear. His disapproval that she was talking with Dennis was clear, but the tone in his voice was urgent.

"I am sorry, this is my brother. He tells me we have somehow mistakenly boarded the wrong train. We are going east to Charleston. You are going west to Memphis. This is so embarrassing, Dennis. Au revoir, au revoir!

"Your name! I didn't get your name!"

"Camille Dumond! Enchante!"

"Wait, what does Enchante means!?"

She blew him a kiss and Dennis watched with disappointment as the two of them deboarded, crossing to the train going to Charleston on the opposite side of the platform. The interaction with the beautiful young woman had been a tonic; she even seemed attracted to him despite his plain clothes.

Minutes later, the train pulled out of Collierville. Memphis was only thirty miles away. They would be there in no time. Dennis returned to studying this puzzling relationship Charles had with the fashionable stranger. All he could see were the backs of their heads, yet he detected intimate communication between them. He again elected not to interrupt. The conundrum was the unpredictable reactions of his father.

Everyone stood up when the train pulled into Memphis station and passengers filled the aisle before he could reach the two. He tried to catch his father's attention, but before he knew it, his father and the stranger disembarked, yet he was still making his way forward with the baggage.

Stepping off the train onto the platform, he could see his father and the stranger deep in conversation by the curb. Charles looked directly at him, even making eye contact, but he acted as if Dennis did not exist. Struggling with the baggage, Dennis came up beside them. The stranger did not acknowledge him. Dennis broke in, "Da! We have things to do!"

His father was oblivious, and the dark haired stranger ignored him. The two were in a world unto themselves. If he was to control situations with his father, he would have to be more forceful. He needed a way to change the dynamic. He decided to call his father by his first name.

"Charles, your friend, introduce me to your friend!"

It didn't work. Still no acknowledgment. It was alarming. The two kept up a low-toned conversation. They were making plans to see one another again. Abruptly, the dashingly dressed stranger bid "Adieu" and walked away, spinning a silver topped cane. With his departure, Dennis reverted to calling his father Da again.

"Da! Who is that man, and what's happening? Why?"

Finally, his father seemed shaken out of his disregard.

"Oh, Denny boy! Where have you been? A most wonderful thing. I found my captain. We are to meet again tonight at the De Soto Hotel! You won't mind if we stay there, will you? It's just over there." He pointed across a busy, dusty street clogged with riders, coaches and pedestrians. It was an elegant, imposing three story building.

Immediately, his mind went to the cost this would involve, and he slapped his waist to feel the money belt. He could not deny his father. He was intent on seeing more of his former commander. They climbed the steps of the huge stone structure and entered the foyer. The check-in counter was straight in front of them, the dining room off to the right. The hotel was opulent, and Dennis felt out of place, but his father looked well-to-do enough, so they stepped up to the concierge at the desk. Dennis requested the price of a room, and the man replied it was five dollars a night.

"Don't you have anything cheaper than that?" Dennis asked aghast.

His father made a maddening response, as if his personality had changed. Charles interjected before the concierge could answer, "Son, there will no bickerin' about price in a place like this. Pay the man."

Dennis pulled out a wallet that he kept a few bills in. The situation with his father was getting out of control. The night's stay was substantial. They had to make their money stretch as far as possible. Dennis bit his lip in anguish and proceeded upstairs to the second floor behind his father and the Negro porter. When they got inside the room, Dennis could not stop himself from lambasting his father.

"You have no idea what you've done! We need to get to New Orleans, and you are squandering our money!"

His father did not reply. Once again he went into a detached state of mind. He flopped down upon the bed. In moments he was out cold. Dennis watched incredulously as his father began to snore. He sat down in a chair, dumbfounded. Then his father mumbled in his sleep, "Captain, oh, Captain. I shall be in your service forever."

Dennis laboriously took off his father's suit of clothes and hung them in a chifferobe, picked up his own bag, and set it in the chifferobe. In exhaustion, he sagged onto the bed and succumbed to sleep next to his father.

He did not know where he was when he awoke. It took a while to orient himself. He reached his arm over to his side, expecting to touch his father, but touched empty space. Alarmed, he shot upright and looked around the room. His father was gone, the chifferobe was open, and his father's suit was gone. He recalled that his father was to meet "the Captain." They must be in the dining room. Going to the window and looking below, it was night with little activity on the street. He could see only the silhouettes of a few passersby, a couple of horses tied to hitching posts outside a tavern, and the cast of the gas lights on the street. He hid the money under the chifferobe and quickly headed downstairs. The dining room was closed, and the concierge was drowsy.

To check the possibility that they were in front of the hotel, he stepped outside. Maybe they were just enjoying the cool night air under the awning. He found two colored men in elegant uniforms with long tails, acting as doormen. As he was going back in, he stopped, hearing something familiar. On the still night air came a sorrowful refrain. The mournful harmonies did not make sense. This was not a plantation. It was eerie to hear the voices in the dark.

"Where is that coming from?" He asked the doorman, an older black man with graying temples.

"The auction, suh."

"Auction?"

"Slave auction, suh. Yes, suh. It's a few blocks over yonder, suh."

"Is it like this every night?"

"Most, suh."

"Do they sing all night?"

"Oh, they be stoppin' befo long."

The white desk clerk called out to the doorman. "Is there a problem?"

Dennis went to the desk and said, "Maybe you can help. I am looking for my father, Mr. O'Brien."

"Oh yes, he is with Captain Adair."

"Can you tell me where they are?"

"They stepped out earlier this evening. Other than that I cannot say. I have told you what I know. You will have to find out for yourself, I am afraid."

Dennis headed for the exit, now more disturbed than ever over his father's whereabouts.

After searching fruitlessly for several minutes, he recognized the foolishness of trying to find his father at night, in a place he knew nothing of in a town this size. He would have to trust that his father returned to the Hotel, so Dennis headed back. As he walked, those melancholy voices were like a siren's call in the breezeless night. Their sound was far more mournful than the spirituals he had heard from the plantation fields. As he drew closer to their source, the voices ceased. He became very aware of his vulnerability. Shadows in the entrances of buildings and alleyways put him in a trepid state. He was glad he did not have the money with him. Thoughtlessly, something made him go on, something beyond his own will.

When he had paced nearly two blocks, he came to a street called Adams. There was a stench that brought his hand over his nose. It smelled like a full outhouse pit. Lantern light illuminated the front of a brick building. On the upper reaches of the two story structure there was stenciled in whitewash "Negro Mart" along with the names of owners of the establishment. It looked to be *Hill & Forrest*. There was something like a stockade next to the building, and next to it was another brick structure that looked like a warehouse. He heard weeping coming from within, then a collective groan. It gave him goose bumps and in his head he pleaded. *Dear God! What is this? Why am I here?*

With that, a pale arm extended out a barred window and to his shock, it was accompanied by a weak voice, "Dennis. Dennis."

He nearly wet himself. The voice came again. This time with greater strength, clearly feminine and vaguely familiar.

"Dennis. Dennis."

He cautiously stepped nearer the building. The complexion of the arm and the upturned palm in the lantern light were now unmistakable to him.

"Elizabeth? In God's name, could it possibly be?"

"It is. Tell me that you are an angel." Her voice grew weaker.

"Angel. I am no angel."

He reached out and took her fingers. They felt cold. Horror flooded his mind. He saw no way he would be able to help. Dryness in his throat allowed him only to croak, "Why are you here? What happened at the Robert's? You're to be sold!?"

"It was because of this." Elizabeth stepped forward out of the shadows and pressed her left cheek up to the bars. A long gash went from the corner of her mouth all the way up to her ear.

"Dear God in heaven! Mr. Roberts did this!?"

"No, it was Elmore. When Mr. Roberts found out what Elmore was doing behind his back, he fired Elmore and drove him off the property. Two nights later, he sneaked back and slit my cheek with his Bowie knife, so I'm not fancy anymore."

Rage came up inside Dennis. He wanted to find Elmore and kill him.

"What can I do for you? How can I help?" he asked desperately. Grabbing the bars on the windows, he shook them violently in fruitless effort.

"You must not trouble yourself. It is enough that I have laid my eyes upon you again. My fingers have touched your fingers. I know there are angels for sure. You have surely been a messenger. Now you must go. Go quickly," and with that she stepped back into the darkness. Dennis was so transfixed, he did not see the three white men come up behind him. They grabbed him in a hail of curses.

Thinkin' of freein' niggers, eh? Well, we'll see about that!"

One put him in a choke hold while the others took turns punching him in the gut. He took the blows, but he didn't go unconscious. Instead he fell to the ground and played possum, and the men left.

23

━━►‹‹◉››◄━━

Friends

D ennis cautiously stirred. His rib-cage was bruised, wincing, he got to his feet. Dusting himself off, he saw that two great shutters had been closed over the barred windows of the Negro Mart warehouse. Filled with a torrent of feelings, he stumbled gingerly back to the De Soto Hotel.

At the entrance, the doormen, seeing his condition, moved forward to help him through the door. Standing under a crystal chandelier in the lobby, the prisms dangling from the lighting fixture cast little rainbows on the walls. It was bizarrely opposite to what he had experienced at the slave mart. The clock over the desk in early morning read 2:30. The clerk stared at his disheveled condition skeptically.

He ascended the stairs slowly to the third floor, hoping to find his father back in their room. When he inserted the key in the lock, another door opened at the far end of the hallway. The silhouette of a man could be seen slowly backing out the door. He recognized the body shape to be his father. Dennis was relieved and started down the hallway. Then a second silhouette appeared. Dennis paused. The contour was slender and graceful. Ever so slowly his sylphlike silhouette moved toward his father. Then the Captain brought his head forward and kissed his father's mouth. Dennis sickeningly dropped to his knees. The thumping caused Charles O'Brien and Captain Adair, now in embrace, to look down the dim hallway.

He had not witnessed this. He had not seen anything. He quickly opened the door to their room and closed it behind him. Dennis put his hands frantically over his ears, over his eyes, then his mouth. He paced back and forth. He heard footsteps coming rapidly down the hall. His father opened the door with a wild look in his eye. It was not possible to process what had just happened with his father and this, this Captain Adair. In order not to deal with it, Dennis pretended a yawn, but inside felt like screaming. Feigning still further, he blandly said.

"Da! I hope you didn't get worried. I went out for a walk. I missed you when I woke up. I knew you were with the Captain (he almost choked on the words), and I didn't want to infringe on your reunion, so I just took a walk, took a walk."

Charles O'Brien looked desperately at his son, but Dennis remained impassive. He had to suppress this incident. It was too much to comprehend. If he were to cope with all the implications, it had to be at a distant place and time. Dennis continued the charade, but his brain was branded by what he had seen in the hallway.

"Da, I hope you had a good time tonight. While out I got a taste of what the town is like." Everything he said masked the bombshell, the altered image of his father.

Charles was taking dry gulps of air, trying to hold back anxiety. He fumbled, playing along with the charade.

"Ya, ah, ah ya. That sounds interestin'."

"When I came back, I chatted with the night attendant. He says there is mercantile a few blocks over. I would like to get some things for the trip to New Orleans and some gifts to send back to everyone in Corinth."

"We shall have a grand time. I cannot wait to see what we might get fer Ma, Adam, and Beulah, and oh, fer Robert and his girls, of course.'"

Charles continued to eye his son anxiously for signs that he had witnessed him and the Captain. A guilty strain showed on his brow. Not being able to take the stress, he began searching for the elixir that helped him cope. He found the bottle of laudanum bought in Corinth in the luggage and swigged some down. In a couple of minutes, it started taking effect. Dennis helped his father get out of his suit, which was wrinkled now. He hung up the suit and made sure the money was still hidden. His mind was racing, so he looked for other tasks to do.

His father began to snore, and Dennis knew he would remain on his back until he woke up from his drugged sleep. In an effort to quiet his thoughts, he went to the window and looked out at the city bathed in the light of the moon and stars. The moon produced a sheen on the Mississippi River. Smoke curled into the sky from a dozen steamboats. His mind churned over the events that had taken place in just a few days. From the simplicity of Shiloh to the flooding at home. The assault on the road to the comfort of Corinth. From Corinth to these incomprehensible experiences in Memphis. To try and block out the image of what had happened in the hallway, he concentrated on his reconnection with Elizabeth. A steely resolve came over him as he lay down beside his father. He lay staring into the darkness, thinking and rethinking what he was going to do and how he was going to go about it.

Dennis was just dozing off at dawn when a knock came at the door. He quickly put on his pants and found a young porter standing at his door with a folded paper his hand.

"A message for Mr. Charles O'Brien," the porter said politely, and after handing him the note, he excused himself.

Dennis looked over at his father, knowing that he would still be unconscious for hours and then read the message:

"Captain Adair gives you his respects. He wishes to cover your accommodations and meals for as long as you wish at the De Soto. Please accept his thanks and regards. Come to the desk for a refund for last evening's stay." - The Management"

The scene of his father and the Captain in the hallway returned vividly. Dennis stared at the note then tore it up, then stepped back out to catch the porter.

"Excuse me. I should have given this to you at the door. I forgot my manners." Dennis handed him a dime. "Could you tell me when the auction at the Negro Mart takes place today?"

"If you are talking about Mr. Hill's and Mr. Forrest's establishment, it is open at 9am. The sale is at 1pm."

Dennis was convinced that his father would sleep until late afternoon. He had a plan of action for the day. He put on his father's suit. Looking at himself in the mirror, a self-possessed young man was looking back him.

He had not eaten since yesterday and was famished, so he went downstairs to the dining room. The waiter supplied him with a complimentary newspaper, the *Memphis Avalanche*. After looking at the front page with talk of war, he found on the back page this advertisement:

Mr. Nathan Bedford Forrest announces new partnership at 89 Adams Street

Buying and Selling Negroes, both on commission and on private account, in new quarters with Mr. S.S. Jones of Desoto Mississippi, and my brother, Wm. H. Forrest, of Memphis. Our buildings are located at 89 Adams Street, next door east of my old Mart; they are spacious, combining convenience, comfort and safety--are superior to any establishment of the kind in the State, and equal to any that I have ever inspected. Will board and sell on commission, and keep constantly on hand, a good assortment of Virginia, Georgia, and Carolina Negroes. 500 NEGROS WANTED, I WILL PAY MORE THAN ANY OTHER PERSON, FOR No. 1 NEGROES, suited to the New Orleans market.

The ad turned his stomach. Ignoring his breakfast, he pushed back from the table, taking the newspaper with him. This time he was going to the mart in daylight.

Arriving at the mart, the barred window was now un-shuttered and open for the public to view the slaves inside. He looked, but could not see Elizabeth. In the courtyard was a long line of black men, women, and children, queued up for a climb onto a stage at the center of the yard. On the platform already was a magnificent muscular black man. Midway down the line of slaves, he spotted Elizabeth.

Inquiring of a spectator, Dennis queried how he might bid. The man pointed to a billboard on the front of the building.

We *have constantly on hand the best selected assortment of* FIELD HANDS, HOUSE SERVANTS & MECHANICS. *We are receiving daily from Virginia, Kentucky and Missouri, fresh supplies of likely young Negroes. Negroes Sold on Commission and the highest market price is always paid for good stock. The Jail here is capable of containing Three Hundred, and for comfort, neatness and safety, is the best arrayed in the Union. Persons wishing to purchase, are invited to examine the stock before purchasing elsewhere. We have on hand at present Fifty likely young Negroes, Comprising Field Hands, Mechanics, Home and body Servants Etc.*

He entered the office and waited in line behind three finely attired men waiting to register as bidders. Having initially intended just an inquiry, he found that all bidders must be bona fide. When his turn came, a Mr. S.S Jones looked up in anticipation at Dennis. Seeing his youthful appearance, he exclaimed, "Ah, I have not seen you before. I hope you have someone that may vouch for you."

"Sir, if you require a deposit, then I am prepared to present one."

"No, young man. A man's word is as good as his bond. However, since you are unknown here, just provide a known resident of this city that can affirm your reliability and stand good for you, and that will be sufficient. Now a name?"

"Captain Adair," he replied with crossed fingers behind his back, using the only name he knew that might be a resident of Memphis. To his surprise, Jones answered:

"Captain Jack Adair? Of course. You know him? Well regarded among us! As I am sure you are aware, he is recruiting a company of militia that will serve to thwart northern aggression. We will be pleased to accept your bids. Are you interested in any particular kind of stock?"

Dennis tried to come across as old and experienced as he could: "Female, octaroon, house servant."

A wry smile spread across Jones' face. "A connoisseur I see. I regret to say in today's sale we have but one *high yellow*, she does have a mar on her face, and you may not find her suitable. However, she is fresh on the market and could be an asset when not in social situations. Go to the yard and make an inspection. She might be had at a bargain price. Go ahead! Take a look. She has been examined by a doctor, teeth all there and pearly white, hands and feet un-calloused, just like a baby."

"I will take a look, Mr. Jones." Dennis replied, trying to sound well-heeled, though hearing Elizabeth spoken of in this way brought back the discomfiting night he first saw her at the Robert's plantation.

He exited the side door of the office into the auction pen. The sale was already in progress. Stepping quickly, he skirted the crowd of planters and business men who were all furiously bidding for slaves on the auction block. Also offering bids were refined hoop-skirted wives holding perfumed scarves to their noses. By contrast, a group of five people stood away from the others. These were dressed in black as if in mourning.

The first slave on the block brought $1000. Dennis's heart sank as he thought of the $250 in his belt. The ones that followed, while decreasing in price, were still being sold for many hundreds of dollars. Powerful field hands went first, then a blacksmith, and a mechanic. Two lots of three were sold, and then it came Elizabeth's turn on the stand. She was trembling, and it seemed from more than fear.

"Ladies and Gentleman. Behold a fine specimen. Raised on one of the best plantations in Hardin County and only 20 years of age, she has been sheltered and groomed for elegant service."

Grumbles went up from the crowd because of the vicious gash that ran from the corner of her mouth almost to her ear. Someone cried out "Ha! Damaged Goods!"

The auctioneer continued, "Now, now, she has received a little scratch, and it will soon heal. What am I bid for the mullato, a rare high yellow girl! Let's open the bid at $500." Disappointment gripped Dennis. He could not hope to compete.

But the starting bid caused another groan of dissatisfaction from onlookers. Then a ruffian jumped up on the scaffolding. At first guards held him back, but the auctioneer told them to hold off, saying, "If he has money, he has a right to examine the merchandise." The brute circled Elizabeth. Looking at the festering wound, he bayed like a hound, "Scratch!? Scratch!? This ain't no scratch!! Just look at her shakin! If someone takes this wretch home, she'll die in a week! I'll take a chance and pay $50 dollars. And that's a deal!"

"Get that man out of here!!" The auctioneer hollered, and this time bodyguards leapt on him and put him on the street.

"A thousand pardons, ladies and gentlemen. We promised safety, and we have delivered. If we have kept true to our word, then you will know that this young Negress will be an asset to any household."

The words fell on deaf ears. The crowd was grumbling until a plump tuxedoed man called out, "Seventy-five dollars!"

"You more than disappoint the house, sir. You insult the house!" A laugh went up. Another man yelled, "One hundred dollars!"

Dennis pushed his way to the front and with a stuttering voice called out, "One...One hundred and twenty-five!" The crowd sensed a contest.

The rotund man called out again, "One-fifty!"

Then another bidder volunteered loudly, "One-seventy five!"

Dennis's heart beat faster, "Two hundred!"

"Ah folks, you see, we are heating up. Who will make it two hundred and twenty five dollars?"

"Two hundred twenty dollars!" came the call of the rotund man.

Then the competing bidder requested a halt. He asked permission to step up on the platform for a closer look at the girl. Dennis felt nauseated, and he despaired. He could only afford two hundred and fifty dollars.

The bidder on the stage took Elizabeth by the chin, pulled down her lower lip to look at her teeth, then pawed at the gash on her cheek and pushed roughly at her belly. Elizabeth cried out in pain and doubled over, then fell to the lumber floor of the auction block. Blood spread below the waist area of her white cotton dress revealing a previous internal injury. Some of the planter's wives gasped. One cried out, "She has hemorrhaged!"

"I've seen this before. She should never have been put on the block. She will die within the week. The man they threw out was right. I take my bid back, by rules," shouted the bidder on the stage.

"Two hundred and twenty five dollars!" Dennis called out desperately.

The auctioneer beckoned for more bids. Then, noting the bidding had turned quiet, he pronounced slowly and deliberately, "Two hundred and twenty five dollars. Going once! Two hundred twenty five going twice!" Two hundred twenty five going three times!"

Dennis was sweating profusely. In desperation he prayed under his breath, "Please God! Make them accept this as the last bid! Please! Please! Please, dear God!"

Everyone in the compound fell into silence. "Sold to the young man in the spectacles for two hundred and twenty five!" and simultaneously, the gavel came down.

Dennis was overjoyed he had come off the winner, but was extremely concerned as he watched Elizabeth being helped off the block by two other slave women. Before he could go to the office and claim Elizabeth, he felt a tug at his sleeve. It was a woman in a black dress, wearing a distinctively modest bonnet. Next to her were three other women dressed the same way, and a man who had a long, well-groomed beard. The bearded man held out his hand, "Mr. O'Brien. Mr. Dennis O'Brien, we are Friends. The Society of Friends. May we haveth a word with thee, brother?

24

Recoup

Nobody that day recognized the simple garb of these Quakers. Either that, or the intensity of the auction had diverted attention from them. He was bewildered as to why and how they knew his name. He looked from face to face of the five in front of him.

The Society of Friends? These were Abolitionists. Incredibly, they had braved the hazard, entering a slave pen in the Deep South. Not just any slave pen, but as the *Memphis Avalanche* had noted, this one belonged to one of the most renowned traders below the Mason-Dixon Line, Nathan Bedford Forrest. He had a lot to lose if abolitionists achieved their goal.

"Sorry, I don't know any of you. How is it that you know me?"

"Thy reputation is well known," said the woman who had touched his elbow.

"Thy reputation? What reputation? I have no reputation. I'm just a poor farmer's son. How could you possibly know me?"

"Best keepeth thy voice low, brother. But in answer to you, letteth it be known that Douglas said to be on the watch for you."

"Douglas! You know Douglas? How could that be?" he asked

incredulously, while trying to stay attuned to how Elizabeth was being handled.

Despite lowering his voice, they were beginning to attract attention. Some planters' wives in the crowd, growing bored of the palaver of the auctioneer, began eyeing the simple black dresses and modest bonnets of the plain looking women.

One of the Quaker ladies pleaded, "We must leave for now. Let us meeteth at a place more discreet."

"Yes. On the vessel *John J. Rowe*," another of the Quaker women insisted.

Dennis was wary, and the woman continued:

"It is understandable thou art reticent, Mr. O'Brien. Yet a mob is possible, and thou hath not a place to take the girl. We are equipped to help."

He had not given thought to what he would do if he was able to purchase Elizabeth. He had just rushed headlong into it, but were things falling into place? He needed help, and this odd sect was offering a solution. It really was a godsend. He would have no money left after the purchase of Elizabeth. What would he do once he claimed her?

"Goeth to the levee, to the steamer on which we arrived, the *John J. Rowe*. There art facilities for what the poor girl needeth, and a brother from the north who is a doctor. Also, the miscellany of travelers serves to ameliorate attention."

"What is the name of the steamboat again?"

"She is called the *John J. Rowe*. Persueth the welfare of Elizabeth now. We shall returneth with a suitable carriage."

This offer of help and the authority with which his new acquaintances made arrangements brought relief.

"I really appreciate this. I, I really don't know how to thank or address you people."

"Brother O'Brien, calleth us simply friends."

Dennis headed for the slave mart office while the Quakers dispersed. When Dennis stood before the desk, Mr. Jones looked up with a grin, almost a leer.

"I hear you got the bargain merchandise you were seeking. Feed her, bathe her, tend to her abrasion, and you will have a prize that will service your every need. If you understand my meaning."

Dennis was revolted, but gave Jones the stack of bills that he had removed from his money belt at the hotel and put in his wallet.

"Two hundred twenty five-dollars. Count it if you must." He said blandly, trying to mask his distaste and inwardly in turmoil over handing over what amounted to over a year's wages.

"Not to be concerned, we never lose on our investment, and we have no concerns about counting the amount you have tendered. Besides Captain Adair would stand good for you. You can pick up the mulatto at the rear where she is being attended by the doctor. As advertised, we have the best stock and safest establishment in the country."

While he listened, he felt a presence behind him that darkened the doorway. When he turned around, a powerful looking man, over six feet tall, was standing there. The handsome face had a goatee style beard and a fine crop of hair, but his hairline was receding on the upper parts of his temples. Jones gave a salutation, grandly announcing, "Young man, behold my partner, Mr. Nathan Bedford Forrest! Mr. Forrest meet Mr. Dennis O'Brien."

The man with the commanding appearance reached out his hand, and Dennis held out his. It was the firmest grip he had felt since Douglas' muscular hold. He looked Dennis in the eye and in mildness contrasted with his steely visage said, "I'm glad to meet you. Where are you from? I know most of my clients. From Cairo to New Orleans, from Memphis to Charleston. I do not recall ever seeing you before."

"Sir, I am from the Hamburg and Shiloh part of Hardin County, Tennessee."

"I know the area. Most are owners in a small way. I buy and sell stock occasionally to some there. The way you are dressed doesn't square with most of the people out that way. And you are young."

Though Forrest had mildly put it, Dennis tried not to show nervousness under the scrutiny. He scoured his mind to find a way to reply without lying. He need not have concerned himself just now, for Forrest turned his attention to his partner.

"I understand there was an irregularity here today, Jones. Something about an injured high yaller gal."

Jones sat up and took notice. He glanced at Dennis, then requested Forrest to step out the side door to the pen. The cacophony of the sale was increasing. More valuable Negroes were coming on the block, and shouts of approval and competitive banter drowned out most of what the two partners were saying to one another. Outside the front door, two of the Quakers, the man and one of the women had returned.

Dennis stepped to the front door and acted as if watching the commerce on the street. The brother had removed his distinctive hat and was holding it behind his back. He had opened his tight, straight-laced coat, so he did not stand out as he had before. The sister had taken off her modest close fitting bonnet and long raven hair flowed down over her shoulders. She didn't look much different than some of the women passing by on the boardwalk though her dress was not as billowing as other women's. Dennis asked why they had changed their appearance. The man replied, "The Good Book calleth for well arranged, plain dress, but it also sayeth: "Behold I send ye forth as sheep in the midst of wolves: be ye wise as serpents, and harmless as doves."

The female added in an undertone, "Remember ye also when David, before the Philistines, appeared as a madman at the gates of the city and frothed at the mouth in order to fooleth them. So we too fooleth the gentile who enslaves. The Lord shall forgive our deceptions and our vanity."

The Quakers reasoning that God would forgive on the basis of mercy solved Dennis's dilemma. Could he keep fooling the owners of the mart since he was under the legal age to own property? Tennessee laws stated that ownership of property could not be transacted with anyone under the age of 18. He had resolved that he would simply lie, beg God for forgiveness, and hope that he would not be interrogated.

Dennis moved back to the side door to eavesdrop on the partners. The countenance of Forrest had changed, and their discussion had turned to quarrel. They stepped back inside. The argument continued.

Jones asserted strongly, "But the girl still had value! The young man wanted her. Ask him if he wants to keep her. I'm sure he does!"

Forrest didn't turn to look at Dennis, but retorted to Jones with rising but controlled anger. "Now, look here, Jones. I have built my reputation on fairness, cleanliness, safety, and quality Negroes. You sorely disappoint me that you took in a decrepit specimen! Do you see the rich men in that audience out there?! If it gets around that I am selling damaged and diseased stock, the flood of customers we have now will go somewhere else."

Jones withered under the denunciation. "Nathan, now I get it. I will do something to remedy the matter. Young Mr. O'Brien, I will return a discount for the girl. Say ten percent?"

That meant Dennis could get back about $27 dollars. He was ready to accept the refund. But before he could open his mouth, Forrest growled lowly and firmly, "*You will do four things.* You have so misrepresented the firm in this transaction that *first* you will restore to me personally the two-hundred dollars you paid for the mulatto girl. *Second* you will return all the money the young man tendered for her. *Third* you will not take her back into inventory, but will give the dying soul to this young man from Shiloh. And *fourth* you will give him $25 to cover medical expenses or burial costs he may incur.

He is doing us a favor by taking this stock off our hands. Do you understand me?"

Jones was astonished with the consequences and attempted to protest. "This is the likes of which I have never heard. Surely, we can at least take the girl back and try and tend to her ourselves. You have a good mammy on your plantation across the river in Arkansas, and once she is revived, our investment will be safe."

Forrest was breathing heavier and on the verge of an explosion, but he kept control of himself. He turned to Dennis, and in a demonstration of who was the boss and senior partner of the firm, said to Dennis. "Young Mr. O'Brien, I am ashamed of the spectacle that was forced on the public here today by my associate. I regret that you have been shortchanged. Wait here, I will see to it that Jones brings the Negress to you. On the way, he will make an apology to all our clients! Are you hearing me, Jones?"

Forrest took the money Dennis had paid from the desk and put it back in his hand. Then in a surly way, he turned and made out the stock ownership forms. He asked Dennis for his age and signature, signed the bill of sale himself, and laid them forcefully in front of Jones for his witness signature. Jones was flustered. Quickly, he did as Forrest commanded. The peculiar thing was, that in the heat of the moment, he left the description line empty. It did not describe Elizabeth, either by appearance or sex. And with that, Dennis became the owner of another human being.

Jones went sheepishly into the warehouse to do as Forrest had commanded. Forrest then told Dennis he was an alderman of the community and needed to be at the municipal government building for a meeting. He exited past the Quakers without noticing them and mounted a magnificent black Tennessee stud. It was an irony that he tipped his hat to the undetected abolitionists and rode down Adams Street. Coming in the opposite direction was the buck-board with the other women Friends. Forrest glanced at them, then trotted on.

It took half an hour to receive Elizabeth. She was so weak that one of firm's robust private slaves was carrying her. She was brought to the wagon and laid upon a blanket and covered by another. The women Friends began ministering to her.

It was getting late in the afternoon, and Dennis's mind suddenly went to his father, lying on the bed back at the De Soto. He wondered if he would get back before his father came out of his laudanum sleep. And what about Elizabeth?

25

━━●(())●━━

Pilot

With the precious load of damaged Elizabeth on board, the wagon trundled down Adams Street toward the levee and steamboat landing below. Before they left, Dennis gave the Quakers the twenty five dollars from the slave trader meant to cover Elizabeth's "expenses" and started back to The De Soto Hotel. Lost in heavy thought and looking down at the boardwalk, Dennis did not see the tall black tramp leaning against the pole of the gaslight near an alleyway. A begging hand came forward.

A gravelly voice spoke from underneath a rumpled black hat, "Massuh, coulds ya heps a po colored man? I's been wanderin' the streets of dis great big town wit no muny in mah pocket an ifn da High Sheriff kitches me, dey is gonna puts me in jail or worse. A free negrah needs muny in his pocket. Kins ya heps me?"

Dennis had all his money on him, he was respectably dressed, young and alone, so he was a good mark to be robbed. He stepped back, but felt a strange familiarity. Then he saw several coins in the man's outstretched palm. The scruffy freeman spoke in a velvet tone with perfect English, "There are six shiny pennies and a tarnished dime. Which one would you pick as most valuable?"

Dennis was so startled, he stumbled back. It was Douglas, once again appearing incomprehensibly.

"Where did you come from this time?! You scared the livin' daylights out of me! Are you following me all over the country?!"

"Do you think that's what I'm doing? Did you ever look down the tracks of a railroad line? There are two rails that run parallel to one another. They seem to come together toward the horizon, but they are still separate in reality. Likewise, you travel a track parallel to the one I am on, and it appears that they are meeting. You have come to this place for one purpose, and I for another."

"Do you always have to use these parables when you talk? Why don't you just get to the point and say it's a coincidence?"

A broad smile came across Douglas's face. He rubbed the stubble of his chin and replied, "I guess I should apologize. Railroads are on my mind all the time."

"They're on my mind, too. It was my first time on the *Memphis – Charleston*."

"Oh, I know, I was in the boxcar, where my people have to ride, but I saw you on the platform."

Dennis pricked up his ears. "That doesn't seem like coincidence to me."

"There is coincidence, and then there is providence."

"There you go again. Can't you just speak plainly what you're getting at?"

Douglas let out a belly laugh. Then he got very serious. "Sometimes providence uses coincidence. You did not know about Elizabeth when you got on that train. I did not know to what purpose you were traveling with your father. I was going for one purpose and you another. We got on the train by coincidence."

"Ok. I buy that. So where's the providence?'

"For me as a pastor, the true master says: "What man of you, having a hundred sheep, if he loseth one of them, doth not leave the ninety and nine in the wilderness, and go after that which is lost, until he find it?" I went to the help the lost lamb Elizabeth; she was not hard to find, but I did not know how I could save her. I was ministering to her in the night at the slave mart when you came. I knew *that* was providence."

Two intense men were coming up the boardwalk. On the belt of one was a holstered pistol. Upon reaching them, he said, "Bothering you, isn't he? We know how to take care of these free negrahs. They are a plague in any big town they come to. He better have papers."

Dennis raised his finger and shook it in Douglas' face as if he were threatening him. "Don't bother, men, I just gave him money to get him out of town. I'll see that he does." Douglas dropped his head as if he was withering under Dennis's condemnation.

The two men were amused at Dennis's youth, but seemed satisfied with what he said. They spit tobacco at Douglas's feet, and stomped down the boardwalk, disappearing around the corner. Waiting to make sure they were gone, he told Douglas what had happened.

"Douglas, I have the official papers from the slave mart that say she belongs to me."

As the words came out of his mouth, he could not describe the way it made him feel. He was stating that Elizabeth was owned by himself. He felt unclean. He wanted to free her immediately. Douglas eased his mind.

"You don't need to worry. The Friends will take care of everything. Manumission down here is a complicated process, and we have to get Elizabeth out of here now. A leg of a different kind of railroad has been built. This one extends to Earlham, Indiana. The people you met are a delegation from the Friends College there. You do not know their names, and it is best you do not. Just be content that Elizabeth is in the best possible hands. I should go now."

With that Douglas ambled away, continuing his farce. Watching, it was interesting to see what a chameleon he could be. "I's be a goin'. I's be a goin,' boss. Don't yas worry bouts me, boss. I be on that boat jus as soon as I kin!"

On the way back to the hotel, Dennis picked up the pace, concerned his father was likely awake. When he opened the door to their room, he saw his father in his underwear, asleep uncharacteristically on his belly. There was something shiny on his father's back. It was a gold coin, as brilliant as if it had just come from the mint. Someone else had been in the room and put it there. He stared at the twenty dollar gold piece. A realization that something sordid had taken place in the room came over him. Dennis tried to rouse his father, who only mumbled into the pillow. The coin slipped off and rolled on its edge until it touched the door where it fell over flat. He picked it up, stepping into the hallway with it in his palm. He walked purposely to the room where he had seen his father and Captain Adair. When he reached it, he rapped on the door hard. It opened, and there stood debonair Captain Adair, stroking his mustache.

Dennis, speaking through gritted teeth, seethed, and his face quivered, "Take your money back, and if you ever get near my father again, you, you," (he did not know what word to use). Not able to find words of enough threatening weight, futility overwhelmed Dennis. Turning away he walked back down the hallway, his footsteps vibrating on the hardwood floor.

To his back, Adair called out, "Tsk, tsk, tsk. Are you any different? Prostituting my good name to transact business for a pathetic yellow maid. Did you think I would not find out? I was in the crowd at the mart while your mouth watered at the little beauty. And here, I did in fact vouch for you. Look at you, a dog with his tail between his legs," and he closed the door.

Rage was not the word, nor was cursing adequate. Dennis took his father's suit off himself and threw it at his father, who had awakened because of the shouting down the hallway. He put on his own clothes, making sure to secure the cash in his money belt. Then he gathered up all their belongings and stuffed them in their bags.

His father was sheepish as he struggled to get dressed. It was a turning point. Never again would Charles O'Brien beat him. Never again would their relationship be the same. He felt only sorrow. His father was unstable and vulnerable. Dennis was fully taking charge. It was on to New Orleans. Maybe there he would find out what else lurked in his father's history.

It was a strange sight to see the father following the son that day. In late afternoon they trudged toward the landing. Charles looked like a puppy following Dennis. Dennis thought of providence and coincidence as he passed the gaslight where he'd spoken with Douglas. Where was providence involved in his father's life, why had the coincidence of Adair showing up resulted in what it had? What kind of God was this who seemed to be two sides of the same coin?

When they got to the levee that day, April 6, 1860, there were at least two dozen paddle wheelers beached against the shore in shallow water. Under a clear blue sky, smoke belched from the stacks on each vessel. The smell was of burnt wood and the muddy, frothing water of the wide Mississippi. Steam whistles split the air, hundreds of black stevedores hustled and shouted while loading or unloading cargos. A few vessels stood silent with most of their crews gone on leave to the city above with its four and five-story buildings visible over the top of the bluff.

On shore were stacked bales of cotton. The roustabouts shouldered barrels of whiskey, flour, cornmeal, and other foodstuffs, taking them to the ships. Top-hatted gentlemen and refined ladies sported their fashions, watching the goings on from the boiler decks. Dennis and his father walked, baggage in hand, while looking at the names emblazoned on the sides of the vessels. Lined up were the *John Warner,* the *J.C. Swon, Tigress, Hiawatha, Iatan, Crescent City, Planet, Galena, Vicksburg, William M. Morrison, J.M. White, Missouri Democrat, St. Louis, Rufus J. Lackland, D.A. January, John H. Dickey, A.B.Chambers, Paul Jones,* and finally at the southern end of the collection of steamboats, there was the side wheeler *Alonzo Child,* but no *John J. Roe.*

Dennis, glum and sweating on the embankment next to his abashed and forlorn father, saw a man on the main deck, close enough to call to. The racket of commerce along the landing made it difficult to hear. Dennis shouted "Sir! I am looking for the *John J. Roe.* Can you tell me where to find her!?"

The man was about 25, wearing a white uniform and monogramed black cap with a bill, smoking a cigar. He called back with a hand cupped to his ear, "Say again!!"

"Sir! I am looking for the *John J. Roe.* Can you tell me where to find her!?"

"Say again!" repeated the young man, who blandly puffed three smoke rings into the sultry air.

"I am looking for the *John J. Roe.* Can you tell me where to find her!?"

Dennis gave up. He picked up the baggage, directing his father to go back up the landing when the young pilot trotted down the gangway calling, "Wait! Wait! I'll tell you about the *John J. Roe.* She left a half-hour ago, going up to Cairo."

"I promised some people I would meet them here on the *John J. Roe.* I thought there was time to reach her before she left, but I guess there is nothing that can be done now. My father and I must get to New Orleans as soon as we can."

"If you are wanting to go to New Orleans, you can take this vessel, *Alonzo Child.* We will be backing out tomorrow morning at 8, once we have taken on all passengers."

Dennis patted his money belt. Noticing him touch his waist, the young pilot urged, "I wouldn't do that if I were you. It's a dead giveaway. There are a lot of confidence men and expert pickpockets that ply their trade on these boats. You could be ransacked in a moment. Report up on the texas when you get aboard, that's where the safe is. When you see the purser, you can check it with him. You can pay your fare at the same time."

"The texas? I don't understand."

"It's jargon for quarters just below the pilot house. The purser's name is Cassius. He will be glad to take your cash. Tell him I sent you personally." The pilot smiled.

"My name is Dennis O'Brien and this is my father Charles."

"Excuse my question, but is your father ill?"

It was becoming increasingly evident that others could tell something was askew with his father. Dennis didn't know any other way to answer, but to say: "No, he is not well, Mister, I am taking him to a special doctor in New Orleans."

"I see. Sorry to hear that. I've been told three ways to keep your health is to eat what you don't want, drink what you don't like, and do what you'd rather not. I don't do any of them. Don't call me mister. The name is Sam, Sam Clemens. See you aboard."

26

———◄(◐)►———

Dreamland

Reporting to the texas, Dennis warily removed the money from his belt and deposited it with the purser. From behind came a baritone voice effected by cigar smoke. It was again the young pilot.

"Cassius, call the porter and settle this fellow and his father into quarters next to mine here on the texas. Charge them only the going rate for the lower deck. Order up this evening's meal for all of us at the captain's table. They will be my guests."

A breeze picked up, flowing across the deck with a hint of honeysuckle. A porter picked up their bags and escorted them to their room. Dennis, now regretful of his rough actions toward his father, made a weak apology, putting his father gently to bed. He lay down, curled into a ball, and to Dennis's amazement, started sucking his thumb, yet a new symptom. He would not let it spoil the refreshment he felt at meeting this Sam Clemens.

When suppertime came, his father couldn't rise. He had gone into some sort of hibernation and not because of laudanum. Dennis pushed at his shoulder, but his whole body was as stiff as a beeswax sculpture. After several attempts to raise a response, there was a knock on the door and a friendly salutation. It was Sam calling him to dinner. He chanced leaving his father alone and followed Sam on the texas deck.

As they sat through supper, a beautiful relationship began to unfold. They traded experiences. There was a difference of nine years between them, but there was never any mention of it by Sam. They exchanged stories of their travails, and laughed about the peculiarities of people they had encountered. As the conversation continued, Dennis began living vicariously through Sam's vivid descriptions, things he thought would never happen to him, but it caused him to express his own longing to be totally free. Trying to encourage Dennis, Sam, in referring to his own struggle and final success, gave vent.

"I tried hard, but could not get on the river- my parents would not let me. I was disconsolate. Boy after boy managed to get on the river. The minister's son became an engineer. The doctor's and the post-master's sons became 'mud clerks;' the wholesale liquor dealer's son became a barkeeper on a boat; four sons of the chief merchant, and two sons of the county judge became pilots. Pilot was the grandest position of all. King of a kingdom almost as grand that is promised to come, with a princely salary—from a hundred and fifty to two hundred and fifty dollars a month and no board to pay. Two months the same as a preacher's salary for a year."

After Sam's admission of how much he was making, Dennis's jaw dropped, but he did not want to interrupt nor show envy. He composed his face and listened on.

"Despite my parents' opposition, I apprenticed. In these few short years on the Mississippi, the water has become a wonderful book--a book that is a dead language to the uneducated passenger, but which tells its mind to me without reserve, delivering its most cherished secrets as clearly as if it uttered them with a voice. And it is not a book to be read once and thrown aside, for it has a new story to tell every day. The Mississippi River towns are comely, clean, well-built, and pleasing to the eye, and cheering to the spirit. The Mississippi Valley is as reposeful as a dreamland, nothing worldly about it . . . nothing to hang a fret or a worry upon."

Nothing to hang a fret or worry upon, a dreamland. With that Dennis wistfully said goodnight and a "see you tomorrow" to Sam, for he could not neglect his father, though he told himself if his father fell overboard he would not cry an alarm. He wanted to spend all of his time with Sam Clemens, but what he needed was help with his father.

Charles O'Brien, in that waxy inflexibility, now presented the problems of normal bodily function. He'd wet the bed. He'd messed himself. He needed food and water. The only liquid Dennis could get in him were trickles down his tongue until natural reflex caused him to swallow. Food was an impossibility, and cleaning his father was nauseating.

Next evening from the pilot house Sam spied a distressed Dennis leaning over the railing. Sam left the wheel in charge of the steersman and came down to find out the reason. Dennis took him to their quarters and opened the door. The smell that flowed out was stomach churning. Sam let out an expletive and plugged his nose. He took Dennis by the shoulders and looked him in the eye:

"You can't do this alone."

"I don't know what to do," and Dennis nearly cried.

"I know of a family on board who has a nanny. I will see if we can hire her to help you!"

"I can't afford it. I will take care of him by myself."

"Look, do you think what I said about having nothing to hang a fret or worry upon is the whole story, that life on the river is only dreamland? I see the look in your eye, and I'm sorry I painted a picture without shadows. You don't have to suffer in silence. I have tried to do that. The fact of the matter is the river bottom is littered with wrecks of once glorious steamboats. It happens all the time: fires, boiler explosions, snags, and collisions. My own brother was scalded to death two years ago when the boiler on the *Pennsylvania* blew up. I tried to bear the grief alone, and all it has done for me is make me doubt the existence of a loving God. Don't let that happen to you! Get help when you need it. Don't be so proud. Find as many friends as you can. Count me as one."

Sam returned to the texas with the nanny whose owners were happy to pocket the money she would earn them. She shooed Sam and Dennis out of the room and went about this new job dutifully. Sam put a hand on his shoulder and walked him round the deck. Giving Dennis a cigar, he tried to teach him how to blow smoke rings and slapped him on the back when he coughed. To help Dennis get his mind off his troubles, he related humorous stories of people he'd encountered on board and along the river. He contrasted the upper part of the Mississippi to its southern course:

"The river below St. Louis is the least interesting part. Here you can sit in the pilot-house for a few hours and watch the low shores, the ungainly trees and the democratic buzzards, and then might as well go to bed. You've seen everything there is to see. Along the Upper Mississippi every hour brings something new. There are crowds of odd islands, bluffs, prairies, hills, woods and villages…"

Dennis was getting sleepy from tobacco smoke in his eyes. As they passed others strolling the deck in the moonlight, the soothing music of southern accents blended with Sam's Missourian yarns. When they had made several circuits round the texas, they came back to find his father restored to sanitary conditions and breathing like Rip Van Winkle. The nurse looked like an ebony angel, and it brought to mind when Elizabeth had called him an angel.

Before he returned to the pilot house, Sam reminisced more about his upbringing and then warned him. "Remember, don't stay long on the river with me. It will give you a hope that if we live and are good, God will permit us to be pirates."

For the next few days the, *Alonzo Child* stopped, loaded and unloaded cargo and passengers at picturesque landings. At some, it was necessary to stay overnight. All the while their friendship grew. With his father under the care of the nanny, Dennis suspended reality and let himself think he could actually be a pilot himself. He fantasized he could apprentice to Sam, but when he started asking him about the intricacies of the boat one morning at breakfast, he was surprised when Sam revealed he was not a true master of all things nautical.

"Don't ask me about parts of boats. I am so indolent, and all forms of study are so hateful to me, that although I've been several years constantly on steamboats, I've not learned all the parts of the steamboat. Names of parts are in my ear daily, I don't inquire the meaning of those names. For I fear it will reveal my ignorance. I cannot describe the marks on a lead line. I don't know what "in the run" means—a negro deck hand could tell you more than me about the parts of a steamboat. Please don't ask again. I do not want reveal to anyone my secret ignorance."

Dennis was a little bit unsettled at hearing this. He did not know whether Sam was bamboozling him or not. What he did learn was that it was not necessary to know every dot and tittle to become competent. He had felt until now his own destiny would be only a menial existence of hard labor. Maybe it could be more. Sam's comments were encouraging, but they seemed in opposition to freedman preacher Douglas's beliefs about being faithful in the little things. Sorting it out, bringing the two together, caused heartburn.

The conversation turned to slavery, and Dennis related all his personal experiences with it from Shiloh to the slave market in Memphis. He told everything, from the ruse his family kept up to keep Beulah from the slave catchers to the rescue of Elizabeth from the slave market. He displayed his disgust for the way some Shiloh owners excused their own complicity with slavery by saying it was only *slavery in a small way.*

Hearing his own words, Dennis put his fork down and took a drink of water. There was unfinished business. Sam's refreshing association had given him respite from unceasing dutiful earnestness, but technically Dennis was a slave owner himself. He still had Elizabeth's bill of sale in his baggage. It didn't matter that Douglas had said not to worry, that she was in good hands with the Quakers on the *John J. Roe.* Seeing that Dennis was getting internally anxious after the long discussion, Sam thought it best to divert attention away from the "peculiar institution" of slavery. It was not going away overnight. To change subject, he once again waxed nostalgic. Mention of the *John J. Roe* made it possible.

"The *John J. Roe,* there is not a better boat to ride upon to freedom. As slow as she is, Elizabeth will get to where she is going with heavenly company. Not just the Quakers, but a dear family of steam boating backwoodsmen and hay-seeds I would love to have as blood kin. One of the times I was aboard her, we were at the same place that is your destination, New Orleans. On a memorable trip, I had been working on the Pennsylvania. We arrived at New Orleans, and when she was berthed, I discovered that her stern lapped the fo'castle of the *John J. Roe.* I went aft, climbed over the rail of the ladies' cabin, and from that point jumped upon the Roe, landing on that spacious boiler-deck of hers. It was like arriving at home at the farm-house after a long absence. It was a delight to meet and shake hands with Captain Leavenworth, a giant of a man. There were a dozen passengers, male and female, young and old; the hearty and likeable sort affected by the *John J. Roe* farmers. Now, out of their midst, floated the enchanting vision of a girl of 15. She was a slip of a girl with dangling plaited tails hanging from her young head, and her white summer frock puffed in the wind. Frank and winsome, comely and charming, she had a fragrance of distant regions of Missouri, freshness and fragrance of her own prairies. Her name was Laura M. Wright, and I can see her with perfect distinctness. I instantly wanted to be her sweetheart.

I can state the rest, I think, in very few words. I was not four inches from that girl's elbow during our waking hours for the next three days. Then there came a sudden interruption. Zeb Leavenworth came flying aft, shouting, "The PENNSYLVANIA is backing out." I fled at my best speed, and as I broke out upon that great boiler-deck, the PENNSYLVANIA was gliding sternward past it. I made a flying leap and just did manage to make the connection, and nothing to spare. My toes found room on the guard; my finger-ends hooked themselves upon the guard-rail, and a quartermaster made a snatch for me and hauled me aboard. I have not seen that girl since."

The story paralleled his feelings for Jane. Dennis spent the remainder of the day, wistfully wandering the decks. He wondered about the cotillion where Jane would mark her official entrance into womanhood. In a vision of it, she was just stepping down off the staircase in her mint green gown, her gloved hand on the bannister. She was reaching for his hand.

He had more conversations with Sam as they drew ever closer to New Orleans, but knew he probably would never see him again. When they arrived at the Crescent City April 15th, the river had reached the high water mark, and Sam had to stay in the pilot house to steady the *Alonzo Child*. Dennis took the now mobile, but still mentally vacant Charles O'Brien to the staging plank on the shore and walked down the gangway. He turned and saw that Sam had stepped out of the pilot house, and from the skylight deck he hollered, "Do the right thing. It will gratify some people and astonish the rest."

27

Asylum

Dennis faced a dilemma after debarking from the *Alonzo Child* with his father. Dennis knew there was an insane asylum in New Orleans. It was certainly common knowledge. But the uncommon question was: How do you go about finding the place in this unfamiliar, spectacular city, where you know nobody? Do you just walk up to a stranger and say, "Where is the nearest asylum?" He uttered a prayer as they descended the gangplank.

The apron of the metropolis was a massive levee that extended for miles north and south. Scores upon scores of steamboats lined it, and tall mast ships were anchored in the middle of the river ready to deliver or take on cargo. The slope of the levee was covered with all sorts of freight organized for either incoming or outgoing packet vessels. Men of all shapes, sizes, and colors swarmed around the goods, examining and conveying, slaving, or resting with legs dangling from the cotton bales. Immense stacks of cotton bound for foreign ports stood like miniature castles. After ascending the slope in wonder with their meager baggage, Dennis and his father came to a broad commercial thoroughfare, Tchapitoulas Street. Signs over small stores bore German and Irish names. Lager-beer saloons were frequent along the way. Progressing southward, these tackier tin roofed structures gave way to more impressive and uniform structures of commission merchants, mercantile wholesalers, and banks.

They came upon a man seated in front of one of the stores, reading a newspaper. Dennis asked him where he might buy a copy.

"You are in luck, young man, I have just finished reading this one and you may have it, consider it lagniappe."

"Lagniappe? What's that?"

"A small gift given to a customer by a merchant gratuitously or by way of good measure! Think nothing of it, young man."

Thanking the man, Dennis folded it and put it under his arm as they continued along the way looking for a place to eat. Turning on a street called Poydras, they found a splendid boarding house. Deciding to splurge over a spread of okra soup, grits, sweet potatoes, and ham, Dennis tried to engage his father in conversation. His father ate but was dazed. Dennis tried to prompt him.

"Da, do you know where we are?"

"Where we are?" Charles repeated, more than questioned.

"We are in New Orleans"

"We are in New Orleans."

"Da, I am going to try and find a place for you to stay for a while."

"Stay for a while."

"Do you know what that means?"

"What that means," Charles said, toying with his food.

Seeing that his father was in his own world, Dennis opened the folded newspaper. The masthead read: *New Orleans Daily Picayune April 15, 1860.* The center columns of the page were dedicated to news, but the periphery columns contained advertisements. Suddenly his eye was arrested by the following ad:

Luzenberg Hospital - Situated on the Pontchartrain Railroad
The above hospital, in past, under the skillful and attentive

management of the late Dr. C. A. Luzenberg, is now open under the care of Dr. J. Rhodes, for the reception of patients. Terms of Admission:

In the upper wards, one dollar per day.

In private wards, from two to three dollars per day.

Surgical capital operations will be charged as extra.

Within the large enclosure is an Insane Hospital devoted only to the treatment of those afflicted with insanity.

A separate and distinct building for Small Pox and other contagious diseases.

For further particulars, apply to Dr. W. Irvine, at the hospital, or to Dr. J. Rhodes, 27 Royal Street.

It seemed remarkable that he had found the notice so soon after his quickly uttered prayer. Now he had specific answers about where to go: 27 Royal St.

Banking on providence, and seeing as how they were already at a boarding house, he inquired for a room, but found the rate higher than he wanted to spend. First, he must take his father to the hospital which was fortuitously close. At 27 Royal Street, the gold lettering on the door said modestly:

Offices of Luzenburg Hospital.
Dr. J. Rhodes
Dr. W. Irvine

Entering the office, a distinguished looking gentleman sat behind a large desk, engrossed in writing. Stacks of papers had weights placed on them. The man did not look up as Dennis and his father entered. Finally, he raised his head and said:

"Hello. I am Dr. Irvine. May I help you?"

"Yes sir, I am Dennis O'Brien, and this is my father, Charles. I am seeking to get treatment for him in the asylum. I saw the adver-tisement in the paper, and it says you have wards for the insane."

"We prefer to call it a hospital, young man. Though the word asylum does mean a place of refuge, the word has become a pejora-tive and produces stigma when used."

"Oh, thank God! This is just the kind of place I had hoped for my father. There is a good man somewhere in his clouded mind. I know it. I hope you can help restore him to normalcy."

"Thanking God is a good idea. As far as normalcy goes, that is subjective, and we can make no promises. We, however, have had some success in the treatment of melancholia, mania, and other dis-eases of the mind. Some, however, can be quite hopeless. First let me put your father through a simple physical examination."

The doctor led them to an examination room. Using a stetho-scope, he listened to Charles's lungs and heart and then used a small hammer like device to check for reflexes.

"This is good. At least no current signs of consumption or other physical malady. Now tell me his symptoms."

"Where to begin? Currently, he is easy to handle, but is some-times wild. He has been physically violent in the past. On the other hand, he can become silent and unresponsive. He goes into dazes and tells of mysterious events. He cries profusely sometimes."

"What events?" asked the doctor as he took out a notepad and pencil.

"Some of them relate to the Mexican War, but others are of Ireland. A twin brother died. Something happened with his parents. He has both a love and hate for the Catholic Church. I have wit-nessed things and heard things that no one else in the family knows about. He confides in me. I have a hard time talking about some things he has said and done. They all tumble together in a ball of confusion for me."

"I see. You, young man, have been through much yourself." the doctor said kindly, looking over his spectacles, thoughtfully tapping his pencil on the note pad. But it made Dennis feel uncomfortable as the doctor looked piercingly at him.

"Please, what can you do to help?"

"As I said, as far as help is concerned, I cannot make promises. We have a variety of therapies. Sometimes methods seem cruel but are only applied out of necessity. We do not beat the patients. However, we do have to resort to the use of force on occasion. We rely on the help of very large Negro men in some of these matters. The camisole is used sometimes to restrain the patient from hurting himself and others. You will have to trust us. If you have objections to a black man handling your father in a rough way, this is not the place to leave him."

"Everything you have said, I have no objections about. It is your profession. Please, will you accept him?"

"We are not a charity at this hospital. You must pay one half in advance, plus some other security. If not, there is another hospital in the city of less reputable reputation."

Dennis took all of the money from his belt, held back twenty dollars for himself, and gave the rest to the doctor. From his baggage, he withdrew the silver platter. The doctor secured the valuables in a safe behind his desk. Then he reached up and pulled a cord. Upstairs was the ringing of a bell. Moments later a large black man with a stoic face descended a short flight of stairs. He gently took Charles O'Brien by the hand and led him upstairs.

"We have temporary accommodations here at 27 Royal St., but only for patients. I hope you have lodging elsewhere for the night. Tomorrow we will take your father out to Milneburg where Luzenberg Hospital is located. It is best to make the separation between the two of you now. He is not cognizant and will not miss you because of his condition. Come to the hospital at the end of month. There is a train on Elysian Fields Avenue that will take you to the hospital. It is quite convenient, and the fare is very reasonable. Now the next order of business is to do the paper work for your father's admission."

Dennis spent the next half hour providing the information needed. Then he asked to see his father before he left. Peeking into the upstairs room, he saw his father asleep on a cot under the watchful eye of the negro. He did not disturb them. He shouldered the duffle bag, went downstairs, and stepped out onto Royal Street, to search for a boarding house.

28

Henry

Dennis left the doctor's office with the remaining twenty dollars; it was a tidy enough sum, but he needed to conserve.

After searching dozens of blocks for cheap boarding, he stopped on a corner. The street was dry, and the dust of the street rose in little poofs under clopping horses' hoofs. A throng of humanity passed and he earnestly inquired of those who would stop about cheap room and board. The dust had settled on his face and clothes, giving him an ashen appearance. Well-dressed businessmen looked askance at him, and ladies turned their faces away. Finally, a cheery young fellow came along. Though he was smartly dressed and spoke with a British accent, he told a grubby looking Dennis, "You should check the darkies' part of town. That's the way I found accommodations when I arrived here."

"Darkies part of town? I've never known them to own property."

"Then welcome to old New Orleans. There is a sizable free black population here, some with means. Even some slaves have a certain amount of autonomy. On St. Thomas Street, Mrs. Williams has a boarding house. Perhaps she has room."

"How far to St. Thomas Street from here?'

"Oh, not far. I am going that way, running errands for my father. I'll show you."

"I'd appreciate it. By the way, I'm Dennis O'Brien from Shiloh, Tennessee."

"Henry Stanley here. Late of Denbigh, North Wales. Pleased to meet you."

As they cut across town, Dennis learned Henry was seventeen, only a year older than himself, and contrary to what his clothes suggested, his life had been pretty rough. He was orphaned as a child and forced into a poor house. At fourteen he escaped and stowed away on an English ship, but when he was discovered, they made him a cabin boy. He had been born Henry Rowlands, and fended for himself in New Orleans. While working for a merchant, he met a pious man who unofficially adopted and baptized him. Henry had taken the man's last name, Stanley.

"You will like Mrs. Williams," Henry said enthusiastically as they came to St. Thomas Street. "After I jumped ship, I slept between cotton bales at the levee until I found work. Her boarding house was my first night in a comfortable bed. She provides room and board and will even do some laundry for you. All at the rate of thirty-five cents a day. She even has a washroom with a full copper lined bath. Quite extraordinary. Do you have the coin for that?"

Dennis balked. He had only just met this Henry Stanley. Seeing his hesitancy, Henry put his hand on his shoulder and said, "Never mind. It was not a proper question. You're wise to be cautious. I just hope you have the same experience as myself. There are a couple of attic rooms in her two-story house."

Shortly, they arrived at Mrs. Williams' house. A garden welcomed them in the front and a spacious tree-shaded yard evident at the rear. Mrs. Williams appeared at the door. She was a relatively young black woman with an intelligent, no-nonsense look on her face. She acted maternally warm when she saw Henry. Then giving her attention to Dennis, she agreed to take him on, at same rate of thirty five cents a day. He paid for a week in advance. She led them upstairs to the very attic room where Henry had stayed. Then looking Dennis up and down, she recommended he wash his clothes and get spruced up. He was already feeling at home.

"Look, my book shelves are still here! Built them myself!" Henry exclaimed. "I spent many an hour by candlelight pouring over books I purchased at a second hand bookseller. I shall take you there and introduce you to him. You can begin building your own library on these shelves."

"I'm not sure I can afford that. I have yet to find a job, but the idea sounds nice."

"I'll introduce you to Mr. Speake and Mr. McCreary, my former employers, tomorrow then. I would not be surprised if you find an opening at their store. Thievery has been a problem in his warehouse, sorry to say. Finding solid help is the dilemma of many of these merchants. I will vouch for you."

"Vouch for me? We have not known each other long enough."

"I feel we have known one another for a long time. Tomorrow there will be much vouching!"

In his first night completely away from his father or any family members, Dennis lay sleepless, staring up at the slanted ceiling of the attic room. An orchestra of katydids, crickets, and tree frogs ramped up outside the open window as he kicked off covers in the heat and humidity. He was totally independent for the first time in his life and tried to assess his feelings about that.

At last his father was in a place where he could be taken care without him. He was freed of the encumbrances of Charles O'Brien. But he could not call it a true liberation, for his innate sense of responsibility had not left him and probably never would. He still needed to check on his father and communicate regularly with his mother in Corinth, but there was a sense that invisible shackles had been released, and ropes binding his mindset had been loosened. He could move about as he pleased, even if there was uncertainty where his feet might take him, and he could take in the world without the strictures of someone else closely dictating how he should see that world. For at least the summer there were, for the first time, personal possibilities.

Henry had given hope that he would find him a place to work. If he was to get that decent job, he needed to look fresh, well rested. He couldn't look like something the cat had just dragged in, so he started counting sheep in an effort to quiet his mind. The technique didn't work. He had to stop his mind from racing. He rubbed his temples with his fingertips. At last his thoughts became restful, ironically, by permitting himself to think about Jane Winningham and seeing her that first day at Shiloh Spring.

The next thing he knew, morning rays of sunshine warmed his cheeks, coming through the eastward facing window. As he yawned, he became aware someone else was in the room. At first startled, he then saw Henry hunched over the shelves he had built. He strangely felt as if he had known Henry all his life. Henry was placing an array of books on the shelf, mumbling the titles as he did so:

"Gibbons: Decline and Fall of the Roman Empire. Spenser: Faerey Queen. Tasso: Jerusalem Delivered. The Iliad, the Odyssey, Paradise Lost. Ah, this is a good start."

"What are you are doing, Henry?" Dennis spoke, continuing to yawn.

"Providing you an expansive world! With the loan of these volumes, you will be in the company of kings, emperors, knights, warriors, heroes, and angels."

"All that, eh? I think I should like breakfast first."

At that very moment, Mrs. Williams came to the door and

announced the morning meal, "You boys have got a real appetite worked up, I hope. I have a treat comin' for you this mornin'," she said cheerfully in a soft drawl.

"And here Mas' Dennis, I finished yah laundry. You will look fine fo job huntin'."

"Your cooking is *always* a treat, Mrs. Williams," Henry grinned.

Dennis dressed quickly, and the both of them nearly tumbled downstairs in a hurry to get to the table. There they found a spread of scrambled eggs, bacon, grits, hush puppies, and liver mush. There was coffee and a large pitcher of milk to wash it down.

Dennis was as famished as he could remember and started shoveling food into his mouth. He was quaffing a large glass of milk when Henry, who had been watching, bemusedly asked, "Are you heathen? Don't you say grace?"

Dennis, embarrassed, immediately bowed his head, but rushed through the words. "Great Jehovah, we thank you for these vittles and the hands of Mrs. Williams that prepared them. In Jesus' name. Amen."

There was little conversation while Dennis scarfed down his breakfast. Finally, feeling gorged, Dennis pushed himself back from the table and took in a deep breath, "Delicious, Mrs. Williams, absolutely delicious!" and he patted his belly.

Henry added, "I know just how you feel. The first real meal I had here in New Orleans was here at Mrs. William's. But for now, we must go see Mr. Speake or McCreary, my former employers. It's important we get there early in the morning, otherwise the bustle will make it unfavorable for a good interview."

Fully fueled, Dennis and Henry returned to the main artery of the city, Tchapitoulas Street, and proceeded on the boardwalk as establishments opened for business. As they walked, Henry narrated details of what to expect at Mr. Speake's. Negroes swept alleys between piles of goods, pushing dust and debris from the previous day's traffic out into the gutter. Whiskey and rum barrels, marked and branded, were rolled out and arranged near the curbstone. Sixty-two gallon hogsheads of molasses and forty-two gallon tierces of wine were set on end. Cases of goods were built up, flour sacks laid in orderly layers awaiting removal by low-lying carts without sides called drays. All waiting to be conveyed to the river steamers.

In short order they arrived in front of a store marked No. 3 where a middle-aged gentleman in a dark alpaca suit and tall hat sat reading a newspaper. Over the door the sign read: *Speake and McCreary, Wholesale and Commission Merchants.*

"Mr. McCreary, are you looking for a boy?"

The respectable, but genial face brightened, "Why Henry, where have you been since I last saw you?"

"With my father, dealing goods on the river towns mostly. I have someone I want you to meet. This is Dennis O'Brien of Shiloh, Tennessee. He is looking for work for at least the summer. Do you possibly have a place for him?"

"Can you read?" Mr. McCreary asked, handing Dennis the newspaper. "If so, read that!"

Dennis complied as instructed: "SUCCESSION OF GREER P. DUNCAN- Sale of the fine offices known as the "Duncan's Buildings" and the Splendid Residence on Apollo street, between Euterpe and Terpsichore streets. Also a Desirable Pew in St. Paul's Church..."

"Correctly enough, you even came close on pronunciation of the Greek names of those streets. Now can you write?"

"Well enough, I reckon."

"Then let me see you mark that coffee-sack with the same address you see on the one near it. Over there by the desk is the marking pot and brush."

In a few moments, Dennis traced out a triangular symbol followed by block letters, MEMPHIS, TENNESSEE. Mr.

McCreary commended the work with a "neatly done." Then he told him to mark the other sacks in the same way. There were about twenty of them, and Henry smiled as Dennis swiftly repeated the procedure.

"Excellent. You do it as well as young Stanley here did when he was in my employ. Now there is less chance of them getting pilfered. As Henry may tell you, we have been the victims of thievery in past. If you are half the worker that he was when working for me, you will be well worth the same wage; that's 10 cents an hour, ten hours a day, six days a week. Now, is that acceptable to you? You may start immediately, after you have had a hair-cut. Here is an advance to take care of that. Now is that acceptable to you?"

Dennis thanked Mr. McCreary profusely and told him repeatedly he would not regret hiring him although he anxiously felt he had to give Mr. McCreary one caveat.

"Sir, this opportunity means more to me than anything, but I would not be fair to your offer without mentioning a difficult situation that exists for me."

"Out with it then," McCreary said sternly. Dennis became downcast with the possibility of losing this incredible opportunity. His eyes began to glisten.

"My father currently is in residence in Luzenberg Hospital on the Lake for a dire condition of the mind. It may be necessary at times for me to attend to an emergency."

McCreary's face softened, and in a response that shocked Dennis, Mr. McCreary's eyes too began to tear up.

"O'Brien. We'll cross that bridge when we come to it. By my reckoning you are about fifteen years old, are you not?"

"Sixteen, sir."

"Then you'll be a son of the famine."

"I don't understand, sir."

"When I arrived here in the mid-forties there were two options for the famine Irish. Either work in the swamps diggin' the canals or go off to the Mexican War."

"Yes sir, Mr. McCreary, my father served in that war."

McCreary nodded his head knowingly. "I worked the swamps and nearly died of fever. Well-nigh 10,000 others did die. I hung on by the skin of my teeth, saved every cent. I was taken in by a well-to-do sugar merchant and that is how I have ultimately come to own this enterprise. Well, I can't help but have a soft spot for the sons of Ireland. Now be on your way to the barber, but be on your way back quickly," and he winked.

Henry bore him away to find a tonsorial parlor. They located one at the corner of a building, with a barber pole painted with red, white and blue swirls outside the door. This was the first time Dennis had ever had a professional hair-cut. As he lay back in the luxurious chair, he at first was rigid, but soon relaxed. The gentlemanly barber operated as if Dennis was a work of art. As Dennis watched his locks fall away over the linen apron, he felt like he was coming out of a cocoon. All the while Henry watched with amusement as the barber shampooed his head and neck and then performed a semi-scouring of his face that made his cheeks glow. Looking into the mirror, the transformation gave Dennis a feeling never experienced. He could not help but admire his own face. Henry laughed: "You look first rate, Dennis!"

When they emerged from the shop, Henry hurried to get back to his father's business while Dennis returned to Speake and McCreary's store. Henry promised to see him "on the morrow," and in parting, put his hand Dennis's shoulder and said quietly. "You know McCreary's a millionaire. One of many in this city."

The rest of the day, Dennis assisted two slaves, Isaiah and Samuel, in rolling liquor and flour barrels, and taking groceries on hand trucks from the depths of the long store to the sidewalk. Dennis did all the marking of the sundry lots since the two Negroes could neither read nor write.

The good fortune he had found that day left him buoyed. He had gainful employment. He assessed his new situation. There was a young gentleman named Mr. Richardson who made out bills of lading and arranged with the pursers of the steamers for their transportation. Dennis felt he was already in "high cotton," but he thought *I could do that and make even more money if I could work my way into that position.* He could care for himself, save some for his father's care, and who knows, maybe there would be something leftover for something frivolous.

Over the next few weeks, the world opened up for Dennis. Some of it was adventuresome and exhilarating, other times taxing and difficult. Regularly, Henry came after work and took him out on excursions into the city as the spring turned into summer and the daylight afforded longer hours. However, he kept reminding himself that he was not here in New Orleans on a lark. Once a week he mailed a letter to his mother in Corinth. Early every Sunday morning, he dutifully checked on his father at the Luzenberg asylum, but there was time, glorious time, after seeing his father, to do as he pleased the rest of the day.

The trips out to the asylum involved a train trip of several miles that ran from the base of Elysian Fields Avenue at the river through the eastern part of the city, then out across an expanse of swampland along the edge of Lake Ponchartrain. The trip on the clacking carriage cars behind the little locomotive "Smokey Mary" proved to be a pleasant, meditative experience until he got to the hospital. Then things at times became bizarre.

Luzenburg asylum was an all-purpose facility, dealing with all sorts of maladies, wounds, and operations. The outer building of the hospital administered to the needs of these regular patients. They were a different world from the center of the compound. While waiting to see his father or his father's doctor in the waiting room of the center building, it was not uncommon for the intermittent anguished screams of mental patients to be heard. This portion of the hospital was devoted only to the treatment of those afflicted with insanity. At times while waiting, he recognized the timbre of his father's voice in these cries.

At mid-June, Doctor Irvine delivered to Dennis a diagnosis of "variegated psychosis" and said that it might stabilize. It was the first time Dennis had heard such words. They were complex terms. When defined by the doctor, it was nothing new to Dennis. He already knew this about his Da; that he was possessed of a variety of subterranean traumas inhabiting his mind. At least hope had been offered that his father would stabilize. Sometimes he was allowed to see his father, other times not. Their times were awkward and brief for the presence of outsiders sometimes caused general pandemonium among the other patients.

By day, he worked alongside the slaves, Isaiah and Samuel at the mercantile. He learned that they were essentially leased labor to *Speake and McCreary*, and it was puzzling to whom they actually "belonged." This merchants' store was a kind of cooperative with various brokers and merchants maintaining desks for business in a warehouse of goods. Isaiah and Samuel were semi-autonomous in their forced servitude with freedoms he had never seen with the slaves back home, yet it was clear they were still under the thumb of owners. They were called 'boys' though they were able bodied men, and not given the respect that he was given, though he was an adolescent. They always asked or answered using the word 'massuh.' They even addressed Dennis as 'little boss,' though he was just hired. This was a constant reminder to Dennis of the "peculiar institution" of slavery.

When he worked alongside them, Dennis sprang upon his work with avid desire to complete a task, but they did their utmost to suppress his eager exuberance, "Take it easy, li'l boss! Don' kills yo'sef! Plenty of time. Leave somethin' fo tomorrow."

This rankled Dennis at first, thinking them lazy, but as he ana-lyzed their behavior, he realized it was a clever passive resistance to their forced servitude. He tried to put himself in their place and could see that the harder and more swiftly they worked, more might be expected of them to no advantage. He could try and be friends with them on some level, but their bondage inhibited true camara-derie. They tried to stay at a distance, either upstairs or in the back yard of the building, and they pretended not to hear. It was a fatigu-ing task to call and then wait for them.

After a few weeks, the difference between white and black was impressed on him even more. He was commended for his prompt-ness and was engaged at the rate of twenty-five dollars a month. He came to learn that the 'boys' were allotted thirty cents a day each, the balance of the value of their rented labor given to their owners. It was a lesson in freedom. Dennis as a sixteen year old white male earned enough after his room and board to have fifteen dollars a month available for other purposes. The black 'boys' made few dol-lars, along with "free" room and board wherever it was that they were living.

It was conflicting to Dennis, so he threw himself into his work, but the wonder of which made him feel as if it was not work. Henry had apprised him of all the variety, but now he was experiencing it for himself. He marked sundry lots for shipment to a multitude of Mississippi river ports such as Bayou Plaquemine, Attakapas, Opelousas, as well as the major docks of St. Louis, Memphis, and Cincinnati. He oversaw Samuel and Isaiah in taking groceries on hand trucks from the one hundred foot depth of the store to the sidewalk. There were three lofts above the ground floor where goods were stored. They contained piles and piles of groceries, besides wines and brandies, liqueurs and syrups. The ground floor was piled high almost to the ceiling with sacks of coffee-berries with their characteristic fresh scent. The seminal aroma of grains and the sap smell of wooden cases blended together in the nostrils as a heady mixture. The brandings on the cases read of bottled fruit, tinned jams, and berries of all kinds, scented soaps, candles, vermicelli, macaroni, and many other foods Dennis had never heard of before. It was an intoxicating environment, and the summer lay before Dennis with many delicious possibilities.

29

Liberty

Delicious possibilities? To say that the summer of 1860 was unfettered liberty would be an overstatement. In order to obtain those delicious possibilities, he had to start living a double life and compartmentalize his existence. There was the life of visiting the hospital, and the life he could pursue outside of it.

The stay at Luzenberg on Lake Ponchartrain was definitely therapeutic for his father. Dr. Irvine capsulized his father's status in late June:

"As you know from your regular visitations, we did not know from day to day whether he would be in a state of catatonic staring, stupor, mutism, food refusal, defiance, chronic masturbation, or violent rage and self-harm. For the last three weeks, he has shown a steady progress towards an equilibrium of sorts. We established a regimen which has enabled us to taper off the laudanum."

These were not grand revelations to Dennis, for he had experienced dealing with his father up close and personal from his tender years forward, including catching his father in the act of self-abuse. The things he did not understand were the love-hate relationship with the Catholic Church, and what had happened with his parents and twin brother, and the matter of the relationship his father had with Captain Adair. His father had only spoken of these matters in abstract. Dennis wanted to know the root causes of these things but did not relish the process. Divorcing his mind from the briefings on Sunday mornings at the hospital, Dennis sallied forth into the depths of the metropolis, sometimes with Henry, other times not.

Dennis at first resisted Henry's invitation to Lafayette Square the first Sunday of July. There was to be an artillery demonstration there. The mention of cannons being fired conjured up the haunting images that he had lived vicariously through his father's episodes. Still there was an overwhelming curiosity for Dennis of what it would be like to hear them fire in real life. He gave in, and they arrived at the park near noon.

"That, Dennis, is the famous Washington Artillery of New Orleans!" Henry had to shout because of the crowd. There were four cannon lined up, side by side, pointing toward the Mississippi River. Attending to them was a company of about 100 men. All were obeying strict military etiquette, ignoring the crowd while focusing on their military task at hand.

Dennis studied the soldier closest to himself. On his head was a red kepi, circled by a peacock blue band with two brass cannons crossed in the front and the letters "WA." He wore a royal blue frock coat and sky blue pants with a wide red stripe down the outer seams. The frock's red collar also had crossed cannons sewn on to it. The jacket's cuffs were red. He wore brass epaulettes attached to the shoulders, buttons with pelicans embossed on them adorned the front, with a white buff belt and shoulder strap. The brass rectangular buckle had a pelican within a circle. White gloves and white gaiters completed the exquisite outfit. The soldier smartly wore his sword and pistol. Dennis found himself enamored with the look and wondered what it would feel like to be in one of those uniforms.

His little daydream was suddenly and literally blown apart when the full battery fired. Startled was not the word. It wasn't just the noise, but a concussion wave that compressed his chest. He felt as if his soul left his body in the behemoth thundercloud of the smoking, belching beasts. It took a moment for Dennis to realize he was not in some other realm. When he regained his bearings, Henry was laughing at the look on his face, as was the soldier under Dennis's scrutiny earlier. They locked their arms over each other's in camaraderie.

"Dennis, let me introduce you to Private Francisco Moreno Jr.," the young soldier moved forward with a friendly hand outstretched:

"Mucho gusto; pleased to meet you," and clicked his heels together.

The young private toured Dennis and Henry around the head-quarters of the Washington Artillery, relating its history. Moreno was clearly proud to be part of the Artilleries 5th company, but was not overly serious. He spoke perfect English but occasionally flourished it with short Spanish expressions. He seemed to be as interested in Dennis's remarks as Dennis was in the explanations. Francisco pointed out that the regimental flag had been awarded in August of 1846 after serving under Zachary Taylor in the Mexican-American War. Dennis felt a jolt in his subconscious about his father's service. He looked around at all the strutting officers and internally wondered what was to become of these men if secession occurred. He could not help asking, "What will you do if the South secedes?"

"Dios no lo quiera! God forbid that happens! But my loyalties will be with the regiment and the South."

Dennis tried to be dispassionate. "How is it that you, a Spaniard, feel that way?"

Moreno bristled slightly and replied: "You do not understand this yet? As J.T Bickford said in the novel Scandal "Home is where the heart is.""

Henry interjected that he should read the book. It was in the library he had given Dennis.

Dennis was confused, "I can sort of see what you are saying, but I try to stay neutral."

"We're getting too serious here. We should discuss this more genially over a meal."

After being dismissed by his commanding officer, a tour of a different sort began. Francisco took them to quarters and carefully put away his uniform, donned more informal attire, and they set off in search of refreshments.

So came to be an unusual alliance. Dennis, 16; Henry, 17; and Francisco, 18. Their association through the summer was one of exploration, both philosophical and geographical. Being near the same age contributed to the chemistry of their friendship, but this association was quite unusual for Dennis. He viewed himself as the odd-man-out. Henry "was on his way" because his adoptive father, Mr. Stanley, was a successful merchant. He could never have imagined becoming friends with a young man of Moreno's social stature. His great-grandfather had commanded one of the Spanish colonies in Louisiana in 1778. His grandfather had been a surgeon in the Spanish Army stationed in Pensacola before the ceding to the United States. His father was a banker in Pensacola, Florida, and it was primarily the relationship between Mr. Stanley, the merchant, and Don Francisco Moreno Sr., the banker, which had enabled them to come together. Dennis, Henry and Frances came to call themselves, the "little triumvirate." At restaurants and on outings about town on Sundays, the "little triumvirate" enjoyed long discussions about philosophers, current events, and promises to ever maintain their friendships. However, on Sunday July 29th 1860, Dennis missed their usual outing.

It started in the early morning with a confrontation between Dr. Irvine and Dennis. He had impatiently expressed to the doctor that he did not think the treatments were showing much improvement for his father. The doctor responded indignantly, "Until Christ comes down out of heaven and lays his healing hands on all of the poor souls of this world, I can only triage the ones that he seems to funnel into our institution."

Dennis took the rebuke to heart and profusely apologized. Then he asked to see his father. His father was in a syrupy, sentimental mood. "You have become just like a father to me, Denny. Just like a father," and he held out his arms to be embraced.

There could not have been crueler words uttered to him. He was quite aware that a role reversal with his father had inexorably taken place over the years, but this, the raw truth coming through his father's mouth caused a suffocating constriction in his chest. As he allowed his father to put his arms around himself, he felt injected with venom of an unfeeling serpent. He felt the fangs and the toxins as they killed his hopes for long term independence. All his hopes were once again being swallowed by the constricting viper of duty. Dennis firmly gripped his father's arms, removing them from his shoulders. "Da, I must hurry to catch the train," he said tersely, and fled out the entrance of the hospital, frantically jumping onto the little train back to New Orleans.

The trip back home allowed him to decompress. By the time he got back to the Elysian Fields station, he was in a state of acceptance; the time to mediate on the train caused him to feel that there may have even been a breakthrough. For now he would put it completely out of mind and try to find something pleasant to occupy the rest of the day. He would splurge. He entered a hostelry and ordered lunch and a julep. While waiting for his order, he looked across the room to see a familiar female face. The girl was alone. He walked over to her and recalled what Douglas had said about coincidence and providence.

"Tu te souviens de moi, Camille?" Dennis asked tentatively, with the stay in New Orleans having added a few new French expressions to his vocabulary.

"Why, Dennis, of course, I remember you. Isn't this extraordinary that we meet again? And listen to you. You have learned more French. I am impressed."

"Well, don't get too impressed. I am sorry to say that the main words I have been taught by some rascal friends of mine are not so savory. May I join you at your table?"

"Oui! But of course."

Their initial interaction was somewhat trite, but as the conversation progressed, the two of them found increasing enjoyment in one another's company. However, she had an air that something was troubling her. He tried to prompt what was wrong. She spoke tentatively. He learned that her home was in Charleston, South Carolina, but her uncle, her father's brother, lived here in New Orleans. After they finished their lunch, Dennis asked, "Is your brother chaperoning you today?"

"Chaperone? I am so mad at my brother. He wants to continue escorting me about, but I have turned eighteen, and plan to do as I please." She did not sound as sure as her words. "I have a monthly stipend from my father's estate, and I am quite independent now." Again her voice was not so confident.

"Pardon me, but your father's estate? I thought when we met on the train near Memphis you were going to join him in Charleston?"

At that Camille's eyes welled up, and she brought a handkerchief to her face. Speaking through the cloth, her voice broke. "He had been suffering with ague in Charleston for some time. He succumbed to it shortly after we arrived home."

Dennis put his hand on her arm. She responded by leaning forward and weeping into his sleeve. He looked around the room. They were attracting attention from other patrons.

"Come, let's go for a walk together. Have you been to Congo Square? "

"Of course. I know the place. It is the liveliest and most interesting place I know in the city. On a Sunday, anyway!" Camille recovered her pleasant demeanor and put the handkerchief back into her purse.

He rose, and she took his arm. They stepped into the light of the early afternoon sun, and both of them squinted. She lifted a pink ruffled parasol over her head. The avenue was bustling with a different pace than business days. People were out and about after church, looking for entertainment. Horses pulled fine open carriages occupied by top-hatted men and women dressed in their Sunday best. The pastel pink and blue colors of the French Quarter buildings were soothing. On the overhanging balconies, the designs in white-washed wrought iron balustrades looked like the dripping frosting on wedding cakes. The morning humidity climbed, and battalions of clouds rolled in from the Gulf of Mexico.

When they arrived at Congo Square, it was alive with throbbing syncopated rhythms of several competing drum groups. In turn, the clearly African beats spawned competitive, uninhibited, very suggestive dancing contests. Flutes of the strangest kind were being played by exceedingly black men, and the music lilted above the sound of the crowd. There was giddy pandemonium in the air.

Women of all shades of skin walked around selling baskets of freshly made "calas," fried rice cakes covered in powdered sugar. Dennis bought one for Camille and himself. It was his first taste of these sweet cakes. He licked his lips, savoring the sweetness. She reached up with her index finger and brushed away a bit of powder at the corner of his mouth. Her touch discombobulated him. He took her hand and brought it up to his forehead as feigning she had given him a fever. She gave him a gentle push and pretended pshaw, and they continued meandering.

The square was surrounded by uncountable little make-shift and collapsible shops where slaves and free blacks were hawking their goods including pottery ware. They strolled among them, sampling foods and at others trying on odd trinkets that the vendors called *nkisi*. The objects were intriguing. One seller explained that these animal tails and dangling objects contained spiritual properties of healing. After hearing this, Dennis stopped trying them on because they gave him the willies.

Meantime the clouds had piled up on themselves and a continuous rumbling indicated downpours were imminent. The vendors began closing up their shops, and the crowd thinned. Then came a tremendous clap of thunder, and instantaneously the square was deluged. Dennis put his arm around Camille and hurried her to an enclosed carriage for hire. They both climbed in drenched.

"Where would you like to go from here? We've got to get you there before the streets are completely awash."

"Return me to the hotel where you found me please," Camille begged, shivering, though the afternoon temperature was warm.

"To Rue Dumaine!" Dennis requested of the colored coachman, reaching through the window and handing him a coin. Rain dripped profusely off the driver's stove pipe hat.

As they sat together, he kept his arm around Camille. She leaned into his chest for warmth. He put his face into her saturated, perfumed tresses and kissed the crown of her head. The sound of splashing horses' hoofs and the sensual motion of the carriage and groaning thunder coalesced. Camille raised her head and looked into Dennis's face and smiled at the droplets on his glasses. She reached up to remove them, and as she did their lips came closer. He ran his fingers through her wet hair. Their mouths closed upon one another. For Dennis, he had fallen into a universe he did not know existed.

That universe evaporated as the coach came to an abrupt halt in front of the hotel, causing the coach to rock violently, bringing them out of their intimacy. It was still pouring, and Dennis jumped out, then helped Camille onto the boardwalk. They ducked into the foyer. The few people in the lobby had their faces close up to the windows, awed by the quantity of water inundating the streets. Dennis and Camille looked at one another questioningly. Then she quickly took his hand and whispered to him to discreetly tiptoe down a hallway to a room on the first floor with the number seven on the door. She took a key from her purse, turned it in the lock, and they stepped inside a modest room with a brass bed, an armoire, and a privacy screen. With clothes dripping, they resumed embracing and kissing. It continued to the point where Dennis realized they were heading toward the inevitable. He broke off necking and invited her to sit down next to him on the bed.

Camille was nervously gripping the quilt. Dennis felt like his head was going to explode and finally said, "I think we are having an awkward silence."

She giggled and replied, "That is one of the most truthful statements I have ever heard!"

"Yes, yes, we have got to be truthful. Tell me what you are feeling," Dennis said earnestly.

Camille hedged, "I think we need to get out of these wet clothes or we will catch our deaths!"

"We certainly should not catch our deaths!" Dennis teased.

Camille giggled.

Next to the armoire leaned a folded privacy screen. Camille set it up between them, then stepped behind it and removed her wet long cotton skirt and high necked blouse. She hung them to dry over the top of the screen. He kept his head down respectfully. It was one of the hardest things he had ever done. However, as she dropped her undergarments on the floor, he caught a glimpse of her peach colored calves, and provocative aspects of her feminine shadow cast across the floor. It was then that he felt he had to make a wrenching decision.

"Camille. We have promised to be truthful." He said in a low serious tone. "You are truly beautiful, and I have never felt such a powerful attraction for anyone before."

"I feel the same way, mon amour. Comprenez-vous?"

"Of course, I understand. I want you more than anything today. But you are in grief, and we are really only acquaintances. Should I take advantage of you at this time, I fear that in the future you should come to despise me. We should wait for a better time."

There was a long silence on Camille's part. Then he saw her reach into the armoire and draw out a dressing gown. After donning it, she stepped from behind the partition.

"Dennis, I have never met anyone like you before," she said with a mixture of frustration and admiration. "I have had suitors before, their mouths watering, but you are the first true gentleman I have ever known. You say that in the future I should come to despise you if you were to take my flower now, but I say, you shall always be my love… bien que nous n'ayons pas consommé."

"I don't know what that means."

"Though we have not consummated our passion," and she took his face in her hands and kissed him for one last time that day. He caressed her cheek with his palm, promised to see her the following Sunday, and took his leave into the driving rain.

30

$$\scriptstyle\blacktriangleright\!\!\!\!\gg\!\!\!(\!\langle 0 \rangle\!)\!\!\!\ll\!\!\!\!\blacktriangleleft$$

Salvage

The week after the storm was one of the most exhausting stretches of work that Dennis had ever experienced. The levee along the crescent had been breached, and portions of the city were under water for three days. All the stores along Tchapitoulas Street, including *Speake and McCreary's* warehouse, flooded up to two feet, ruining much merchandise. After the water subsided, the job of salvage required hiring more laborers. Mr. McCreary put Dennis in charge of three more slaves besides Isaiah and Thomas.

Misters Speake and McCreary made it mandatory that they work from to dawn to dark. They were required to sleep in one of the lofts and not go back to their places of residence. When Dennis asked Mr. McCreary for permission to check on Camille, under duress Mr. McCreary angrily told him that if he wanted to check on "a slip of a girl" he did not need to return. Then he softened, "You say she resides in the French Quarter? She is on higher ground and need not worry 'til you see her."

Had it not been for the fact there were three lofts above the

ground floor, where piles upon piles of the most valuable groceries, rare wines, liqueurs, and syrups were stored, the loss would have
been inestimable. As it was, the ground floor had been turned into
a muddy mélange of ruined sacks of coffee berries and grains, cases
of miscellanea, barrels of saturated flour, and hundreds of pounds
of unrecoverable bacon and hams. There was some consolation that
many cases had been filled mason jars and foods in tinned cans and
bottles, and therefore, had been preserved. However, the stink of the
perishables mixed with sewage and flotsam from the river was so
bad that wearing a neckerchief pulled up over the nose was a must
for days.

Dennis took pride that he had been counted worthy by Mr.
McCreary to give direction to the laborers, but the fact that they
were permanently indentured pained his conscience. They had no
choice. He was now an overseer. With revulsion, he recalled Elmore
at the Robert's plantation and began shoveling sludge himself. There
was a quiet astonishment by the black men at seeing him do the
dirty work. Isaiah and Samuel who had previously always found
something to do at a distance, either upstairs or in the back yard,
had pretended not to hear him when he called, trying patience, now
seemed sincerely willing to help him. They frequently cried out to
the other slaves, "Now listen to 'lil boss!'"

Throughout this week of compulsory drudgery, Dennis's
thoughts were filled with concern about the status of Luzenberg
Hospital, and especially how Camille had fared. When the work load
finally eased off late Saturday afternoon, he raced to Mrs. Williams's
house for a bath and a change of clothes, with the intention of then
going on to see Camille. Upon seeing Dennis's pitiable condition,
Mrs. Williams sent him upstairs to bring fresh clothes while she
pumped water for the bath and heated it on the stove. When he
came down and went into the washroom, the water was steaming.
He stepped into the copper lined tub, delicately at first, then finding

the water deliciously warm, sat down in his nakedness. Enveloped in the warmth, the tension in his muscles eased. He gently stirred the water on each side of his body and felt the week's fatigue dissolving away. A sense of tranquility came over him. His eyelids became like lead and the needs of his taxed and weary physique overpowered the intentions of his heart. He inescapably fell asleep.

He was awakened by the pounding on the washroom door by another tenant in the house. In a panic, Dennis dried off with a hemp towel and hurriedly got dressed. When he opened the door, a white-whiskered oaf of a man, naked as a jaybird, stared at him and curmudgeonly complained, "Do you think you're the only one in the need of a scrub? Out of the way!" and he pushed past Dennis and slammed the door behind him.

With little time to spare before dark, Dennis jogged all the way to the French Quarter. When he arrived at the hotel, he was out of breath and had to stop with his hands on his knees in the foyer, wheezing. The white concierge at the desk watched him somewhat disgustedly.

"Can I help you…*sir?*"

"Oh, thank you. I am here to see Miss Camille Laurent. Room No. 7."

"And your name?" the clerk dubiously asked.

"Dennis O'Brien. I should like to see her right away."

The concierge turned around to a cubby-hole cabinet behind the desk and withdrew an envelope marked with Dennis's name on it. He handed it disdainfully to Dennis. Ignoring the steward, he sat down in a wing-back chair in the lobby. He studied the script that read *Monsieur Dennis O'Brien* on the envelope for a long time before opening it. He removed the note that was on perfumed stationery and read what had been composed only two days after they had been together:

July 31, 1860

Mon Cheri,

It is with great reluctance that I pen this message. Even as I write, my brother and uncle stand impatiently waiting for me. I am yet a captive of their protection. Under protest, they are to taking me back to Charleston. I will forever remember our precious time together.

Au revoir,
Camille Dumond

Dennis brought the letter to his nose and sniffed the floral scent on the paper once again. Rising from the chair he approached the concierge

"Did Miss Dumond leave a forwarding address?" She had not. He removed his bi-fold wallet from his front pants pocket. He withdrew a dime and placed it on the counter. Then he carefully folded the letter and placed it in his wallet and walked quietly away from the hotel.

When he arrived after dusk at Mrs. Williams, he was so weary he could barely greet her and trudged upstairs. Opening the door and flopping on the bed, he fell into a deep slumber.

Through the next week, Mr. McCreary praised him for his performance during the previous week's flooding, but Dennis remained glum. He stayed so until Henry popped in on Saturday, having just returned from a trip up-river with his adoptive father, Mr. Stanley.

He was anxious to plan ahead for the rest of the summer with the little triumvirate. Henry had already seen Frances Moreno, so to say he wanted to "plan" with Dennis was moot. There was already a fixed agenda, mainly because Francisco was footing the bill. A prime thing was going to see what the political clubs were doing. Late Sunday morning after Dennis had checked on his father at the hospital, they sat in the restaurant of the four story *City Hotel* having a late breakfast and trading off reading the contents of the local newspapers: *Daily Picayune, The Bee, Daily True Delta, New Orleans Daily Crescent.*

The reports of the upcoming election were particularly heated, and the *Daily Picayune* referred to the campaign as the most intense canvass seen in the city for twenty-four years. While Henry and Francisco were enthralled with some of the articles pitching the merits of each political party, Dennis sought out other news, specifically the weather. The rains were continuing intermittingly since the great storm, and he hoped there would not be another experience like the one he had just been through. When the third paper was passed to him, he smiled, reading:

New Orleans Daily Crescent
Thursday August, 12 1860,
Local Intelligence

There Was More Rain yesterday, and plenty of it. Quite a freakish display came on in the afternoon – a violent squall of wind with a deluge of rain, and the fiercest thunder and lightning, the whole of which lasted more than 30 minutes. The frogs sing joyously and the mosquitoes multiply by myriads.

The message was upbeat and sardonic, but then Dennis turned the page. There was a sickening notice, and his face showed it. Henry and Francisco looked questioningly at him. Dennis said that it was nothing and went on reading. He had known these two young men now for several weeks, and was beginning to discern their proclivities. Francisco was definitely partial to pro-States Rights articles, but Henry was maddeningly laissez-faire. Wanting to keep the camaraderie, Dennis was torn about revealing his affinity for anti-slavery sentiments, but flying in the face of all that he opposed, was the following announcement.

> **Important Notice to Persons of Color**
> An announcement is made that
> from the 1st of September: all
> free persons of color arriving-
> in the city must immediately
> be lodged in jail, and there remain
> until the departure of the boat or
> vessel on which they came.

Dennis skimmed a second article that disparaged owners of slaves giving monthly passes. It was a new policy, this time affecting negroes in all of Louisiana. "It is now the policy of this State to diminish as fast as possible the number of free Negroes. It is now apparent that the habit of giving monthly passes creates a mongrel class of black population in our State." Next to it was yet another article that also riled him.

Editors Appeal: The news via the Europa, received here on Saturday, is reported to have had no effect on the cotton market. For the most part, this is true; but after the receipt of it, a concession was demanded, particularly on the lower grade of cotton. The opinion among other factors is that for grades below middling, there will be a reduction. For middling and better grades prices will probably be sustained – even running lists of middling will bring 11 ¼ to 11 ½ c.; good middling 12c. For our great Louisiana staple, sugar and molasses, there is a heavy demand, with an upward tendency in prices; in fact, everything for sale here seems to be on the advance. A-No.1 field hands are selling here from $1500 to $1700 each. Planters complain loudly of the high prices, but buy at last. This is a hard market to sell an unsound Negro in; slaves not fully guaranteed bring little or nothing, comparatively.

Dennis picked up *THE NEW ORLEANS BEE,* and discovered an article that was not as inflammatory. He showed it to Henry and Francisco. It hailed the creation of a new political club called the *BUNKER HILL RANGERS.* It was trying a middle road policy because of the vehement animosity between North and South. The club had taken the first part of the name *BUNKER HILL* from the Revolutionary War Battle in Boston, "expressing a hearty and constitutional remembrance of the North." It was juxtaposed with *RANGERS* as a nod to the increasing number of Southern militia who romantically fashioned themselves after the legendary Texas Rangers.

Though Dennis tried to suggest the article was a way to tamp down the tensions, it bored Francisco, whose eyes seemed to lightly sparkle when the suggestion of war was mentioned in the other papers. Dennis felt a flash of ire.

"Moreno, you seem to have no idea what war can do to a man. It's not all shiny brass buttons and epaulettes on frock coats! My father served in the Mexican War, and I tell you, you have no idea..." and he became lost for words.

Francisco was slightly taken aback, but then smiled.

"Volvemos a ser demasiado serios. We are getting too serious, again" Francisco announced, slapping the table with both hands, then getting up. "Let us be on our way to Jackson Square!"

After the heated discussion, Dennis looked forward to something lighthearted the rest of the afternoon. He thought that going to Jackson Square would be just the tonic. To the contrary, it turned out that opposing political club rallies were squared off against one another in various parts of the park. On one side of the Andrew Jackson equestrian statue, The Southern Rights Association was advocating for secession; on the other side The Friends of United Southern *Action* were calling for clear heads and preservation of the Union. That did not set well with the SRA, and a pushing match developed. It might have only been pushing, but then a contingent of the *Société d'Economie et d'Assistance Mutuelle* arrived. The presence of this multi-ethnic benevolent organization included Creoles of African descent, who had some wealth and influence. A tinderbox ignited.

From somewhere in the crowd, a brick flew through the air and hit a proponent of FUSA who was standing on a soap box calling for peace. The man speaking crashed to the ground, his head bloodied in the extreme. The SRA blamed the *Société*,. Soon a real melee broke out.

Dennis, Henry, and Francisco worked their way out of the frenzied mob. When they reached the edge of the square, Dennis found out why they were able to escape. The crowd had parted because of a stoical looking man with a very French coiffure, well angled broad mustache and goatee. He was wearing the uniform of a Federal army officer. Francisco strode forward, and though not in uniform, he stood at attention and gave a salute. Francisco then turned and announced to Dennis and Henry, "Let me introduce you to my mentor, Major Beauregard, Chief Engineer at the Customs House and well known for strengthening the forts around New Orleans."

The major nodded and shook hands, but was not overly cordial.

He spoke with a Creole accent. It was not clear if he was associated with *Société d'Economie et d'Assistance Mutuelle*, but he seemed to have the respect of everyone regardless. In fact, his calm presence had a ripple effect across the gathering. What had been a riled throng gradually dissipated to smaller groups murmuring a few curses, then there with a fair amount of cordial back-slapping. It was an intriguing way to end another Sunday as Beauregard took Francisco by the elbow and said, "Come walk with me. I should like to discuss your promotion."

31

Landslide

The last Sunday of August, Henry Stanley and Dennis O'Brien rode in the direction of St. Louis Cathedral along with Francisco Moreno Jr. in a fine Spanish carriage. The horses drawing the carriage were not ordinary. The measured high-steps of the horses' hooves exhibited classical dressage. Nothing but the best for the Southern Spanish aristocrats of the Moreno family.

Ostensibly, this outing today was with pious intent to attend mass at the historic Catholic Church. In addition to the religious services, Francisco wanted to go to confession. They had dressed for the occasion. He had gifted suits for Henry and Dennis from his own wardrobe for this outing, the three of them being of similar build, young men growing into their adult bodies. On the face of it, their attire was a respectful nod to their purpose of going to church, but these duds also gave an opportunity to go peacocking. Francisco's striking and immaculate clothing were like his natural skin. Henry was living it up, luxuriating in the feel of the fine garments, but Dennis felt like a fish out of water. Francisco was a "good" Catholic, Henry had some interest in religious matters, while

Dennis was in turmoil since his Catholic father had not taught him much about the liturgy of the Church. Dennis wondered if priests really provided heavenly direction, much less absolution. Maybe he needed absoluton because he had come here today instead of going to see his father.

As they circled the crowded city square, vendors hawked goods and refreshments. All shapes, sizes, and shades of people meandered about. There was a riot of sound. Hansom cabs, lone riders, mule drawn wagons, and carriages reflecting class stature choked the streets. The conversation and shouts of hundreds of people blended into a low roar that sounded like falling water. It was entertaining, but then the young men's eyes were simultaneously drawn to a petite blonde girl, hair shining in the sun. She wore a practical dress and blouse, but she was so fetching, Francisco had the driver halt the horses. She stepped out to wait on a customer from under a frilled umbrella that was atop a wheeled beverage cart with a sign in French that read "glacée boissons," *Iced Drinks*. She exchanged a cool glass of liquid with a lady for a coin. The girl chatted for a few moments while the lady sipped. When she finished and returned the glass, the flaxen haired girl took the used glass and put it in a compartment in the cart. She put her hands on her hips. Her sleeves were rolled up, arms tanned. Surveying for the next customer, she fixed on their coach and squinted her eyes, raising her palm to shield them from afternoon glare. Watching her wince in that moment, Dennis felt like he had been hit by a landslide. Closing his eyes tight, then opening them, he expected a mirage, but the girl looked like Jane.

If Francisco and Henry actually had pious intents, they evaporated in the afternoon sun. They saw the dazed look in Dennis's eyes and laughed, not knowing what had produced his dumbfounded expression. His hesitancy was an opportunity to squeeze him out in friendly rivalry for the attention of this female. As Francisco and Henry exited the coach, they nudged one another to see who could get the advantage. Henry did a quick step and purposely strode toward her. Francisco's breeding made him yield to Henry's boyish enthusiasm, so he coyly pretended disinterest.

As the scene unfolded, Dennis was unable to move, like he had been injected with a poisoned dart. The situation was cruelly familiar. If this was indeed Jane, in order to talk with her, he would have to vie once again with suitors for her attention. The acute sense of joy at seeing her contrasted with a conflicting rage of having to see her under these circumstances. But how could she really be Jane? The two young men with whom he had a reasonably good relationship transformed into thorny obstacles in his mind. Why couldn't he have found her without these companions being present? He could not hear what was being said, but he watched as Henry and Francisco each purchased a refreshment and winsomely engaged with the girl in coquetry.

While he watched, it was of some comfort that the girl seemed undistracted from her business. While clearly aware of their attentions, she responded to them as polite rather than flirty. She gazed beyond Francisco and Henry as they talked, looking for the next customer. Her eyes seemed to be looking his way in the carriage. He stared back, heart racing. He felt the urge to leap from the carriage and run to her like some awkward colt, but his body was unresponsive and numb. Besides, it couldn't be Jane, could it? How could she possibly be here when she was supposed to be in Clarksville, Tennessee? Was this coincidence or providence? Maybe it was some divine joke.

Seeing that they were getting nowhere with the girl, Francisco and Henry disengaged nonchalantly and headed back for the coach. It was at this point, with the words *divine joke* still in his mind that he heard "the voice." It was clear, gentle, but authoritative: "If you are ashamed of me, I will be ashamed you." The mysterious words conveyed both encouragement and a warning. Should he jump out of the carriage and go the blonde girl? Henry opened the door to the carriage and seeing the peculiar look on his face and crouched posture he asked in a puzzled tone, "What's wrong with you, Dennis?"

Feeling a pronounced embarrassment, Dennis straightened up. He could not explain his glut of feelings, but he blurted out, "I think I know that girl!"

"Introduce her to me then!"

"No, I am probably mistaken," came Dennis's abashed reply.

With a shrug, Henry climbed back in the carriage followed by Francisco.

When they were all together again in the cabin, Francisco called to the carriage driver: "To the cathedral!"

As the carriage set in motion, Dennis turned his face toward the girl's cart and saw her pushing it away. He stayed fixed on the girl until she was assimilated in the crowd. Then he decided to go after her. He told a half truth.

"Francisco, tell the driver to stop. I have to go to the hospital to see my father. I've been having a good time with you, but I have neglected him. I really must check on him. If you could please stop the carriage, I'll just walk to the Ponchartrain rail station."

Francisco gave the command, and Dennis stepped down onto the dusty street.

"Are you sure this is what you want, Dennis?" Francisco asked with concern, and Henry looked incredulous. "We can take you there." Dennis adamantly turned them down and waved his hand goodbye. He acknowledged their farewells, and watched the carriage roll away.

Standing there in the early afternoon sun, Dennis sorted the jumble of emotions. Uppermost he wanted to find out if the girl was Jane, but there was also the urgent need to check on his father. The stifling heat gagged him, and seeking relief, he yanked loose the blue velvet string tie that held his crisp white collar closed. Regret surged.

This was the finest suit he would probably ever own, and he remembered how Francisco had looked them up and down admirably when he outfitted Dennis and Henry. He had thanked him then, but he should have thanked Francisco again for the clothes at this parting, but it was too late, the carriage had disappeared among the throng of other vehicles.

He had stranded himself now. All over him a phantom assumption that girl was Jane. He must make a critical decision: go look for the girl or out to Luzenberg Hospital before visiting hours were over. He was afoot, anxiety rising. He wished he could just dismiss his father as a concern. He took a kerchief from his vest pocket, wiped it across his brow, and gave up the idea of looking for the girl.

At Elysian Fields Avenue where the rail line began, he paid his fare, pushed his way through the arriving crowd of people coming back from Lake Ponchartrain, and got on board. He took a rough bench seat in the open coach behind the small stout engine, known as "Smoky Mary". The boiler hissed steam. Shortly the bell clanged, the whistle snorted, and the little locomotive got underway. Out across swampland toward Pontchartrain Lake, the roiling smoke rising from the black stack made him think of the 'pillar of cloud by day' that went before the Israelites to lead them. Was he being led also? Maybe "the voice" was about to speak again and tell him where to find Jane, if it was indeed her.

He begged the time of another passenger. It was 2:30 pm. Maybe there was yet time for a return to New Orleans to conceivably look for that girl. Yes, yes, he would make it happen.

When the train approached Luzenberg, Dennis didn't wait for a complete halt. He jumped off and trotted to the gate between the two white washed sentry houses. The sun, moving westward, caused the fence posts to cast long bar-like shadows across the great green lawn in front of the facility. The Negro sentry in white uniform waved him through to the administrative big house. He advanced to the admittance desk. Tapping his fingers anxiously on the counter, he waited for the white middle-aged matron tending paperwork to turn around. When she finally did, exhaustion showed on her face. In a lackluster voice, she said without pleasantries,

"Mr. O'Brien, the doctor left you a message. I know I have it here somewhere."

"A message? I need a briefing! Please, I need to see him as soon a possible!"

"Oh, don't be concerned. I believe it will be good news for you. Just take a seat over there, I will be right with you when I find it." Then she returned to her paperwork with no sense of urgency. Dennis went into the waiting room, realizing that no amount of pressure was going to speed things along with the matron.

What was the "good news" she had spoken about? There was a large clock on the wall of the waiting area. It read 3:30. He sat down, fidgeting while time ticked away. He became absorbed in thoughts of the girl that looked like Jane. In no time the clock gonged 4:00.

Miffed and gritting his teeth, he rose to inquire what was the hold up, but as he approached, the matron stepped out of the room and walked briskly away down a hallway, entered a room, and closed the door behind her. He waited at the desk while the minute hand labored on to 4:30. Outside he heard the train approaching on its return trip to the city.

"Hey! Hey!! Maam! Have you forgotten me?!" He shouted down the hall, and his words reverberated. The matron burst out of the door with an armload of files.

"Hold your horses, just hold your horses!" she said, placing a folded sheet of foolscap in his palm. "There has been such a crush of new admittances! Here, I found the message in Dr. Irvine's office!"

Dennis quickly unfolded the paper, but had difficulty reading the poorly scrawled cursive script. More than agitated, he said to the matron.

"I can't read this ! What does it say?!"
She took it and read perfunctorily :

Master O'Brien, I am pleased to tell you that after today's evaluation, I have decided to discharge your father. While this might seem somewhat premature, we must make room for others in more dire condition. I am taking him to the 27 Royal St. address where you may retrieve him. Please be there poste haste i.e. 9pm.

Your obedient servant,
Dr. Irvine

Dennis was thunderstruck. "What time did the Doctor and my father leave here?"

"At 1:30!" she said oblivious to the fact she could have simply told him that earlier.

It was unbelievable. His father and the doctor had arrived at Elysian Fields station at the same time he was heading the opposite direction to the asylum. Somehow in the crush of boarding and deboarding, he had walked right past them. He blasted out the door and ran for the train as it started to churn away from Luzenburg back to New Orleans. A conductor grabbed his wrist and pulled him aboard.

Panting and disheveled, he sat out of breath as "Smoky Mary" chugged back to the city across deceptively beautiful swampland. Alligators slithered off the banks of the levy as the train passed. He became depressed as he calculated how much time remained before dusk. He wanted to hunt for the girl. Dennis muttered "God, if the voice was you, what is this all about?" He listened for an answer from the voice, but there was none.

When the train arrived at Elysian Fields station, he had not brought enough money for a cab ride back to the square, so he had to walk. With all the perspiration, his fine clothing looked like he had been swimming in them.

Shops were closing, carriages with respectable folk were heading home, the crowds had thinned. A sort of changing of the guard was taking place. Creatures of daylight were giving way to the denizens of the evening. Gamblers and prostitutes were making their appearance. Too late to get to the square.

Exhausted, he leaned against a red brick wall next to an alcove for a few moments. When he did, a woman with caramel skin and a turban-like head covering stepped out of the recessed opening.

"You are looking for a girl?" The purr in her voice was marked by the distinctive Creole accent.

Startled, he immediately assumed she was a madam, plying her trade.

"No, no, I am not interested in what you are selling."

"I did not say I was selling anything. I am not the kind of Madame you assume. I merely asked if you are looking for a girl. You are looking for a a particular girl, are you not?"

"Yes, yes, I am. But of what is that to you?"

"Ah! If you knew to whom you speak, it would be apparent. You seek a blonde girl, Jeanne? A concessionaire in Jackson Square?" Dennis was astonished. She was saying Jane's name in French.

"Why, yes, that's her. Please tell me where she is if you know!"

"If you step inside, you will get the answers you seek. Step inside, step inside, and for a silver coin, I will provide the conjure."

The hair raised on the back of Dennis's neck. The mysterious way the woman spoke, her curious knowldege about his search, knowing Jane's name, and the invitation to conjure? The words of beloved Beulah came to his mind *Watch out for the hooba dooba… stay away from the hooba dooba.* Dennis backed up. As he did, the woman kept enticing him.

"Young O'Brien, do not be afraid. Step inside, please, and you will know all. Marie will see to it the desire of your heart is fulfilled. Step inside, step inside." Not only did she know Jane's name, she knew his!

Beulah's words were ringing in his ears as he violated her warning, but the chances of finding out if it was Jane were slim, and he was desperate. So he nervously followed the woman inside. Maybe a quick answer would be alright. Dennis nervously followed into the alcove and then through an ornately carved door. They stepped into a foyer. On the right side was a great room, on the left was a stairway. He would certainly not go up there! Marie saw the look on his face and smiled knowingly.

"Oh no, mon cher. You have a fleshly mind. You still think I am a queen of the night. I am Madame Laveau. I assure you, I take no one to my boudoir. No, no, mon cher. Step into the great room." In the middle of the room was a round oak table with feet carved like lions' paws. It sat upon a purple Algerian berber rug. She motioned him to take a seat. He took one opposite from her. On the sideboard sat a collection of small bones, a stack of large rectangular cards, a curious looking doll, and some glass bottles. Dennis now was even more nervous. Where he was flew in the face of the things he had been taught to avoid. Yet, here he was face to face with the *hooba dooba*. This Marie then took the bones from the table and cast them out across the table. Dennis recoiled at the sight while the woman began a low chant and her face went blank.

"No!" Dennis broke through her trance "I just want a straight answer! Where is Jane? You say you know where she is. Simply tell me where she is, and how she got to New Orleans, and I will leave."

"It is not that simple!" The woman retorted. "The loa speak on their own terms. Here, let us read the cards instead."

Dennis had reached the limit of his compromise. He got up to leave, but as he did, the room became frigid.

"You see, you have angered them. They were warm to you, mon cher. Now it will be difficult to get the answers you seek. Please, do not try to leave. They will not like it. You must at least pay me for my moment of hospitality."

Dennis was completely spooked, but he realized he'd better compensate the woman to extricate himself.

"Look, I am sorry. Here!"and he placed a quarter dollar on the table. She reached for it, placed it between both her palms, and then rubbed them together. Then she placed the coin back on the table. When she did, the coin began to vibrate. Seeing that, he headed terrified for the door.

"Never mind! I don't want to know anymore!" he called as he opened the door, but she grabbed his wrist and held it.

"You say you no longer want this, but the coin has spoken, and you will hear it. The girl you seek, you will not find again. I saw her in Jackson Square like you. She was in the city looking for you, but you will not be together now." She put her hand on his forearm. "It would have been so easy for you, but you have scorned me and the loa. Now you will not find the girl. The one to whom I am pledged, Papa Legba, will see to it that it turns out his way."

Dennis wrested himself away from the woman. He almost broke the doorglass getting out. He hit the cobblestones running. He had to get to 27 Royal St. He cursed everything about the day as he ran, even the fact that he had seen that girl. It could not have been her. Everything turned bitter. There was only duty left. He had reversed roles with his father long ago; he would now go pick up his child. There was only wretched duty.

———— ⊰◉⊱ ————

32

Seventh

Mindful now that he had encountered the *hooba dooba*, Dennis hustled down the street. Gradually he slowed, trying to overcome his fear and analyze the encounter. As darkness closed in, the St. Louis Cathedral bell gonged in the distance. He paused to count the peals. It was eight o'clock; the final hour before darkness this late summer day. The overhanging balconies, with their wrought iron balustrades created patterns of shadow on the worn brick walls that looked like faces mocking him.

A negro lamplighter was going about his rounds. "Gud evenin,' Massuh!" the man said, voice deeply resonating. He doffed a well-worn top hat and bowed ceremoniously, holding his lighting wand like it was a scepter. However, Dennis was so pent-up that he did not respond to the presence of the lamplighter.

He pulled Dr. Irvin's note from his pocket. Maybe the matron had not deciphered the message correctly, maybe there was a mistake. Maybe this sweet summer of independence did not have to end abruptly. Maybe there was more than duty left. He tried in the lamplight to read it. He squinted at the cursive scrawls on the lined paper. It was futile. All that he could remember was he had to be at 27 Royal St. by *9pm to retrieve your father.* He let the paper slip from his hands and looked skyward where there was only a sliver of moon.

"Excuse me, sir, but did you mean to discard this muniment?" the lamplighter asked in a low velvet tone. Dennis was jolted The voice was unmistakable. Not only was it familiar, but it was the use of the word 'muniment' instead of paper. Dennis knew no black man, even any white man that had the command of language like the traveling preacher and freedman, Douglas. Ubiquitous Douglas. Dennis was dumbfounded once again.

"You look to be troubled, Dennis."

"Wha...wha...wha? Whe whe where...ha ha how?" he stammered in surpise.

"I must admit that when I saw you, I was taken aback, too. When I saw you last in Memphis I thought I was headed to Indiana with the precious cargo of Elizabeth, but the Friends turned me back, and told me I would do better for the cause if I stayed south of the Mason-Dixon Line. And so, here I am. I sought employment in the Crescent City as a lantern lighter."

Dennis was overwhelmed. Douglas had become a friend of the heart, showing up when needed most. He wanted to grab Douglas, hug him, but even here in New Orleans, it would be unwise. Tears welled up. He put his palm over his eyes.

"You, you have no idea how much I need a friend right now. You have no idea how low I have sunk since I saw you last."

"Hmm, no idea?" Douglas chuckled. "Considering that I saw you coming out of Madame Marie Laveau's establishment, I have a couple of ideas."

Dennis raised his head in surprise, then lowered it again in shame. "You saw me coming out of there? Beulah told me to stay away from the *hooba dooba,* and I didn't."

"Ah, Beulah, a wise woman. Indeed! You should have steered

clear of the modern day witch of Endor. Beulah knows from experience, she worked hard to rid herself of spiritism. She gave you good advice. Why didn't you listen?"

"I had to do something. I felt like I was falling apart! Falling apart! She told me, that woman, she told me…" and he began madly hitting himself. Douglas made him stop it.

"Tell me, if you can, what she said."

"The words are pounding over and over in my brain! She said something like, 'The girl you seek, you will not find. Like you, I saw her in Jackson Square. Petite Jeanne was in the city looking for you. It would have been so easy for you, but you have offended me and the other realm. The one to whom I am pledged, Papa Legba, will see to it that it turns out his way." Dennis banged his head with his knuckles again.

"Stop, Dennis! Just listen to me. I can help, but you need to stop doing this to yourself. You are reinforcing the power of suggestion she used on you. She put a semblance of truth in your head, seeds of facts, but that is all they are…seeds. Once planted, you are the one that makes them sprout."

"Oh yeah, then how did she know about Jane? Wait, wait you don't know about Jane yourself, do you?"

"Of course I know who Jane is. Have you forgotten when we met at Sarah Bell's cotton field and the Indian mounds? I saw you being bullied. You confessed your anguish about a girl. Up there black folks all know the children. It was not from something supernatural I know about Jane. Really the names of all the children of Shiloh are common knowledge among members of my congregation at shake-a-rag church. That is how I came to know Jane's name."

"Well, a lot has happened, but of course I remember how we met, but you always appear out of nowhere. I also recall the coins you carry and when you spoke of the seventh love. Are you ever going to explain all that clearly? What about that?"

"It is an appropriate time to tell you, but first let me recount more about the voodoo woman. She is a keen observer with instinctive hunches. Madam Laveau does not have pure motives, and she has minions that slave for her all over this city, giving her valuable information. Some help her by giving her knowledge of vulnerable newcomers to the city. It provides her a good living as you could well see from her elegant quarters. Yes, some of her power lies in keen observations and intimate knowledge of humans and their needs. Are you getting what I am saying?"

"Yes, yes. The girl that looked like Jane in the Square. Someone must have been watching my reactions."

"This is a big town, but it is also a small one for those who ply the evil trade of divination. Where would you go if you were a pickpocket, scammer, or swindler, and wanted to find an easy mark?"

"Jackson Square is loaded with them. The Square is one of the first places newcomers visit when coming to the city, so they stand out. That girl with her blonde hair and blue eyes, she stood out in the crowd. Bees drawn to a flower. Yes, they are aware that you are new here. No doubt they have eavesdropped, too, because they prey especially on the naïve, uninitiated to this place. Such is the stock and trade that keeps conjurers in business. Listen and make no mistake, though, there is more to this than a person understanding human nature; there is true evil afoot, and there are wicked spirit forces in heavenly places that wish you no good. Do you think that the descriptions of demon possession in the Gospels were mere old wives' tales?"

Douglas's insights made Dennis uncomfortable, but not in the way Madame Laveau had made him squirm. Douglas truly cared for him because he was a man of God. The reflection of the lamplight made the preacher's eyes sparkle like gold dust.

He sighed, "I wish I could be like you, Douglas."

Douglas looked kindly at him, then surprised him. "You have heard the voice, haven't you? It is not like the one Laveau would have you hear, it is the true voice that speaks to one as a father would to a son. I heard the voice and have followed it without disappointment. Will you keep seeking the true voice of the seventh love?"

"The seventh love. There you go again. What about seven coins?" Douglas took them out of his pocket and displayed them symbolically in his palm like he had before.

"The Greeks defined seven kinds of love. The seventh is the most important. Agape.

The highest form of love embodies selflessness, sacrifice, and unconditional care for others. This profound concept transcends mere feelings, emphasizing actions and commitment. It is love you do not give up on. It can encompass all the other kinds of love. For you see, in scripture the number seven represents completeness and perfection. You must never give up in your search for answers, pursue them. Love never fails. If you desire to be like me, first you must never give up on the voice."

Every word that Douglas said resounded with Dennis, but the witch's words still haunted him. He voiced his final fear to Douglas.

"Will I find Jane? She said I would not find her."

"Forget what she said. Just remember the seventh love. It covers all. You have someplace to be very soon. Walk with me and listen." He explained, "A spiritual attack is coming on you that you will feel keenly if you desire to achieve the seventh love. You must endure it, Dennis, because from the beginning, a spiritual war has been waged against you."

"Why, why does this have to happen?! I still don't understand!"

The two arrived at the next lantern. Douglas turned the valve and raised the lighting wand. The gas hissed and ignited. Douglas looked at Dennis's puzzled face and answered: "You will understand when the attack comes. Find a place to stay with your father. I will see you here tommorow evening at this lamp post. For now I must say goodbye." Dennis mourrnfully bid farewell.

When he looked at the street clock, there was time to spare. Soon the familiar gold lettering on the downtown offices of the hospital glinted from lantern light as he knocked on the door of 27 Royal St. The door opened and the familiar face of Dr. Irvine greeted Dennis. The doctor ushered him in. His father was bemusedly looking around the room.

"I was beginning to give up on you. I asked you to be here, and you have surely used every last minute."

"I am sorry, doctor, but when I went to the hospital this afternoon, it took me by complete surprise that you were releasing my father. We are paid through the whole of September. Why this early release? I beg of you. There are important things I want to do before I am ready to take him back home."

Dr. Irvine took umbrage. "Things you have to do? You have no idea the amount of things we have to do *at the hospital*. The talk of war, the firing of cannon, the rallies in the streets have brought a crush of new admissions."

"But can't you keep him at least until the first of the month? I beg of you."

The doctor spoke tersely, "Here is your refund." He put a small stack of red-backed banknotes on the desk. "And you can be confident they are legal tender anywhere because as you can see they are DIX banknotes of the Citizens Bank of Louisiana."

Dennis gathered them up and placed them in the hidden pocket of his vest. With some reluctance, he said, "I must thank you for all the care you have given my father. He is cured then?"

"I have never seen a case truly cured, young man."

"Then why have you released him? You have no idea what my father is capable of!"

Dennis checked himself, for surely after three months of hospitization, the doctor did know of what his father was capable. The doctor replied, "Your father is not the only Mexican War veteran to come to us with melancholia and mania. You may recall we even have a veteran of Napolean's disaster at Waterloo at the hospital. Your father has seen improvement, and we must triage our capacity."

"Triage? What does that mean?"

"It means we must treat the most serious cases first. Your father has seen improvement to the point where we think he is capable of functioning on his own. You may be surprised. I believe that he can speak of his traumas now in more objective ways."

Dennis was downcast at the personal restriction this would now mean for him because of his desire to search for the girl that looked like Jane. He was able to take some solace in the statement that his father "was capable of functioning on his own."

Relunctantly, he signed the papers that released his father. The doctor shook his hand and Dennis stepped outside the office with his father. Dr. Irvine softened at seeing the dispirited expression on Dennis's face.

"If you deem it absolutely necessary, bring him back to Luzenburg for evaluation before you decide to leave the city. In all our briefings, you should have come to know that love is the best therapy that can be adminstered. If your family had not already been applying this remedy, your father would long ago have been consigned to one of the institutions, trash heaps, that pretend to be places of asylum. Never give up. You are a fine young man, Mr. Dennis O'Brien. Keep him from becoming overstimulated, especially when it comes to political and military matters. He will exhibit some amnesia. We have tapered him off the laudanum, so please, try to use it sparingly. Good night to you both and may God go with you!"

33

⚊⚊))◉((⚊⚊

Epoch

Standing in front of the hospital office, Dennis wondered how to start a conversation with his father. He need not have been concerned. His father had perked up at the change in surroundings. Recognizing the predicament they were both in at this hour of night, he said with a little cough and in his Irish accent, "Well, Denny, this is a fine how do ya do!"

After all the tension and time, to hear something normal and down to earth coming out of his father's mouth, Dennis burst out laughing. His father continued, "It's just the cherry on top of a perfectly upside-down day," and he broke into laughter, too. It was just the kind of release they both needed. Was his father really cured?

Since leaving Hamburg, Charles had been in a kind of limbo. Dennis, even before his visitations at Luzenberg Hospital, realized that his father had experienced normalcy of mind at times. No, his father was not out of his mind all the time. He still had feelings about his family but could not express them while in that limbo. He seemed somewhat restored. Dennis wanted to continue that restoration.

"Da. You were right about New Orleans. It is the grandest place. Maybe the grandest on earth. I know it has been a long time since you first came here, but do you know a place where we both might lodge tonight?"

And so it was that Dennis and his father began to sew up the torn garment of their relationship. This start of reconnection with his father was encouraging, but he steeled himself in case the "old Charles" re-emerged. His father's sudden release from the hospital caused a whirlwind of logistics. He could not be sentimental about leaving. His time in New Orleans was over. It had to be forsaken and dealt with realistically. They found an inexpensive place his father recalled only a block away from the doctor's office, for it was far too late to go to Mrs. Williams's boarding house, and with the amount of refunded cash that he was carrying, too dangerous to walk across town at night.

When they settled in, his father said something he thought he would never hear,

"Denny, I'm sorry I have put you through so much. Maybe 'tis' a new epoch."

"A new epoch, Da? May we live long, and may we be in heaven a half hour before the Devil knows we're dead." They both laughed at the old Irish proverb.

"Might I have a little of the money, Denny?" Charles asked through a cough. "I'll be lookin' the fool if I have ta be askin' it of you all the way back home."

Dennis opened his money belt and gave his father half of 200 dollars that was in it. His father was aghast and protested he did not need so much. Dennis said, "It's best we do it this way, Da. Should we somehow get separated, we will both be in good stead."

Though he was exhausted, Dennis lay awake until the wee hours, thinking of all the things that had transpired since they had come to New Orleans and what the coming day might hold. The hopes of saying goodbye to the other members of the triumvirate were nil. He knew Henry was headed up river as he usually did with his father at the first of the week. As for Francisco, to see him would involve taking his father to the headquarters of the Washington Artillery. They dare not do that.

Despite his lack of sleep, Dennis was up and ready for breakfast the next morning. As they ate, it was reassuring that his father was still as chipper as he had been last night. An adult relationship with his father took root.

At Mrs. William's boarding house, he introduced his father and told her he had to leave. She was dismayed, but having had roomers come and go, not troubled. Charles brightened at meeting her, and the two of them engaged in a lively interchange about the size of the town and how it had grown since 1848. Dennis was surprised that Mrs. Williams was old enough to remember that. Because of the smoothness of her skin and lack of wrinkles, he had thought her to be younger. It was heartening to see his father functioning quite well. While they continued to talk, Dennis gathered his belongings. He looked wistfully at the little library he had gathered because of Henry. As he and Charles said their goodbyes, he asked that Mrs. Williams return Henry's books to him. In leaving, she gave him a huge hug as if he were her son. He teared up.

It was on to Tchapitoulis Street and *Speake and McCreary*. Here was the place that Dennis took most heart and began to feel a new resolve. On introducing his father to Mr. McCreary, they both lit up at their shared nationality and began a conversation in Gaelic, the likes of which he had never heard. He listened for a while, but then thought it best to let the Irishmen be, so he found Isaiah and Samuel to say goodbye. They were both surprised and regretful to see him go. He did not know how to express the affection that he had for them after the summer's labors. He shook hands with them and warned them not to call him "lil boss."

"Ok's den. We's gonna call ya big boss now," they laughed and slapped their knees.

"Young O'Brien!" Mr. McCreary called out to Dennis at the back of the store. "I'll be sorry to say goodbye to you, son. It's going to be hard to find a replacement. Come here I have something for you!"

When Dennis got to the front of the store, his father was beaming. "Look what the man has for ye Denny. Tis a letter of recommendation. You'll be havin' little trouble findin' a good job with this!" Mr. McCreary handed him an unsealed envelope.

On the front of the envelope was embossed the name of the business, *Speake and McCreary, Wholesale and Commission Merchants.* On the letter within it read: To *whom it may concern.* Then a glowing report about his work during the summer. Mr. McCreary especially emphasized the salvage operation and the way Dennis had handled the slaves, "getting the most out of them."

"I have never gotten such production out those boys before. You will be missed young O'Brien, truly missed" and he shook Dennis's hand vigorously.

The next plan had to be about what form of transportation they should take in getting back to Corinth? Should they return upriver by paddle-wheeler or go by train? During the summer, he had learned about the new rail line that went from New Orleans to La Grange, Tennessee, the *New Orleans, Jackson and Great Northern Railroad.* That meant a connection to the *Memphis to Charleston* rail line that would then get him and his father back to Corinth. It was, therefore, the least expensive and most efficient way to get home. They bought the tickets.

Home? What was home now? Did the farm still exist after the great flood? Dennis felt he could have stayed in New Orleans forever and make it his home. He had good friends and a good job here. He had grown to know the city like the back of his hand. Then he thought of Douglas. He had promised to meet him tonight. Douglas would understand if he did not show up, he told himself, but then he had an idea. *The New Orleans Gas Light Company* was the only one in the city. Approaching a porter, he asked if he knew any of the lamp lighters. The porter answered yes. He gave the man Douglas's name and description. When the porter said he was acquainted with him, Dennis somehow was not surprised. There was coincidence and there was providence. They had come together once again. Dennis asked the porter to tell Douglas that he was sorry he had not made their appointment and tell him he hoped to see him at Shiloh.

So with one foot on the platform and the other on the train, Dennis looked out over the skyline of New Orleans and gave up the idea that Jane was in the Crescent City somewhere. It could not possibly have been her anyway. In his imagination he saw Sam Clemens, the riverboat pilot and knew what to say departing New Orleans. To the city, and all he knew in it, he called out Sam's parting words, "Do the right thing. It will gratify some people and astonish the rest!"

34

Return

"How long does it take to get from New Orleans to the *Memphis and Charleston* railway line?" Dennis asked as the conductor punched their tickets.

"Should take but two days with all the stops," he replied with an Irish accent.

His father, hearing the accent, chimed in cheerily, "I always tell me son, 'May you have the hindsight ta know where you've been, the foresight ta know where you are goin', and the insight ta know when you've gone too far.'"

"Éirinn go Brách!" the conductor pronounced with gusto.

Dennis winced at the conductor's pledge of allegiance to Ireland. Would it trigger his father? Would the militancy in which the conductor pronounce the Irish homage get an unhappy rise in his father's temperament? He braced to see how his father would react. To his relief, Charles O'Brien just wished the conductor well and called him "Mo Chara" (my friend).

As they settled in, the train hooted repetitively while lumbering out of the metropolis. With each blast of the whistle, Dennis resolved to gently probe the solidity of his father's recuperation. The evaluations that Dr. Irvine had given him had not been comprehensive. Maybe it was unfair to say they were not. Dennis had to acknowledge there were facets of his father's problems that he had not relished exploring during the briefings. To get a better understanding, it had to be done at a pace that would allow for his father to get rest. Too much stimulation was what the doctor had warned against. Even now his father's forehead was bobbing, his eyes closed after the long day.

It indeed had been a long day, having walked through much of the city while taking care of the necessary business of ending their sojourn in New Orleans. As the locomotive reached its optimum speed, the monotonous rhythm of the rails and the rocking of the coach produced a mesmerizing affect. Dennis scooched down in the seat, closed his own eyes as darkness closed in, and fell asleep. Periodically through the night, the train stopped at communities along the way to take on passengers, freight, and water for the engine. It made for a fitful rest for Dennis, but his father weathered the interruptions with no apparent disturbance to his slumber. His head went from bobbing up and down, to forehead against the window glass, to laying it on Dennis's shoulder. Dennis felt both discomfited and yet at the same time a comfort that he had not known since he was a little boy.

In the early morning, the train slowed to a stop at Canton, Mississippi with its characteristic grinding squeal, releasing of steam, and telescoping of the cars. This time everybody onboard awoke, with a mixture of cheerful "good mornings!" groans, curses, and audible yawns. Dennis rubbed his eyes while his father wiped the sleep from his. The conductor came down the aisle, slapping at the seats and announcing that everyone should get off the coach as it was the end of the line. Connections needed to be made to get to Corinth.

"Da, at this rate we'll be home before we know it."

"Denny, we need to get some gifts for everyone." Charles said thoughtfully. "A mercantile of great variety is to be found in this town."

"You have been here before, Da?"

"Indeed, when I came back from Mexico, I spent two days here. Like ever 'ting else the town is bigger than t'was back then. There's no tellin' where 'twill all end. Maybe 'twill be as big as New Orleans one day," Charles exaggerated. "Now breakfast is in order!"

They inquired at the station desk about the train to La Grange and found that it was close to four hours before it would arrive. The clerk directed them to an establishment two blocks from the station. Charles seemed to be coming back into his own after so long a gap in his sensibilities. This was not like the trip on the way to New Orleans that had been more like a nightmare. Charles was like a young man again, eager to show Dennis around the village. As they walked, Dennis began to let his guard down. They came to a relatively impressive wooden building. On the side of the clapboard structure, painted in neat black letters and bold font was *Eichelstine's Mercantile and Eating House.*

On entering, other passengers they had been with were already dining in a room that was impressive. While not as elegant as the ones in New Orleans, care had been taken in its maintenance and general presentation was designed to please, especially the planters. The sturdy, functional tables and chairs were spread with coarse cotton cloths and tableware already set for waiting customers, including pitchers of sweet tea punch. The place was intended to be open long hours since there were sconces on the walls, containing extinguished candles from the night before. Charles remarked about the framed artwork and mirrors and shelves displaying decorative items. The shellacked wooden floors were covered with mats in hallways to reduce wear in high traffic areas and especially at the entrance to cut down on the amount of dust. Noticing that Charles was admiring the place, a customer at a nearby table leaned over and wryly commented: "You know, the owner is *a Jew*." Dennis had never met a Jew, and though the other customer had strangely implied something disparaging about the proprietor, he looked about and wondered to himself that "the Jew" who owned the place was certainly enterprising and industrious.

The restaurant was not separated from the general store by a wall, so when they finished breakfast, they merely stepped out of the open dining area into the retail setting to find gifts for the family back in Corinth.

The store was laid out in orderly aisles, and they took their time perusing them. The first aisle next to the eatery was lined with foodstuffs: sugar, tea, canned tomatoes, jams, coffee, and other items of common consumption. Dennis was used to seeing such goods in bulk containers, bags, and crates back at *Speake and McCreary's*. The next aisle was stocked with bolts of denim, cotton, and even silk. Charles ran his hands thoughtfully over the fabrics. Complementing the materials for home garment making were notions like thread, needles, and buttons. There was also ready-made clothing, from denim dungarees to dresses.

When they came to the housewares aisle, Charles examined with wonder the crockery, dishes, pots, pans, lanterns, and washboards. Dennis took note, and it caused him to feel somewhat ashamed that the institutionalization of his father had deprived him of enjoyment of the most elementary items of daily life. It was even harder to watch as his father wander down the tools, hardware and farm equipment aisle, overcome with emotion upon picking up a mere hoe.

On the far aisle, Dennis located some toys among the miscellaneous stacks of school supplies like slate and chalk. Behind a glass shelf were arrayed cigars and patent medicines including laudanum.

After carefully selecting and paying the cashier for presents and laudanum, Mr. Eichelstine himself stalled them at the door with profuse pleasantries. He thanked them for coming. He asked if they enjoyed the meal. He thanked them for their reply. He asked where they had come from and where they were going. That spurred him to tell a couple of anecdotes about the times he had been in New Orleans. He asked forgiveness for going on and on. Again thanking them for their business, and again how much he appreciated them patronizing his establishment. Finally he wished them well on their journey with a "*Shalom!*"

They stepped out of the store with the prizes individually wrapped in brown paper, tied with string, inserted into a bag also purchased at the store. Returning to the rail station, the clerk deposited the packages in the common storage room with their baggage. There was much time left before the next train arrived, so they took a stroll outside of town.

Halfway down the block, which was becoming choked with slaves driving wagons loaded with cotton to the rail head, a perspiring and frustrated man approached them. He asked if they knew by chance how to get to the road leading to Yazoo City. "I am trying to finish the census for this county," he told them.

"Census? We're not from around here. You'll have ta talk to the locals." Charles replied in his lilting brogue

"Ah, the locals. When they see me with this book and hear I'm taking information for the government, they balk, and some won't even speak to me. The fact that I am a northerner makes it even worse."

"Well, then, try the rail station or over at Eichelstine's emporium. You'll find no shortage of information from him." Charles chuckled. Charles then became absorbed in learning more about the man's job and engaged him Dennis strained to hear them over the growing cacophony of the streets.

"Yes sir, this the blackest county I have canvassed." The man pushed his hat back on his head and wiped his brow. "The blackest. I shouldn't be telling you anything, but there are almost four Negroes to every white man in Madison County. Well, I've said too much. Thank you. I'll be on my way over to this Eichelstine's."

Getting to the edge of town proved to be a hazard. More and more wagons were coming in from the plantations with the cotton harvest.

"T'was truly clear the census man was right," Charles remarked, shaking his head. "There's nary a white man among these teamsters coming to the depot. 'Tis hard to understand how these darky's can be so thoroughly controlled. There's a day of reckonin' coming!"

His father's words more than hinted that he was aware of the increasing animosity and clash between north and south. Dennis tried to steer the conversation in another direction. Charles, realizing this, tried to allay his son's fears. "Ya know, Denny, when I was in that place in New Orleans, ya know that asylum…"

His father's acknowledgement that he had been in an asylum caused Dennis to listen attentively.

"I came to a measure of peace about some things. Dr. Irvine and his people provided a good routine, and an environment t'was not so bad. I got to confess some things I've never been able to talk about with anyone. Things bottled up as tight as a genie's bottle, and the good doctor was like Aladdin his self."

Dennis berated himself. He recalled missed opportunities he'd had with Dr. Irvine, the rushed way he had asked for reports about his father. He had missed a couple of Sundays. There were the times his mind had been somewhere else. Every visit had counted. He had not taken advantage to the fullest extent of the valuable nuggets picked out of his father's rocky mind. He decided to broach the subjects he wanted to know about most, but ironically had begged off learning about.

"Da, can I ask you some things?" he probed gently.

"There's nothin' I would keep from you, Denny. As I told you once before, and I know it is a strange maddening sentiment, but you've become like a father to me. Same t'was said to me by my own Da long ago in Ireland."

The statement jolted Dennis. It was the first time Charles had spoken about his own father since his Chapultepec delusions on the river. He also had looked after his own father in some dire circumstance.

"I don't understand. What happened?"

"Me Da, at only 14 years of age, was a follower of Robert Emmet in the 1803 rebellion against the Brits."

"Yes, Da, you named the dapple gray after him."

"The rebellion failed. Emmet was captured, tried, and executed. They searched for everyone involved. Suffice it to say, me father was hounded. When I was your age, I helped him escape numerous difficulties. Finally the strain caused his mind to fail him, and he said those words to me, that I had become like a father to him. Mother decided to take him to France, but they were killed, the both of them, before they could get away. I buried them both beside a wall at Laraghbryan cemetery in County Kildare."

Dennis searched his father's heavily lined face in the morning sun, and it revealed no strain in the telling of the story. Rather, there was a tranquility, but then he began to cough heavily. Dennis asked if he was alright.

"Tis nothing, Denny," his father replied, bringing a hankie to his mouth. "Tis just all that cotton dust" and in a sweeping gesture, he waved at the cloud churned up on the road by the loaded wagons. "And just look at those dry, crackly, denuded plants that stretch for miles out there! It's gonna get worse when they start plowin' them under. The Almanac is predicting a dry year comin."

Charles's coughing calmed, and they continued down the road. It felt good to be with his father, something he had not experienced in a long time. They came to a fork in the road after about a mile and decided to turn around. With his father in such an extraordinary state of mind, Dennis decided to pursue more of a resolution in respect to his father's Chapultepec delirium.

"Da. You had a twin brother. What became of him?" There came a pronounced change in Charles's countenance. He seemed to age another ten years in a moment's time. "Oh, Da, I'm sorry I asked. I will not do so again."

"No, no, Denny, you should be the keeper of the flame. Just let me gather me self."

As they walked, his father started coughing once again. When it calmed, he spoke slowly and deliberately. "We were not identical twins, but we so much resembled one another that people said we must be. Because of that, I suppose we were selected by a priest to be altar boys at the tender age of six, after our first communion, when we should have been at least seven to ten. He took us under his wing, so to speak, and taught us enough Latin to understand all the parts of the Mass. And believe it or not, we both understood. I suppose we looked like two little angels on either side of the altar during Mass."

"It must have been amazing, Da. I never knew you understood Latin. You have never spoken of it before."

"I have only begun to tell ya. Ya notice I said the priest "took us under his wing." Well, our times at church started out with teaching Latin and the parts of the Mass. We quite frankly enjoyed it, and we rapidly learned because we were twins and shared a bond that we could not explain to anyone. Even our play involved practicing our Latin. When we went home, we acted out the intonations, the pomp and ceremony, the gestures of the priest. My brother professed he wanted to be a priest."

"But Da, that sounds wonderful. Why aren't you a Catholic today?"

There was a harsh change in Charles's demeanor. "Therein lies the rub. It was one thing to go to the church! It was another when the father took us to the rectory. At that point Charles clammed up. He turned and put his hands on Dennis' shoulders and looking him in his eyes, his voice became resolute. "What that man did to me and my brother. Do you understand, Denny? I don't want to have to delineate. The man diddled us. Do you understand? Time after time. For years it went on. We could not tell my Da or Ma. He said if we did, he would deny it, and we would burn in hell forever and ever. We kept silent. When we turned twelve, my brother ran away. I don't know where he is to this day."

"I wish I had understood all of this before, Da. It's horrendous! You have had a hurricane of a life."

"For me, Denny? It is you, more than me who has suffered. It's you, your brother John, your brother Adam, your mother. You ask why I am not a Catholic. Now you know. I could not speak of these thing before. I know it was you, Denny, that was responsible for gettin' me into that asylum. For that I am forever grateful. I have been granted a remission. You and Dr. Irvine are the true saints."

35

———◦(◦)◦———

Overtaken

They heard the clanging bell and wailing of the locomotive whistle in the distance. It meant hurrying, but it was worth it. The four hour layover had been filled with the most meaningful and significant conversations between father and son. Dennis had answers to questions for which he had long wished: what had happened to Charles's parents in Ireland, the mystery of the twin brother, and the reason for his father's struggle about all things Catholic. One major issue still needed to be addressed, and that one could prove to be thorny, if not explosive. The enigma of Captain Adair.

"All aboard! All aboard for Grenada, Water Valley, Oxford, Holly Springs, Corinth, and all points in between! All aboard!" cried the conductor. With that, the train dragged itself laboriously north out of Canton station. The physical exertion of getting quickly to the station in time affected both Dennis and Charles. Dennis was wheezing, his father coughed and bent over with fatigue as they sat uncomfortably on the wooden hard-backed benches of the passenger car. It caused a male passenger across from them to get up and change seats. He looked disdainfully back at them as he did. The look provoked Dennis, and he got up to take issue with the man, but his father calmed him down.

Because of the number of stops along the way, it meant two days travel to get home, but that was better than taking more than a week by horse-drawn wagon. Really, it was remarkable how fast distances so far apart could be covered by train, Dennis thought.

The vacated seat ended up helping the situation. Dennis helped his father lie down on the empty bench. Despite the harshness of the surface, in short order, he fell asleep. The afternoon heat and humidity was becoming oppressive and the flies were a plague, so Dennis slid the double hung window open like others were doing. The air flow helped stagnation of air in the coach compartment, but it did not help the mugginess. Dennis unbuttoned the top buttons of his shirt.

The scenery became almost monotonous because of the omnipresent cotton fields. Every acre seemed to be exploited. "It's like a blizzard has passed over!" a woman at the front of the car blurted for all to hear. Others echoed the comparison of cotton crops to snow. Then a conversation broke out about slaves. As the train passed the plantations, clusters of black men and women working the rows appeared as colonies of ants. A few seats up the aisle, a planter began a dissertation to some finely dressed women sitting across from him.

"Look out there, ladies. That owner possesses some fine stock. There must be twenty-five big black bucks working that one tract alone, all good pickers. And look at the quality of the crop. Each one of those bucks is going to bring in more than a 200 lbs. per day, that's 5000 lbs. not counting what a hundred biddies, mamas and picanninies bring in, and you've got another 5000 lbs. That's 10,000 lbs. a day. Let's see, it looks to be a 1000 acre farm. That planter is going to make more than a million dollars this year." The women gasped approvingly and fluttered silk fans in front of their faces. One giggled. "That is truly *high cotton*."

Dennis continued doing calculations in his head as the train rolled over the miles. He had never been able to estimate what the Southern economy was like outside of Shiloh and their little 40 acre farm on the Tennessee River. It was staggering him now. It explained why planters didn't bat an eye at auction when paying $1700 for a big muscular "No.1 man." No wonder these people were ready to go to war over such wealthy livelihoods.

Over the next several hours, the train progressed through the railway stations of Grenada, Water Valley, and Oxford. At each stop all aboard debarked to use toilets and get some form of refreshment. At Oxford they were informed there was a problem on the tracks ahead. A section of the rail bed had deteriorated, and the train ahead of the one they were on lost its caboose. It had been fortunate that there had not been a complete derailment. The station master informed everyone that the repair had been underway since the previous day, but the crews were efficient, and they would be underway just as soon as word came over telegraph. Dennis and his father took a meal and went for another walk.

"Da, it's still light out right now at almost 8:00. I hate to see winter coming."

"Aye, Denny, the changing of the hours gives pause. It's odd how the slant of the sun can affect ya. When I think of it, this is the same time of year that we took Chapultepec Castle in '47."

Dennis was startled, his father was matter of fact like any normal conversation. Had his time at the hospital truly changed things for him? The last allusion dealing with Chapultepec had been when his father, in a delusional state, spoke of the seven falling Mexican boys. He was not sure how to take his father's state of mind. Was it going to be a prelude to a breakdown again? His father continued on.

"Major Robert Lee said it was a beautiful thing to watch the taking of the rampart, even wondrous; but a terrible thing, to see those patriotic young Mexican cadets die rather than capitulate. I wonder how he feels now."

"Major Lee, Da?'

"He was a major then, he is a Colonel now. Stopped John Brown at Harper's Ferry last year. Or did we talk about that?"

"Yes, you brought the news about it home and read it aloud to the whole family. I had just started at the Shiloh school. You actually knew him, did you?"

"Oh, I knew him, and others who have come under the limelight recently. I would prefer company with a Captain I served with."

At the mention of *a Captain,* Dennis clinched up. He could barely move. Was his father going to say it was the man who was now the head of a militia in Memphis? The man who had.... his father continued:

"He was my regimental quartermaster. Sam Grant. He muttered to me once that he thought we were fighting a most unjust war against a weaker nation. It was a good thing nobody else heard him say it."

His father was onion-like, Dennis thought. Get one layer peeled back, and there was another layer to pare away. He was talking fondly now of some of his fellow veterans. They sounded more than interesting. If ever there was a time to confront his father about Captain Adair this was it, while he was lucid. However his stomach churned at the prospect.

"Da, there is something I need to ask about." His father noticed the change in tone immediately.

"Denny, what's got into you. I won't hold anything back from you."

"I need to know about Adair."

His father was confused. "Jack Adair? Why, how do you know of Captain Adair? I haven't seen him since Mexico. I don't think I have ever spoken of him."

It was now brought home to Dennis just how completely detached from his senses his father had been on the way from Hamburg to New Orleans, especially Memphis. His father remembered little. Ironically, it gave Dennis a sense of relief, but it was still daunting how he should approach the real history of his father and that man.

Dennis was aware of homosexuality before he had seen what he had seen in Memphis with his father and Adair. Once, when the family had lived in Corinth, his mother had allowed him to go to a church with a neighbor. He heard that day a Bible sermon about Sodom and Gomorrah. The preacher spoke vehemently against *men laying with men*. The whole congregation had pronounced amens, shaking their heads in disapproval. Subsequently, Dennis had read the place in scripture repeatedly. It was hard for him to imagine a man being attracted to another man in such a way; so when Adair kissed his father on the mouth in the hallway, it was the shock of his life.

After they had arrived in New Orleans, and Dennis got established, he often walked past a club in the French Quarter. It was called the Achillean Inn. He thought little about it since so many Southern streets and towns had Greek cultural references. Many streets in New Orleans were named after Greek gods and goddesses: Apollo, Euterpe, Terpsichore, and others. There was an aura that emanated from the Achillean Inn. These were the thoughts he had as he tried to compose an answer for his father.

"Yes, Da. You did speak of Adair. You said you would have liked to have stayed in his service."

It was truthful the way he framed the answer, but Dennis was begging off. In anger, he wanted to berate his father. There was no idiom strong enough to describe what he wanted to say. But as he looked at the quizzical, almost pathetic expression on his father's face, he thought of the Seventh Love. He could remember crystal clear, nearly verbatim, what Douglas had said. *Agape, the highest form of love, embodies selflessness, sacrifice, and unconditional care for others, transcending mere feelings.* Could he do that for his father, a sodomite?

A strange calm came over him, and as it did, he finally heard the voice again. *If it be possible, as much as it depends on you, be peaceable with all men.* Dennis interpreted it to mean he did not have to approve the incident of his father with Adair. Certainly it had not been his fault. Nonetheless, Dennis sensed his father wanted to talk about it.

"Denny, I was but a very young man when I went off to war. I had no friends at the time, and I was but a private. I started out as infantry. The Mexicans utilized poorly trained peons to a great extent in their defense. We had all the advantages in trained men and equipment. I came to see we were to the Mexicans what the British were to the Irish. I understood what Captain Grant said about it being an unjust war. What with all I had been through with my father, my allegiance to the war was getting thin as gruel. I gave up me musket and begged to become a litter bearer. The commanding officer called me a coward and was ready to put me before a firing squad. That was when Captain Adair stepped in on my behalf. Said we needed all the bodies we could utilize."

"Da, I had no idea. Captain Adair saved your life, did he?"

"My deliverance came at great cost. Captain Adair made me his personal orderly, his valet; some call it body servant. I was at his bidding in everything. He was an elegant man. I admired him at first. If you want me to stop talking, Denny, I will stop."

"Da, I want to know. Please go on."

"I had your mother, you, and John back home. I would've done anything to get back to you. At night he began invitin' me into his tent, sleepin' on a spare cot. He had me hold a lantern as he wrote orders and correspondence at first. It advanced to more personal duties. He started having me shave him and comb his hair. All the while his eyes fixed on mine. 'Twas a look quite familiar. Then he put his hands on me thigh and moved upward. You know, Denny, one can get used to almost anything if one has to. Whenever he demanded, I submitted. I had developed that kind of thing long ago. To get through it, I pictured being somewhere else. It was like I was out of me own body, with someone honorable, and I would say to that fantasy, "I will be in your service forever."

"Da, Da. Couldn't you have called out to someone? Couldn't you have reported it?"

"Remember, son, I was a traitor in the commanding officers' eyes. Anyway, Captain Adair cast me off after a few weeks and took a new novitiate in his service. Somehow I was allowed to finish the war as a non-combatant. I even saved a couple of lives. That meant a lot to me."

Dennis was overwhelmed with compassion for his father. He grabbed and embraced him, squeezing hard, but it caused his father to start coughing again. They heard the locomotive whistle sounding its commanding call. It meant they would be in Corinth by the following morning.

36

Crossroads

Ida at the post office, picking up the mail,
Daddy at the station, pounding on a rail,
Beulah in the kitchen, filling up a box,
And Adam in bed with the chicken pox.

T he Garrett girls were skipping rope to a little ditty they made up when Charles and Dennis came walking down the street. Dennis called out to Connie and Marcie. They dropped the rope, came running and screaming, almost tackling him. Adam, hearing the ruckus, came round from back of the house. Seeing his father and brother, he hollered to his mother Ida, Peg, and Beulah.

"They're here! They're really here! Everybody, quick! Come quick! Come see!"

All met together in the middle of the yard. Dennis and his father were surrounded by jumping, squealing, hugging kin. It was a reception they had not imagined. With the grim departure they had all had when they were last together, it might have been subdued. Yet here they were, seemingly an ideal family. When the initial unhampered joy cooled, they all went into the house, bringing in the baggage and presents.

Everyone demanded the telling of tales of their absence. Dennis and his father looked across the room at one another with knowing glances and gave abridged, sanitized versions of their time away. Their stories were cute and anecdotal, unlike the ones that they had confessed to Robert down at the Corinth roundhouse when they arrived.

The little sisters received their gifts first. Charles reached in the bag and pulled out two paper wrapped objects with the names Marcie and Connie on them. The girls ravaged the packaging. Each received a cloth, cotton filled, home-made doll. One was white, the other black. They had hand-sewn facial features. The girls were tickled and retreated upstairs to play with them, all the while arguing over which of them got the best doll. Adam took his Noah's Ark toy and ran off to float it in the horse trough. There were shawls for Ida, Peg and Beulah.

With the gifts dispensed, Dennis and his father excused themselves and went out to the carriage house. When they stepped into the yard, they were amazed to see that Robert had put a second story onto it with sleeping quarters for Beulah over the stalls and wagon space below.

Charles's coughing started up again. When it calmed, he told Dennis he'd had a dream of the farm and was eager to get back to it. It was evening now. The adults gathered at the dining room table and pooled together what money was available. Ida had managed to save some money, thanks to Robert who refused to let her spend it on household expenses. Dennis and Charles had come home with $150. Robert tossed another $50 onto the table. They were amazed that they had so much. It would be perfect to set themselves back up at the farm in Hamburg.

"Da, I'll take Bobby up there tomorrow to scout things out first," Dennis insisted.

"I'll start getting provisions ready, Denny! When you come back for us, we'll be on our way to normal!" The enthusiastic emphasis Charles put on the words caused him to cough once more, but he would not hear concerns about his health. "No, go away, and leave me alone! I am just fine!" he protested, but the sputum on his handkerchief was pink in color this time. Seeing that, Ida refused to listen to his protests and made him delay going back to the farm.

One of the town doctors made a house call and after learning where Charles had been from spring through summer, he diagnosed consumption. The prescription was mandatory rest until he showed improvement. He also told them to leave the windows open no matter the weather with fresh air flowing at all times. His diet should contain as many vegetables as possible, and suggested they think about a visit to a drier climate. Charles would not hear of going somewhere else.

The postponement of his visit to Hamburg made Dennis antsy. He was anxious to get up to Hamburg and Shiloh to assess the farm, On the evening of November 8, he could stand it no longer. He would go up to Tennessee tomorrow.

Robert was just coming in from a night shift at the roundhouse when he saw Dennis saddling up the dapple gray. Rather than go inside for breakfast, he pressed a newspaper into his hand. Dennis unfolded it, and the headline made his head spin.

THE CORINTHIAN
Nov. 9, 1860
Secession Guaranteed!

"The Presidential election throughout the Union is over & the people have learned by means of the telegraph that the Black Republican ticket, headed by Abraham Lincoln of Illinois...has triumphed...this has been a sectional contest. The entire North, excepting perhaps the states of New Jersey & Delaware, has gone for the Black Republican candidates while the entire South has cast its strength against that ticket..."

"We best not show this to your father, eh?" Robert queried. He had started treating his nephew with a new respect.

"No, Uncle Robert. He will know it, regardless, in short time. We'll break it to him gently, but his reactions are not so volatile anymore. The coughing seems to have let up some. Maybe it won't be so bad to show him the newspaper."

Dennis did not need to spur Bobby heading out of Corinth. The horse responded to the slightest movement of Dennis's direction. They talked to one another as they ambled along. Dennis told Bobby he was sorry for his absence and patted his big neck. Bobby responded with a low guttural noise as if he was accepting the apology. Dennis told the splendid gelding how much he had missed him. Bobby replied with a whinny and tossed his head. The 'conversation' became more vivid as they continued to saunter. There was no real need to hurry. The sky was azure, and the roads were dry. Midway to where they were going, Dennis brought Bobby to a halt. It was where the bushwhacking had occurred last spring. He dismounted and looked over the area and found shards of pottery partially buried in the roadbed. Continuing to survey the site, he picked up what had been a book. Its back was broken, and the paper was nothing but mush, but as he brushed off the spine, the gold embossing stood out clearly enough to read: *Leaves of Grass*. Ironically gazing at the dry field of grass, he recalled a portion of a poem he had memorized from the demolished volume. He recited it aloud to the horse:

> *Or I guess the grass is itself a child, the produced babe of the vegetation.*
> *Or I guess it is a uniform hieroglyphic,*
> *And it means, sprouting alike in broad zones and narrow zone,*
> *Growing among black folks as among white,*

No response. Dennis chuckled, "Don't like poetry, eh Bobby?" They had come nearly ten miles, and Bobby was fatigued. Dennis led him to a nearby creek where they stayed for about an hour until both of them were rested. It was now just after noon, and in a couple of hours they would reach Hamburg. Just a half mile north of town lay the farm.

Once in Hamburg, Dennis went into the only public house in town and had something to eat. There were a few people there, but he recognized none of them. All were just waiting for the next steamer to come to the landing. Even the keeper was unknown to him. The place had changed hands. It gave him an uneasy feeling. Surely, someone he knew could be found. When he walked out-side and unhitched Bobby, another rider arrived at the inn and dis-mounted. It was their nearest neighbor, Mr. McCorkle, a genial man of few words.

"G'day' Dennis!" he said surprised.

"Good day, Mr. McCorkle! You are just the person I would like to see!"

There was a change in McCorkle's demeanor. He put his head down and thought for a moment, then dismounted.

"How have you been, and how is your father? Haven't seen ya'll in a coon's age."

Dennis just feigned that his father was well and doing fine. The man shifted his weight from foot to foot.

"Y'all comin' back to the farm, I reckon?"

"Yes sir, as you well know we left in a fever pitch in the middle of the storm last spring. How did you fare through it all? And can you tell me what shape our place is in?"

"We're makin' out alright, but about your farm…best you find out for yourself," McCorkle's face flushed and he excused himself curtly, going into the pub.

He tried not to think the worst, but the neighbor's response had all the earmarks of what to expect. Dennis mounted Bobby and plodded north out of town, confiding his fears to the gelding. When they reached the high road above the farm, Dennis braced himself. He took in several breaths, came over a slight rise, and looked down.

The cabin was still there. Yes, the cabin was still there, but everything else of what had been their homestead was now an inlet of the Tennessee River. The upper part of what had been a fertile little bowl was now a steep bluff. The cabin was on slightly higher ground, but that would not last long. Balanced precariously on the edge of the lapping lagoon, it could only survive through the next rain. Dennis thought of going down to find out if anything was salvageable, but even as considered it, he heard a massive snap and crackle. The cabin collapsed on itself and slid into the water. It startled Bobby, so Dennis pulled him back from the bluff. The pathway north to Shiloh lay ahead. They broke into a gallop. Dennis bawled for a mile up the road.

At Lick Creek, they stopped. Getting off the horse, Dennis, still shuddering from grief, tried to lead him to water, but Bobby would not have it. Instead he nudged Dennis, forcing him to pet his muzzle. They made camp for the night in a little copse of trees. Dennis reclined on his bedroll. He prayed hard that night, something he had not done in a long time. He begged why had this all happened. He begged for the misery to stop. He demanded that God speak to him. He heard no voice in reply.

Falling autumn leaves on his face awoke Dennis the next morning. He brushed them off. His mouth felt like muck. He got the canteen, swirled some water around in his mouth, and spit it out. It dawned on him it was near time for the harvest festival, but he could not remember a specific date.

When he got to McCullers' Orchard, there was something strange. The apples were curiously still on the branches with some rotting on the ground. It was not likely any farmer would let that happen. He looked to see if anyone was about the property and saw a lone slave picking the fruit, tossing them into a basket. It was strange the McCuller boys were not involved in the harvest. They were nowhere to be seen.

Up the road at the Stuart's and Larkin Bell's place, it was little different. Only a black man and woman were garnering apples. There was an eerie feeling in the air. Dennis shook it off and continued. When he came to Sarah Bell's, the group of slaves that he had seen last year were bringing in the last of the cotton harvest, but no white foreman. He strained to see if Douglas might be among them, but he was not. His heartbeat began to pick up, because farther up the on the left was the Barnes's place. He held Bobby up, deliberating. He unconsciously put his hand on his chest and rubbed his pectoral muscles. His physique was strong, because of all of the heavy lifting he had put in at *Speake and McCreary's*. Cognizant of his own brawn, he felt he could best James if it came to that. He did not have to wait long for the test of whether he could remain peaceable with his old nemesis. As he came up the road, James was standing at the corner of the family property in a butternut uniform as if he was waiting for someone. Dennis dismounted, tied Bobby to a branch, and walked directly up to him.

"Hello, James," Dennis said with a mix of caution and resolution. He braced himself for belligerence.

"Dennis O'Brien. I didn't think you would ever come back here!" The timbre of his voice sounded plaintive.

"Yeah, yeah, well, I am back."

The next reply was so unexpected, Dennis could have been bowled over with a feather.

"I'm so glad to see you, Dennis. How have you been? Everyone at the school wondered what happened to you!"

Dennis was not convinced of his attitude had truly changeed, so he responded harshly.

"Like you care?"

"Dennis. I know things were rocky between us before. Please believe me all that is in the past. With the storm last year, everybody took a hard hit around here. When it was over, everybody had to look out for everybody else. We all heard about your farm and everyone was really sorry for what happened. I'm glad you're still alive and kickin'."

Dennis let his guard down and asked who was still at the school. James rattled off some names. He asked whether Miss Sornby was still teaching. She was. Then all of a sudden, James interrupted and asked Dennis anxiously:

"Have you seen Nellie Devine? Tell me you've seen her!"

"No, I'm sorry, I haven't."

"Did you know we vowed to marry each other? No, of course, you couldn't know that. It was after the storm and you were gone. Well, you see, we went into the woods and tied our twigs together. I asked her father for her hand honorably, but he said I wasn't good enough for her. He then decided to take her to their other plantation down in Tishomingo County. He's a Captain of a company of Rangers forming there, outfitting them with his own money. You've got kin down there, I think? Please, if you see her..." His voice trailed off. "Well anyway, it's good to see you."

"Wait, James. I will make every effort to let you know if I do see her. Maybe you could return the favor?"

"Sure," he said though having lost interest in their interchange.

"What happened to Jane? She was supposed to be going up to Clarksville"

"Oh, yeah. You liked her, didn't you? She went to New Orleans after the storm to stay with relatives. Didn't you know? Oh, that's right, you couldn't. That storm changed a lot of people's plans."

As James walked away, Dennis mounted Bobby and then sat motionless in the saddle in a daze. He couldn't process what James had just said about Jane. Why had she never said anything to him about having relatives in New Orleans? If he had known it might have changed everything. Bobby, sensing his mood, began to twitch.

"It's nothing, Bobby. Let's go up to the school and see Miss Sornby."

When he got to the school, it was still in session. He waited outside the door for her, hoping it would let out soon. She saw him outside and turned the classroom over to an older girl he did not recognize. She came toward him hurriedly and then hugged him rather stiffly.

"Dennis, as you can see, I am quite under the gun here. I am glad you are well. I am aware of what happened to your family and am so sorry. God bless you and keep you. Now you will have to go." She said it in a way that indicated she was trying to remain emotionally distant.

"But I never finished school here!"

"Oh, oh my, Dennis. What are you thinking? You want to go backwards? You don't need any more schooling here. You belong in a university. You will have no problem making it in this world. Just don't go for a soldier. Almost all the boys you know are up at a militia camp in McNairy County, the cream of the southern crop. They will become mere cannon fodder. All my boys, all my boys. Please, now, just go." There were tears in her eyes as she turned away.

Dennis mounted Bobby soberly. He desired not to go back by way of Hamburg road and by the remains of the farm. He trotted down the Pittsburg Landing-Corinth road past Shiloh Spring, deeply depressed.

37

———<>———

Underground

A man reduced to despair by a series of misfortunes feels wearied of life, but is still so far in possession of his reason that he can ask himself whether it would not be contrary to his duty to himself to take his own life.

The memorized words came into Dennis's mind as he plodded home in the dark; Dennis was contemplating the worst. He thought back to why he remembered. During the summer, the little triumvirate had delved into various philosophies. Henry challenged him to read some of the more dense books in the library he had loaned. They sat across from one another in New Orleans restaurants and examined treatises of the European thinkers. It had all been heady, mind expanding. Francisco Moreno had encouraged him to retain one of the essentials of philosopher Emmanuel Kant about duty.

"From self-love I adopt it as a principle to shorten my life when its longer duration is likely to bring more evil than satisfaction. It is asked then simply whether this principle founded on self-love can become a universal law of nature. Now we see at once that a system of nature cannot consist of a law to destroy life by means of the very feeling whose

special nature it is to the improvement of life. Those laws contradict and, therefore, could not exist as a system of nature; hence that maxim cannot possibly exist as a universal law of nature and, consequently, be wholly inconsistent with the supreme principle of all: duty."

What was the gist of this heavy imperative, boiling down the density of the subject matter? They had all agreed that, indeed, it was worth going on in life because 'duty was the supreme principle.' After mulling it over further and thinking of his friends, Dennis began to emerge from his abyss. His frame of mind became much better. Riding on, he heard the sound of a rider approaching from behind. He turned around and saw a mule, but could not make out a rider. Thinking it was an escaped animal, he resolved to capture it. Instead as he drew closer, he made out the shape of a black man ensconced in the saddle.

"You've looked pretty gloomy since you left Shiloh, Dennis," came the velvet voice. At once Dennis recognized Douglas.

"Gloomy? How would you know? This is the first I've seen you. I can never get over how you seem to appear out of nowhere."

"Then you don't understand the rules of the road for black folk on the run."

"No, wait a minute. Why would you be on the run? You're a free man of color."

"Don't you remember the rule enforced in New Orleans: freedmen just arrived are subject to arrest and put back on the boat they came in on? I was under that umbrella, so here I am. It's just as well, for it facilitates the mission to which the Lord has entrusted me."

"So you have been watching me for all these miles? It's amazing you are able to stay out of sight."

"The Lord says: "Behold, I send you forth as sheep in the midst of wolves: be ye therefore wise as serpents, and harmless as doves.'"

"You've been paralleling me on the road all this time?"

"It's a skill you should utilize. The scene of this world is changing,

Dennis. It's time you make up your mind. Don't you realize you are being called?"

"Called? What are you talking about?"

"You well know what I am talking about. You've heard the voice again, haven't you? Those of us who have heard it are in search of those who have evidenced having heard it as well. Stop resisting. You need to be *on the road.*"

"What road? I'm on one right now." Dennis looked around and down at the Corinth road beneath him, bewildered.

"The *underground* one," Douglas emphasized. "Really, you stepped onto it when you set Elizabeth free."

"I don't see how I can, Douglas. I have so much to figure out already."

"Need I tell you the way that makes it feasible? Have we not been together enough times that you still don't know the path? Need I draw the coins from my pocket to show you again?"

With that a commotion was heard coming up the road from Corinth. The sound of at least half dozen riders moving swiftly.

"That will be bounty hunters," Douglas said, backing up his mule. "Just remember what I said about the road," and he deftly guided his mule off the road to where he would be screened from sight by trees.

Dennis clicked his tongue, and Bobby responded. He met up with the trackers about a short distance from where Douglas was hiding. They hailed him and then interrogated.

"Seen any runaways?!"

"No, I am the only one on the road that I know of. You're the first people I've seen since Shiloh." Dennis lied, wondering whether he had committed a sin in doing so.

"Too bad. It's gettin' pretty profitable to catch these maroons, and it's gonna get more so, because once Mississippi secedes, they ain't gonna be no more manumissions. We won't just be getting' bounty money; we can sell on the open market. You should be like us."

"That's quite an idea, but I just got an offer to work on the railroad," Dennis replied with a quick unplanned answer that surprised him, coming out of his mouth.

"You sure about that kid? It's hard to get on the crew down in Corinth."

"Sure enough." He fibbed again. "I'm gonna be a conductor on a new line. My Uncle Robert got me on as a trainee."

"Rob Garrett by any chance?!"

"Yes sir!"

"You are one lucky son of a gun. That Robert Garrett is one good ol' boy!"

The self-appointed posse rode off in the direction where Douglas had gone into the trees, but went past the place. It would have made no difference, for Dennis could now see Douglas's silhouette just off the road and within earshot.

"I see you are on the real road now, Dennis!" he called out. "The Lord will bring us together again. Don't be thinking *"to be or not be"* like Hamlet anymore! " and he turned his mule off on a cow path, ambling away in the dark.

Dennis rode on for about a mile and then bedded down. His mind, body, and spirit were sore. He turned over and over on the ground, berating himself about that last day in in New Orleans. The last day the triumvirate had been together. The day he had surely seen Jane. Finally, he fell asleep to the song of the last surviving crickets of the year, trilling and chirping in the brush nearby.

He arose at break of day and variously ambled, trotted, and cantered the rest of the way home. He cooled Bobby down the last few blocks, dismounting and walking the horse. From a distance he saw his brother in the front of the house, waiting. It struck him how much his brother had grown while he and his Da had been in New Orleans. Even in the last two months it seemed he had grown two inches. When he arrived in the expansive yard, Adam helped put

Bobby away in the stall, removing tack and hanging it up. Dennis didn't know how to break the news to his brother that the farm was gone. He put off giving him news about the farm, hoping to break the news to everyone all at once.

"Adam, I won't tell you what the farm looks like just now, we'll just wait and all go up together. Just suffice it to say you will be surprised." The words caught in his throat, and he tried to think of something else to say. Then it dawned on him that it was a special day.

"Well, little brother, you turn twelve today, don't you? November 13, 1860."

"I'm surprised you noticed, Denny. You've been paying little attention to me since you got back. I know you've been doing a lot, but what am I, chicken feed?"

Dennis was taken aback. He realized that once again he had been behaving like John. It pained him even more because of the farm. He decided to tell his brother.

"You're right, Adam. You deserve better. I felt like an adult at your age, and I'm sure you feel that way now. You're going to have to brace yourself, Adam. We won't be going back to the farm."

"Why not? Tell me, why not? I can take it."

"It's part of the Tennessee River now."

"Well, I figured as much, the way we left and all. Cotton pick! Don't you coddle me anymore! All that time you were away, I had to do your chores and mine, too. You never gave me enough credit. The farm is gone?! Well, good riddance to bad rubbish. I'm glad we'll never see it again!" then he began to shudder, disguising grief.

Dennis grabbed and hugged him. Adam tried to break away, but Dennis hugged even harder and just kept saying over and over, "Adam, you're right. I'm sorry. I sold you short. You carried a huge load. I was not paying enough attention these last years. I am sorry, so sorry."

Adam let down and returned the hug just as hard. Adam had grim news of his own. "I was surprised how skinny Da was when you got back from New Orleans. We've all been watching how he only eats little bits, so tired all the time. After you left three days ago, Da took a turn for the worse. He stopped eating altogether. That's three days now he hasn't had any food. The doctor came to see him and said he needed to drink more liquids, but he started refusing even that. The only thing he wanted was to hear the news from the papers. Ma kept saying no but finally gave up because he began shivering more than usual. After Uncle Robert showed him the newspaper, he started coughing so hard the blood came up in plugs."

No sooner had Adam spoken when they heard their mother's scream from the house coming from the open upstairs window.

"Charles! Charles! Charles! Don't leave us now! Not now!"

Dennis and Adam ran for the front door, racing up the stairs. All the women were gathered round the bed, and Ida was weeping on Charles's chest. Peg had her hand on Ida's shoulder, and Beulah was humming mournfully, rocking back and forth. Dennis put his arm around Adam who had leaned into him. For the longest time, no one said anything; there were only Ida's sobs and Beulah's plaintive spiritual tune. Beulah broke into singing a spontaneous predictable dirge: "Mmmm, mmmm sweet Lawd, sweet Lawd take him home. Sweet Lawd take him home." Dennis stepped forward, drew his mother lovingly away from the body, then closed his father's open eyelids and brought the sheet up over his head.

The next few days involved the grim necessary details of death. The men did the heavy lifting, all the men, including Adam. They carried the body downstairs, placed it in the wagon, and took it to the undertaker. While downtown, Robert encountered a man whom Charles had known at the post office years ago named Sullivan, and when he found out about Charles and the disaster at Hamburg, he offered a spot on his farm just outside of town for burial in the family enclosure. He pronounced the Irish proverb: "Under the shelter of each other we live. Under the shelter of each other we die."

Dennis, Adam, and Robert returned a day later to retrieve the remains of Charles O'Brien, enclosed in a simple pine box with no handles. They brought him home to the Garrett's to lie in state in the parlor in the suit Robert had given him for the trip to New Orleans. It was a much modified Irish wake, for Charles had long ranted that he didn't even want one. "Just stick me in the ground and be done with it," he'd repeatedly said, usually in one of his maniacal states.

There was singing and the telling of stories, the reciting of Irish proverbs. Ida even allowed Charles's off color maxims to be repeated with curses by Uncle Robert, told laughing while strumming a guitar. The little girls related how they loved that Charles could make a pencil disappear magically behind his ear. Beulah poignantly recounted the story of how Charles had found her by the riverbank. Peg told how when he had been best man at their wedding, he passed gas at the pronouncement of 'man and wife.' The women prepared a small buffet for visitors. Neighbors did come into the house, but it proved to be more gawking at the open coffin than comfort. Other than Mr. Sullivan who patted the coffin and kissed Ida on the cheek before excusing himself, there were three negroes who stood at the edge of the road to pay respects at a distance. It was an unexpected tribute. Nobody knew who they were.

Early Wednesday morning all walked the wagon to the burial. The bereft family circled around the open grave after Dennis, Robert, and Adam lowered the coffin by ropes. Certainly there was no Catholic priest, nor Protestant pastor. It was only Robert, Peg, Connie, Marcie, Ida, Beulah, Dennis, and Adam. Then out of brushy thicket, a big black man strode forth with a Bible in his hand. Dennis introduced Douglas, but of course, Beulah knew him already. Robert had no qualms about shaking the black man's hand. Dennis mused about his Uncle. The head of the bounty hunters had called him a "good ol' boy." That man did not know that Robert Garrett was a magnanimous, unprejudiced man. Douglas opened the Bible and read:

"From the Revelation to John. Chapter 21, verses 1 through 4:

"And *I saw a new heaven and a new earth: for the first heaven and the first earth were passed away; and there was no more sea. And I John saw the holy city, New Jerusalem, coming down from God out of heaven, prepared as a bride adorned for her husband. And I heard a great voice out of heaven saying, Behold, the tabernacle of God is with men, and he will dwell with them, and they shall be his people, and God himself shall be with them, and be their God. And he will wipe out every tear from their eyes, and death will be no more, neither will mourning nor outcry nor pain be anymore. The former things have passed away.*"

They all said "Amen" in chorus and thanked Douglas. Dennis picked up a shovel and stove it into the fresh mound of earth beside the grave. Before he could pitch the first shovelful into the pit, Douglas stopped him and took the shovel from his hand.

"It's best you let me finish this. You folks should be in the land of the living. Go on and leave things to me."

Dennis reluctantly surrendered the spade to Douglas, and the family all got into the wagon, except for Dennis and Adam who rode tandem on Bobby slowly back home. Memories of the good things his father had done or believed came to the fore once again. Each member of the family related different anecdotes of Charles's eccentric humor or bravery, some Irish blessing or curse. It was preferable for them to reminisce in this way rather than around a yawning grave. Preferable to hearing the hollow sounds of clods thumping on top of the man who had loved a woman, fathered three children, saved the lives of a number of men in Mexico, and one black pearl of a woman who was with them now.

"Uncle Robert, do you think there is any chance I could get a job down at the roundhouse?" Dennis asked.

"Maybe, Dennis, the *Memphis to Charleston* has a help wanted sign down at the station now. They are looking for people to whom they can teach the ropes. With all the men draining away to the militias, they are hard pressed for civilian man power. You could be a conductor and rollin' down the road with a good rate of pay." Dennis could hear Douglas's voice in his head - *there is coincidence and there is providence. They sometimes meet; the way it appears in perspective when you are looking down the two rails of a railroad track.*

38

———◄●►———

Conducting

Dennis studied the broadsheet tacked to the wall of the Corinth station:

CONDUCTORS WANTED!
INQUIRE AT STATIONMASTERS OFFICE

Conductors are honest and responsible for overseeing passenger and freight operations. They verify tickets, manage passenger seating arrangement, and ensure the safe boarding and disembarking of passengers. Conductors also supervise the loading and unloading of cargo. All men of an eligible age considered. The conductor will be the boss of a train crew. He reports to the trainmaster, his immediate superior and takes instructions from yardmasters and dispatchers. Those with experience in fields related to the above description and with letters of introduction preferred.

Inquire at Office of Memphis and Charleston Railroad
John Goforth-Stationmaster

"The job is yours, young man. With militias forming like never before and civilian manpower at a premium, you came at just the right time," said the stationmaster after reading the embossed recommendation letter from *Speake and McCreary, Wholesale and Commission Merchants*. "That Mr. McCreary has a high opinion of you. I especially like the way he says you handled the negroes down there in New Orleans. You'll have your work cut out for you up here. Here, nearly every train has a car full of them, either headed to market in Memphis or dropping them off to the various depots. It will be important to see how you manage them." Dennis couldn't help a sour look from creeping over his face. Thinking he understood the reason for his demeanor, Goforth said, "Yeah, I know, they sure do stink, don't they? Especially when there is a car full all packed in like sardines."

It was all Dennis could do to keep from blurting out anti-slavery sentiment, but he checked himself. If he was going to have any impact on black people's lives, he was going to have to carry out the charade of a lifetime. Douglas had been clandestinely meeting with him since the funeral to forge a plan to help slaves escape once he was truly employed by the rail line.

"Oh, and O'Brien, two things."

"What's that, sir?" Dennis tensed up.

"It hasn't hurt that Robert Garrett is your uncle."

"Yes sir, and the other?"

"Don't try to pull the wool over my eyes. I know you're not 18. But report over to the trainmaster at the roundhouse."

Not 18. Did it show that much? He thought his physique convincing enough. He thought the patchy whiskers on his chin, and in front of his ears made him look older. In reality, the sparse hair growth on his face signaled that he was younger. His brother John could grow a full beard by the time he was sixteen. Why had he not inherited the same advantage? He reported for work.

Dennis thought he had learned the meaning of truly hard indus-
trial work when at *Speake and McCreary's*. Working for the railroad
as a conductor was even more intense. He was given little training. It
was sink or swim. Those who had been working the line a few years
resented his position as conductor, telling him he was still wet behind the ears. To gain their respect, he pushed himself, learning fast.
He reminded himself of Uncle Robert's advice: work hard to make
good money, be affable but not a push-over, and stand tall.

The daily grinding routine of the rails had him working like
Jehu driving his chariot. Ticket taking was the easiest part of the job.
Record keeping was draining. Preparing for arrival and departure
was sometimes complicated. In addition, he acted as chief purser.
Continually jumping on and off the train at the various stops to
supervise the loading and unloading of freight was exhausting. The
stops involved more that town depots. There were interim layovers
at large plantations along the line where slaves were taken on and off
loaded. It was emotionally wrenching because he had to endure personally dispatching human cargo of men in chains, weeping women
recently separated from their children, and old black men deemed
of little value being sent off to market. He could not help but feel
complicit, but he did have control of their treatment to some extent.
He disallowed the use of prods and whips, and his commands were
obeyed. He had the authority of the railroad behind him, and after
all he had been through he was no milquetoast. He worked on pro-
jecting professional confidence and an aloof manner to signal that
he was not be engaged in conversation idly. It helped to keep those
eager to talk to him about the rebellion at bay, but it was about to get
harder not to do that. He had only been at work for about six weeks
when South Carolina seceded from the Union.

While based in Corinth, Dennis was on his way to the station
to report for his usual duty the week it happened. People streamed
off the incoming train from Charleston in jubilation, shouting,

cheering, expressing undying support for their sister state's cry of independence. The platform filled with yelling, jumping young militiamen. Planters in top hats shook hands with one another vigorously. Women fluttered fans over their heads joyously. The train whistle blew continuously. "The union is dissolved! South Carolina has seceded! Hurrah for Dixie! Hurrah! Hurrah for the Palmetto State! Mississippi is next! Thank God Almighty!"

Dennis picked up a broadsheet someone had dropped in the pandemonium. It had just been brought from Charleston:

CHARLESTON
MERCURY
****

EXTRA:
Passed Unanimously at 1:15 o'clock, P.M
December 20th 1860
AN ORDINANCE
To dissolve the Union between
the State of South Carolina and
the other States under the compact with her entitled
"The Constitution of the United States of America"

We, the People of the State of South Carolina, in Convention assembled do declare and ordain, and it is hereby declared and ordained, That the Ordinance adopted by us in Convention, on the twenty-third day of May in the year of our Lord One Thousand Seven hundred and eighty eight, whereby the Constitution of the United States of America was ratified, and also all Acts and parts of Acts of the General Assembly of this State, ratifying amendment of the said Constitution, are here by repealed; and that the union now subsisting between South Carolina and other

States, under the name of "The United States of America,"
is hereby dissolved.

****

THE

UNION

is

DISSOLVED!

The riveting effect of the announcement, the celebration over the breakup of South Carolina with the Union meant Mississippi would not be far behind. No hope for a reversal. The political rhetoric would continue to spiral. It would be a challenge on his job in such an atmosphere. Some passengers and soldiers were "fire-eaters" about the Southern cause. They would expect him to have similar sympathies. He would have to appear to be secessionist while going about his business. He needed to thoroughly dedicate himself to his duties, pour himself into the routines of his job while considering surreptitious actions.

When Mississippi seceded from the Union on January 9, 1861, the load increased heavily. Then, on February 8, 1861 the *Confederate States of America* was formed by seven southern states at Montgomery, Alabama. Troops moved by train, many of them were stationed in Corinth because it was at the strategic crossroads of two major supply lines. The *Mobile and Ohio* ran north to south. East and west the *Memphis and Charleston* was the main artery of the South. Many of the soldiers ridiculed Dennis for not joining up. On the other hand, some of the officers commended him for playing one of the most important supporting roles of the new nation.

After working on the *Memphis and Charleston* for months, he began to feel he was coming into his own. That sense of confidence allowed him to turn his attention to the secret work in which Douglas was mentoring him. He hoped in his imagination to liberate a million slaves. At least that was the way he envisioned it. All day long he concocted ideas for releasing men, women, and children from bondage. He even considered the idea of sabotage to gain their release. He pictured uncoupling cars full of slaves, mid trip, enabling them to escape into the wild and free, beyond the beyond. But everything he came up with had a downside that seemed impractical and too hard to overcome. He grew exhausted cooking up plans and discouraged that he had not freed a single slave yet. It was time to confer with Douglas. They had decided the best place to meet was in Beulah's little room above the carriage house on the Garrett property. Robert was above reproach among confederates in town, his property deemed above suspicion.

"Dennis, Dennis, Dennis," Douglas shook his head, hearing all of Dennis's grandiose schemes. "Don't you realize that you had it right from the beginning? The beginning was with Elizabeth. You cannot hope to be Moses. The Lord is pleased with small beginnings. The prophet Daniel says the great liberation will come when the great God Jehovah 'changes the times and the seasons, removes kings, and sets up kings. He gives wisdom unto the wise, and knowledge to them that know understanding.' He will give such wisdom to you if you let him."

"Where do we begin then?" Dennis looked across the room at Beulah's shining black face in the lamp light, her eyes sparkling like sapphires. He remembered Beulah's voice when he sat with her long ago on the bank of the Tennessee River, watching the black swans.

"Yes, suh, young Dennis, I see dem black swans, an' knows Jack and me is gonna be together agin someday."

"Okay, Douglas, Let's start with Jack. Do you think we can find the plantation where Jack is?"

Douglas replied: "We'll get the mustard seeds out of our pockets and see how God makes them grow!"

39

Beginnings

Where to look for Beulah's beloved husband Jack? That involved some serious logic, since it had been untold years since they were separated from one another. Beulah was found by Charles almost lifeless on the riverbank near Pittsburg Landing, not far from Shiloh. The anomaly of the Tennessee River near Shiloh is that it flows north not south. She had therefore floated north from somewhere south. She could have gone into the water somewhere near the muscle shoals of Alabama, for the steamboat she had leapt from could not navigate beyond the shoals.

The nearest town to the shoals was Eastport, Mississippi. Douglas began his search clandestinely from there. He slogged through swampy areas, trod cow paths, and pushed through brushy thickets to reach slave churches held at "brush arbors." Clues to Jack's whereabouts surfaced. A few remembered Jack and Beulah. One old woman recalled Jack as a powerful man, highly valued by his owner, brought directly from Africa despite the law prohibiting it. When away from the owner, at one of these hidden open air worships, Jack sometimes broke into phrases of his tribal dialect. Still another man recalled that after he was separated from Beulah, Jack had contracted small pox, leaving him with pitted scars on his face. Maybe the most useful bit of information came from a house servant of a small plantation. He recounted that Jack had been purchased by a man named Robinson. Armed with that knowledge, Douglas returned to Corinth and rendezvoused with Dennis in Beulah's room above the carriage house. It was just after sundown. Dennis yanked him inside. Beulah sat quietly on the bed, stitching up some worn garments.

"Douglas, I was afraid you wouldn't make it back. Things have drastically changed. South Carolina fired on Fort Sumter April 12th. Freedmen are being seized and sold with increasing frequency. I thought for sure you had been."

"It was bound to come to that. What has Mr. Lincoln done about it?"

"He does not honor the Confederacy as a new sovereign nation. He's calling for 75,000 men to suppress the insurrection."

"Then the earthquake has begun. The prophets said HE will shake the nations. This is a pivotal moment. We shall see whether this is more than union and states' rights. It is the crucial opportunity to end slavery in America. It will be won both on and off the battlefield."

"Is that what the voice is telling you? I thought we were supposed to be peaceable with all men."

"Once Jesus said if you "take the sword you will die by the sword." But on another occasion, he said "let he that has no sword take his money pouch and buy one.""

"Oh, great. Which way am I supposed to choose?"

"You will know when the time comes, Dennis. When the time comes."

"That doesn't help much. I can't abide black people as slaves, but I just can't picture me slinging a sword against people I have grown up with, known all my life. What if those 75,000 end up down here in our back yard? I would feel mighty resentful about that!"

"Suffice to say, you will have to decide if that happens. Meantime the window narrows for finding Jack."

Dennis was so conflicted by the looming war and its ramifications, he had trouble paying attention to the matters about Beulah's husband. He felt panicky. He had just started on the Underground Railroad, trying to free slaves. Douglas studied the look on Dennis's face.

"It appears that you think it is all about you. Isn't that true of what is going through your mind?

Dennis was irritated now and answered half grunting.

"Just go over the details with me again about Jack," so Douglas reviewed them. The pertinent details were Jack was still likely a powerful man, even if he had grown older. He had smallpox scars on his face. He could still speak an African tongue. The key that narrowed things down was the information about his owner, a man named Robinson. As Dennis let the facts sink in, he felt guilty. Here he was speculating over the future, when right in front of him sat Douglas, in danger of being put back into bonds.

"We've got to get you out of here somehow, Douglas, pronto!"

"I can still make my own way, Dennis," Douglas replied tolerantly, showing no fear.

Dennis protested. "It's not like before, bounty hunters are one thing, now average citizens can trash your freedman papers and demand your arrest. I have an idea. I'll be back in a minute."

Dennis left the carriage house and ran across the yard to the house. Quietly but anxiously, he asked everyone to help him find a small box for storing papers. His mother found it in the baggage brought home from New Orleans. Dennis grabbed it and quickly flipped through the contents. Some of them were evaluations from Dr. Irvine, but in the middle of the bundle he found what he was looking for: the ownership document given him at the time Elizabeth was turned over to him. He examined it in the lamplight. It was just as he remembered. In the rush and pressure that Nathan Bedford Forrest had put his partner Jones under, Jones had left the line for the slave's name and date of sale blank. It was perfect. He could fill in Douglas's name, and it would appear that he, Dennis, was legal owner of Douglas. It could protect Douglas if arrested. Then his idea expanded. Dennis begged his mother and Aunt Peggy to make careful copies of the document, as many copies they had stationary for with special attention given to the signature, N. B. Forrest. He left them with the task and returned to the carriage house. Beulah was humming contentedly, still sewing. Douglas was gone.

This time Dennis was especially disappointed with Douglas's disappearance. He was anxious to tell him about his idea of using forged documents. Thinking about the visit they'd just had, he reflected on Douglas's counsel. "It appears that you think it is all about you. Isn't that true of what is going through your mind?" It was true. He had the habit of thinking everything fell on his shoulders alone. It was the same complaint Adam had expressed. It caused him to recall a discussion of the 'little triumvirate.' Francisco and Henry had brought up the philosopher Kierkegaard who had said: *"forget Christianity for a moment and think of what you ordinarily know as love; call to mind what you read in the poets, what you yourself can find out...Only when it is a duty to love, only then is love eternally secured against every change..."*

Dennis examined himself now in the light of that heady discussion with Henry and Francisco. Duty and love must go together. His care for his father had been only drudging duty over the summer, that *"Duty! Duty! Duty!"* feeling that plagued him. On the way back to Corinth, it became love. He needed to strengthen his love for others by *freely choosing* duty, to take it upon himself to love them, care for them, and work for their good. The words of the philosopher were not far off from the *seventh love* that Douglas had emphasized, *agape.*

However, this duty was a contradiction given the present climate in the country. He felt it was his duty to free slaves, but he also felt obligation for the places and people where he had grown up. What would he do should hordes of armed northerners come south? What was he going to do about these contradictions? Douglas, the man who had more self-control and forbearance than anyone he had ever known, had repeated the admonition, "You will know when the time comes." For now duty was the matter of doing work on two kinds of railroad.

Reasoning on Douglas's whereabouts, Dennis saw obvious things. Douglas served congregations in the hinterlands, traveling far and wide. He had been in New Orleans and Indiana where the Friends had their base. Of course, Dennis was not his only white contact! Until Douglas communicated again, Dennis needed patient awareness. If Douglas did not show up, someone else would. Until then he would be alone in figuring the best use of the forgeries.

The advantage of the papers he possessed was that anywhere he traveled they would be accepted. The Bill of Sale showed ownership by one Dennis O'Brien and was signed by one N. B. Forrest. Although it was risky, a bogus ownership paper with the slave's name improved chances of making a way through the southern states without detection. However, it also required the help of others sympathetic to the clandestine mission. Importantly, too, he was a uniformed officer of the railroad, so had to maintain the comportment of one. Patience and vigilance was the course of action. Some situation would present itself, some person. Douglas had always said with faith he would know when the time came.

While Dennis longed to go the full length of the *Memphis and Charleston*, the railroad superintendent had up to this point only assigned him runs covering Corinth to Memphis or Corinth to Huntsville, Alabama. "Don't bite off more than you can chew right now," his Uncle Robert told him. "Time will come when you'll make the long run."

While the train schedules were exactingly prompt every day, his job was never monotonous. As conductor, he was immersed in frenetic activity. By contrast, the constancy and sameness of the simple architecture of the depots was somehow comforting, a welcome sight to those coming home. With the exception of the larger towns, depots were basically built the same way, simple gabled structures made of wood, sometimes brick. There was a large open space for handling cargo and a separate area for passengers. The exteriors were painted occasionally with decorated elements. Raised platforms ran alongside the tracks to facilitate the loading and unloading of passengers and goods. Some were covered by a roof extending from the main structure, providing shelter from rain and sun. Inside, there was a waiting room for passengers with wooden benches along the walls. Behind the counter, the ticket clerk counted money, and the telegraph operator clicked away messages in Morse code. Newspapers were also available. A separate area was designated for freight, with large doors that opened directly onto the platform for easy transfer of goods to and from the trains.

He began to notice a peculiarity at some stations. Lanterns were still lighted though it was still daytime. He thought little of it at first. When he commented to a station attendant about the matter, he got a curious reply: "The lantern is only a candle, but Thy word *is* a lamp unto my feet, and a light unto my path." The first time this happened, he dismissed it as the man being merely religiously minded, piously quoting one of the Psalms. The next time it happened, he was scratching his head while looking up at the lit lantern. A passenger approached him with the same words: "The lantern is only a candle, but Thy word *is* a lamp unto my feet, and a light unto my path." It just seemed coincidence. When he heard the words the third time, in a peculiar circumstance, he realized it was some sort of code.

A man, in the elegant clothes of a planter, was standing next to a lighted lantern. Dennis went to extinguish it. The gentleman said under his breath, "This lantern is only a candle, but Thy word *is* a lamp unto my feet, and a light unto my path." The man then went on, "When you notice the still burning candle, know that a friend of peace is here. That friend will give you instructions about what is required."

"Are you a Quaker?" Dennis asked, also in an undertone.

"No, there are Friends and there are friends. I am just a sinner trying to make compensation."

"What do you mean?"

"I once owned slaves. You know the song, don't you? Amazing Grace. I was blind but now I see."

Dennis was staggered that a planter was saying this to him. This was "the situation" he had been waiting to present itself. He and the planter stood away from others to carry on a longer conversation without coming under scrutiny by anyone. It would be perceived that he was just giving deference to a rich man.

"Do you know anyone named Douglas?" he cautiously probed. "Mr.? I'm sorry, may I ask your name?"

"I do know him, but it best you do not know my name. However, I do know yours, Dennis O'Brien. Do you have something useful you wish to pass along? I am expecting him at an agreed upon rendezvous."

"Tell him this. I have facsimiles of Elizabeth's papers." Dennis opened his ledger book and handed forged documents to the man as if he was merely providing a railroad schedule. "Give these to Douglas. I know you and he will understand how to use them."

He wanted to continue the conversation, but the bell was clanging, and he had to attend to the loading of passengers. He bowed to the planter courteously, pronounced a loud "Thank you, sir! I am pleased to be of service!" and excused himself. Armed with the simple information of the code, he now knew he was definitely not alone in the mission he had embraced. He also knew he could not be far behind Douglas.

It was April 30th, 1861 when he saw the lantern still on at the Collierville depot. Going to the desk, he informed the clerk that the wick needed to be put out. The clerk replied "The lantern is only a candle, but "Thy word *is* a lamp unto my feet, and a light unto my path." The clerk motioned to a white man who was sitting with a muscular young slave in shackles to come up to the counter. It proved to be the first time Dennis was able to use one of the forged ownership papers himself. Dennis heard the slave's name, entered it on the forged Bill of Sale, and handed it to the "owner." He escorted them to the passenger car, dedicated to the transportation of slaves. He had freed Elizabeth; now with her papers, he had set in motion another rescue.

40

Railroads

"You're as bad as John!" Adam declared on a rare day that Dennis was home from the railroad.

"What do you mean? I'm here, now!" Dennis blurted, shocked by the words.

"We never see you. You hardly talk to me. Ma says you think you're really something."

Some things don't die in a family. Sometimes you can't win. Dennis felt like storming in and confronting his mother, giving her a piece of his mind. Wasn't it enough that he was contributing his wages to support the family, hoping to get them a house of their own? Wasn't it enough that he was working on more than the physical railroad? Everyone in the family except Connie and Marcie knew about his efforts to help Beulah and other slaves get free.

He stopped for a moment to think about it. He had neglected his brother. He had not spoken with him enough. He was always in a rush and should have at least given his mother more than quick hugs. After all, she was still in grief over her husband. He had not even allowed himself time to process the fact that their father was dead. He decided to make corrections.

"Adam, maybe you will understand if I do take the time to talk right now."

"Well, what is it?"

"There has been some success in looking for Beulah's husband. The problem is that I have to keep things secret, and it keeps me pent up. I don't mean to be so brusque with you, it's just that if I'm not careful, well… let me tell you something a friend in New Orleans said to me: "Beware of silent dogs and still waters.""

Adam's expression changed, and he thoughtfully responded. "I like that, and I get it. I'm sorry, Denny. Do you think Jack will be found soon?"

"Beulah should be the first to know. Let's go out to the carriage house so that you and she will know what's happening. Then we'll go in and tell Ma and Peggy. We will just need to keep things quiet from the girls. They're too innocent and might let word get out." Dennis punched his brother lightly, then put his arm around his shoulders. They walked across the yard and upstairs to see Beulah.

Suppressing excitement, Dennis revealed to them that someone in the Underground Railroad network had located a Robinson plantation in South Carolina. It was not known whether this was the same Robinson that had purchased Jack so many years ago, but it was promising. Beulah grabbed Dennis and squeezed him tightly, crying with hope. Adam joined in the hug.

The three of them crossed to the house. Although there was still light this summer's evening, Connie and Marcie, after a busy day of hard play with friends down by the creek, were already in bed sleeping. When Ida and Aunt Peggy heard the hopeful news, both were happy, but had misgivings. Finding Jack was fraught with danger. Before Dennis left the following morning, he reassured his mother of his love by hugging her long and hard. He did the same with Aunt

Peggy and the girls. He took Adam aside, encouraged him, and then slapped him lovingly on the back.

Arriving at the station, he met Uncle Robert, but he was not his usual genial self. With a concerned look in his eye, he handed Dennis the latest copy of the *Corinthian*. Three days earlier, July 21, 1861, a major battle between Union and Confederate forces had taken place at Manassas, Virginia. It was a resounding southern victory, with General P.G.T. Beauregard credited with vanquishing the enemy and exhibiting heroic leadership. Dennis felt a twinge in his chest. He clearly remembered encountering then Major Beauregard in New Orleans last summer. He had shown favor to Francisco Moreno, personally discussing his promotion. No doubt Francisco had been at the general's side.

The paper went on to state that Lincoln took immediate action to strengthen the Union's military efforts. He called for enlistment of 500,000 new troops. To counter, Confederate President Jefferson Davis appointed General Albert Sydney Johnston to command all Confederate troops west of the Appalachians. Johnston was in process of spreading his forces across a vast area to protect key locations, and trains became prime to moving large bodies of troops.

Dennis had been restricted to conducting routes either from Corinth to Memphis or Corinth to Huntsville, Alabama. His repeated requests to work the distance all the way to Charleston, South Carolina had been ignored by the Superintendent of the *Memphis and Charleston*. Now the Superintendent needed conductors to help handle the logistics of uptick in civilian traffic and military activity. Much to his surprise, Dennis was assigned to the Charleston route. It would be no lark for Dennis, but maybe it would afford more opportunities to liberate some slaves, and he could hopefully investigate the Robinson lead in South Carolina. Was this another incident of providence and coincidence working in tandem?

During the rest of the sultry summer into September, the train churned across the black belt of the south to Charleston. It was difficult to maintain enthusiasm for the underground work in the heat and humidity. He sweated a river. Raucous, young rebel volunteers made life more difficult, ridiculing Dennis, telling him to "sign up like a man." Additionally, after a couple of runs to Charleston, Dennis found none of the stations had lanterns with wicks left burning. He even employed the code but got no response. Up until the battle of Manassas the use of the forged documents had proved effective. So effective, in fact, that once when in route to Memphis, Dennis overheard two railroad financial officers in a discussion that left him alarmed, but a little amused. The men kept track of all freight, including slaves. They casually noted the name of a slave owner, Dennis O'Brien, who came up frequently on their ledgers. Though curious, the two accountants concluded that this Dennis O'Brien must be a wealthy planter who bought a lot of slaves from the well-known dealer N.B. Forrest. With the transport of troops becoming ever more frequent, monopolizing all space on the train, he realized it was going to be very difficult to keep the original liberation plan in effect. It was even more dangerous now that his name was recognized along the line. It was time to refocus on finding Jack.

The grind of working the unrelenting schedules on the railway was punctuated by short leaves from work. He often did not have a choice as to when. At last the opportunity came in mid-September at the eastern head of the railway, Charleston. Anticipation was not the word to describe his feeling getting off the train. There was Jack, of course, but Charleston was on his mind for more than that, there was Camille Dumond.

The chances of finding someone in particular seemed slim, but he was reminded of Douglas's admonition to have faith. Charleston was not the size of New Orleans, but the city made for a daunting search in the little time he had available. It was cotton harvest time, and despite a Union marine blockade, the city was swelling with an influx of slaves bringing cotton to market. Dennis estimated there were at least two slaves for every white person on the streets. In his official uniform, he decided to take a walk along the promenade of the high sea wall, East Battery Street. Upper class residents were strolling in the balm of the late summer evening light. Looking out over the harbor in the distance was Ft. Sumter. He tried to imagine the festive atmosphere that he had read about in the newspaper when the hostilities began. People were excited that the North was being taught a lesson. They had reacted to the bombing as if it was a grand fireworks display.

The port was choked with blockade runners. As he counted them, a merchant stepped up beside him on the seawall and informed him that they were specialized steam-propelled vessels that could outrun the enemy, carrying 500 to 2000 bales. Noticing Dennis's conductor's uniform, the man introduced himself, and a conversation ensued.

"Yes, Mr. O'Brien," the man who was a British import and export merchant named Trenholm bragged. "Without your employer, the *Memphis and Charleston* railroad, and the firms I operate, *John Fraser and Company* and its Liverpool office, the South would literally be sunk in the deep blue sea."

"How much cotton is getting through?" Dennis earnestly inquired.

"If you keep things confidential, as I know you will, we have more than thirty-five blockade runners. We are shipping twenty percent of all cotton leaving the South. In return we bring in tons of civilian and military goods."

"That is more than impressive, sir. Dare I ask what that amounts to in profits?" Dennis tried to sound important. The man raised himself to his full height and slightly puffed out his chest.

"We project more than five million dollars this year, and that is not in Confederate notes. If you should like to change professions, I would gladly make a place for you since you know the workings of the rails. A young man like you could become quite well off." The offer stunned Dennis, and he briefly entertained the idea, but could not picture himself in such a rarefied setting and circle of associates.

"Let me consider!" Dennis feigned. "I have some railway business to attend to first. Where might I find you?" The man gave Dennis a business card and then ambled down the cobblestone street, drawing in smoke from a cigar and blowing it out in a way that drew attention to himself. While following the man's departure, Dennis looked down the promenade and saw a lovely couple strolling toward him. The young woman was wearing a hooped dress, frilly and pink, twirling a matching pink parasol. The young man was wearing a loose fitting frock, stylishly loose trousers and high topped boots. They were both laughing without care. From a distance, Dennis had a faint sense of recognition.

As the couple came closer, he felt both thrilled and let down. It was, in fact, Camille Dumond, walking with a beau. She could not know it was him, dressed as he was in his conductor's outfit, or so he thought. Ten yards away from him, she stopped twirling her parasol. It was hard to describe the look she gave him. It was not a blush, nor was it a rush to greet him. She turned to the handsome young man with her and clasped his arm more tightly. Then she led him forward unhesitatingly. As she did, she said, "Brook, I want to introduce you to a friend of heart, Dennis O'Brien. He is the true gentleman I told you about that I met in New Orleans." Brook held his hand out to Dennis.

"I have heard good things about you." He said sincerely, with a slight bow. "You saw Camille through a vulnerable time in New Orleans in an honorable way."

Dennis was nonplussed, but he avoided stuttering.

"I am pleased to meet you. Brook, is it?"

"Yes, Brook Aiken."

Still uncertain how much this Brook knew about Camille's experience with him, Dennis sought only to exchange pleasantries. When she had heard enough, Camille interrupted.

"Dennis, mon tres cher, Brook and I keep nothing from each other. He knows of our summer's dalliance. As he has said, he knows you acted honorably."

Once again Brook nodded his head in the affirmative. Deflated, Dennis could not tell Camille how much he had wanted to see her – alone. He turned his face toward the harbor.

"You live in a beautiful city. I should like to visit more than once."

"But you can visit and frequently," said Brook. "I see you are an officer of the railroad. When you are in Charleston, you are ever so welcome to stay with my family. I am quite serious."

"Yes, please, Dennis, stay at the Aiken house. It is less than a thirty minute walk from here. You and Brook can escort me home, then walk together to his home. Please, I want us all to be friends, friends forevermore. As they say in France, Liberte! Egalite! Fraternite!"

Dennis began to decompress after the initial shock and disappointment of seeing Camille under these circumstances. He, after all, did not feel the kind of profound attachment for Camille that he had felt for Jane that day he saw her in Jackson Square.

"Come, walk with us," Camille said, and she enveloped his arm with hers and with her other arm enveloped Brook's as well.

As they continued down the promenade, Dennis began to feel more comfortable, even somewhat relieved. Here was Camille in a relationship that she had not been forced into by her uncle and brother. She was her own woman, she was happy. His feeling of embarrassment gave way to a sense of liberation, and he looked realistically at his situation. He had no place to stay that evening. He could seek out a hostel, but it was getting late. The waterfront was filled with ruffians, and he looked like an easy mark. Swallowing pride and surrendering reluctance, he accepted Brook's invitation. The two young men escorted Camille to her home with a gated garden and saw her to her door. As it was now dark, Brook and Dennis hurried their pace until they came to Elizabeth Street where stood the three story structure that was Brook's home. It wreaked of wealth. Entering the mansion, a maid and doorman greeted them. "Good evenin,' Massuh. Welcome home, Massuh"

"Tom, show Mr. O'Brien to sleeping quarters on the second floor. He will be our guest through tomorrow." Brook instructed the servant. "And provide him a sleeping gown, Dorcas," he asked of the maid. His manner was kind and he did not demand. It was somewhat surprising to Dennis.

He thanked Brook as graciously as he could, given the unease he felt. He also thanked the slaves. He settled into a broad four post bed. It was comfortable beyond anything he had ever felt, but he was still unsettled, given the surroundings. He was just not used to such luxury, and it had been a long and eventful day. He was soon enveloped in sleep, hugged by the feather bed mattress.

In the morning, Brook rapped lightly on his bedroom door and invited him to tour the house before breakfast. Francisco Moreno's Spanish aristocracy had dazzled Dennis. Now he'd entered another realm of the Southern elite, and this mansion put to shame the plantation houses of the Shiloh area. It was an immense three story structure with columned verandas facing Elizabeth Street. There was a large preparatory kitchen, an expansive dining room off an equally spacious parlor, several bedrooms, a carriage block, and quarters on the back lot for more than thirteen slaves. It even had its own art gallery.

When they sat down for breakfast, their acquaintance warmed. He learned that Brook was the grandson of a former governor of South Carolina, William Aiken Jr. That was a little bit potent for Dennis to absorb. He had never been this close to power, but Brook was unassuming about this and other aspects of the family and their fortune. In fact, as they continued eating, Brook treated him as an equal. He genuinely considered Dennis's association with *the Memphis and Charleston* very important. He spoke as if Dennis's job was on a plane with his own heritage. His great grandfather, William Aiken Sr. had pioneered one of the first railroads chartered in the United States, the *South Carolina Canal and Railroad Company*

Dennis complimented Brook, "Your great grandfather must have been remarkable, building that line the way he did. And he built this elegant home, too. It's a magnificent credit to him."

Brook corrected him. "Oh, no, my great grandfather did not build this residence. He purchased it and the plantation lands from a Charleston merchant and planter by the name of John Robinson. People still commonly refer to it as the Robinson House and lands."

41

———◦—

Destinations

D ennis was stunned. If this wasn't providence, nothing was. The issue now was to find out if Jack was among the slaves the Aiken family owned. Time was a factor. He had to get back to work on the *Memphis and Charleston* tomorrow night. If he did not find Jack now, the state of flux in the country might not allow him get back to Charleston to search again.

Douglas had alluded to Jesus' saying that if you have faith the size of a mustard seed, you can move mountains. In the brief time that he had been acquainted with Brook, he had proved to be a decent enough person, but in this situation there was indeed a mountain to be moved. How to explain his mission? He would know when time came, Douglas always said. He did not have to wait long.

"Dennis, I should like to take you out to the fields today. The city swelters more than the countryside. We can pick up Camille and go for a ride out to one of our plantations," Brook suggested in an offhand way.

He was speaking nonchalantly of plural lands the way Dennis would have spoken of bales of hay. Dennis had to keep his jaw from dropping. Soon after picking up Camille, the three of them were clip-clopping along a country lane in a surrey drawn by two black horses.

"Brook, you have more than one plantation?" Dennis ventured.

"Yes, my friend, we have. In fact, I should like to take you out to Jehossee Island one day. It is one of the largest rice plantations in the state, and we have more than 700 slaves there living in their own village."

"A village for slaves?" exclaimed Dennis, mind boggled. "I could never have imagined such a thing!"

"Oh, Dennis, yes, you should go there," Camille interposed. "Among the buildings there are 84 wood-frame houses, a church, a hospital, a store, and an overseer's house."

"We treat our Negroes the way God would want us to," Brook said with strangely innocent certitude. He was genuinely proud of the family's holdings, both agricultural and human, viewing them as a stewardship. Dennis masked the way he really felt about slavery, for he needed to maintain common ground in the conversation.

"I have to say, all that's quite overwhelming to me. You see, my family only has one black servant. She is all that my Irish immigrant father could acquire while he was alive." The moral absurdity of this "white" lie made him almost nauseous.

"Well, Dennis, that is nothing to be ashamed of. It's a start. My great grandfather was an Irish immigrant, too, and as you have become familiar, this grand land of opportunity and God have blessed my family immeasurably. Now that we are friends, maybe we can work something to your advantage. Are you in need of another servant?"

Dennis couldn't believe his ears. Was this mustard seeds and mountains? Was there providence and coincidence in all this? He tried not to sound skittish and continued his little lie. "Well, I had been thinking of buying an older male servant. I have savings enough. I just need to find the right stock."

"A mile from here is a small parcel of ours, only a 100 acres. There are a few of our boys working it, field hands, but trainable. You can look them over and see if there is something suitable for your needs."

Dennis had a hard time using the word "stock" and hearing this intelligent young man speak of grown black men as "boys," so he turned the conversation in a different direction.

"Well, you two, do you have any announcement to make for the foreseeable future?" He winked at Camille, and she gently bashed him with her closed parasol.

"Brook, shall we tell him?" Camille glanced at Brook for his assent, and he smiled with a slight nod of his head and turned to Dennis.

"Dennis, you should be the first to know. It was only yesterday before we encountered you on the promenade that I proposed to Camille. That is why we were filled with gaiety. Yes, we are to be married in the spring. We have not set a date, yet. We are waiting for my grandfather and mother to get back from Europe."

"Oh, and Dennis, you must come."

"I will if I can, I'd be most pleased to do that Camille."

When they got to the tract of land, Brook drew up on the reins, stepped off the surrey, and helped Camille down. While they engaged in pitching woo, Dennis stood looking out over the acreage. It was comparatively small cotton field, with a log cabin at its forested edge. There were several slaves at work, bent over picking. All he could see of the slaves were bowed heads and arms in motion.

"Excuse me, Brook, may I go look them over?"

"I'll go with you, Dennis," Brook said. "Camille, my dear, do you think you will be alright here, if we excuse ourselves a few minutes?"

Camille harrumphed, "Mon Dieu, Good Heavens, Brook! Do you not remember? I was free in New Orleans, and I have certainly been in a cotton field before. You are not leaving me behind! I can function as well as any man! Liberte, Egalite, and Fraternite!"

"She is fond of saying that, isn't she?" Brook winced good-naturedly.

He turned back to Camille, "I would never want to tame your spirit" and he quickly kissed her on the mouth. She batted him away playfully.

"I can agree. There is a girl at Shiloh I feel the same way about."

They made their way through the rows of cotton plants. Camille in her riding habit gloried at the excursion into the field. Coming upon the slaves, Brook called out to one who seemed to be acting as overseer. "Virgil, call a water break. I have a man here that is looking for a certain kind of stock. Maybe you could have everyone line up along the row."

Dennis had not felt this uncomfortable, even revolted, since he had been at Forrest's slave mart in Memphis.

"Virgil, please call out their names as he looks them all over."

With that instruction Dennis agonized even more. "Everyone line up" for an examination was an imperative that he was sure no slave ever wanted to hear. He tried to appear collected. The penetrating sun caused profuse perspiration to drip down the half-naked bodies of the slaves. He had to shield his eyes from the glare as Virgil called out their names.

"Titus! Cato! Cicero! Hector! Jeremiah! Ezekiel!"

Dennis walked down the row in front of them, but saw only young slaves. It had been too much to ask of providence. All he could hope for was a chance to return to Charleston, and go out to look among the hundreds on Jehossee Island. Brook saw the disappointment on Dennis's face and misread it.

"Don't see any that you like, Dennis? I will entertain any offer from you."

"I would not take advantage of you, Brook. If I could, I would buy them all."

"Then we can make an arrangement. I know you will stand good for it."

Standing in the glaring sun in the middle of that cotton field, things came to a head for Dennis. A summer of sweat and well-meaning deceits, the waning success on the Underground Railroad, the grinding schedule, the loss of the farm, the loss of his father, the disappointment of not finding Jane, and finally the failure to find Jack came to a bitter end. He could no longer pretend.

"Brook, I can't thank you enough for having such faith in me, but I am a fraud. I have something to admit. The servant I told you about is no slave at all and is more like a second mother to me. My father found her nearly drowned many years ago, along the banks of the Tennessee River. Her name is Beulah. I'm here looking for one particular slave. Beulah's husband. He is not here among these strong black men, so I won't trouble you anymore."

Brook stood there, looking at him with amazement.

"Are you by any chance looking for a slave with small pox scars on his face?"

Dennis returned an equally dumbfounded look. All he could do was nod his head up and down, yes.

"Ever since I was a little boy, my "Uncle" Jack has talked to me about his wife Beulah. I sat on his lap many times, and he told me the story of how they were separated. He always said that swans mate for life and that is what he and Beulah were, black swans. I promised him one day I would reunite them if I could. That you have been put together with me is providence. I have someone for you to meet."

Brook whistled loudly several times and called out: "Uncle Jack!" From the cabin at the edge of the field came a brawny white-headed black man. He stepped over row after row until he reached Brook. Dennis could see the pox marks on his face now. He looked to be at least sixty years old but still strong.

"Uncle Jack, I have something to tell you. We have found Beulah."

"Child, don't be playin' with an old man now! Tell me you be lyin."

"I made a promise to you, Uncle Jack. That promise is coming true today. I want you to meet Dennis O' Brien. He is going to take you to be with your wife."

Jack fell to his knees and gripped Brook around the waist, weeping uncontrollably.

Brook raised the old man up, and embraced him like a father.

"You will be going away from me now. Dennis will reunite you with Beulah. Come, let's go. He will take you to her where you belong."

42

Passage

There were only two options when transporting slaves by train. One was riding in a segregated passenger car while being watched over by an overseer or master. The other was to be loaded into a boxcar as cargo. Obviously, Dennis could not personally watch over Jack while acting in his capacity as conductor, so it left only the grievous alternative.

Dennis had supervised the process of loading slaves many times. It was a terrible irony that while he was working in the Underground Railroad, he had to play a part in the machinery of enslavement. It required mental detachment to accomplish the job of saving some while leaving others behind to suffer. It became even more excruciating with the transport of Jack.

Brook delivered Dennis and Jack to the station very early in the morning after signing Jack's papers over to Dennis. It had been an emotional parting between Brook and Jack at the Aiken house. Brook choked up, then wept like a child, as he personally put the obligatory foot shackles and iron neck ring on the white haired older man he knew as his Uncle Jack. That parting had been away from prying eyes. At the station both Dennis and Brook had to maintain decorum of southern norms. Brook pretended aloofness, as he handed the leading chain connected to the neck ring to Dennis. Dennis asked that his regards be given to Camille. They shook hands and exchanged a look of unspoken recognition that they would probably not see one another again. Through it all Jack showed uncommon dignity and calm, his eyes aglow with the prospect of being with Beulah.

On the platform at least 100 other slaves stood fettered in the morning sun, waiting to be loaded into three 30 foot long by seven foot wide boxcars. Profuse sweat dripped down the chests of the half-naked black men. As part of his duties recording freight, Dennis stood at the base of the ramp to count and check collar badges for each slave. He could show no favoritism for Jack, but then what favor could be shown, with the concentration of bodies crammed into confined spaces? Once loaded, it was practically standing room only in the early autumn humidity. Even Nathan Bedford Forrest might not have stood for this, but Thomas Ryan's Charleston slave mart seemed not to care about shipping slaves this way. As Jack walked up the ramp, all Dennis could do was pray for his well-being.

There were some 650 miles of rails to travel between Charleston and Corinth. With all the transfers and stops, it would be almost October when Dennis arrived home. The war was engaged fully now. Confederate soldiers were assigned to each train because bands of Union scouts were scoping the line. It was not unknown to have a Union bullet ping against the boiler of a locomotive. The threat of a boiler explosion was real.

At each stop Dennis did his best to check on Jack. Jack was always cheerful despite dire conditions. Some of the slaves had succumbed to heat exhaustion. Others had had bouts of vomiting and diarrhea. The boxcar wreaked with the smell of sickness. Dennis insisted with his superiors at Chattanooga to have a doctor check them, for losses of property would look very bad for the line. Several were taken from the train. Dennis did not know where, but he hoped that they would receive the care they needed.

At Huntsville station, the train had a three day layover, required for necessary repairs and maintenance. All slaves were offloaded and taken to a nearby creek to wash. Two escaped into the woods, but were quickly tracked down by the sheriff with the use of blood-hounds. Dennis successfully prevented them from being whipped, pleading with the law officer that damaged property did nobody any good. He began to wonder how long he could keep this up. He tele-graphed ahead to let Uncle Robert know of their projected arrival.

When they pulled into the Corinth depot on September 28th, Dennis had wired ahead, so Uncle Robert was there to meet them. He brought a buckboard with Bobby harnessed to it. They helped a weakened Jack get down the ramp, but as they did, he turned back to the slaves still aboard, giving them a wave while calling out, "Change is comin'!" A couple of men who worked with Robert came to look Jack over. They ribbed him about how he was "comin' up in the world" because he now had two slaves. He replied, "Ain't my servant, boys. Jack here belongs to my nephew Dennis."

"Well, well, well," the roundhouse men continued flippantly, "The young conductor is building an empire."

Dennis tried to brush them off, to act as if he enjoyed the teas-ing, but they continued on. "He's got his first slave. It's a start," and they walked off raucously laughing.

Little was said as they drove home. When they arrived at the Garrett's house, everyone was in the yard to greet them except Beulah. Dennis's heart sank.

"Where is Beulah? Please tell me she's alright!" Dennis pleaded.

"Don't worry," his mother said emphatically. "She is just beside herself upstairs in the carriage house. She has been preparing and re-preparing the room. She is in bloom with joy, but concerned about what she looks like after all these years. She has said "'Lawd! Lawd! Lawd!' so many times, I think she is going to usher in the Second Coming. Precious woman, precious woman."

Hearing that, Jack asked permission to get down off the buckboard.

"You don't need my permission, Jack, not now or at any other time," Dennis admonished Jack. "You are not a slave in this household."

Robert added, "You will not be treated as such by anyone here on this property." Then he pointed to where Beulah lived and urged gently. "Now go on up and see your woman."

Everyone retreated into the house as Jack went around back and stood at the base of the stairs, looking up at the room. The family stationed themselves at the windows in the house below. He seemed frozen for a minute or two, then started to climb the stairs slowly. Step by careful step, he gingerly approached the door. He knocked, then pushed it open, and stepped inside.

Early next morning Ida and Peg fixed a large breakfast for Beulah and Jack and took it up to the carriage house. They set the tray down, rapped on the door, and then skittered gleefully down the stairs. Dennis, Adam, and the girls, peeking through the curtains in the house, watched as the door opened gradually. Jack stuck his head out warily, hair white as lamb's wool. He picked up the tray in wonder, his massive biceps and large hands dwarfing the size of the platter. A broad smile broke across his pockmarked face. Beulah stepped out the door in her dressing gown, and bouncing on the balls of her feet, gave a delighted wave of thanks.

In the following days, Jack easily integrated himself into the family. His way was not with many words, speaking only when spoken to. He had an unusual accent which reflected his country of origin. When finding that Robert had begun adding a new bedroom onto the back of the house, he took over the project that had stalled numerous times due to railway work schedules. Adam helped some, but was now enrolled in one of the schools in Corinth, as were the girls. Jack was a skilled carpenter and had served in that role at the Aiken properties. In fact, it had been Jack who was largely responsible for the buildings of the slave village on Jehossee Island. He finished the addition on the house single-handedly in less than a week.

Dennis requested and was granted shorter runs on the *Memphis and Charleston*. He was primarily assigned the Corinth to Memphis route. He returned to the rail line and his clandestine efforts, but something had changed on the Underground Railroad. As it had been with the Charleston run, there were no lights left on at the depots, no furtive meet ups with those who knew the code. It was worrisome. He kept hoping to catch a glimpse of Douglas along the line, but to no avail. Then a clerk at the Memphis station hailed him. A message had come over the telegraph for him. The message was cryptic: *From the rising of the sun unto the going down of the same the LORD'S name is to be praised*. It had no sender information.

It was, of course, a scriptural reference and was probably from Douglas, but its meaning was ambiguous. Staring at it did nothing to clear up the mystery, so Dennis put it his vest pocket. At that moment two uniformed men, senior officers of the *Memphis and Charleston* stepped up from behind him and took hold of his elbows.

"Come with us. We have some questions for you," said the taller of the mustachioed men.

"If you come quietly, there will be no scene," said the short, stouter one, as he pointed to a young confederate lieutenant with his hand on a pistol.

"What do you want with me? I'm just doing my job," Dennis replied with alarm.

"We told you to come quietly. Make things easy for yourself and for us, and you can be on your way."

"But I'll miss my schedule. I have duties to perform. I will miss my train."

"We have taken care of all that," they both said in unison.

They released their hold on him and escorted him to an office above the telegraph operator. The lieutenant took a station at the bottom of the stairs. Sitting him down on a hard chair, they stood over him in an intimidating manner. For about thirty minutes, they grilled him about whether he had seen any suspicious activity at any time during his employment with the railway. He played dumb for a while, then feeling he had nothing to lose, stood up to try a deceitful offensive. All the while he was acutely aware of the documents used for forgery in the ledger he held in his hands.

"Gentlemen, in my time on the *Memphis and Charleston,* I have done everything asked of me and more. I could go about my job doing only what is expected: verifying tickets, keeping account of fares, and managing passenger seating arrangements. I ensure the safe boarding and disembarking of passengers as well as supervise the loading and unloading of cargo. I am the boss of a train crew and report irregularities to my superiors, taking instructions from yardmasters and dispatchers. Those are daily responsibilities. I take pride in my work as if I were the owner of the line. I protect the interests of planters by seeing that their stock arrives healthy and in good stead. I cooperate with the commanders of troops and put up with derisions of the soldiers. I may be young, but I am certainly not stupid nor disloyal."

As he said the words, he felt something odd happening to him, a call to southern fealty. Could he inwardly be a rebel? He certainly didn't believe in slavery, but he loved the south where he had grown up. Maybe all the things he had been through were just driving him insane. Although conflicted, he was impelled to mouth words he had heard many times. He pronounced the motto of the Confederacy.

"Deo Vindice! Under God as our Vindicator." We in the south

have to maintain solidarity. Perhaps you have heard of Governor Aiken of South Carolina? His grandson only recently promised me financial backing. You can telegraph him for confirmation. Why would I act against my own self-interest?"

The aplomb Dennis demonstrated took them aback. The two stepped out of the office for a few minutes. Dennis could see them through the glass in an animated discussion on the stairwell landing. They came back inside after an apparent resolution.

"Well, young man. You have passed the test. You are obviously a patriot. We just have one more matter to check, and that is the message in your pocket that came over the wire." Dennis handed it over to them as if it meant nothing. They each took a turn examining it.

"According to this telegram, you seem to be a religious man," the taller man said half apologetically.

The short stout man added: "Your message reads *From the rising of the sun unto the going down of the same the LORD'S name is to be praised.*" Indeed "Deo Vindice! Under God as our Vindicator."

They all went downstairs to the loading platform. The officials walked away with the young lieutenant, and he heard the taller man say half seriously, "That young man is going places. He knows the Aikens, he might own this railroad someday."

"Stranger things have happened," echoed the shorter official. "You have the advantage when you're young. He's got youth behind him, the Aikens, and God on his side."

Dennis did miss his train. It would be two hours before he would be able to take his return trip to Corinth. He leaned over with his hands on his knees, relieved, yet also ashamed for what he had mouthed aloud and the compulsion that had overtaken him.

"It is apparent that you have learned the lesson to be as "wise as the serpents," came a velvet voice from behind a pillar. Dennis nearly leaped out of his skin.

"I won't ask where you came from this time," Dennis said, trying to calm his heart. "But how can you travel alone with the way things are?" Then he noticed shackles on Douglas's bare feet.

"I am not alone." Douglas motioned to a white man on a bench beside the pillar. "He is a friend of the cause, pretending to be my owner."

"The telegram. What does it mean?"

Douglas replied. "*From the rising of the sun unto the going down of the same.* The sun rises in the east. It goes down in the west. The route to the west is the one you will pursue from now on. You will understand when the time comes. Now may the LORD'S name be praised and may HE be with you."

The interrogation had been somewhat terrorizing, and his encounter with Douglas had been less than satisfying. Dennis's nerves settled as he went about his duties there in Memphis, preparing for the journey on the next train back to Corinth. It was unusual that there were no slaves to board on this one. He asked the stationmaster why. He replied, "Nathan Bedford Forrest has outfitted a whole battalion of cavalry at his own expense and is riding reconnaissance against the Yankees. He has turned over the operation of his slave trading business to one of his brothers. It has not fared nearly as well under his management. Far fewer slaves are being shipped from Memphis by his firm with this war on."

Dennis remembered the fierceness displayed by Forrest against his own partner the day he rescued Elizabeth. With that attitude, Dennis could see trouble was in store for anyone that crossed Forrest's path, and how much more so with a battalion of cavalry at his command.

Dennis meditated on Douglas's message as he traveled home to Corinth. The stress of the trip took a toll on him especially this time. Refusing supper, he went upstairs and flopped on the bed next to Adam's. He slept fitfully and a dream unfolded. In the dream the sun was rising in the east, and it was going down in the west. He saw a trail; it led through Texas and beyond. He slept late while everyone else had breakfast.

He awoke to the sound of pounding on the door and the screaming of the females in the household. Disoriented, he ran down stairs, expecting armed men had come to get him. Instead, standing in the doorframe, was his brother John.

43

Express

Yes, there stood John in the doorway. Twenty years old now, he was wiry, about five foot ten. He wore a broad brimmed, high crowned hat that made him look taller. When he took it off, it revealed his normally dark brown hair was sun-bleached, and his face was so tanned and dry there were crow's feet at the corners of his eyes. He was wearing a leather shirt and pants with fringes along the outer seams and high topped, square toed boots with spurs. He'd left a strawberry roan grazing in the Garrett's front yard.

Dennis waited at the foot of the stairs while everyone else mobbed John at the door. Ida was the first to embrace him. She hugged him long and hard, blurting out and sobbing about the loss of Da and the farm. John broke down, apologizing profusely for not having been home when he passed. They both lamented the loss of the farm and resolved to go on somehow with God's help.

Next Aunt Peggy, who had not seen him since he was seventeen, slowly peeled Ida away from John and dabbed the tears trailing down his cheeks. When the grief had subsided, Adam jumped him like a wildcat, shouting his name. The little girls were standoffish and shy, not remembering him well. Finally Beulah took her turn. She pulled him maternally toward her and kissed him tenderly on both cheeks, commenting on how much he had grown.

"Where's Denny?" John said, faking that he could not see Dennis only steps away.

"So the Pony Express Rider comes home!" Dennis, stepped forward and stood face to face with John. He was now a few inches taller than John.

"Let me correct you. The Pony Express is officially called the Central Overland California and Pike's Peak Express Company or C.O.C & P.P. It's unofficially known by its riders as "Clean Out of Cash and Poor Pay."" Dennis laughed, and they looked at one another for a few moments somewhat awkwardly. Finally they embraced with the kind of bear hug that Uncle Robert had taught them as boys.

The women repaired to the kitchen to make a spread of food for John. Adam took the roan around back and put the horse away in an empty stall. He told Jack about John and urged him to go to the house to meet his brother. Jack stood respectfully at the back door. Dennis brought him inside. John stood up, his leather coat fringes dangling, strode across the room, and shook Jack's hand.

"John, I want to introduce you to a new member of the household. Beulah's husband Jack. Jack..." It dawned on Dennis that he didn't know if Jack or Beulah had a surname, so he didn't know what to say. Jack, recognizing the situation, quietly said, "Aiken. Mos' black folk take the name of their owner."

"What is your African name, Jack? Maybe we should call you by that."

"I don' think tha's a good idea. White folks don't like that. It would not be good for me or you. Aiken is good."

"Well, tell me the name anyway, Jack,"

"In Yoruba language, my name is Agbara. It means strength."

"It's a good name, Jack, but if you think we should, we'll call you Jack Aiken. I know you had affection for Brook, and Brook loved you."

When Uncle Robert got home from the roundhouse, he was overjoyed to see John. They took a walk down the street with Dennis and Adam. During the jaunt, John explained that each ride on the Pony Express had been an arduous journey of 2,000 miles. There were 80 riders, 184 stations, and over 400 horses. Each rider rode 75 to 100 miles at a stretch in a day with a change of horses every 15 miles. There was a rest, while another rider took over in a relay. Then another hundred mile stretch, another rest while the next rider took over, and so on and so on until San Francisco was reached. Little food was available at some stations along the way. There were times across desert without water for neither man nor horse. He related how his horse had reared near Julesburg, Colorado. Thrown onto the rocky ground, he just escaped being bitten by a rattlesnake. There had been brutal encounters with Paiute Indians at Pyramid Lake, Nevada. One of his friends had been shot with an arrow and had ridden all the way to Sacramento, California with the projectile imbedded in his arm. In San Francisco, John found a dime novel with embellished stories of the Pony Express. He and his fellow riders guffawed at the accounts.

Dennis was taken with all his brother's feats until they started walking back to the house. John inquired, "So, Denny. What have you been up to? I hear you have a nice comfortable job with the railroad."

John was so flippant. Dennis was crestfallen. Just yesterday at the Memphis Station, he had been forcibly interrogated and threatened with arrest. For nearly a year, he had essentially risked all, trying to free slaves. It wasn't that he did not think John had undergone hardships, it was that John thought he was the only one who had endured them. John did not even ask about his and his father's time in New Orleans.

"Yeah, it's pretty happy-go-lucky," Dennis sighed with resignation, not feeling he should proclaim what he had been through. It had been nearly two years since his brother left in a fever, full of himself. John had not changed, only grown more so.

"Well, maybe someday you'll get to have the kind of experiences I've had. It will sure make you grow up fast," John condescended.

That statement stung. He was glad he was scheduled to leave on his next run. Trying not to show his anger, Dennis bade goodbye to them all. He turned around in the street and walked away briskly.

"Must be nice to have such a cushy job!" John called after him, laughing.

He stalked back to the house so mad, he spit every few yards. When home he spoke briskly to his mother, telling her, too, that he had to get to his next run. She could tell something was wrong and tried to pry it out of him. He brushed her off, went upstairs, changed into a fresh uniform, and walked to the station.

When he got to the station, he saw a small militia had just boarded, most of them in homemade butternut uniforms. They were commanded by none other than Captain Joseph Devine, Nellie's father. He was just about to step aboard when he saw Dennis approach in his conductor's uniform.

"You look familiar to me, young man," Devine said, keeping military demeanor.

"Yes, sir, my family lived near Hamburg, not far from your plantation. My name is Dennis O'Brien."

"Of course, your father was with me in Mexico under my first command as brevet lieutenant; a good man your father, saved some men. We sometimes met at the tavern in Hamburg. I gave your father advice about that little farm of yours. Sorry to know what the storm did to you all, but it looks like you have bounced back. How is your father?"

"Deceased, sir, consumption took him over a year ago."

"Accept my condolences then. As I said, he was a good man."
Devine seemed to let down some of his military bearing.

"I went to school with your daughter at Shiloh School. How is
Nellie?"

"Off at the Academy in Clarksville, Tennessee."

Dennis's heart leaped, but he calmly inquired. "I have often wondered why some go to Clarksville when we have an academy here in
Corinth."

"It is a preferred school for young women, and she has a friend
from Shiloh School who is also attending there. Winningham is her
name, I believe."

The safety inspection by the crew was finished, and they gave
the go ahead to Dennis. Captain Devine stepped up on the train.

"I will join you aboard shortly, Captain."

Meanwhile back at the Garrett's after supper, Uncle Robert took
John aside out by the stalls. They talked about the horses for a while.
John explained the strawberry roan had been given to him by the
C.O.C. & P.P. in appreciation for his service with the company. He
also explained that he had been let go early. The company was experiencing financial difficulties because the telegraph lines were nearly
complete, and it was not viable to keep all riders employed. As he
spoke of it, he seemed a bit deflated. Uncle Robert, having listened
carefully to everything John related, began shaking his head:

"A little disappointed you didn't get to stay on to the last? I know
what that's like. I'll tell you the story about a job I loved and lost
some time, but you can't feel sorry for yourself. You could take a page
out of your brother's book. Dennis has been through quite a lot,
John. It's clear you don't realize that."

"Well sure, I know Da died and all, we're all broke up about that,
but you got him a nice job on the railroad, didn't you, and he's doin'
real good."

"You don't understand what he went through with your Da. I

know your Ma didn't tell you everything in her letters. She thought you should be care free. You should ask Dennis about everything when he gets back. About the storm, New Orleans, and the asylum. And while you're at it, get him to tell you about the bushwhacking, how it was that Jack came to be with us, the risks he's been taking. Oh, and Dennis has saved most of his wages to put toward buying you all a house." John scratched his head thoughtfully, and said he would take his Uncle's advice. Then Uncle Robert added, "I believe your brother has a leave coming to him. Why don't you take a ride up to Shiloh with him? It'll do you both good."

On board Dennis walked the length of the train, hopping from car to car, but with the soldiers he took no tickets. Their fares were covered by the Confederate government. In the first coach car sat Captain Devine. He nodded to Dennis as he went past. However, there was the usual taunting as he passed by some of the cadre of confederates. When entering the next car, he recognized boys from Shiloh. Some sniggered as he went by. Among them were Bradley Sowell, Patrick Spain, George Howell, Clifton Jones, and James Wood and the Wicker brothers. Then he came to a young immaculately uniformed second lieutenant who stood up and commanded everyone to stop the harassment.

"Dennis O'Brien is performing a valuable government service. Leave him alone!" commanded James Barnes. The train lurched, and both of them steadied themselves. Dennis approached James.

"I see you got what you wanted, James. Do you remember challenging me in a mock duel back in Shiloh School? You're actually a real lieutenant now. How did that happen?"

"Captain Devine came up to Shiloh and recruited a bunch of us for the Corinth Rangers. When it came to electing officers, I got voted as second lieutenant."

"Congratulations! You have promotion written all over you," Dennis sincerely complimented. "Next time I see you, you'll have risen through the ranks. Did you get to see Nellie?"

"Yes, I did. When I was able to assist Captain Devine in recruiting a bunch of us boys, he warmed to me and invited me to his house. I asked for her hand again, and he said he would consider it after she graduated from the academy in Clarkesville. I saw her off at Eastport just last month. Oh, and yes, for sure. Jane is up there, too. Who knows what the future holds for all of us?"

44

Butternuts

These boys from Shiloh in their home made butternut gray uniforms, part of the Corinth Rangers, were all headed to an assignment to who knows where. Memphis would be a layover for sure, but that would not be their final destination. Too much fighting was taking place over a wide area. Dennis felt a pang. That feeling of being left behind. Sure, some of them had razzed him, but for the most part it was good natured camaraderie. He thought about their personalities.

Bradley Sowell was painfully quiet, with a permanent blonde cowlick on the back of his head. Patrick Spain was a handsome fellow with jet black hair but not given to vanity. George Howell, as stocky as a log, had been an earnest student and had requested Dennis's tutoring. Clifton Jones was the best shot he had ever seen and helped on the trap line once. James Wood worked hard at his father's cotton gin during harvest and enjoyed a good laugh. He wondered where others were now. What about Frank Walker and the Wicker brothers?

Dennis had some soul searching to do. He had been through

much with his father, living war vicariously through him and had the knowledge that the asylums were populated with veterans. That was enough to make him never want to see war, much less participate in it. Yet deep down he wanted to be with these boys with whom he had grown up. He abhorred slavery and its worst manifestations, but he loved the south. He had never been outside of it and felt tied to the land and its people by birth and upbringing. There were more than twice as many people in the north. With war on, that had the effect of making the north seem like a dark storm cloud threatening death and destruction. It brought to mind what Francisco Moreno had said to him: *Home is where the heart is.*

When the Corinth Rangers got off the train, Dennis was depressed. On the way back to Corinth, he was unusually inattentive, and some passengers actually had to call out to him to punch their tickets. At Collierville, a telltale lamp was still lit at the station, and he took no note of it. He watched the passing landscapes in a daze. The forests looked like standing regiments of soldiers, the sky was denim blue. When he arrived at Corinth, he set about preparation for the next run, not remembering he had been granted a week's leave. He had to be shaken out of his state of distraction.

"Denny! Denny!" Uncle Robert urgently patted his cheek. "What's come over you?"

"Oh, nothing, I'm just a little more tired than usual," Dennis blinked repeatedly.

"Well son, you ought to be gettin' some good rest tonight. Your brother John wants you to go with him to Shiloh tomorrow."

Uncle Robert rarely addressed him as "son" and he recalled the way his brother had talked down to him. It irritated Dennis, and he retorted, "Oh yeah, I'm sure that will be fun."

"What's the matter, Denny? Your eyes are so bleary. There's somethin' you're not sayin'." Uncle Robert softened. "You wanna tell your Uncle about it?"

Dennis sighed. "I'm tired of working the rail line, I guess. It's been non-stop. Maybe I'm not cut out for this in the long run."

"That's not like you, Denny. You've always been able to do anything you set your mind to. The railroad could take care of you for life. What's really goin' on?"

"I don't really know. I guess watching them going off in their uniforms, I wanted to go with them."

"By them, you mean?"

"The Corinth Rangers, especially the boys from Shiloh who are among them. I feel odd, like a horse of a different color. Miss Sornby warned me not to go off soldiering, but it looks like everybody I ever knew is going off to fight. Maybe I should go, too."

"Well, Denny, the horse doesn't feel odd because he's a different color. Just take a look at Bobby. That dapple gray is about as odd as it gets with horses. He has never shown aggression to anyone except that bushwhacker. And why? He was protecting his family and did it instinctively. Like him, you'll know what to do if the time comes."

The next morning John rousted Dennis out of bed. He aggressively pulled off his blankets, full of noise and bluster. Dennis would have liked to take it easy for the week he had leave, but detected there were things bothering his brother. For one, John could not openly admit it, but he needed to lay to rest the loss of his father and the farm. After breakfast, they set out for the cemetery on Bobby and the strawberry roan. Arriving at Mr. Sullivan's little farm, John was reluctant to dismount, so Dennis slid off and tied off Bobby's reins to the iron fence that surrounded the little graveyard. He offered to take John's reins, prompting John to get off his horse.

John stood speechless at the gate, reluctant to go in, so Dennis took the lead, walking past the Sullivan family graves to where their father's tombstone stood. He placed his hand atop the marble and patted it gently. John's face was gaunt as he looked at where their father was buried. He looked at Dennis. He looked at the ground. He looked at Dennis and looked at the ground again. He dropped to his knees, and from within him arose a primal groan, "Da! Da! Oh, Da!" and falling prostrate, he pounded the earth.

Dennis waited for his brother's grief to subside. Finally, John rose, and they stood before the stone together.

"Where do you think Da is, Denny? Is he in heaven or hell?"

"He's resting, John. That's what R.I.P. means. Rest in Peace."

"Yeah, that's what Ma always said. A God of love doesn't torture people. Remember that Scripture she always quoted? "Whatsoever thy hand findeth to do, do *it* with thy might; for *there is* no work, nor device, nor knowledge, nor wisdom, in the grave, whither thou goest."

"So it stands to reason," Dennis joked, pointing downward, "If there is no work, no device, he's not down there somewhere shoveling coal to keep the hell fires burning."

"Nope," John pointed heavenward. "And if there's no knowledge or wisdom, he's not up there right now reading books." They both chuckled, then went silent again.

Never great huggers, they slapped one another on the back and mounted their horses. When they arrived at the crossroads about mid-day, Dennis described the whole bushwhacking episode in detail, how Bobby had saved them. John reached over to the dapple gray and patted him on the neck.

"This horse was the best investment Da ever made," John said heartily.

"The Irish know their horses," Dennis agreed.

They were halfway to Hamburg now, and John seemed to be reconciled to his grief. As they rode along, John told Dennis more about his Pony Express experience. This time it was more reflective. "Denny, you should have seen the buffalo. Millions of them are out there on the plains. At one place in Kansas Territory, the mass of them was so great that you could have walked on their backs for miles."

"How did you make it through them all?"

"The herds in the valleys got sullenly out of my way, turning and staring stupidly, sometimes only a few yards distant. On one occasion in the hills, some big bulls saw me as a strange threat and started at full speed toward me, stampeding and bringing with them the numerous smaller herds through which they passed, pouring down on me in one immense compact mass, mad with fright and as irresistible as an avalanche. Reining my horse, I waited until the front of the mass was within 50 yards. I carefully aimed my gun and with a few well directed shots split the herd, sending it pouring off in two streams to my right and left. When all had passed me, they stopped, and apparently satisfied, simply returned to grazing."

Dennis suspected his brother was spinning a yarn, but it was a gripping story. After relating the tale, John was energized. He challenged Dennis to race. Dennis had not ridden in a while, so was hesitant. John took the end of his reins and purposely whipped Bobby's hip. The gelding bolted ahead, almost throwing Dennis off., but he quickly recovered, leaning forward to achieve full gallop ahead on the road. John quickly caught up to Dennis on the roan and easily passed him. John was an exceptional rider after his time on the Pony Express, and the roan was in top shape. He continued to outdistance Dennis on Bobby by several lengths, then by 50 yards, then out of sight in a cloud of dust. Dennis slowed Bobby, for it made no sense to try and catch his brother. When they finally caught up to where John and the roan had stopped, they dismounted and walked the horses to cool them down.

"You know, Denny, I can't stay here. I've seen too much of the country!" John exhaled invigorated.

"I figured as much. When do you plan to leave?"

"That depends on what happens when we get to Shiloh!" John smiled broadly.

"Does it have to do with a certain girl with long blonde hair?"

"How did you possibly guess?"

"Well, let me see. As a participant in the delivery of the U.S. mail, you somehow found time to send her a letter."

"Yeah, I sent and received more than one letter. We're getting hitched, Abby knew I was coming back. I should've mailed ma about it and all. Now I have to figure out how to break it to her that we plan to wed."

The news dumbfounded Dennis.

"Yep. We want to go west and settle. They're goin' to be practically giving land away. Congress is talking about what they call the Homestead Act. Don't worry, it's comin'. Just wait and see. You should go and get you some land, too."

"Hold on, hold on. Plan to wed!? I'm just finding out you are going to marry Abby Davis, and in the same breath, you suddenly want me to leave here and go west. I don't think so."

"Come on, Denny, you've got to think bigger. If you could only see how vast this country is! There is so much land. You can take your pick of acres and stake your claim!"

"What about Ma, Adam, and Jack and Beulah?"

"They can go, too. Once this war is over, even negroes will have no problem owning land."

"That's assuming a lot, John. This war is just getting started."

"That's why I'm saying leave now. The sooner the better!"

All this was too much to consider. They remounted and urged the horses on. When they reached Hamburg, they stopped for a meal at the tavern. As evening approached, they rode out to where the farm used to be. The sight was ghastly to behold. It was a veritable cliff down to the water. All that remained of the land was a portion of the road that had gone down to where the cabin had once stood. There was not a splinter of the cabin or barn left. John did not seem moved by the sight.

"See what I mean! That's our inheritance down there. Are the O'Brien's going be catfish farmers? Come harvest time, we'll just bale 'em up!"

The absurdity of his brother's joke made Dennis laugh.

"Well, maybe you're right, John. The west may be the place for a young man to go."

They bedded down for the night near Lick Creek. Having packed some food and coffee in their saddle bags, they built a fire and enjoyed the warmth it gave in the cool crisp air of the Tennessee autumn. When they awoke next morning, Dennis was a little stiff from hard riding the day before. John, however was quite spry and tended to the horses while Dennis roused himself. After breakfast, they rode north up the Hamburg road, past McCullers's and Larkin Bell's properties. Young men were noticeably absent, and like the year before, the orchards were neglected. They turned west at Sarah Bell's cotton field where even here there was no activity. The cotton was already picked and no slaves present, but John perked up. Just ahead lay Davis's wheat field, and Abby Davis was running toward them. Handing the reins to Dennis, John flew out of the saddle and sprinted toward her.

45

Ashes

Dennis felt like a fifth wheel when Abby leaped into John's arms, and he swung her round and round. It reminded Dennis of being with Jane in the hay field when she and Dennis were 16. The difference was Abby and John were kissing, they were in love, and there was no question how it would turn out. Dennis waited for their intimate moment to end, then came forward with the horses and dismounted. Abby tore herself away from John to greet him.

"Dennis, Dennis. It's been so long since I've seen you. We're going to be kin now!" She embraced him. "You are the best brother-in-law a girl could ever hope for," and she kissed him on the cheek.

"I feel the same way about you, Abby," he said wistfully and looked down at his boots. "Congratulations."

"Oh, I see, the two of us together makes you think about Jane." She lifted his chin. "There's hope for you two yet. There's still time. Just look at me and your brother."

"Still time? The last time I talked with her on the day of the picnic she was headed to Belle Meade for the cotillion there."

"Things changed Dennis. Look how things changed around here after the storm. It's almost a ghost community."

That was what James Barnes had said. Things changed after the storm. He could only wonder about the details that took Jane to New Orleans. He put it out his mind; obviously, Abby had.

"I'd like to go up to the school and see Miss Sornby. Is she still teaching?'

"No, Dennis, she's gone. Went to Missouri. You need to prepare yourself. The school burned down."

The pit of his stomach clinched. The best months of his young life had been spent at Shiloh School. Not just learning, but teaching other kids alongside Jane. How much he had wanted to see Miss Sornby again.

"Burned down!? Why!? How did it happen!? When!?"

"Nobody knows for certain. It happened just before school was supposed to start. Whoever it was wanted to burn down the church, too. Some say it was Unionists from the other side of the river who hate Shiloh because it's pro slavery."

"Who do you think it was?"

"I think it was just some kid who hated going to school and church," Abby said unconcerned, more starry-eyed about John than caring about what had happened to the school.

"You can find out about all that later!" John said impatiently. Abby was losing interest, too. It was clear the young lovers wanted to be alone and there were a multitude of things to sort out. Not the least was how this was going over with Abby's folks. Dennis did not want to be anywhere near that possibly volatile situation.

After spending a few more minutes with John and Abby, who were oblivious to him, Dennis rode off at a trot, calling back to them, "I'll be back before long!"

Dennis reached Barnes field. It did not appear anyone was currently living at the house. As he passed it, knowing James was gone soldiering, he felt forlorn. As he rode on, the feeling became accentuated. He came to the place where the boys had circled him that day so long ago, bullied him, and broke his glasses. He found himself oddly wishing that the boys who had been his nemeses should be here: James Barnes, Allen McCuller, Larry Tilghman, Joe Hagy, and Bruce and Will Wicker.

When he got to the crossroads of the Hamburg-Purdy and the Pittsburg Landing-Corinth roads, there was no traffic. There were no negroes driving wagons loaded with cotton to Pittsburgh Landing. Had anyone around Shiloh even harvested cotton this year? Of course, there were no students going to or from school, no lone riders. Nobody. Downright unnatural.

Turning south on the Corinth-Pittsburg Landing Road, Dennis got off and walked Bobby. In the distance he could see the log church, but no schoolhouse across the road. His heart ached at the emptiness of the site. In the little cemetery next to where the school had been, there were fresh mounds of earth. He could not bring himself to look at who had recently been buried there. When he reached the site where the school had stood, there was nothing left except a blackened mass of burnt wood. Stricken, he stepped gingerly into the pile of cinders. They crunched underfoot and an acrid smell rose. His foot hit something hard, and he reached down to pull out a slate board that somehow had escaped intact, despite the heat of the fire. He continued to kick about in the ashes and found a few more. He wondered if among these were the ones that he and Jane had used to chalk their names. While he was preoccupied, someone came up from behind.

"You there, would you know who might be responsible for this?" came the commanding tone of the preacher.

Dennis recalled some interaction with the preacher while tutoring inside the church with Jane, but for the most part, he knew little of this man of the cloth. Still Dennis was glad see him and encouraged that he was on the scene.

"I have no idea who would want to do this." Dennis said bewildered.

"You don't think I know who you are, do you?" the preacher asked.

"I hope you do, sir"

"Oh yes, I remember that day in the school yard when you as a skinny kid mocked me and the sacrament of baptism."

"Well, if that's the way you took it, I'm truly sorry, but "Imitation is the sincerest form of flattery." Or so said Charles Caleb Cotton."

The preacher softened. "How is it you know of the cleric Cotton? Of his maxims, that is one of my favorites."

"I have read books," Dennis said ruefully.

"I certainly hope you have read the Good Book."

"Can't say I have memorized it, but my mother and a preacher I know have taught me the essence of it." He reached out his hand to shake the preacher's hand.

"Good. Then keep it up."

Dennis and the preacher continued their conversation about the destruction of the school, the departure of Miss Sornby, and began to touch on the subject of the war. The preacher lamented.

"Recently, I have pondered on James the 4th chapter: *From whence come wars and fightings among you?* Three of our boys came back to us, you know. They are over there now in the cemetery. Died in a useless skirmish. I wish I had not been so vehement, encouraging them to pick up the sword. I should have been 'no part of the world' as the Lord said. After the deaths of those boys, their families up and moved away. Others are thinking the same. I have little congregation left."

The preacher was bereft, and his shoulders drooped. They walked across to the church together, with Dennis holding the little stack of slates. Dennis stepped inside and placed them on a bench. There was a scorched spot in the corner where someone had attempted to start a fire to burn this place down, too. He offered to help scour it off, but the preacher said to leave it as a reminder of the temporary condition of things made with hands, that the Lord did not dwell in handmade temples. He invited Dennis to Sunday services. Dennis thanked him, but said he had to be on his way back to Corinth.

He trotted back to the Davis property. Upon arriving, to his relief, he saw John and Abby and Mr. and Mrs. Davis standing in front of the cabin, all looking peaceful. If there had been any upset about John and Abby marrying, they had become reconciled to the situation. Mr. Davis said he had long ago become fond of John when the O'Brien's had run the trap line through the Davis property. He was happy to have John as his son-in-law. It was typical that John had everything fall in place. Of course, John wanted Dennis to break the news to their mother.

"She'll take it better from you than me." John coaxed. "You ride on ahead of us, and tell Ma we're getting married."

"You have got to be kidding me! Ride on ahead of you! What does that mean?"

"I mean, that you go break the news while I stay up here. The Davises are looking after the Barnes' place while they are gone to Arkansas. I will be staying over there until we get married in a couple of weeks."

"You know it's not that simple. Ma will never agree to setting foot inside that church. You'll never change, will you? You'll let me take the brunt of the explosion when she finds out about you and Abby! Thanks a lot!"

Mr. and Mrs. Davis just smiled. Abby, batted her brown eyes like a fawn and begged "Please." He succumbed to her humorous pleading and agreed to break the news to everyone back in Corinth. John said he could stay at the Barnes' house with him that night, but that was just too strange for Dennis. It was midafternoon. He reckoned with a little extra effort, he and Bobby could ride to Corinth by a little after sundown this early day in November of 1861. He remounted and turned Bobby around while saying good bye.

It took longer than he expected to get back to the Garrett house. All were down for the night. After putting Bobby away, he went directly to bed himself wrestling personally with the things that the preacher had quoted from scripture. *From whence come wars and fightings among you?*

46

Farewell

Dennis awoke to the sound of an ax; Jack was chopping wood at the back of the Garrett's property. From the window, he could see there was already more than a cord stacked. It would certainly be needed this winter. Over Friday night the mild weather had turned cold, evidenced by the vapor from Jack's breath. Adam stirred, yawning and rubbing his eyes. Dennis sat down next to him. With the intention of letting him be first to know about John's engagement, he quietly broke the news. Adam went bolt upright.

"Married! John's getting married!?"

Before Dennis could explain further, Adam leapt out of bed and ran downstairs screaming, "John's getting married! John's getting married!"

It was not the way Dennis imagined breaking the news to his mother, but there was no escaping it now. Maybe this was the best and quickest way for all of the family to receive the startling news.

"Why didn't you tell me about this before you left?" Ida complained.

"Why are you looking at me, Ma? John should have told you. I didn't know until we got up to Shiloh."

"Now don't tell me that. You boys must have been in cahoots to keep this from me!" and she began to weep.

Dennis felt no compunction to comfort his mother. He sat down at the breakfast table head between his hands, waiting for his mother to become reconciled to the idea. She grilled him with repetitive questions. He told her over and over the questions were better answered by John and Abby themselves. She finally stopped when he told everyone that the school had been burned down. She sobered, thankful that nobody had been hurt, sorrowful that Miss Sornby was gone. Then she started up again about John. Exasperated, Dennis went out back to help Jack stack wood. Adam followed, still pestering him for more information. Jack just smiled.

With winter closing in, making the trip up to Shiloh for the wedding would be quite an effort. Dennis had to keep working. His leave was almost over and he would not get another one for a couple of months. He figured he would just have to miss the wedding. For all the sibling animosity that existed between them, Dennis would have liked to stand next to his brother during the nuptials. Uncle Robert had time off coming and he could serve as best man.

The anxieties proved to be for nothing. The day before Dennis had to return to work, John and Abby rode up to the Garrett's house on the strawberry roan. Anxious to move ahead with their plans, they had not wanted to wait two weeks to wed. The very next day after Dennis left, they were married by the preacher at Shiloh Church, recruiting an old man who lived near the church as best man. The household was burgeoning. It was propitious that Jack had finished the addition to the house. John and Abby were quickly absorbed into the family and its routines.

As Dennis returned to his duties on the rail line, snow flurries dusted Corinth. They melted quickly when the sun appeared.

He was traveling east to Huntsville, Alabama this second week in November. At Huntsville, he picked up the latest newspaper. There was an account about a significant battle that had taken place at Belmont, Missouri on November 7, 1861. Although the paper proclaimed a southern victory, a Union brigadier general named U.S. Grant had inflicted serious losses before withdrawing. There were more than 600 casualties on each side.

There was a dramatic uptick in military activity in Huntsville, Alabama. The entire train back to Corinth was packed with confederate soldiers, even the boxcars. At Memphis they would transfer and head north on the *Memphis, Clarksville & Louisville Railroad* to a line of defenses that ran from Columbus, Kentucky to Nashville, Tennessee. Dennis wished his job allowed him to go to Clarksville with a chance to see Jane, but no opportunity came.

Activity on the Underground Railroad became nil along the *Memphis and Charleston* line. No lights were left burning in the daytime at depots anywhere along the way. He wished that Douglas would make an appearance, for he had not seen him in a long time, and he needed guidance.

Dennis was away from Corinth for almost two weeks after John and Abby arrived. He had a brief stopover at Corinth on the way back from Huntsville, but it was not enough time to go to the Garrett's. He talked to his Uncle Robert at the station, however. Big decisions had been made while he was gone.

"The scene of the world is always changing, Denny!" Robert began, "While you've been gone, John and Abby announced they want to go west as soon as they can."

"Well, that sounds just like my brother and Abby."

"Prepare yourself Denny. They want Adam, Jack and Beulah to go with them, and your ma. They figure you would want to stay here."

That stopped Dennis in his tracks. He felt like dropping his duties, and heading for the house to argue that it wasn't the right time. Then he remembered Douglas's last communication: "From the rising of the sun unto the going down of the same. The sun rises in the east. It goes down in the west. The route to the west is the one you will pursue from now on. You will understand when the time comes." He understood. The time had come. This had to be providence. He said so to his uncle. His uncle laughed, "Well, there is Divine providence, and then there's providin' for the trip. It's fine for them to want to go, but the means is yet to be decided."

"Well, I am all for it. Have them count all the money we have. There is some reward left, money I made in New Orleans, and much of the money I've made on the railway that I have put away for the house. All that should amount to several hundred dollars in hard coin, not confederate notes. That should be enough to get all of them to Texas, even farther, but I have to keep Bobby."

"No worries there, Denny. I'll contribute by buying them a mule."

"Tell them all I can't wait to get back to talk about it. Hopefully, I should be back in a few days, but with all the troops being transported, it has upset the schedule. There are delays. The trains are so packed that soldiers are sometimes riding on top of the cars."

"I know, and I hope all goes well with your trip, Denny. But they can't wait long. The winter is closing in and so are the developments of this war. There is talk of drafting all healthy men from 18 to 35. Your brother is 20 years old and needs to get away from here if he is not to be forced into a confederate uniform. You should be okay, exempted because of your work on the rail line."

When the train left Corinth Station, Dennis's mind raced with the ramifications of this newest development. His anxiety increased with every delay along the way. The locomotive experienced problems and was taking longer stops for maintenance. All seemed chaos. Three days turned into four, then five. When he finally got back to Corinth, it was the first week in December. He was off for two days.

He did not find his uncle at the roundhouse, so he ran that morning all the way to the Garrett's. Fearful about the weather and not knowing when Dennis would arrive, they had grievously prepared to leave without seeing him, but he got there just in time. Everyone was relieved to see him as they were about to get underway. The covered wagon was packed and ready to roll with a new white canvas bonnet, and a mule was harnessed to the wagon. John was on the strawberry roan. Jack was at the wagon reins with Adam next to him. Beulah, Ida, and Abby were ensconced in the back of the wagon. Robert, Peggy and the girls were all standing on the porch, having said their goodbyes already.

When they got underway, Dennis rode with them for several miles west of town. As they rolled along, everyone spoke of grand prospects for the future. John had their sights set on the frontier of Texas, but it was not certain where they would end up. Everyone urged Dennis to come out west as soon as possible. When it came time for him to ride back to Corinth, they stopped, and the women got off the wagon. They each embraced Dennis in turn with tears streaming down their cheeks. Dennis remounted, reined Bobby around and started back for Corinth. As he did, snow began to fall.

47

———— ⬧◉⬧ ————

Letters

When he got back, Uncle Robert, Aunt Peggy, and the girls were subdued. With much of the family gone away, probably forever, it was haunting. Every time he turned a corner, sat down at the dinner table, went through the yard to the carriage house, there was a sense that his mother and Adam, John and Abby, or Jack and Beulah were going to somehow appear. Their absence left him with an empty feeling similar to when he stood among the ashes of Shiloh school.

Back on the train, his mood changed. With less obligation to family, it dawned on him he had other choices. Thoughts he had never entertained seriously came to the fore in a kind of mania. With the Underground Railroad at a virtual standstill, he mulled over discontinuing the work. He was less resolute, with so little contact from Douglas. He reasoned maybe life would be better if he tried to get on with his uncle at the roundhouse. Maybe he could go back to New Orleans and work for *Speake and McCreary, Wholesale and Commission Merchants,* working his way up in the business and making lots of money. Somewhere he still had the card that Mr.

Trenholme had given him in Charleston. Maybe there was still an opportunity to be part of the blockade running company of *John Fraser and Company*. He could make even bigger money and maybe get to see England. What about the financial backing Brook had offered? There were no limits.

When he got back to Corinth, he dropped by the post office to get mail and was handed an envelope. It stopped all his wild thoughts of business. It was a letter to Abby, come too late and forwarded to Corinth from Pittsburg Landing. It was from Jane in Clarkesville. He took it home and put it on his bed and stared at it. He paced back and forth. After finally convincing himself to do it, he slowly pulled the letter out from its envelope. There, curling across the page, was the cursive script that was so familiar. He touched it as he read it, knowing her fingers had also touched the page.

"Dear Abby,

How much I wish I could come to Shiloh to share the joy of your marriage to Dennis's brother John...

He stopped reading. She actually had referenced him in the first sentence. He cautiously continued, forbidding himself to read no more than one sentence at a time. His heart began to race.

...to stand at your side as your maid of honor, with Dennis on the other side as his brother's best man. I miss him. All the young men I have met

since then do not measure up to him. I remember the day he swung me around in the meadow. I did not really understand how much he meant to me. I cannot come to be with you because they are training us as nurses. There are very many sick men brought here. War is a terrible thing. Nearby at Ft. Donelson, there are thousands of troops ready to fight the Yankees. Life was so serene in the days we were in school. Maybe this war will be over soon. I hate to see so many afflicted men. I do not want to imagine what it will be like when it comes to a really big battle. I am planning to come back to Shiloh in the spring. I love you, Abby. Best of luck to you and John in your married life - whenever and wherever that happens.

Yours, Jane Winningham

He put the letter in the breast pocket of his conductor's uniform, taking it with him on his next trip to Memphis, repetitively reading it. Now he knew for sure where she was, how she felt. He would write her as soon as he got back to Corinth. That was his intention anyway. On his return, the *Memphis and Charleston* line suffered its first passenger fatality when a rail broke, curved up through the floor of a passenger car, and struck a passenger. Dennis was also seriously injured in the tragic mishap, knocked unconscious. When he awoke in a hospital in Memphis, all was blurry. After his vision cleared, he saw a black man staring down at him. In that familiar velvet tone, Douglas spoke. Dennis lifted his hand and felt the bandage that encircled his skull.

"You have given us all quite a scare, Dennis," Douglas said softly.

"How long have I been here?"

"It has been almost three weeks."

"Three weeks? What day is it?"

"Thursday, January 2, 1862."

"Then I am eighteen years old today."

Looking down at the hospital dressing gown, he panicked. "The letter? Where is Jane's letter? " he begged.

Douglas pulled out a piece of luggage from beneath the bed and carefully went through his torn uniform. From the vest pocket he found, remarkably, Dennis's intact glasses. Then he produced a tattered piece of paper, covered in dried blood. He gave it to Dennis. Dennis examined it carefully. All that was legible on the remains of the page were two words *Jane Winningham.* He ran his finger over the name, brought the blood stained paper to his lips. He sat up carefully.

"I need to get out of here."

"Soon enough, but you need more rest. Your uncle has been coming every weekend to check on you. He will be here on Saturday. Meanwhile, I will call the doctor over to examine your head. I have been acting as your servant."

The hospital was basically a long hall with dozens of beds. All of them were filled, mostly with soldiers who were ill or injured. When the doctor came to his bedside, he slowly unwrapped the bandage and examined the wound. Dennis went to feel it, but the doctor prevented him. He asked for a mirror, and the doctor produced a small one from his medical bag. His head had been shaved bald. There was a long gash running across the top of his head.

"You are a very lucky young man," The doctor's response was matter of fact. "An injury such as this might have been fatal. Your servant has conscientiously cared for you. You will be discharged on Saturday and go home. Meanwhile, get up and walk with the assistance of your servant."

Douglas helped him to slowly get out of bed. His legs were quite weak, and he nearly collapsed, but with Douglas's help he steadied himself, and the two of them were able to walk outside. They sat down on a bench underneath a tree.

"Your work is done on the Underground Railroad here," Douglas said, looking straight forward.

Dennis was shaken by the statement and attempted to rise. Douglas steadied him.

"Please! Just give me time, and I will recover well enough to continue the work!"

"No, Dennis that is not what I mean. I know your tenacity. The issue is this leg of the Underground Railroad is being discontinued for the time being. Too much troop movement along the line."

"When will I see you again, Douglas?"

"You well know the answer to that, Dennis," Douglas smiled.

"Yes, yes, I do know. When providence and coincidence meet."

Douglas helped an exhausted Dennis back to his bed. The next time he awoke, Douglas was gone, and his Uncle Robert was smiling at him. They took the train back to Corinth with his head still bandaged. It looked as if he was a casualty of war. Dennis winced when others aboard thanked him for his patriotism. His uncle just played along, telling fallacious tales of how Dennis received the wound. He bragged: "One southern boy is as good as ten Yankee hirelings." Then he spun outrageous accounts of how his nephew had shown bravery in battle.

Arriving home at the Garrett's, his Aunt Peggy handed him a letter from his mother. Everyone crowded around as he read it aloud:

> *My loving son Dennis, I hope this letter finds you, Robert, Peggy and the girls well. I write to you from Springfield Missouri. We have been traveling for it seems like a year. The weather is very cold, but, we acquired some buffalo blankets and they keep us warm. Your brother John has made up his mind to take us to California, following the pony express route. I guess that is for the best as he says the Comanche Indians in Texas are too dangerous to deal with. It is so good to have such men as John, Jack, and your brother Adam. We women are nothing to sneeze at either. I wish we had never left Corinth, but he says California is the best place we can be because of the war and he knows the way well. It will just take us longer to get there. When we reach St. Joseph, we will winter there. We passed a place called Wilson's Creek where a big battle took place last August and the confederacy won. It is near Springfield. Missouri from whence I send this letter. When we get to St. Joseph, I will send another letter. You may direct all letters to the post office at St. Joseph. All give their love to all of you.*
>
> *Your mother.*

The letter from his mother eased Dennis's mind. He sat down and composed a return letter that concentrated on pleasant generalities, minimizing his accident in order not to worry his mother. Then he began writing a letter to Jane. After composing a couple of sentences, he set it aside to mull over what he wanted to say.

Dennis's hand trembled so much with his first attempts to compose the letter, he tipped over the bottle of ink onto the paper. In subsequent attempts, he was dissatisfied and fearful that he said things stupidly. An accumulation of balled and torn up letters lay in the corner like some woodland creature that was building a nest for the winter. Finally, he gave up and just decided to settle on what came out of his next draft.

Dear Jane,

I hope this letter finds you well. It seems like a long time since we knew one other at Shiloh. A lot has happened to me and I am sure a lot has happened with you. You may know by now that my brother John and Abby are married and along with the rest of my family are moving out west. After they left, a letter from you to Abby was forwarded to Corinth. I must confess I read it. In it I was pleased to read that you missed me. I surely have missed you. Something you may not know is that I was in New Orleans at the same time you were there. It is so strange. I saw you in the square, but could not believe it was you. I was so foolish. If we had found each other in that great city, I would have said things to you that I should have back in Shiloh. I can no longer keep from telling you how I feel about you. We do not know what is going to happen tomorrow. There are so many *ways I want to say it, but still have trouble. Even as I write, my hand trembles. I love you. There it is. I love you Jane Winningham. I know you are coming back to Shiloh in the spring. I want to meet you at Shiloh the first week in April. Please write me back and tell me you will meet me. Send your letter to Corinth post office.*

Very truly Yours, Dennis O'Brien

After deciding this was his best effort, he slipped the letter in the envelope, addressed it, and took it to the post office. Now came the tortuous wait for a reply.

48

Requited

After being gone for so long, he was not sure he still had a job. Instead, he found that because of the accident, he was the talk of the rail line, and everyone he knew was glad to see him return. Mr. Goforth said he could work as his assistant until he was fully recovered. Working in that capacity allowed him to heal, but it drove him crazy. Being a conductor had involved heavy mental and physical tasks. He also had an endless variety of scenery as the train moved along its course. Added to that was the strange intoxicating excitement he felt while running risks on the Underground Railroad. Now, with the exception of running errands as an assistant, he was largely confined in an office. He worked alongside Goforth, scheduling arrival and departure times. He participated in consolidating the records involving freight and passengers on many train routes.

However, there was one matter that was especially intriguing. He communicated with the Quartermaster General of the Confederate government. This meant sending and receiving telegraph messages that were not privy to everyone. Troop movements on three different railroad lines had to be coordinated: the *Memphis and Charleston*, the *Nashville and Chattanooga,* and the *Memphis and Clarksville.* These routes formed a triangle whose northern point was the town of Clarksville, a short distance from Ft. Donelson. Dennis was in a perfect position to monitor what was going on. As he daily awaited Jane's letter, he was alarmed when he read of a massive buildup of Confederate troops at Ft. Henry and nearby Ft. Donelson. Finally, he received her reply the third week in January. He hastily opened it at the post office, tearing the envelope in the process. He held his breath as he read.

Dear Dennis,

I received your letter with great gladness here at Clarksville. As of late the Academy has become more than I ever expected. It is being prepared as a hospital. You, my dear Dennis, are also more than I ever expected. I remember when you teased me, telling me to go to a fictitious academy, promising me a Yankee dime if I did. I smile when I think of how you kissed my cheek. I have read and re-read your letter. I have lain awake at night thinking of what I should say. With your words of love, my heart is affected in a way that no other person has touched. I have been fickle. I do not know why you should ever want to see me again. My heart has been treacherous, while yours has been true. I am reminded of the words of Pascal – The heart has its reasons which reason knows nothing of... We know the truth not only by reason but by the heart.

Dennis, my reason and my heart tell me that I love you too. We will confirm our love when I return to Shiloh. It is difficult to know how, but with providence we will meet at Shiloh Spring the first week of April.

Very Truly Yours, Jane Winningham

Jane's reply was like falling face first into a cherry pie. Dennis at first crushed the letter into his chest, then pulled it away in horror when he wrinkled it. He needed a place to read it again in total privacy. When he got home, he put it on the table in his room and smoothed it out, then he brought it to his face. He smelled perfume. He flashed back to the time he first faintly smelled that very fragrance on her neck in the schoolhouse, the first day he sat behind her in the humidity of the fall morning at Shiloh. This was incredible. Jane Winningham loved him. He fell back on his bed and stared at the flower and grass pattern of the ceiling wallpaper. He and Jane were meant to be together forever. Going to sleep, he dreamed they bounded toward the field of hay where he had swung her around.

Only this time they fell together passionately to the ground. He awoke the next morning with his Uncle Robert gently shaking him.

"Wake up, Denny. You'll be late. You've got to get to the station. Is your head hurting you?"

Dennis raised himself up in the bed. "A little," he replied. He still had the letter on his chest.

"Oh, now I understand," Uncle Robert gently observed. "It's about that little filly you were calling out to in your sleep when I came in. You said a few things in your sleep. Jane is her name?"

Embarrassed, Dennis took the letter, folded it, and put it back in the envelope. In muffled reply, he said, "Yeah, Jane is her name."

"Mmmm. Reminds me of myself and Peg. Did I ever tell you she didn't seem to care anything about me when we first met?"

It was the first time his uncle had ever let on anything about him and his aunt. He had always thought that with them it had been love at first sight.

"Yep, I didn't think she knew I existed. She had some boyfriends before I finally just outed that she was for me and that she needed to understand that I was for her. That's all it took. I should have told her straight the first time I saw her. I wasted time. Time gets wasted when you don't tell the truth of a matter. But on the other hand, you may have to fight. I fought a couple of boys in my journey to get to her heart. I think it may have been the same with you. Now let's get you up and off to work."

When he got to the station, Mr. Goforth was agitated, but not because Dennis had arrived late. In fact, he expressed gladness that Dennis was alright. Over the telegraph he had received a worrisome message, stating that a Union ironclad gunboat had fired on Ft. Henry on January 22, 1862. The ironclad had withdrawn, but the damage it inflicted on the fort was severe, and it could not repel a sustained attack. The Confederate High Command expected Ft. Henry to fall should another assault come from more than one gunboat. General Albert Sydney Johnston was reinforcing both Ft. Henry and nearby Ft. Donelson with several thousand more troops. This meant there would be increased troop movement passing through Corinth. To his horror, Goforth also informed Dennis that mail service going north and south was suspended. Dennis was crushed, because he had hoped to write an answer to Jane as soon as he could. Now all communication had been cut off, and a big battle was brewing near Clarksville.

49

—●(◉)●—

Changes

Day after day Dennis monitored the messages coming across the telegraph. The tension it created inhibited the healing of his head wound. Headaches plagued him with worry about Jane, but he continued to discharge his duties as assistant. On February 17, 1862, word came that Ft. Henry had fallen to the Yankees; soon thereafter, Ft. Donelson unconditionally surrendered after a fierce battle. More than 12,000 Confederates were taken captive, over 300 were killed, and over a thousand were wounded. Dennis was hardly able to keep his mind on his work. Jane would be nursing both Yankee and Confederate wounded. Accounts and southern rage over the loss of Donelson came via a newspaper from Richmond. An angry passenger slapped it on the stationmaster's desk. Everyone in the office crowded around as Mr. Goforth read it aloud.

"THE RUIN OF OUR ARMY"

"Days of adversity prove the worth of men and of nations...if the inhabitants of the South have any real manhood these reverses

will inspire them with determination. They will cease to palter between the laws of peace & the measures of war...we shall sink under it, be subjugated by Lincoln and ruled forevermore by foreigners, after having been insulted, plundered and reduced to misery by Yankee general Grant and soldiers. We shall be conquered because we deserve to be conquered...No powerful nation has ever been lost except by its own cowardice..."

As he read on, the paper demanded that General Albert Sidney Johnston be replaced in the west because of the losses at Ft. Donelson.

"Listen to this," Goforth emphasized. "A Confederate congressmen has complained that Johnston is "no general." President Jefferson Davis angrily replied, "If Sidney Johnston is not a general, then the Confederacy has none to give you.""

More reports came in across the telegraph. Along with forts Henry and Donelson, many other points of the Confederate defense had fallen, including a small fort at Clarksville. It was taken without resistance. The Ladies Academy was flooded with wounded men.

Jane Winningham, now 18, was taking her nursing duties very seriously toward both Union and Confederate wounded. Gone was the bouncing blonde schoolgirl she had been. She hastily glided from wounded soldier to wounded soldier. The extent of their injuries was appalling, the shortage of medical supplies maddening. Some had been shot in the arm or leg, lead Minie balls completely destroying bone. Long shrieks emanated from the operating area as limbs were sawed off without benefit of sulfuric ether or chloroform. Even worse, others had sustained disfiguring wounds to the face, one had his jaw shot off. The man mercifully died as she gripped his hand.

In the long room to which Jane was assigned, most were unconscious but moaning in pain. She developed grit in dealing with so much horror, going from bed to bed, bandaging wounds and bringing what comfort she could. However, one suffering young Union officer affected Jane so emotionally, she found herself returning to his bedside more frequently than others. His horse had fallen on top of him. Externally he looked to be fine, internally it was only a guess. He was handsome and fit with dark brown wavy hair and mustache, and his name was Valentine, Owen Valentine.

"Miss Winningham. You are the most beautiful woman I have ever seen," the young officer said with a pained, winsome smile at the outset of his care. Then he dropped away into unconsciousness.

She did not feel beautiful. She felt old, haggard, and plain after two weeks of caring for these men and boys whose lives had been forever changed or ended too soon. Yet those simple words revived her in a way she did not expect. Jane unprofessionally kissed him on his fevered forehead every time she came to his bedside. When she did, he returned to cognizance, and their conversations became more intimate.

Meanwhile, on March 1, two Union ironclad gunboats approached Pittsburg Landing. A regiment of Louisiana troops with a battery of six field cannons engaged them, but proved no match for the six and eight inch heavy naval guns. There were fatalities on both sides, and the Louisiana regiment drew back to Shiloh church three miles from the river. Soon they retreated all the way back to Corinth. An exodus of families around Shiloh ensued, and it was not just there. The appearance of Federal troops deep in Confederate territory created panic among other communities adjacent to the river, causing their residents to flee, spurred on by reports of burning and plundering by the gunboat crews.

These reports quickly reached Corinth, creating massive uproar. All railroad operations were placed under military control. Confederate troops arrived by the tens of thousands and began camping in and around town. As an assistant to the stationmaster, Dennis was now inexorably part of the Confederate war machine.

Then cavalry scouts brought news that Union soldiers were set-ting up camps around Shiloh Church. This was what he had long wondered about: How he would feel if the North came down en masse? It had literally happened. He was furious and frantic since he was supposed meet Jane in only weeks. How would that be pos-sible now?

While going back and forth to work, he was emotionally stirred by the throngs of Confederates being drilled. He wanted to join them. The desire spiraled when he encountered an old friend in a company of the 6th Arkansas Regiment, "the Dixie Grays," drill-ing in the street. It was Henry Stanley calling out to him as Dennis walked to the station.

"Why, Dennis O'Brien! I knew this was where you are from. I had wondered if there was any chance I would encounter you...and here, like a bad penny, you have turned up!"

Dennis ran and shook Henry's hand vigorously "I could not have imagined you, an Englishman, would be standing here in such a uni-form! How did this come about?"

"I spent several months in Arkansas looking after my father's business. The war separated me from him, and suffice it to say I was caught up in all this. No, I dare say, I am here of my own volition. Partly because of resentment. I had wished to return home, but all communication was stopped, normal commerce was greatly inhib-ited. One day I heard that enlistment was going on. In but a short time, it seemed that all of Arkansas was being emptied of all the youth and men I knew. I was forlorn, I suppose. When a doctor I was fond of asked me if I did not intend to join the valiant children of Arkansas to fight, I answered, 'Yes' and so here I am."

Their reunion was cut short by a shout from a commander for all the Dixie Grays to line up for inspection. As Henry queued up with his unit, he called out to Dennis.

"Francisco Moreno is here, too! He is a lieutenant aide-de-camp to General Beauregard, now 2nd in command to General Albert Sydney Johnston!"

When he got to the railway office, he approached the Confederate officer charged with oversight of Corinth station. He requested to enlist. He was told that he could best serve by helping to keep the rail lines running smoothly. He consulted with his Uncle Robert at the roundhouse. His uncle advised him to stay put, but he was feeling wild, especially because of his vow to meet Jane at Shiloh Spring. He had to do something. Despite what he knew of his father's experience in war, he told himself this was different, not what his Da had experienced in Mexico. This was an unpredictable horde of Northerners coming down literally into his own back yard.

On March 21st a cavalry colonel named Wirt Adams came canvassing door to door, looking for anyone not enlisted yet, especially accomplished riders with their own mounts and a knowledge of the area. He found Dennis caring for Bobby, the dapple gray, in the rear of the Garrett's house. It took little for Colonel Adams to convince Dennis to be a civilian scout and be a part of defending the place where he had grown up. There was no time to waste. With great misgiving, the family saw him off. He was put at the forefront of Colonel Adams' regiment for a foray into the area he knew so well.

Unbeknownst to Dennis, something else was playing out nearly two hundred miles to the north. In Clarkesville, Jane and Lieutenant Owen Valentine were taking comfort in one another's company. Though Jane's conscience kept striking her about her profession of love for Dennis, she continued to tenderly minister to the young lieutenant beyond the requirements of her duties. They spoke of plans together after Lieutenant Valentine's recovery although his abdomen had become severely distended with a buildup of fluid. Though neither of them admitted it, more and more evidence presented itself that the young lieutenant was not long for this world. He was light headed and weak, had shortness of breath. His hands and feet tingled. Speech became slurred. Then he slipped into unconsciousness. She held his hand, waiting for him to come to. His breathing became shallower. Then he delivered up a wheezing exhalation. She wept profusely as she covered Owen Valentine's face with a sheet.

After Adams' cavalry made its first reconnaissance to the Hamburg-Shiloh area, it became apparent that almost all of the home population had gone somewhere else. They confirmed a full Union Division of over 8,000 had set up camps from Owl Creek in the west, camping all around Shiloh church, and some of its troops stretched as far east as McCullers's property on the Hamburg road. Dennis was keen to help gather further information. Because he was wearing civilian clothes, he pleaded with Colonel Adams to give him permission to go alone into the encampment by the church. He was warned of the risk, but his request was granted. Colonel Adams told him to be as discreet as possible and report back to the main body of cavalry at Hamburg if all went well.

At first he received surprisingly little reaction from the encamped Union troops that early morning as he ambled Bobby past tee pee like tents and campfires. It was staggering to see how many soldiers were in the place where only children had romped months before. They were fully equipped, and their provisions were amazingly plentiful. Their crisp blue uniforms in comparison with Confederate homemade uniforms were enviable. They seemed nonchalant as they polished their brass buttons with campfire ashes. After he made a wide circle around the church, a sentry stopped him and made him dismount. Forced to leave Bobby with another soldier, he was brought to a tent on top of a familiar knoll behind the church. He had thought he was fully recovered, but his head began to throb.

When Dennis entered the tent, a high ranking officer in a white shirt was about to put on his military jacket, but on seeing Dennis, he sat down on a strange looking chair, draping his jacket over one forearm. The man's hair was reddish and tousled, and he had a roughly trimmed beard.

"Who are you, sir?" Dennis asked the officer.

"I ask the questions," the officer replied. With that the sentry slapped his head and pushed him, saying, "Have more respect for General Sherman."

"What is your name and what are you doing here?" the general asked. Dennis's head throbbed even more, and a resentment like he had never felt before rose in him. He was not inclined to be discreet as Colonel Adams had advised. It took all his might to restrain his anger. As it was, he answered with gritted teeth and made a provocative reply.

"Dennis O'Brien's the name, if it's any of your business. I could ask you the same thing. What are you doing here? And I mean all of you! Who do you think you are? This is my home, where I went to school."

This caused the general's aide to slap the back of his head again. His head began to swim, then he fell to the ground. The scene had played out like his dream of long ago. He got to his knees and raised himself back up. The interrogation continued.

"So, you know this area well, do you? That could be good thing or a bad thing for you, son."

"I'm not your son, mister!" and he ducked another attempt to slap him.

"Hold on lieutenant, let the young man be. As they say 'you can draw more flies with honey.'" The general chuckled. "Very well then, Dennis O' Brien, since you know the area so well, maybe you can give us some information."

Dennis looked steely eyed at this Sherman. "What can I tell you that you don't already know? You have driven off most of the neighbors around here. You're all squatting on land that's not yours."

"Couldn't be helped. If you people hadn't rebelled against the union, we wouldn't be here. And as far as squatting on this land is concerned, you have not seen anything yet."

Dennis was infuriated that the general had referred to everyone he'd ever known abstractly as "you people."

"Then you don't really care if you sweep away the wheat with the chaff?"

"That is not my decision to make. I simply follow orders. You are at odds with the Union."

"Have you no decency, sir? Of the people you have displaced here, few had slaves. I see you have no problem with the Cherry family across the river at Savannah, who favor the Union. They have well over fifty. If you want the slaves, take them. What makes you think you have the right to destroy a whole community on this side of the river? Do you believe in God and the golden rule? What have these people here done to you?"

"My family is strongly Roman Catholic. I am not. As I said, I simply follow orders. Come what may, I will prosecute this war until the south bends its knee to the Union. There are tens of thousands more coming to 'squat on your land,' and you will get used to it." The general grew impatient. "Lieutenant, this young man is obviously a belligerent. Escort him to one of the steamers on the river as a prisoner of war."

The aide forced him down a path, not realizing just how familiar Dennis was with the terrain. As he passed Bobby, the horse gave out a long, alarmed whinny. It stabbed Dennis to the heart. A ravine on the Pittsburg landing road was so familiar to him from his days on the trap line that Dennis bolted down the steep side of the hill ravine. The aide fired his pistol and missed. Dennis continued to run jaggedly down the creek bed until he fell into the beaver pond. He heaved an anguished moan over losing Bobby. He scrambled clandestinely on foot through the bushes, trees, and ravines the rest of the day. At times he was close enough to encamped troops that he could hear their conversations. What Sherman had said was confirmed by the scuttlebutt of the soldiers. There were five more divisions of Union troops arriving by April 1st at Pittsburg Landing. At Hamburg that evening, he breathlessly reported to Colonel Adams the coming buildup of the enemy. Pleased with the report, the Colonel gave him his spare mount.

50

—=»((◉))«=—

Shiloh Spring

By April 1st, river steamers had transported most of the wounded from Clarkesville to hospitals in the north. For Jane the days since the Donelson battle were a horrific heart wrenching blur. After Owen Valentine died, she'd had time to think about what had passed between them. They had been in a poignant relationship, a dreadful intensity of feelings, and now she realized that because of her physical disconnection from Dennis, she had vicariously transferred what she felt for Dennis to the young lieutenant. What she had felt for Owen took a pendulum swing back to Dennis's faithful love for her. Nonetheless, she was tormented by her emotional unfaithfulness. She needed to prove to Dennis and herself that she could be faithful. She was determined to rendezvous with Dennis on Sunday, April 6th. Her resolve stiffened to make it on time to Shiloh Spring, not knowing that Federal soldiers at that very moment were drinking from its water.

On April 3rd from Corinth, over 43,000 Confederates began marching toward Pittsburg Landing where 40,000 Union troops were now encamped. While the Confederates knew what lay before them, astonishingly, the Union cavalry had not detected the vast host of their enemy that had reached and positioned themselves less than three miles from Shiloh Church. In his positon with Wirt Adams' cavalry on the Hamburg road at Lick Creek, not far from McCullers' property, Dennis was trying to get used to a strange horse and wearing a pistol on his hip. They were issued to him by Colonel Adams after his perilous reconnoitering of Shiloh Church. He had used a firearm many times while hunting game, but the real possibility of firing to kill a man was something far different. It was that old dilemma. How would he know if he could really do it? Would he be able to use it? He would find out when the time came. Then came another one of the surprises of his young life. Several more companies of cavalry joined Wirt Adams to guard the Hamburg road, and they were commanded by none other than Colonel Nathan Bedford Forrest.

Jane was struggling mightily to find a way home. She made a successful get away from Clarksville on the Cumberland River by way of a small steamer. However April 3rd, she had great difficulty getting transferred to another boat at Paducah at the mouth of the Ohio and Tennessee Rivers. Astonished to find all transports were completely reserved for military purposes and headed for Pittsburg Landing, she began to lose hope. Then a steamboat called the *Minnehaha* stopped to take on fuel for the boiler. She tried to get aboard and was refused. Seeing her frantic pleading, a young woman on the vessel interceded. Her name was Ann Wallace. She was making a surprise trip to see her husband, a high ranking Union army officer, General W.H. L. Wallace. Spying Jane at the boarding ramp, obviously distraught, she went to her, and upon learning her circumstances, arranged to have her brought on as her cabin mate for the trip to Pittsburg Landing. About midnight on Saturday, April 5th, the *Minnehaha* stopped for the night at Savannah, less than ten miles from its destination. In the early morning before daylight, the two lovesick women arrived at Pittsburg Landing. Soon the sound of gunfire was heard, and word came that a large battle was in progress.

Confined by orders to the vicinity of Lick Creek and the approach from Hamburg, Dennis waited with hundreds of cavalrymen all morning, agitating to join a fight that from its sound was growing more ferocious by the hour. At 11:00 they watched as two infantry regiments passed them, marching for the battlefield. After more time passed, Forrest was furious.

"Boys! Do you hear that rattle of musketry and the roar of artillery!?"

Dennis joined in a resounding collective Rebel yell that echoed through the woods. "Yes! Yes!"

"Do you know what it means?! It means our friends and brothers are falling by the hundreds at the hands of the enemy and we are here guarding a damn creek! We did not enter the service for such work...we are needed elsewhere. Let's go help them! What do you say?!"

Again came wild hollers of agreement. Suddenly all were in motion. Dennis bent forward in his saddle and goaded his horse into action along with the rest of the cavalry. Thousands of pounding hoof beats along the Hamburg road shook the ground. Flying quickly over familiar territory to Dennis, they soon arrived at Sarah Bell's cotton field along the Hamburg-Purdy road. Its fences were fallen down or blown apart.

Orders came to fire only within close proximity to the enemy since their pistols did not have the range necessary to reach the distant Union line. This was of some relief to Dennis as he had been waving his pistol over his head wildly. As he beheld the field, it was littered with so many dead bodies, Union and Confederate, it was difficult to move forward without horses stepping on them. They came under artillery fire. Explosions of cannon balls devastated men and horses, smoke roiled across the field, making it impossible to truly aim at anything.

Forrest ordered a charge, changing the column of fours into an extended line across open ground. Swift movement remarkably enabled them to avoid most of the Federal volleys. Riding and firing, they rushed over a regiment of Union soldiers who were falling back. For the first time, Dennis lowered his gun and pointed at a soldier in blue about the same age as himself. The young Yankee stared up in wide eyed terror, while pointing his own gun at Dennis. Dennis hesitated. In an instant the cavalryman next to him fired, killing the young Yankee.

"Why didn't you shoot, you stupid fool?!" his compatriot shouted as the cavalry continued to ride forward. The moment had come, and Dennis had not been up to the task of killing another man point blank. There was no time to linger over the situation, the charge continued. As they reached a black jack thicket of underbrush, the cavalryman who had saved him was shot from his saddle. Dennis jumped down from his horse to come to his aid, but it was too late. He was overcome with guilt. The entire contingent of cavalry slowed to a walk because of the underbrush and were ordered to fall back.

As they regrouped along the Hamburg-Purdy road, word came that General Albert Sydney Johnston had been killed nearby at the southeast corner of a peach orchard that Dennis knew so well. A noticeable lull in the fighting occurred on the Confederate side. The news had to be carried to second in command General Beauregard. A small group of cavalry was chosen to accompany General Johnston's chief of staff to carry the stunning message, and Dennis was among them. It was about 3:00 when they reached Beauregard. The momentum of the Confederate army slowed as word passed to the other generals.

While at Beauregard's field headquarters, Dennis looked for Lt. Francisco Moreno. His heart sank when he found him among the hundreds of fallen. He had been shot through both legs and was bleeding out despite receiving rudimentary first aid being administered by a surgeon. Dennis got down on his knees and lifted his head as his life ebbed away.

"Francisco! Francisco! Do you know me! Do you know me?" Dennis pleaded over and over.

Francisco Moreno's eyelids opened to slits, but he recognized Dennis and gave a weak smile. His last words in his Spanish accent were, "Dennis, Dennis, it is so good to see you. Always remember our talks. Always remember: "Home is where the heart is"… and I see you are now home."

Because of the time that he spent with Francisco, he became separated from his small band of cavalry. Frantically, he pulled himself away from his dead friend and tried to catch up with them, but they were too far ahead. Using his knowledge of the terrain, he rode through the woods trying to catch up with them. The desperate character of the day's battle was especially brought home to him as he unavoidably had to cross a field. Some twenty bodies were lying in various postures, each in its own viscous pool of blood. Beyond was a still larger group, body overlying body, knees crooked, arms erect or wide stretched and rigid. Among the corpses he heard a groaning. Someone was still alive. He dismounted and tied off the reins to a bush. There must be something he could do to help. Had he not done this, he would have never known the fate of someone especially dear to him. The cries turned out to be coming from none other than his cousin Randy. Once again he got down on his knees and lifted the head of someone beloved. Once again it was too late. As his cousin expired, he screamed into the air in agony.

"Come on, Randy, sit up! Sit up! Tell me you're just playin' possum!"

He brought Randy's torso forward, put his arms completely around him and started swaying back and forth as though to cause a resurrection. He continued to rock Randy in his arms until his grief gave way to numb acceptance. Dennis lay him back down amid the hideous carnage, arranging his cousin's body in the customary position with hands on his chest. At that moment he felt a hand on his shoulder.

"Dennis, I can't believe it's you," came a voice with an English accent. Dennis turned to find Henry Stanley incredulously looking at him. It took Dennis a moment to determine it was not an apparition. He looked Henry up and down, then poked at his belly to make sure he was real. Henry winced. "There now," and he pushed Dennis's hand away. "That's a bit sore. A ball hit my belt-clasp a little while ago."

"Henry? Henry? Then you are alright?"

"It's a wonder any of us are, what with bullets flying about like hornets. Come let us get out of this heat."

The two of them walked to the tree where Dennis's horse was tied. In its shade they sank down together, backs to the trunk. Henry plunged his hand into his haversack and pulled out his rations to share with Dennis. They both ate ravenously.

"I had pictured the circumstances of our meeting again much differently, my friend," Henry panted between bites of hard tack.

"Yes, I thought it would be more philosophical," Dennis replied, trying to smile after the death of his cousin. "How do you feel now in that butternut uniform, Henry? This need not to have been your fight."

"I was inexorably drawn into this conflict by bad associations. As St. Paul said to the Corinthians "evil communications corrupt good manners," Henry replied stoically.

The absurd understatement in Henry's British accent caused Dennis to start laughing ironically, and he nearly choked on the hard tack. Henry handed him his canteen of precious water.

Amid the ghastly casualties of the conflict, they continued to renew their acquaintance. They related to one another various anecdotes as if they were abstractly not on the battlefield. However, when Dennis told him what had happened to Francisco Moreno, it gave pause to their conversation. The ugly reality was they had to return to their units. They both rose. Hugging seemed a macabre exercise to do amid the corpses, but they did. Then Henry struck out north in the direction his regiment had taken, and Dennis got back on his horse and headed east to rendezvous with his cavalry command.

At Pittsburg landing, wounded were being brought by the hundreds onto the *Minnehaha* and all the other steamboats docked along the riverbank. The only females on board, Jane and Mrs. Wallace, passed from soldier to soldier, providing water and bandages for the surgeons. They did so until it became so crowded they went to the upper deck, the texas. Amid the deafening roar of cannon and musketry, they tried to carry on a conversation, both exceedingly worried. Jane told Ann all about Dennis. She related the way they had taught the younger children together at Shiloh School, and the day he swung her around in the field of hay and spelled out their names in the grass. Ann recounted the last letter she had received from her husband, Will. He described this place as filled with dogwood trees whose delicate young leaves and white blossoms made him think how pleasant it would be to be with her and share her love. As bloodied men were now brought to the upper deck and placed in tiers in the staterooms like bricks in a brickyard, they hugged one another and resumed assistance to the overtaxed surgeons.

Upon returning to the main cavalry group, Dennis found them all in celebration. A key line of resistance had collapsed along a sunken road, a Union General Wallace had been thought killed, and two thousand prisoners had been taken captive. Grant had formed a last line of defense along the Pittsburg Landing Road, but Colonel Forrest was not taking comfort. He called for a detachment of scouts to reconnoiter the Federal line. Colonel Adams recommended that

Dennis be among them because he was so familiar with the terrain. The moon was coming up in the east while the sun in the west went down like a diver. Darkness enveloped the landscape. Dennis led the detachment to the best vantage point possible, the Indian mounds. Unable to ride a horse up the sides of any of the mounds, Dennis and a Lieutenant Sheridan clambered to the top of the tallest one. From that vantage point, they observed innumerable Union troops debarking from transports at the landing, and two Union ironclad gunboats. The gunboats began firing regularly about every fifteen minutes up a long ravine perhaps a hundred yards away.

About 10:00 that night a steady rain began to fall. Beyond lay the fleet of steamboats, including the *Minnehaha*. Dennis and Jane did not know how tantalizingly close they were to one another. As the storm strengthened, Lieutenant Sheridan urged him to follow quickly back to Forrest to make their report, and he scrambled back down the mound. Dennis was mesmerized by the firing of the gunboats and told the Lieutenant he would be along. As the squad rode away, the night sky vibrated with lightning and a bolt struck a tree nearby. He watched as his own mount startled, broke free, galloping off into the darkness. Dennis turned to go down the mound, tripping on a root in the dark. He was thrown down the wet hill and rolled rapidly like a log until he bumped against something in the ravine. It was long and covered with cloth. He turned his head to find a stark white face staring back with fixed glazed eyes. Its mouth was frozen in an o-shape as if surprised at Dennis's sudden arrival. The thunderstorm illuminated the landscape and revealed a vale clogged with other bodies.

He rose numbed and climbed back up the embankment to get his bearings. He trudged in the mud down a farm road in what he hoped would be the way to Shiloh Church. His ears rung from the periodic bursting of shells coming from the gunboats on the Tennessee River; dizziness made him feel like a toy top. His mouth was parched. He licked at rain droplets catching on his lips, but it was not enough to quench his thirst. All across the field, he could hear distressed cries of the wounded.

"Water! Water! Oh please, could someone just bring me a canteen…just a little…please just a drink." And then, as if heaven answered, came a downpour.

Along the road among the trees, were clusters of men bivouacked around stacked rifles, nursing sputtering fires. Solitary soldiers shivered, huddled against tree trunks, trying to sleep. Miserably wet Confederates stood guard over cheerless Union prisoners sitting on the soaked ground with knees pulled up under their chins. Then came a long whistling shriek of a cannonball.

It exploded in a concussive wave slamming him into a dense thicket. Incredibly, he remained conscious, but his left ear was bleeding. Others were not so lucky. He made out a tall oak split from top to root with a human leg dangling from a branch. Grabbing bushes to raise himself, he pushed his way through the tangled underbrush back to the road. He took hold of a handful of leaves, only to feel a jelly-like substance. He screamed with horror at the human remains and wretched.

Emerging from the undergrowth, he could see at least a dozen men, both Yankee and Rebel, contorted in death as a result of that one explosion. Dennis staggered through the mud as the outcries of the wounded and groans of the dying created a strange orchestra amidst the storm, a symphony of the damned. He broke into an arm-flailing, mud splattering run. As he distanced himself from the massacre, he slowed up with chest heaving, but he cursed God unrestrained. As he did, he heard his mother's religious admonitions. *Never use the Lord's name in vain. Don't blame God for the sins of man.* There came a panicked repentance, and he begged forgiveness for his blasphemy. A quiet set in, and he could only hear the squishing of his shoes in the sludge. It was a short reprieve. There was a great racket, and a wounded but magnificent white horse, blood streaming down its back, burst out of the bushes with a throat rattle, snorting like Apocalypse fulfilled. Could the other horses of the Revelation be far behind? Indeed he found them as he walked on. Two artillery horses floundered, still in their harnesses on the ground, emitting shrieking whinnies, but then something familiar. A dapple gray animal lay heaving on its side, letting out labored snuffles in the mire. That was the crowning horror for him. The beautiful animal looked to be his family's lone horse.

"Bobby! Bobby!" he ran, crying out to the horse his father had named after the Irish revolutionary, Robert Emmet. "Oh, Bobby, what have they done to you?"

Falling to his knees, he threw himself over the side of the animal, sobbing. Its huge mid-section quivered, then relaxed. As the horse expired, steam rose from its hide, and the horse's warmth ironically revived Dennis in the chill of the rainy night. He rose sobbing. He plodded on, hoping it was westward, but not knowing which point of the compass he might be facing. He had to maintain his sanity. He passed destroyed cabins. Neither Union nor Confederate armies had spared the domiciles around Shiloh. What had happened to the residents? Especially, what had happened to *her*? A strong resolve came over him. It did not matter that he, too, might die tonight; he had to keep going as long as he was alive and find out what had happened to her. Scant hope drove him. Jane might be out here somewhere in the miles of altered landscape. Now maybe the Great Jehovah would answer prayer. He fell to his knees and begged.

"Dear God, Dear God. If you would only help me find her."

He kept repeating it, hoping for a God of love who rescues out of trial, but his mother's words loomed in his mind again as he said "amen." "God helps those that help themselves," his mother had repeated time after time.

That's how Dennis was helping himself, by pursuing Jane, but she discouraged him not to go after that girl. His mother intimated that girls like Jane were not wholesome enough, not devout enough. She implied that he would help himself by leaving her alone. But that aside, how could he have brought her home anyway into the house where, of course, his father also resided? That man of unpredictable temperament possessed peculiarities that at times were embarrassing or even revolting. He had taken his father himself to the lunatic asylum in New Orleans. He had reasoned if Jane had seen any of his father's idiosyncrasies, it would have made any chance of being with her a moot pursuit.

He should have ignored all that when it came to Jane. He should have gone after her. He shouldn't have displayed reluctance about her in the earlier years. If he had, she would not have looked upon him as a mere friend. He would not be in this place right now, searching for his unrequited love. He was going after her now under the worst possible circumstances. He would find her somewhere out here. He would run to her. He would hold her. He would tell her all he had ever wanted to tell her. He would take her away from this wretched place.

Then he heard the distinctive trickling of water. Its sound in the darkness brought an overwhelming realization. He knew where he was. He was where he had first met Jane. At Shiloh Spring.

He staggered into the little stream, then tripped and fell head first into the gurgling water. He coughed as he drew in the sweet liquid. He splashed in it vigorously, careless of enemy eyes and ears. The perdition of the night seemed to melt away as the rivulets of cold water soothed his parched tongue and burning throat. His heart beat slower with the succor of water. Hope returned and merged present with past, transporting him back to that wonderful day when he met her at the spring years before.

Two soldiers, one in blue, the other in gray, heard the sound of the raucous splashing that early spring night. They fired their rifles at their unseen foe, and there was stillness at Shiloh Spring.

www.ingramcontent.com/pod-product-compliance
Lightning Source LLC
La Vergne TN
LVHW091519290325
807158LV00001B/34